Praise for *Come with Me*

Praise for *Black Mouth*

"Riveting, bloody, and cosmic,
this novel will tear you apart in all the best ways."
PHILIP FRACASSI

"*Black Mouth* is good magic about dark magic...Smart,
character-driven horror."
ANDREW PYPER

"Full of malevolence and dread, and peopled by truly
compelling characters, the book locks in Malfi's place
as one of the best writers in the genre."
CHRISTOPHER GOLDEN

"The well-done cosmic horror and mix of mundane
and magical scares make this a standout."
PUBLISHERS WEEKLY

"Expertly crafted and thoroughly engrossing,
Black Mouth is a sure-fire contender for the book of 2022."
BLOODY FLICKS

GHOSTWRITTEN

Also by Ronald Malfi and available from Titan Books

Come with Me

Black Mouth

Ghostwritten

Also by Ronald Malfi

FOUR NOVELLAS

GHOSTWRITTEN

RONALD
MALFI

TITAN BOOKS

Ghostwritten
Print edition ISBN: 9781789099591
E-book edition ISBN: 9781789099607

Published by Titan Books
A division of Titan Publishing Group Ltd.
144 Southwark Street, London SE1 0UP

First Titan edition: October 2022
10 9 8 7 6 5 4 3 2

A CIP catalogue record for this title is available
from the British Library.

Printed and bound in the United Kingdom.

CONTENTS

This one's for my girls—Deb, Maddie, and Hayden.

A part of every story…

"The most essential gift for a good writer is a built-in, shockproof, shit detector."
ERNEST HEMINGWAY

"Books have *power*."
THE CLEANER

THE SKIN OF
HER TEETH

1

"We've got a problem," said Jack Baer. They were the first words out of his mouth, even before he sat down at the table. Gloria eyed him coolly as she steeped her tea. They were at Antoine's—Jack's request—and the breakfast crowd was queuing up at the door and curling around the block on this warm September morning. Jack Baer queued for no one; in fact, he seemed oblivious to the people filing into the restaurant all around him. Gloria Grossman had known Jack for the better part of a decade, though his reputation in the industry had preceded any formal introduction. He'd been a top player at CAA before opening his own boutique literary agency, and he had, from time to time, courted Gloria, enticing her to join him. *Merger*, was how Jack put it, framing the word in the air with his big hands to get her to visualize the marquee. But Jack had a reputation for representing difficult clients, which presented a whole host of headaches Gloria did not feel like shouldering. Ironically, it was *her* client, the screenwriter Davis McElroy, who was the cause of today's meeting, and any headache that would inevitably follow.

"Hello to you, too, Jack," Gloria said, plucking her teabag from the cup and tucking it along the rim of the saucer.

"I'm sorry, Glor," Jack said, reaching across the table and squeezing her hand. "I'm a bit frazzled this morning. How've you been? How's Becca? Is everyone well?"

Gloria pulled her hand out from beneath his, enjoying the sound of his heavy Rolex knocking against the tabletop.

A waiter came over and Jack ordered an espresso and a bagel.

"Davis McElroy," Jack said, once the waiter had departed. "What are we going to do here, Glor? Any word from him? Please say yes."

"No, I haven't heard from him." She was careful not to make it sound like some sort of admission of failure on her part. Also, she was cautious not to allow her own aggravation to show. If she was going to curse her client, she'd do it in private.

Jack cleared his throat. "Haven't you tried to reach—"

"Of course I have," she said, cutting him off. "I've sent emails, I've left voicemails. Although I'll be honest, Jack—it's not unusual for him to be unresponsive when he's up at the house working on a project."

"*Is* he, though?" Jack said, arching one slender, steel wool eyebrow. "*Is* he working on the project? Because he's a month past his deadline and the studio doesn't want to renew the option. Not with McElroy attached. He's been MIA for several weeks, maybe more, from what I can tell, and the execs aren't getting the old warm and fuzzy anymore. He's put the whole project in jeopardy."

"Don't exaggerate, Jack," she said, and now she reached out and squeezed *his* hand, grinning condescendingly. *Don't play me, Jacky-boy*, she thought. Thing was, Jack Baer was right—Davis McElroy *had* been MIA. Hell, McElroy might have fallen off the face of the earth for all Gloria knew at the moment. She hadn't heard from McElroy in over a month, he'd missed his last few scheduled Zoom meetings with the studio execs at Paramount, and he had been unresponsive to Gloria's repeated emails and phone calls warning him that his deadline to turn in his draft of the screenplay had come and gone and that the option period was coming to a close, too. Had it been another one of her former clients—old George Lee Poach, for example, who was infamous for his cocaine-fueled benders and periods of reclusiveness—Gloria wouldn't have been surprised. But Davis McElroy had always exhibited a steadfast work ethic and he'd never missed a deadline. He was also six or seven years into recovery, and as far as Gloria Grossman knew, he no longer ingested anything more potent than ibuprofen. True, he did not like to be bothered when he went up to the house—the Hole in the Wall, as he called it—to work on a project, but even his time up there had never precluded him from returning her calls or responding to her emails. Was it possible he'd fallen off the wagon? Lord knew Gloria had seen it a million times before. It was a goddamn cliché in this industry, and hardly the most unexpected thing to happen to a writer.

"Mr. Fish has also attempted to reach out to him *personally*," Jack said.

"The illustrious John Fish makes personal phone calls? I just assumed you did all the dialing for him, Jack. Just like you cut and chew his filet mignon."

"Quip all you want, Gloria, but that should clue you in to the severity of the situation."

"I'm not quipping, Jack. I just don't want you to pop a gasket."

Jack frowned, rubbed a set of plump, hairy-knuckled fingers across the mottled ridge of his brow. John Fish was just the type of client that dissuaded Gloria from merging her agency with Jack's—the epitome of the pampered, pompous novelist, who'd spent the bulk of his career marinating in white male privilege. She'd heard rumors that, while on a book tour, Fish insisted his hotel rooms be cleaned by his own team of hired professionals, and that the rooms themselves be stocked with a supply of assorted nuts, dried fruits, charcuterie, a vase of fresh daisies, scented toilet paper, and bed sheets whose thread count was never to be lower than a thousand.

He was an asshole, in other words. But John Fish—and Jack, for that matter—was right to be concerned. Davis McElroy had been hired by the studio to adapt Fish's bestselling novel, *The Skin of Her Teeth*, and he hadn't delivered. It was a mess all the way around.

"Is it possible something could've happened to the guy out there?" Jack continued. "Could he have had a heart attack or a stroke or something out there at the house?"

"He seemed in good health to me, last time I saw him," Gloria said. Anyway, it wasn't a heart attack or stroke she was worried about. To the best of her knowledge, McElroy didn't attend NA or AA meetings while tucked away up there in the Hole in the Wall like he did when he was here in the city. Maybe the damn fool *had* slipped up.

"Well, *somebody* needs to get in touch with the son of a bitch," Jack insisted. "Maybe you should call the local police up there, have them drop by for a welfare check or something. Make sure the poor bastard isn't lying dead on the floor and that his dog hasn't made a meal of his corpse."

"I don't believe he has a dog." It was meant to be humorous, but it missed the mark.

"I wish I could share your confidence here, Gloria. Whatever is going on, it's bad business, and it's making Fish uncharacteristically… let's say, itchy?"

Gloria laughed. "Itchy, huh?"

"He's troubled by this whole thing. He keeps asking if we've heard from McElroy. It's not like him to give such a shit, to speak frankly. I didn't even think he knew Davis McElroy's name, let alone the guy's phone number."

Jack's espresso and bagel arrived, borne on a linen-covered tray. The waiter set the items on the table and Jack picked up the espresso, his squat, rectangular pinky extended. The cup looked like a miniature novelty in his oversized hand.

"No one's calling the police," she told him. If McElroy *had* relapsed, she didn't want to invite any legal complications into the equation. McElroy could be up there feasting on a buffet of cocaine and Jim Beam, for all she knew. Cops would just muddy the waters. "But I agree that enough's enough. I've already made up my mind to go out there myself and check up on him."

Jack's eyes widened over the rim of his espresso. "To the house?" he said, setting the cup down.

"It's not Beirut, Jack," she said. She'd been up to the Hole in the Wall on a few occasions, whenever McElroy would throw one of his solemn, somewhat self-pitying get-togethers. She had the address in her phone. It was only a few hours' drive, and it would do her good to get out of the city for a while. She didn't own a car, though, so she'd have to butter up to Becca.

Jack just shook his head. "This whole thing sets me on edge," he commented, gazing at the traffic in the street now. His small eyes darted here and there, here and there. "I don't want to lose this deal."

"We're not going to lose the deal. I'll handle it, Jack. In the meantime," she said, "you take care of the studio. Keep them placated and on the line. I'll deal with McElroy. I won't come back from that house without the script."

"And what if he hasn't written the damn thing?"

"You're such a pessimist, Jack," she said, but was already thinking the exact same thing.

2

"A day trip," Becca said, not a question, half-moon glasses perched along the edge of her slender, ski-slope nose. Seated behind an economical aluminum desk—ugly but functional, Gloria supposed—in her office at the university, Rebecca Carroll looked every bit the career academic she'd been for the past two decades.

Somewhat of a bribe, Gloria had brought Becca lunch—a bean sprout and avocado sandwich on rye and a kale shake from Antoine's—and she watched as Becca alternated between nibbling the sandwich and consulting an imposing textbook splayed open on her desk. Behind her, a pair of bookshelves, dense with heavy leather-bound volumes, looked like they might avalanche down on Becca at any moment.

"I wish it was as pleasant as it sounds," Gloria said, and then she explained the situation with Davis McElroy. Becca remembered McElroy and knew of McElroy's house upstate, too—she'd been Gloria's date at one of McElroy's tedious soirees—but she professed concern with the notion of Gloria traveling out there on her own.

"If this guy *is* messed up on drugs or something, I'm not sure it's the smartest thing in the world for you to go waltzing right into the middle of that, Glor," Becca said.

"Worst-case scenario, he's strung out and needs a cold shower," Gloria said.

"No," Becca countered, glancing up from the textbook. "Worst-case scenario, he's dead. Or he comes at you swinging a hammer because he's blotto on smack and thinks you're Julius Caesar."

Gloria laughed. "'Blotto on smack'? Where'd you glean that gem of a phrase?"

"Laugh if you must, my dear, but you know I'm right. Why not wait for the weekend? We can drive up together. Make a mini-vacation out of it."

"What's that word? 'Vacation'? Sounds vaguely familiar…"

"A nice stay at a bed and breakfast, with those crumbly biscuits and a veritable library of teas," Becca continued.

"Sounds nice, but this can't wait. The studio doesn't want to extend the option. But I'm hoping that if he's actually *written* the damn screenplay, I can deliver it and maybe salvage this whole thing."

"You really think that's a possibility?"

"That I can salvage this thing?"

"That he's actually written it. I mean, it would be awfully considerate of the guy to postpone his alleged coke-binge until after he's finished the screenplay, but I seriously doubt that's the case. Addicts aren't generally known for their accountability."

"Well, I can't just throw my hands up in the air and do nothing, Becca. There's a lot riding on this deal. Besides, that's just not my style. You of all people know that."

Becca sighed audibly. She closed her book and wrapped the remaining half of her sandwich in the crinkly brown paper it came in. "Yes, right, I know that, Glor. I'm just concerned, that's all."

"And I really think it will be fine. Now—can I please borrow your car?"

"Of course," Becca said, scooting back in her chair and sliding open a desk drawer. "But I also want you to borrow something else."

The thing Becca placed on the desk looked like a black metal pipe, about four inches in length. It was an expandable baton, like the kind police officers carried. Technically illegal in New York, but Gloria knew Becca didn't much care for laws that impinged upon her personal safety.

Gloria shook her head and smiled. "Aw, Becca, your Penis-Be-Good stick. However will you keep rapists and similarly unsavory characters from assaulting your person as you walk home?"

"Don't patronize me, Gloria. Take the damned thing. Who knows what's happening up at that house? You may need it more than me. And listen—give me a call when you get there, okay? Not that I'm trying to smother, I just want to know you're all right and this McElroy fellow hasn't burned the place to the ground or anything."

Gloria agreed to call, and agreed to take the Penis-Be-Good stick, too. Becca handed over the keys to her Lincoln Nautilus and the cipher code to get it out of the garage. Gloria tucked the keys and the baton into her purse, gave Becca a quick peck on the lips, then hurried off.

3

The only stressful part of the drive was navigating the cumbersome vehicle through downtown traffic, but once she'd fled the city and was on the open road, she felt cool and collected. She ejected Becca's Ani DiFranco CD and replaced it with Sviatoslav Richter performing Chopin. She cranked the windows down, and could almost convince herself that she would ultimately arrive at the Hole in the Wall and be provided with some logical excuse why McElroy had been incommunicado for so long. For all she knew, maybe the guy's cell phone died and he hadn't noticed because he'd been too preoccupied with work. Ditto, why he'd missed the Zoom meetings with the studio executives. Could be that Davis McElroy was simply in the zone.

Yeah, sure, she thought. She was trying not to let her anger overtake her, because really, that's what she was feeling—not concern, not caution for her own well-being, but pure, mounting *rage*. A part of her hoped the son of a bitch *was* lying dead of a heart attack in that house, because he'd put her reputation on the line, not to mention a nice chunk of cash if this deal ultimately died on the vine. She could, in fact, excuse a heart attack or stroke—that sort of thing couldn't be helped—but the selfishness of a relapse? A drug and alcohol binge? That was goddamn inexcusable.

She was reminded again of her former client, George Lee Poach—

he of the pasty face, quivering jowls, and damp, eager hands—and of a specific phone call she had received from a perturbed events coordinator a few years ago, informing her that the venerable Mr. Poach was wholly intoxicated and wearing nothing but a tranquil grin as he attempted to order a calzone and a bottle of Knob Creek from the hotel concierge. Gloria didn't abide such bullshit; she'd dropped Poach as a client immediately after that ordeal. Let Jack Baer juggle the addicts, the booze hounds, the prima donnas; Gloria Grossman did not suffer fools.

Still, Davis McElroy was not George Lee Poach. Yes, she had signed McElroy at the height of his addiction, something she hadn't realized he'd been suffering from at the time. But after a protracted stint in rehab, he had come out clean and sober and, to the best of Gloria's knowledge, had remained that way ever since. She'd seen the AA medallions on a small, wall-mounted shelf in his Manhattan apartment, and recalled the uplifting (if somewhat cult-like) mottos he'd occasionally roll out in his languid, professorial voice. Until now, she would have considered Davis McElroy one of her more dependable clients.

She forced herself to quit thinking about it, because her mounting irritation was ruining an otherwise pleasant drive.

4

She relied on the GPS on her phone to lead her to McElroy's house, although she could have probably found it on her own. It wasn't that she'd been here often enough to remember the way, it was that there was only a single private road that led up to the house, flanked on either side by what looked like charming little peach trees. The house itself—the Hole in the Wall—materialized at the end of the road, a rustic yet well-maintained two-story cedar cabin with a slate roof dappled with skylights and a cobblestone chimney. It was too sophisticated and modern to be quaint, the updated renovations more on par with *Better Homes and Gardens* than *Guns & Ammo*. Davis McElroy had done well for himself, in no small part due to Gloria's own innate talent for landing a solid deal (in some circles, she was known as the hostage negotiator, a moniker she secretly relished). McElroy's banana-yellow Triumph Spitfire was in the gravel driveway, and she could see nothing visibly amiss with the house. Not that she had expected to find it burned to the ground, as Becca had suggested, but still.

She parked the Nautilus beside the Spitfire then shut down the engine. Glancing up at the house, framed now in the Nautilus's polarized windshield, Gloria saw that the blinds on all the windows had been drawn.

She unplugged her cell phone from the portable charger, killed the GPS app, then dialed McElroy's number. It no longer rang, as it had done all week—only went straight to an automated mailbox that was too full to accept new messages.

Climbing out of the car, she took in a lungful of fresh country air, determined to keep her anger at bay. The air smelled of flowers and tasted clean. *We're all killing ourselves living in that city like a bunch of crazed rats nesting in a dump site*, she thought, and not for the first time. *Our lungs are probably caustic from taxicab exhaust and we're all most likely courting a dozen different types of cancer.*

She went up the porch steps and knocked on the front door. A semicircular window stood in the door at eye-level, the glass tinted red like the window of a church. Gloria couldn't get a glimpse inside because the window was covered by an ugly paisley curtain.

A sound then—a high-pitched, motorized *rheee!* Not from inside the house but from someplace out here.

Please don't let that be a chainsaw, she thought, somewhat humorlessly. It would have been the exact thing Becca would have said upon hearing it.

The sound died, revved up again, died once more.

"Hey!" she shouted. "Hello? Davis?"

No answer.

She climbed down the steps and walked around to the side of the house. There was a massive oil tank here, red as a fire engine in a child's storybook, and several large sheets of plywood leaning at an angle against the side of the house. Another couple of steps and she saw an upturned five-gallon bucket and what remained of a fairly large watermelon that looked as if it had been hacked apart by an axe-wielding maniac.

It gave Gloria pause.

Becca's voice piped up in her head: *Worst-case scenario, he's dead. Or he comes at you swinging a hammer because he's blotto on smack and thinks you're Julius Caesar.* Funny at the time; not so funny now. And of course Becca's patented Penis-Be-Good stick was still in her purse, which, in turn, was slumped on the passenger seat of the Nautilus. Fat lot of good it would do her there.

"Davis? Hello? It's Gloria Grossman. Anybody home?"

Davis McElroy was in his late forties—Gloria's age—but exuded the youthful good looks of a man at least ten years his junior. Those looks had earned him more than one cameo in a few of the movies he or his friends wrote—once, even a speaking role—and he may have enjoyed a decent run as a second-tier actor had he not been such an introvert. But the man who stepped out from behind the house and into the harsh daylight looked nothing like Davis McElroy. That rugged frat-boy air had vanished, leaving in its place a dark shiftiness, furtive as a wounded animal. He'd lost considerable weight; the open flannel shirt and Race for the Cure T-shirt hung from his wasted frame. His hair had exploded in a dark, unruly mop, bleeding down his face in the form of a spotty, salt-and-pepper beard. His eyes looked haunted.

Davis McElroy froze upon seeing her. He was holding some sort of tool or weapon in his hand, the sight of which did not help ease Gloria's sudden apprehension.

It's drugs, all right, she had time to think. *Son of a bitch.*

"Gloria," he uttered, and even his voice sounded alien to her. Aggrieved, somehow. He took an unsteady step in her direction, shuffling along like someone unaccustomed to it. His eyes looked like they had strings attached at the back and someone was pulling them deeper into his skull. "Gloria, what the hell are you doing out here?"

"That's the question I came to ask you, Davis. Where the hell have you been?"

"Where—?" It came out as a croak. He seemed confused. As he managed another step in her direction—

"What have you got in your hand, Davis?"

He blinked, then glanced first down at his empty hand, then at the other one. He raised the item but she still couldn't make out what it was. Some sort of metal pole or pipe?

"This?" he said. "It's nothing. It's a wood chisel." As if suddenly disgusted by it, he tossed the chisel on the ground.

"Davis, what the hell have you been doing out here? People have been trying to reach you. *I've* been trying to reach you. I drove up from the city to make sure you weren't dead."

He said nothing, just seemed to tremble there in front of her like something insubstantial enough to be carried off by a strong gust of wind. He glanced at something toward the rear of the house— something beyond Gloria's line of sight—then met her stare again. Those bleak and anxious eyes appeared to quiver in their sockets.

"What is it, Davis? Cocaine? Pills? Or have you just been at the bottle?"

A vertical crease appeared between his eyebrows. He shook his woolly head. "No, no—it's nothing like that."

"You realize you missed your deadline, don't you?"

"My deadline?"

"The *screenplay*, Davis. Please tell me you've got something to show me."

"Jesus," he said, the word wheezing out of him. "Yeah, I know. I mean, I know I missed the deadline. It's just, time got away from me."

"You stopped answering your phone. Even John Fish was trying to call you."

She'd mentioned this to shake him up, maybe drive home just how deep in the shit they were. It had the desired effect, given the expression that overcame his face, but when he opened his mouth, Gloria realized she had miscalculated.

"John *Fiiiish*." The name all but seethed out from between McElroy's teeth. He glanced again at whatever kept attracting his attention behind the house—a tic that was making her increasingly uncomfortable—then scratched nervously at his stubbled neck.

"What have you got back there?" she asked him.

Like a landed trout gasping for air, Davis McElroy's mouth opened and closed, opened and closed. It made a sickening *mawp mawp* sound.

"Davis?" she pushed.

"You shouldn't have come here." He took another step in her direction—a stagger, really. "It's not safe. It's...*dangerous*."

She felt herself take an instinctive step back from him. "What's dangerous?" she asked.

There was a beat of silence. When he spoke, he did so just barely above a whisper, and Gloria couldn't be certain she heard him correctly. Sounded like he'd said, "*The book*."

"I don't even go in the house anymore, except for when I have to put up a new wall," he said, then nodded to a small brick structure no bigger than an outhouse farther down the property. "Been sleeping in there. Where it's safer."

He took another step in her direction and she took another step back.

"Been eating out here, too," he continued, and nodded toward the overturned bucket and the decimated watermelon.

"Davis, I think I should call someone and get you help. Would that be okay?"

"Help," he said, the word sounding like it had come unstuck from the roof of his mouth. "Help would be nice."

To Gloria's horror, he collapsed to a seated position in the grass and began to weep.

Every instinct told her to bolt back to the car and get the hell out of there. She could call the goddamn cops from the highway, have them come and collect the son of a bitch. But she didn't do that. She was on the hook now, her curiosity about what Davis kept glancing at behind the house besting any impulse of survival. Besides, she couldn't leave here without the screenplay.

She stepped around him, one cork-heeled sandal brushing the watermelon rind and setting it rocking. It was a pleasant day on its way toward a cool and clear evening. The air had been scented with lilac just moments ago, but as she turned the corner of the house and crossed into the back yard, she caught a whiff of sawdust and overheated electrical equipment.

There was a flagstone patio back here that led to a set of double doors at the rear of the house. These doors both stood wide open now, and there was some sort of construction project erected on the patio in front of them: a pair of sawhorses hoisting one of those sheets of plywood, a scattering of two-by-fours lying on a bedding of sawdust, a circular saw that must have accounted for the mechanical whine she had heard from the front porch.

She looked down, saw her shoe had gotten tangled around a loop of orange electrical cord, and shook it loose.

There was something inside the house, just beyond those wide-open double doors. That would be the parlor, she recalled, a den with exposed wooden beams in the ceiling and a cobblestone fireplace to match the chimney. When she and Becca had been here last—a year ago?—McElroy had taken to outfitting the entire room in a garish Navajo motif that didn't quite jibe with the rest of the house's modern design. McElroy, clutching a rocks glass of spring water with a twist of lime, had laughed at Gloria's expression as she'd run a hand along the woven Native American blanket folded over the back of his Naugahyde sofa. *Yeah, I know, the place looks like a ski lodge*, McElroy had said. *I never did have a sense for fashion, but I like what I like.*

She stepped over piles of sawdust and a scattering of bent, discarded carpentry nails, and approached the open doorway.

What looked like an enormous wooden crate stood in the center of the room. In fact, it occupied the majority of the room, its top nearly butting against the exposed ceiling beams, its width expansive enough to run flush with the fireplace mantel. The Naugahyde sofa was still here, but the crate had shoved it against one wall, its cushions torn and its frame cracked. The enormity of the thing—the inexplicable nature of what she was looking at—gave her a momentary flutter of vertigo.

Whatever the crate was, whatever purpose it served, Davis McElroy had built it. She'd witnessed people do some crazy things while on drugs, but something about this troubled her on some deeper, inexplicable level.

"I know how this looks," he said, startling her. He'd gotten himself under control, though his face was now mottled in red splotches from crying. He wavered there in the doorway like something insubstantial—like she might reach for him only to have her hand pass unimpeded through his body, ghostlike.

Gloria turned away from him. She didn't like looking at his eyes. It was like someone else staring out from behind the mask of his face.

"What is all this, Davis?"

"Pandora's Box," he said, looking past her and into the house. At the crate he'd built. "Despite the old adage, I guess you could say I'm trying to close it back up."

A terrible notion occurred to her. "Is there something *in* there?" But she wasn't thinking *something*, she was thinking *someone*.

"Christ, yes," he said. His voice sounded raw and exhausted. "I mean, it *should...*I *hope* it's..." He trailed off.

She stepped into the room, could smell the cut wood, could see the pixie-like filaments of sawdust spiraling lazily in a shaft of fading sunlight. Because the crate was so tall, it looked like McElroy had amputated the chandelier from its housing in the ceiling; an eye socket that drooled out lengths of wire was all she could see up there.

She stood on her toes and touched the top surface of the crate. Felt the nail-heads poking up from the wood, the splinters jutting from the two-by-four brace. She looked to her left and saw an antique end table smashed to kindling. There was the chandelier, too—a hideous artifact comprised of antlers—casually discarded on the floor in the hallway. She squeezed past the crate and leaned into the hall, caught a whiff of shit and spoiled food. No scent of booze, and no evidence of empty bottles anywhere. She withdrew back into the parlor.

"Explain this to me," she said.

Davis McElroy gazed at the massive crate. One of his eyelids twitched. He looked apprehensive, like he suddenly didn't want to be too close to it.

"I guess you could say I've trapped it," he said. "Like a wild animal."

"Trapped *what*?"

"The book," he said.

"What book?"

A humorless chuckle burped out of him. "*His* book. John Fish."

"*The Skin of Her*—"

"Don't say it!" he shouted, holding his hands up in a warding off posture.

Gloria flinched, as if he might strike her.

"Don't say it. Don't say it. It'll hear you."

"The…book? The book will hear me?"

"You," he said. "Me. Everyone. *Anyone*." He lowered his voice and said, "It *listens*."

She pointed at the crate. "The book is in there?"

"It should be. I hope so. It was at one time. I haven't seen any new holes. Only…"

"Only what?"

"Only it's been chewing its way out. So I have to keep building walls around it so that it doesn't chew its way out and get free."

"Excuse me," she said. She pushed past him and went back out onto the patio.

McElroy lingered inside a moment longer, then followed her outside. He winced when the sun struck his face. Turning his head, the sunlight reflected off his beard, causing one half of his face to shimmer like gold.

"I'm not crazy and I'm not on drugs. You don't know what it's been like out here, Gloria. The things that have happened…"

"Tell me," she said.

He coughed almost demurely into a fist, then said, "It started soon after I'd begun writing the screenplay. Little things at first, the way a haunting in a movie will start small then gradually ramp up momentum. The book—at first, it would disappear. Or…no, not disappear. *Relocate*. Like something alive, moving about the house. I'd find it in some other room, under a bed, in a kitchen cabinet with the coffee mugs. In the bathtub. I thought I was losing my mind—like, was *I* relocating the book to all these random places only to have no recollection of doing so? Were those memories wiped clean from my mind?"

There was another upturned five-gallon bucket back here in the grass. Gloria went to it and dropped herself down onto it. *There used to be a wooden bench back here*, she recalled. She looked out over the yard, naked and barren except for the unkempt grass, straight out to the swell of woods at the horizon. The yard used to be dotted with bird feeders, too, she remembered. At least a dozen of them. Those were all gone now, too.

She was beginning to feel lightheaded.

"But that wasn't it," McElroy continued. "I realize that now. At first, you see, it was trying to get *away*. Fight or flight. It opted to flee. To escape. I didn't know it then, but that's exactly what it was doing. Was trying to do."

"The book," she said, just to make sure she was actually following this bizarre story.

"Yes. The book." He ran a shaky hand through his mop of hair, then giggled like a child. "My God, Gloria, do you realize? If I'd only understood what it was trying to do back then, I would have let it go. Can you imagine? Can you imagine how differently things would have turned out? I mean, if I'd realized what it was trying to do back then, I would have just let it go. But I didn't know. And then things got worse."

"Worse how?" she asked, though she was not so sure she actually wanted to know.

"It fucking bit me," McElroy said, tugging up the sleeve of his flannel shirt. The wound in his arm looked less like a bite and more like someone had slashed him repeatedly with a blade.

"Jesus, Davis," she said, horrified. Had he done that to *himself*?

"Yeah, I know." He fingered one of the slashes, now a crusty brownish scab. "Doesn't really hurt. Not now. Just…just freaked me out more than anything, you know?"

"How did a book do that to you?"

Again, he chuckled—a nervous titter. "I know, right? But Gloria, it *came at me*. Hungry. Pissed off. I don't know. More than once, too."

He bent and cuffed up one leg of his filthy carpenter's pants with both hands. His shin was swaddled in white gauze, at the center of which was a rose blossom of startling red blood. A much fresher wound than the ones on his arm.

Gloria swallowed an intake of air. She covered her mouth with one hand.

"It wasn't just physical, either," McElroy said, dropping his pant leg. He tapped a finger against his temple, eyes blazing. "It was getting in my head, too. Twisting my thoughts. Waging war on an internal scale, like some kind of parasite. Sneaky fucker, right? I could even *hear* it chattering away inside my head—an insect-like buzzing, like bug wings, but not really, because what it *really* was, you know, was the flittering of its *pages*."

A realization struck her—that she had failed to call Becca upon her arrival, as she had promised.

"It popped something in my head, right behind my eye," he said, and pressed a set of fingers to his left eye socket. For the first time, Gloria noticed his hands were lacerated and bruised, the knuckles ridged with leaky crimson scabs. "Blood gushed from my nose like a faucet. For *hours*. I eventually heated a metal cocktail stirrer on the stovetop then stuck it up my nostril to cauterize—"

"Davis, please," she balked, glancing away from him.

"I burned it in the fireplace," he said. "The book, I mean. It came back. I tore it to shreds. *It came back.*"

She looked back at him. Shook her head.

"Don't you see?" he said. "I can't destroy it. It's impossible." He glanced over his shoulder and at the massive crate he'd built in the parlor.

"Forget about the book. Where's the screenplay, Davis?"

"But listen," he went on, ignoring her. "I tricked it, all right? I baited it like some fucking wild animal, and I caught it. Then I built the walls around it. I could hear it moving around inside, chewing its way through the wood. So I put up more walls. Then more walls. Then *more* walls."

He kept staring at the crate he'd built, a discomfiting mixture of pride and terror in his eyes.

It's like he wants to cry and scream and laugh all at the same time, she thought.

"If it was so bad, why didn't you just leave the house, Davis?"

"I did," he said. "Once. I went back to the city for a few hours. See, a writer friend of mine, he gave me the name of some used bookstore on Worth Street, in the city. Said the proprietor dealt in unusual books, and that he might be able to help me. I laughed. Like, who the hell could help me, right?" He snapped his fingers, loud as a gunshot. "Finter!" he exclaimed. "That was the book dealer's name."

"What did he tell you?" she asked, and thought, *This Finter guy probably called the cops on you, Davis. That's what I should be doing right now, too.*

"That the book wasn't just a book," McElroy said. "That it was actually a vessel, a container, for something else. And whatever was trapped in that book was angry. And dangerous."

"No, Davis, he didn't say these things."

"He did!" McElroy shouted. "He wanted me to bring him the book, but of course I couldn't. I'd already trapped it, *entombed* it. I couldn't let it out again. I couldn't risk transporting it back to the city with me. Too dangerous."

He shambled over to her and sat cross-legged in the grass beside the bucket. "I know you think I've lost my mind out here, Gloria. And maybe you're right. I'm just afraid that if I stop putting up those walls…"

She looked at the construction equipment splayed out along the patio then back at McElroy. "It's time to stop," she told him. "Do you understand? It's time to stop, Davis."

He nodded, then hung his head. His eyes had filled with tears again, and those tears dropped onto the knees of his carpenter's pants as Gloria stared at him.

"Where's your laptop, Davis?"

No answer. He just sobbed quietly, his head downturned.

"Davis? We need the screenplay. Did you write it?"

Something akin to a laugh juddered out of him. "Oh, brother. Yes, Gloria. Yes. I wrote the fucker, all right. I finished it."

Relief flooded her. "So where's your laptop?"

Without looking up, he raised a hand. Pointed toward the brick building that looked like an outhouse.

Gloria got up, crossed the overgrown yard, and saw that the door to the small brick building wasn't fully closed. She pushed against it and it squealed open, revealing a tomb-like, windowless room that reeked of gasoline. Indeed, there was a lawnmower and a can of fuel in here, among similar items—a rake, a shovel, potting soil, some more tools. There was also a bedroll splayed out on a mattress of egg-crate foam. Flies hummed overtop a bucket half-full of discarded food. A mound of unwashed clothes and a pair of Converse sneakers shunted into one corner.

She identified the laptop—or what remained of the laptop—last. Any hope she'd had of salvaging this deal sank into the mire. The instrument McElroy had used to decimate the laptop—a hammer—rested on the concrete floor, surrounded by jagged black teeth of plastic and sparkly bits of metal. The laptop's screen was a spiderweb of cracks, the keys from the keyboard stripped and scattered around like teeth knocked loose after a good punch. Not satisfied with smashing only the exterior, she saw that he had removed the hard drive and had annihilated it with the hammer.

She returned to the patio to find McElroy still seated cross-legged in the grass, his head down.

"Please tell me you've got it saved electronically somewhere," she said. "Please tell me it's in the Cloud or in an email or something, Davis."

"The screenplay?" he said, and glanced up at her, wincing as he faced the sun. "It's gone. I erased it. Destroyed it. It had to be done."

"Why, Davis?"

"I realized that's why it kept eating its way through the boxes. It was to get at the screenplay and destroy it. So I saved it the trouble."

She turned away from him, strumming with anger.

"I had to, Gloria," he said, and hung his head again. "I had to."

5

Gloria piloted Becca's Nautilus down the winding road flanked by peach trees, the visage of the Hole in the Wall shrinking in the rearview mirror. In the passenger seat, looking like someone dragged dazed from a fire, Davis McElroy gazed vacantly out the window and at the encroaching twilight. His eyelids kept sliding shut and his head kept bobbing against the passenger window, as if he might fall asleep at any second. By the looks of him—and by the looks of that uncomfortable bedroll spread atop a mattress of egg-crate foam in the outbuilding—he probably hadn't gotten much sleep lately.

Something occurred to Gloria around the time they were back on the highway.

"Davis?"

He jerked his head up from against the window. He'd been in and out of sleep for much of the drive already.

"You said you baited it, like a wild animal," Gloria said. "What exactly did you use as the bait?"

"Oh," McElroy said, rubbing at the corners of his mouth. "The screenplay."

She glanced at him.

"Yeah," he went on. "The book, it wanted the screenplay. That's what it came down to at the end of the day, you know? It wanted the screenplay so I used it as bait to catch it." His laugh sounded like a shrill bark. "Fooled the son of a bitch real good, didn't I?"

"So," Gloria said, "that means—what? The screenplay is…?"

"In the box," McElroy said. "Pandora's Box. With the book."

"In the box with the book," Gloria repeated.

Son of a bitch, she thought, and felt an inkling of hope buoy back up through the core of her body.

A minute later, Davis McElroy was snoring like a champ.

6

Over the next twenty-four hours, Gloria donned her hostage negotiator's hat and went to work. She held a conference call with the studio execs in charge of the project, during which she relayed— in deliberately broad and ambiguous terms—that the screenwriter,

Davis McElroy, had suffered a debilitating medical condition while at his home upstate. He was recouping now in his Manhattan apartment and under the care of a specialist. She could tell what the execs were all thinking—Hollywood was positively overflowing with screenwriters who suffered from periodic debilitating medical conditions, of course—but she refused to confirm or deny any suspicions. Anyway, they were all happy to know that the screenplay was finished and would be delivered to them before the end of the week. By the end of the call, Gloria felt she had won them over. *Baited* was the term that came reluctantly to mind.

Gloria's assistant tracked down McElroy's ex-wife, whom Gloria phoned immediately following the conference call with the studio. She made the call under the auspice of concern for McElroy's health, but in reality, it was to create a legitimate backstory to the tall tale she'd spun for the studio execs. Gloria knew nothing about McElroy's ex—he had already been divorced from her by the time she'd signed him as a client—but it was clear in the first thirty seconds of the call that this was not a woman who was pining for the man to whom she'd once been married.

"Lady, if you're calling to tell me that bastard is back to snorting junk up his nose and drinking himself blind, I couldn't give a shit. I hope he has a fucking coronary."

Before Gloria could eke out another syllable, McElroy's ex-wife disconnected the call.

Gloria stopped by McElroy's Tenth Avenue apartment with a box of donuts and two coffees later that afternoon. It was a show of goodwill, but she also wanted to observe his condition in case he'd have to be marched out for another meeting with the studio heads in the near future. If he still looked like something that had fallen off a subway platform, she'd work around that, say he was still dealing with his medical condition. Whatever it took. He'd slept for much of the drive back to the city the day before, and when he answered the door, he looked well rested and peaceable. He smiled wearily at her and invited her into the apartment.

"I went to an AA meeting this morning," he told her as she followed him into the cramped kitchen nook. She set the box of donuts and the coffees on the table. "First one in about a month or so. It felt good."

"Is that what all this has been about, Davis? Did you get caught up in all that again?"

He looked down at the box of donuts, its bright pink cardboard like something not of this earth. Gloria could tell he was considering what to say, or whether to say anything at all. Ultimately, he said nothing.

"Well, whatever it is, I'm glad you're seeking help."

"Do you think you could set up a meeting for me?"

"A meeting?" she said, suspicious. "With whom?"

"John Fish."

"Oh," she said. "You know, Davis, John Fish doesn't really take meetings."

"I know, I've heard all about him, but you said something about him trying to get in touch with me, and anyway, I just feel I owe him…I don't know…an apology? Or at least an explanation. I feel like such an asshole for killing this deal."

Gloria chewed on the inside of her cheek. She hadn't told him that she'd saved the deal; all she had to do was deliver McElroy's screenplay, which was currently buried inside a wooden box up at the Hole in the Wall.

"Please," he begged.

"I'll call Jack Baer, see what he says," she told him.

"Thank you."

"Are you sure there isn't a digital copy of that screenplay anywhere? Maybe on a thumb drive or something?"

A shuddery breath escaped him.

"Davis?"

"I told you," he said. "It's gone. I'm sorry about that, Gloria, but it had to be done. That book didn't want me working on it. It was like that book didn't want that screenplay to exist at all. It was trying to *stop* me." He shrugged. He didn't meet her eyes. "So I stopped."

Something like a lead weight descended through the core of Gloria's body. It was in that moment she realized just how hopelessly lost this man was. Right now, he looked sober as an archangel, yet he was still talking about that goddamn *book* like it was the devil himself.

She made a show of looking at her wristwatch then headed for the door. "Anyway, I gotta go," she said.

"You'll call Jack Baer? Promise?"

"Promise," she said, and fled that place.

7

She had no intention of having Davis McElroy meet with anyone, let alone John Fish, although she did pass along McElroy's request to Jack Baer during a phone call from the back seat of a taxicab headed uptown.

"Understand that I'm not *making* this request, but merely relaying this to you as nothing more than an anecdote," Gloria said into her phone. "Whatever he's gotten into, Davis McElroy is in no condition to take a meeting. I was planning to tell him that Fish denied his request and leave it at that."

Jack cleared his throat on the other end of the line. "Not so fast. Believe it or not—and I certainly don't, Gloria—Fish made the same request of me."

"You're shitting me."

"I shit you not, dear. Between you and me, I think there's something playing out behind the scenes here, although I can't for the life of me arrive at what it might be. Fish has been uncharacteristically preoccupied with this whole turn of events. It's not like him to give a shit, to put it bluntly, so of course my hackles are up. Can I ask you something?"

"Sure. I just might not answer."

"What the hell happened out there at that house?"

Jack had been on the call with the studio execs earlier that morning, and although he was pleased that she had rescued the project, it was also evident that he didn't buy her bullshit song and dance routine about some vague medical condition.

"Between you and me, Jack," she said, "he was in the middle of losing his mind out there. No, wait—scratch that. His mind was already gone by the time I got there."

She was recalling what McElroy had said to her back at his apartment: *That book didn't want me working on it. It was like that book didn't want that screenplay to exist at all.*

"Drugs?" Jack suggested.

"Probably. I don't know. I'm not his goddamn physician."

"And the screenplay? You'll email it over this afternoon?"

"Listen, let's pretend we're in the Golden Age of Hollywood, and I'm going to have a handsome young courier run you over a hardcopy as soon as possible."

"The hell are you talking about, Gloria?"

She sighed. "There *is* no digital file, Jack. The only copy has been printed out and is apparently back up at the house."

"*McElroy's* house? What the hell is going on over there?"

"Don't worry, it's all under control. I'm going to retrieve it myself today. You'll have it as soon as I get back to the city and can run off a copy."

"Jesus, Gloria. And you're still of the opinion that *my* clients are the troublemakers?"

"One rotten apple does not a rotten batch make," she told him.

"Who's that, Confucius?"

"Go have a martini, Jack, and let me do what I gotta do."

She heard him exhale on the other end of the line. "The hell's going *on*?" he said, and it came out more as an exasperated sigh than a legitimate question.

I have no idea, she thought. *I have no idea*.

8

She brought Becca a chai tea latte, placing it on the edge of her ugly aluminum desk as a peace offering. They'd already sparred over Gloria's failure to call when she arrived at the Hole in the Wall the day before—a heated phone call that had taken place last night, after Gloria had dumped McElroy off at his apartment. Gloria had downplayed the situation at the house to avoid further chastisement from Becca: yes, the son of a bitch had been hitting the bottle again, but no, she hadn't been in jeopardy. Becca had only sighed. She'd wanted to remain irritated at Gloria, but couldn't. Instead, Becca lamented on the fragile male ego, quick to seek solace in a bottle.

Becca eyed the latte like it might be a plastic explosive. "What's this supposed to be, another bribe?"

Gloria came around the desk, wrapped her arms around Becca's neck, kissed the side of her face.

"I need to borrow the car again today," she said.

"I knew it! You're so predictable."

"You should find that comforting by now."

"I find it manipulative. What do you need the car for this time?"

She explained that the only copy of the screenplay was a printout that was still up at McElroy's house.

Becca lifted Gloria's arms away from her. She looked concerned. "You're going back there?"

"There's nothing to be worried about now, Becca. The place is empty. No fragile male ego to spring from the shadows and attack."

"You couldn't have brought the damn thing home with you yesterday?"

"I didn't know it was there until we were halfway through the drive back to the city."

"The idea just doesn't sit well with me." Becca surveyed the paperwork on her desk. "Maybe I'll take a sick day this time, drive up with you."

She didn't want Becca to see the state of that house.

"Don't be silly," she told Becca. "Save your leave so we can run away together."

"And when will that be?"

"Once I deliver the screenplay."

"You're like the Indiana Jones of talent agents."

"Yeah, well, this sucker doesn't belong in a museum. I need to get it to the brass at Paramount toot sweet."

Just then, Gloria's cell phone chirped. A text message from Jack Baer.

"Well, shit," she uttered.

Becca said, "What?"

"John Fish wants to meet with McElroy this evening. Christ, that was quick."

"Is this good or bad?"

"It's perplexing, is what it is," she admitted. "Looks like I'll have to postpone my road trip until tomorrow. That is, if you'll still let me borrow your wheels."

Becca waved a hand at her.

"Thanks, sweetheart," Gloria said. She picked up the latte. "And I apologize for the crude attempt at bribery."

"Leave the latte," Becca said.

9

She was standing outside Bertoli's in a smart pantsuit when a taxicab pulled up and McElroy climbed out. He had shaved, combed his hair, and put on a shirt and tie. Gloria was pleased—and relieved—to see the change in him. He smiled warmly when he noticed her standing on the sidewalk.

"How do I look?" he asked.

"One dollar shy of a million bucks."

"In that case, you got a dollar I can borrow?"

They were twenty minutes early for the meeting, which was by design. The hostess brought them to a dimly lit corner of the restaurant where candles danced on the table in frosted glass jars. A waiter stood at attention beside the table, ready to serve. McElroy ordered a tonic water and lime juice. Gloria ordered the same, though she felt she could use a stiff drink.

"Couple of things," she said. "I don't know why Fish agreed to this meeting, but here we are. I think it's fine for you to offer your apology or whatever you want to call it, but let's keep things simple. You blame the bottle if you want to offer an explanation, understand? You had a little setback, fell off the wagon, and you're sorry for any trouble or inconvenience. That's it, Davis. John Fish is a notorious booze hound, so maybe he'll be sympathetic. I doubt it, but you never know."

McElroy nodded.

"That shit about the book, and that wooden crate you built around it? You keep that between us. Do you understand?"

Again, McElroy nodded.

"Lastly, the deal isn't dead," she said. "First thing tomorrow, I'm heading back up to that house and retrieving that screenplay. I don't want—"

"No," he said, a look of abject horror falling across his face. He actively withdrew from her, as if she were giving off a poisonous gas. "No, Gloria, you can't *do* that."

"I don't want to discuss it. I'm trying to salvage your career and my reputation, do you understand? I won't humor any opposition on this, Davis. It's a done deal."

"You can't do it." Eyes wide, he just shook his head. "You can't."

"Calm yourself, or I'll cancel this meeting right now."

McElroy just stared at her. Fear gleamed behind his eyes.

She glanced at her wristwatch. "They'll be here soon enough. Go to the restroom, wash your face, gain some composure." When he didn't move from his chair, she said, "Goddamn it, *go*, Davis, or we're done here."

He blinked his eyes, as if to clear his vision, then ratcheted himself up off his chair. She watched him meander across the dark floor of the restaurant toward the restroom alcove, where he disappeared. When ten minutes passed and he didn't return, she wondered if he'd snuck out when she wasn't looking. She found she was relieved by the prospect. But then she saw him small-stepping out from the restroom alcove and across the floor to rejoin her at the table. He looked calmer, but she didn't like the way he drummed his fingers on the tabletop.

Ten minutes later, Jack Baer was led to their table by the hostess. Alongside Jack, the imposing figure of John Fish advanced between the tables. He wore a dark suit and an intricately patterned necktie with a pearl tie clip. Fish was an enormous man, known for his love of food and liquor alike, and his formidable stature and prodigious girth did not fail to meet expectation. Gloria had met the man in person only once, at a lavish party thrown by some publishing executive. Fish had held court, pleased as a pharaoh to command such attention. He'd eaten voraciously at that party, Gloria recalled, the only guest at the host's dining-room table, where he devoured an impressive slab of dinosaur meat, still red and squirting blood. They were ten minutes late now, but Fish was clutching a drink in one meaty paw, which meant they'd been pre-gaming at the bar.

Gloria stood as they approached. McElroy followed suit. The hostess pulled out a chair and Fish levered his bulk onto it. The rest of them sat.

"Pleasure to meet you, Mr. Fish," Gloria said. "I'm a huge admirer of your work."

"Then you have exquisite taste," Fish said. He grinned, and his teeth, although yellow, were filed into perfect rows. His ample jowls bulged above the knot of his necktie.

"Davis," Jack Baer said, and extended a hand to McElroy.

McElroy glanced down at Jack's hand, then looked furtively at Gloria beside him.

Christ, she had time to think, seeing the change come over McElroy's face. This was not the same man who'd stepped out of the taxicab less than a half hour ago. Was it possible he'd actually *tricked* her? Gloria Grossman, the hostage negotiator?

Jack's smile faltered. He retracted his hand slowly, but then McElroy raised his own and gripped Jack's palm in a handshake.

Later, Gloria would opine that John Fish would have been successfully murdered had it not been for that awkward, impromptu handshake.

Davis McElroy was right-handed. As he shook Jack's hand, he

groped for the steak knife that sat beside his plate with his *left* hand. He rose from his seat, still snared in that handshake, and carved a clumsy arc across the table with the steak knife. There was no question as to the intended target: John Fish. More specifically, John Fish's throat.

But it was a stretch. Fish had been seated diagonally from McElroy at the table, and while that allowed for a closer proximity between John Fish's throat and McElroy's knife-wielding left hand, it was a ham-fisted attack.

The knife *did* make contact: it swiped across the front of Fish's shirt, amputating the author's expensive-looking necktie in the process. Fish jerked backward, his drink toppling to the floor. Still pumping Jack's hand in a mad handshake—perhaps having forgotten that he was even shaking hands—McElroy bolted up onto the table, repositioning the knife for a follow-up attack. There was no swipe this time, but a sturdy and decisive downward stabbing motion that ultimately planted the blade of the steak knife in the vast, beefy quarter panel of Fish's left bicep.

Jack Baer shrieked.

Gloria sprung up from her chair. John Fish flailed in his own chair, the soles of his tasseled loafers scrambling for purchase on the lacquered wooden floor.

McElroy advanced across the top of the table toward Fish, still clutching Jack's hand. Jack howled and tried to extract his hand from McElroy's death-grip to no avail.

The table gave way beneath McElroy's weight, sending the man crashing to the floor amid the shatter of glassware and the jangly eruption of clattering utensils.

Jack finally yanked his hand free, and, clutching it to his chest, retreated backward until his backside struck a dessert cart. Plates of cheesecake and chocolate mousse toppled to the floor.

John Fish struggled to raise his formidable girth from his chair, but his panic—coupled with his immense weight—prevented him from executing much more than a frantic little jig in his seat. The steak knife protruded from his upper arm, so preposterous it almost looked like a gag.

On the floor, McElroy was scrambling to his feet, tripping and stumbling over the broken dishware and cutlery, ultimately becoming tangled in the linen tablecloth. Fire burned in his eyes—that same lunatic expression Gloria had seen when he'd first come around the side of the house, that wood chisel like a sword in his hand.

John Fish's chair collapsed beneath him, sending the overlarge man toppling to a heap on the floor. Squeezing his injured arm, Fish's eyes were equally on fire—only with the flames of terror. A full-scale inferno.

Somehow, McElroy managed to get back up on his feet. He loomed over John Fish, advancing like something desperate and ravenous and fueled by single-minded wrath. Someone screamed.

Then Davis McElroy dropped back to the floor. He landed on his hands and knees, tried to get back up, but something drove him straight back down again. A moment later, he was supine atop the tablecloth and broken dishes, moaning in agony.

Gloria didn't know what had happened until she realized she was grasping the handgrip of Becca's Penis-Be-Good stick in one hand. She couldn't even remember retrieving it from her purse and swinging it.

10

Newspapers had a field day with the headlines:

BERTOLI'S NOW SERVING FILET-O-FISH

and

OVERZEALOUS SCREENWRITER CUTS TIES WITH NOVELIST

and

RENOWN AUTHOR SURVIVES BRUTAL ATTACK BY THE SKIN OF HIS TEETH

and so on.

John Fish's wounds were superficial, and required nothing more than a handful of stitches. Repercussions for McElroy were more dire: He was arrested, charged with multiple counts of aggravated assault, attempted murder, and one charge of disturbing the peace. Gloria recommended a very good attorney, who happened to be an old love interest back in the day, but did not insinuate herself in Davis McElroy's legal woes beyond that.

She left the city early the next morning, before Becca happened to hear about what had transpired at Bertoli's on the morning news. Not wishing to stoke those fires, Gloria sent Becca a breezy text from the road, relaying that she had a *crazy* story to tell her once she got back to the city—and did she want to do dinner tonight?

That's it, she told herself. *Keep it light.*

It was midday when she pulled up out front of the Hole in the Wall and parked once again beside McElroy's banana-yellow Spitfire. Despite the bright light of day, the house looked dark and ominous to her now. She got out of the car and popped the hatchback. She took out a pry bar and mallet, which she'd had the forethought to purchase the day before, and carried them around to the side of the house. The overturned five-gallon bucket and sheets of plywood were still here, but something had made off with what had remained of the watermelon.

The equipment on the back patio remained untouched. Two days ago, before they'd left the place, she had closed the double doors to the house, but she hadn't locked them. She went to them now, pulled them open.

During the drive up, a part of her wondered what she would do if she opened these doors and saw that something had eaten a hole in the side of the large wooden crate. But that was not the case—the crate was intact, looking no different than it had when she'd first laid eyes on it.

She pried the Naugahyde sofa away from the wall, dragged it across the floor, and positioned it against the side of the crate. It was crudely constructed, she saw, with two-by-fours forming the framework and the sheets of plywood serving as the walls of this...

This what? *Prison* was the first thought that came to her. *Cage* was the second. But those terms were wrong. Those were terms reserved for items that held living things captive. If what Davis McElroy had told her was accurate, she should find nothing inside this large wooden box but a John Fish novel and the printed pages of McElroy's screenplay.

That book didn't want me working on it. It was like that book didn't want that screenplay to exist at all.

Gloria climbed onto the sofa, wedged the pry bar between the plywood and the two-by-four, and then brought down the mallet.

11

What she found inside the crate was another crate. Small yet similarly constructed as the outer one, the revelation of this crate-within-a-crate reminded her of those Russian nesting dolls. This association was only compounded when she opened *that* crate to find yet *another* inside.

He really did lose his mind out here. And for a moment, she wondered what she would do if she opened the final one only to find…

What?

Pandora's Box, he'd called it. *Despite the old adage, I guess you could say I'm trying to close it back up…*

There was another wooden crate inside the third one, only this one was not comprised of those sturdy two-by-fours and sections of plywood. This one had been rendered more hastily, cobbled together with what appeared to be whatever random scraps of wood McElroy had collected then haphazardly hammered together. It was like the crude Neanderthal ancestor of the outer crates. Instead of two-by-fours for the frame, McElroy had dismantled then utilized pieces from the wooden bench that had once been out back. He'd utilized the birdhouses, too, their little wooden perches still poking out from the woodwork.

She took a break at that point, not because her hands were growing numb and were cultivating blisters (which they were), but because the madness that had fueled McElroy to build this eccentric monstrosity felt like it was needling its way into her own brain. Madness by osmosis.

Her cell phone rang. It was Becca. No doubt she had heard about the brouhaha at Bertoli's last night by now. Gloria didn't have it in her to engage in conversation, particularly about the events of last night, so she let it go to voicemail. As she did so, she recognized that McElroy had probably done the same thing every time *she'd* called. The thought of this made her lightheaded—

(madness by osmosis)

—and she staggered outside to gulp down fresh air before continuing her work.

12

The interior boxes were flimsier, like she was getting to the soft, tender core of this excavation. The fury with which they'd evidently been constructed—not to mention the supplies McElroy had used—made them look *angrier*, too. Bits of chair rail, a scuffed tabletop, a section of headboard, slats from some bookshelf—McElroy had used whatever he'd had on hand at first. It was almost as if—

She froze.

A ragged hole, smaller than a fist, had been chewed through one panel of cheap wood.

Not chewed, she corrected herself. *Why would I think that?*

She busted away that panel and discovered a similarly sized hole in the box within. The wood was no more than cheap particleboard—probably it had once been a bookshelf or something—but sure as shit, it looked undeniably like something had tried to eat its way out.

She dropped the pry bar and mallet on the floor and stood staring at the hole. The impossibility of McElroy's claim echoed back to her now: *I could hear it moving around inside, chewing its way through the wood.*

"No." She said this aloud, with deliberate authority. Outside, her cell phone was ringing again. "No way. I'm just spooking myself."

And she laughed.

Because he had gotten to her, hadn't he? Those bleak, haunted eyes of his. In her head, she kept seeing him launch across the top of the table at Bertoli's, the steak knife gleaming as it tore through the fabric of Fish's necktie. Jack's high-pitched shriek as he tried to extract his hand from McElroy's manic handshake.

Davis McElroy himself had made those holes. Nothing more.

13

The final box wasn't something Davis McElroy had cobbled together himself. It was a large cigar box made of Spanish cedar that, to Gloria, looked for all the world like a miniature coffin. She could see McElroy had nailed the lid shut, creating a perimeter of spiky nail-heads around the circumference of the lid. The jagged hole in the center of the cigar box's lid gave her pause, but simultaneously beckoned her toward it. She resisted the urge to get on her hands and knees and peek inside—

(popped something in my head, right behind my eye)

—and instead went out into the yard and returned with the hammer McElroy had used to demolish his laptop. She could have spent several minutes prying those nails, one by one, out of the cheap cedar lid of the cigar box. Instead, she brought the hammer down once, solidly. The lid collapsed, and she picked away the pieces.

Inside was a tattered paperback edition of John Fish's novel, *The Skin of Her Teeth*. Nothing otherworldly—nothing vile or supernatural or dangerous—about it. Just a book. Beneath the book was a thick stack of white bonded pages bound at the margin by brass pins. She brushed the paperback aside and gazed down at the cover page:

THE SKIN OF HER TEETH

Screenplay by

DAVIS McELROY

Based on the novel by

JOHN FISH

"Thank you, thank you, thank you," she muttered, and scooped it out of the cigar box. She flipped through the pages, gleaning the passages of direction and dialogue, taking it in. That crazy son of a bitch had actually completed it before losing his mind.

Well, not exactly completed—she noticed that the last few pages of the screenplay were blank, and that the text actually ended on page 79. Not quite a full feature-length screenplay, but close. If it held together—if it wasn't a complete shit show, in other words—she could negotiate another writer into the contract to complete it. Hell, she'd pay the goddamn WGA scale out of her own commission just to ensure the deal went through.

There were a few bloody fingerprints on some of the pages, dried to an angry russet color. More peculiar was a damp, pinkish substance on some of the blank pages that adhered to Gloria's fingertips like slime. It was tacky and smelled vaguely organic. She glanced down into the cigar box and noticed the same substance adhering to the fore-edge of the book, too.

Like the rattling chains of Marley's ghost, McElroy's voice once again rose up in her head: *It wasn't just physical*, he had told her. *It was getting in my head, too. Twisting my thoughts. Waging war on an internal scale, like some kind of parasite.*

She forced the voice to be silent. Then she grabbed the screenplay, and shoved it in her purse along with her cell phone. She was about to leave when she looked back at the paperback copy of *The Skin of Her Teeth*. This dog-eared trade paperback that had terrorized her client for the better part of a month.

In the end, she cleaned the slimy gunk from its pages with a Kleenex, then dumped the book into her purse, too.

14

Despite her exhaustion, she sped back to the city that evening buoyed by the satisfaction that, despite all the strange twists and turns of the past few days, she had rescued the Paramount deal after all.

As she drove, she ran through a mental Rolodex of clients whom she could rely on to complete the screenplay. She came up with several, but also realized that each one, no matter how reliable, would need *time*—time to read and digest all that McElroy had written, then even more time to compose their own thoughts on how to finish it. Not to mention even *more* time if they hadn't already read Fish's novel. Time was something Gloria didn't have. If she didn't get this thing to the executives at Paramount before the end of the week, then she'd gone up to the Hole in the Wall and spent the better part of her afternoon dismantling a lunatic's elaborate woodworking project for nothing.

Which left her with only one real solution.

She would finish the damn thing herself.

She wasn't a writer by nature or trade, but it wasn't brain surgery. Based on what she'd glimpsed while flipping through the pages back at the house, she really only needed to tag on an ending. And *she* had read John Fish's novel. She could make it work.

She called Jack Baer, told him she was in possession of the prize, and that she would have it sent to his office before the end of the week. Per his contract with the studio, Fish had final approval of the screenplay, but Jack agreed that she should also send it to the brass at Paramount as soon as possible, too, and not drag their feet on this. She didn't tell Jack that McElroy had failed to write the ending; that secret she would take to her grave.

"So, is the damn thing any good?" he asked, the tone of his voice suggesting he doubted it was.

"I'm going to read it tonight and I'll let you know first thing tomorrow. How's Fish?"

"Stitched up and back home."

"Feel free to call him and give him the good news."

"Right," Jack said. "The good news." She could sense something in his voice—some measure of trepidation, it sounded like.

"Am I missing something, Jack? Is something else going on here?"

"You mean, other than your client's attempt on my client's life? No, Gloria. Everything is just peachy."

He was lying, she knew, but she was in too much of a whirlwind to slow down now. Anyway, she didn't need Jack Baer, that old worrywart, to corrupt her good mood.

She hung up with Jack and immediately called Susan Abrams, vice president of development at the studio. She got Abrams's voicemail, so she relayed her good news and said she'd be in touch.

The hostage negotiator saves another one, she thought as she piloted Becca's Nautilus toward the Lincoln Tunnel and into the city.

15

There was some blowback as a result of her having ignored Becca's phone calls all afternoon, not to mention the fact that Becca had learned about what had transpired the night before at Bertoli's from a Yahoo! News article as opposed to her own girlfriend.

"Becca, I feel like I've been running a relay race for the past few days," she said, her phone on speaker while she dug through a carton of leftover Kung Pao chicken at her kitchen table. She had McElroy's screenplay in front of her, and was skimming the dialogue while she ate and as she attempted to placate Becca. Whatever madness had erupted inside Davis McElroy's head this past month, she was relieved to find that it hadn't translated to the page.

"You could have been *killed* last night, Gloria, and I have to learn about it from the goddamn internet!"

"Look, Becca, I said I was sorry. I didn't use my best judgment, but really, those news articles are full of hyperbole. It really wasn't as crazy as all that."

"Are you kidding me? Your client is in jail on attempted murder charges and that writer was taken away in an ambulance with a steak knife sticking out of his forearm. *And you were there for the whole thing!*"

"He didn't need an ambulance," she clarified, as if that changed anything. "It was just a precaution."

Becca sighed heavily on the other end of the line. "I think I'm going to need some time," she said.

Gloria turned to the next page of the screenplay. "Some time for what?"

"Some time away from all this."

Gloria looked at her phone. "All this?"

"Us," Becca said. "I think I need some time away from us."

"Christ, Becca, don't be like that. Let's have lunch tomorrow, okay?" But then she realized she'd need the day to write, so she amended, "Or how about dinner? Wherever you want to go."

"Not tomorrow," Becca said. "Not this week. You've said it yourself—you've been running a relay race. Go finish your race. We can talk once your schedule clears up."

"Yes," Gloria said. "Perfect. Let's do that. Maybe next weekend we can even hit one of those bed and breakfast places that you talked about, remember? Crumbly biscuits? A library of teas?"

"Maybe," Becca said, but her tone suggested otherwise.

"Becca," Gloria said, and picked up her cell phone.

"Goodnight, Gloria," Becca said, and disconnected the line.

Orville Redenbacher padded silently into the kitchen. The blind old tabby walked with his flank against the cabinets until he reached his food bowl. Despite not being able to see, the old cat looked in Gloria's direction before turning back to his food. As if to judge her.

Gloria put the food away in the refrigerator, exchanging it for a bottle of cheap cabernet, then took the screenplay, the wine, a yellow legal pad, and a ballpoint pen into her bedroom. Propped up against the headboard, she finished reading the screenplay, which concluded abruptly on page 79 in the middle of the climax. Otherwise, the script was *good*. It was almost a shame McElroy had blown a fuse, because it really was a nice piece of work.

The only thing she found odd about the whole thing had nothing to do with the actual writing, and everything to do with those blank pages at the end of the script. She counted them—twenty-two pages. Why attach those blank pages to this draft? Was it some weird writerly ritual?

Nonetheless, it was well written, and her mind was whirling with thoughts and ideas the moment she set the screenplay aside on her nightstand. She took a sip of cabernet, then set the legal pad in her lap. McElroy had taken a number of liberties with Fish's novel, mostly to condense the narrative—a necessity when adapting any book, but particularly when adapting a doorstop like *The Skin of Her Teeth*—so she would have to eschew certain characters and plot points she remembered from the novel. But as long as she continued down the logical path McElroy set into motion, she should run into little difficulty.

Pen poised over the legal pad, she collected her thoughts, then jotted down a series of bullet points that, tomorrow, she could flesh out more fully.

It was 12:55 a.m. when she yawned and peered over at the clock on her nightstand. She'd filled up several pages of detailed notes (and had killed half the bottle of cab) in a few hours' time. She was exhausted, but also satisfied. She'd pull this off yet, and maybe a few years down the road, she'd even cop to what she'd done. She'd get fined by the WGA, but goddamn if it wouldn't make a fantastic anecdote.

Gloria Grossman went to sleep content in the knowledge that she was still at the top of her game.

16

Sometime, in the still-dark hours of an early morning, Gloria awoke to the sound of someone moving around inside her apartment. She sat up in bed, listening, waiting to hear whatever the sound had been that had roused her from a dreamless slumber. She could hear nothing, but knew she wouldn't be able to get back to sleep unless she looked around the place. There'd been some break-ins in the building lately.

She rolled out of bed, flipped on the light, then crept out into the hallway. She turned on more lights, then surveyed her apartment. Everything looked in its place. The windows were still latched and the panes were unbroken. The deadbolt on the door was still engaged. She imagined she'd find Davis McElroy, somehow escaped from jail, standing in her economic little kitchen nook, eyes like grease fires, wood chisel in one hand. But the kitchen was empty, too; there was no one here.

She drank a glass of water from the tap and was on her way back to bed when she noticed the broken lamp. It had stood on the end table beside the sofa, a decorative piece that she'd found at an antiques shop years ago in Los Angeles, emerald-green fish crossing to form a pattern of Xs across its ceramic base. The lamp was on the floor now, its base broken into several pieces, its kitschy, tasseled lampshade having rolled over near the entertainment center.

Blind old Orville Redenbacher had a penchant for knocking over things. Lamps, bottles on the counter, potted plants—anything that she might inadvertently relocate to a place that had been previously vacant. The cat had memorized his passage throughout the entire apartment, but if something suddenly found its way in Orville's path—*smash*. It wasn't the dumb cat's fault.

Thing was, the lamp had been on that end table since she'd bought it. It wasn't something new that had been introduced—that had been *thrust*—into poor Orville's pitch-black world.

She looked around and couldn't find the cat anywhere. That wasn't unusual, either—the old bastard sometimes stayed hidden for days, making an appearance only when he was hungry or felt like coiling himself around Gloria's ankle. She decided not to stew on it, and went back to bed, oblivious to the fact that her perception of the world would change come morning.

17

There was an old George Lee Poach anecdote—a story that had basically become an urban legend in some circles—that went something like this:

During the shooting of the film *Summer Fling* in Honolulu, Poach, who'd been hired by Universal to pen the screenplay, arrived at the lavish Mermaid Hotel where the cast and crew were staying, to the surprise (and dismay) of nearly everyone. Rarely was any screenwriter invited to the set, and even someone of Poach's esteem—he'd earned two Emmys and an Oscar nomination by that point—was conveniently excluded from production. But Poach, who had been midway through an alcohol- and drug-fueled bender, had decided to hop a red-eye to the island unannounced, with only the clothes on his back. Not wanting to make waves, the director notified his studio contacts. The studio people, also not wanting to make waves, decided to allow Poach to hang around on set, provided he kept out of everyone's way. They even paid for his hotel room for the first few nights (before things went bat-shit crazy, as the story goes). As it turned out, Poach had little interest in hanging around on set, and squandered most of his time at the hotel bar, knocking back a procession of neon-colored, coconut-flavored drinks and amassing quite an impressive collection of tiny paper umbrellas.

It was on the third or fourth night at the Mermaid Hotel that Poach, drunk as a lord, arrived at the concierge desk and demanded a change of rooms. When asked why such a change was necessary, Poach calmly informed the concierge that his *current* room was haunted, and that he needed to "get out from that bad juju, son." (George Lee Poach was no longer a client of Gloria's at this point, but when she first heard someone relay this story to her, she could hear Poach's condescending, Midwestern drawl rolling out that exact phrase, verbatim.) The concierge asked him why he believed such a thing, and Poach said that he'd personally *witnessed* the haunting, so there was no question about it. In fact, if the fellow would follow him up to his room right now, Poach would *show* him what had happened.

The concierge, well aware that this old bastard was somehow connected to the Hollywood film being shot here, thought it best to humor him. He followed Poach into the elevator and up to the nineteenth floor. Poach slid his key-card into the door handle of his room and then swung the door wide, beckoning the younger man to enter.

The room looked as if a tornado had blown through: bedclothes were scattered about the floor, the dresser drawers all stood open, and the few articles of clothing Poach had purchased (at the request of the film's director, who informed Poach as delicately as possible that he was beginning to smell a bit ripe) were strewn everywhere. Hands on his hips, George Lee Poach stood there while the young concierge took in the room. "Well?" Poach said, once it was clear the concierge wasn't going to say anything at all. "Look at what the ghost has done to this room, son!"

The state of the room did not necessarily surprise the young concierge. Poach stank like a distillery, his bar tab had quickly become a thing of legend, and the drunk old bastard had even taken quite a remarkable shit in the bathtub. The condition of this room was restrained in comparison.

Before the concierge could flee, Poach snatched him about the lapels. "I. Did. Not. Do. This," Poach exhaled into the poor fellow's face, his breath as acrid as turpentine. "This room is haunted and I need to get out! Do you understand me? I need to get *out*."

The hotel ultimately obliged, and provided Poach with a new room. Things seemed to go all right from then on—well, all right as far as the haunting was concerned; Poach was later arrested for falling asleep naked inside another hotel patron's rental car and soon thereafter traveled back to California, like someone who had sleepwalked through the entire ordeal. The intriguing part of the story was that the young concierge, new to the job and desperate to avoid any similar problems in the future, asked around about Poach's hotel room while relaying Poach's story about a supposed haunting. What the concierge learned was that years earlier, a husband and wife had stayed in Poach's room. They had allegedly run afoul of some local head-bangers—something about stolen money or jewelry or drugs—and these head-bangers, frustrated by the couple's lack of cooperation, had tossed the couple from their balcony, killing them both. Then they had ransacked the room looking for whatever it was they felt had been taken from them—turned out dresser drawers, emptied suitcases of clothing, stripped the bed. Whatever these men had been looking for, they never found it, and they were unceremoniously executed for their failures by whatever kingpin had been running that particular show.

It was this bizarre story that returned to Gloria the following morning, as she stepped out into the main room of her apartment, still tying the sash of her robe around her waist, to find the contents of her purse scattered about the carpet. There was a handful of loose change, a tube of L'Oréal lipstick, a four-count of tampons, and a solitary red-and-white pinwheel mint on the floor surrounding the coffee table. On the table itself was her purse, looking now like something deflated. She picked it up off the coffee table and a cascade of loose coins spilled out from a tear in the side of the purse, startling her. She dropped the bag back onto the coffee table, then peered down at it again—at the fist-sized tear in the bag. She couldn't deny that it looked like something had—

(chewed)

—clawed its way through the fabric.

"Orville?" she called. That damn cat—was he losing his marbles now, too? Clawing at her purse? What was next, slicing her blouses into ribbons?

Blind as a dead bulb, Orville never came scurrying when she called his name, although he often appeared slinking along one wall, his whiskers dictating his passage through the apartment, as he navigated toward the sound of her voice. He did not appear now, however.

"Orville? Where are you, buddy? Come on out."

She went to the kitchen to dump fresh food in his bowl, but saw that there was already food in it from the night before, uneaten.

Concerned now, she searched the apartment—all the little hidden nooks and crannies where Orville liked to hide. He was nowhere. She rechecked all the windows, making sure they were closed tight and that he hadn't wandered outside onto the fire escape. But they were still latched. There was no way that damn cat could have gotten out of the apartment.

Most disconcerting was the damp pile of cat fur on her bedroom floor, at the base of her nightstand. Orville would occasionally shed, or cough up hairballs that he'd deposit randomly throughout the apartment. This was nothing like that—the area where the fur was scattered was contained, almost as if a bolt of lightning had charged out of the sky and zapped the poor fellow into oblivion. Gloria knelt down and snatched up some of the fur. Yes, it was moist, but not from Orville having hacked it up. The moisture was tacky and tinged pink. It possessed an unsettling menthol coolness against the tips of her fingers.

She stood abruptly, wiping the gunk from her hand down the side of her robe. Before she had time to consider just what the hell had happened here, her gaze fell upon McElroy's screenplay. It sat just where she'd left it last night, atop the nightstand, beside the yellow legal pad whose pages she had filled with notes, and the half-empty bottle of cabernet. Only now, the paperback copy of *The Skin of Her Teeth* was right there with it. The book's pages were interlaced with the pages of the screenplay, like shuffling a deck of cards. She'd put that book in her purse back at the Hole in the Wall yesterday, and hadn't taken it out. Yet here it was.

She picked up the book, and the screenplay came with it. Their pages were fused by that inexplicable pink slime. Only now, the slime was still fresh, gummy as taffy. She separated the screenplay from the book and a web of slime stretched between the two items until its weight caused it to droop and break apart. Globs of it pattered to the bedroom floor. She could smell it, just like she had smelled it back at the Hole in the Wall—an organic, almost *vaginal* smell. It repulsed her.

She tossed the book to the floor. Still gripping the screenplay, she took it to the adjoining bathroom and cleaned the gunk from its pages with a damp piece of toilet paper. But mere seconds into that process, she stopped, and stood there trying to reconcile just what the hell she was looking at.

There was the cover page of the screenplay, there were the next dozen or so pages of direction and dialogue…but then a swath of blank pages after that. Like, sixty blank pages. McElroy's bloody thumbprints were still there, stamped right onto the pages, but the text was gone.

18

There was only one bookstore located on Worth Street, an unobtrusive little boutique with a cracked front window. FINTER'S USED BOOKS was stenciled on the tinted glass.

The tiny shop was empty, the tight walls towering above Gloria's head groaning with books. A pair of bifocals rested atop a heap of hardbound books on the small desk beside the front window, but there was no one behind it. The bell above the door that had signaled her arrival was a quaint touch, but it hadn't alerted anyone to her presence.

"Hello?" she called down the length of the shop. Her voice fell flat in the dry and musty air.

A man's face appeared between the stacks. The rest of his diminutive frame followed, stodgily packaged in a pinstriped shirt and sleeve garters. He approached Gloria with an aggrieved expression, as if the tribulations of traversing this shop's narrow corridors caused him physical discomfort.

"Are you Mr. Finter?" she asked the man.

"I'm Ross Finter," he said, settling himself on a stool behind the desk. "What can I do for you, madam?"

She placed the paperback copy of *The Skin of Her Teeth* on the man's desk.

"Sometime in the past month, a man—a client of mine—came to you seeking some sort of information about a book." She nodded at the novel she'd placed on the man's desk. "*This* book."

Finter jostled the bifocals onto his face and scrutinized the book. Said, "John Fish is a popular author. His first editions go for top dollar."

"I don't care about John Fish's first editions. A man named Davis McElroy came to see you recently about this book. He was under the impression that it was…that it was attacking him. He said he spoke to you and you—"

"Ahhh," Finter said, his small, lucid eyes widening behind the glass of his bifocals. "Mr. McElroy, yes. I remember." He looked back down at the book. "Is this it? The, uh…culprit, shall we say?"

"This is it," she said. "What exactly did you say to him?"

Finter rummaged around his desktop until he recovered a wooden ruler. He used it like a cattle prod to poke and jostle the book around on his desk.

"Yes, yes." He was mumbling to himself. "This is her, all right. A naughty girl."

"Her?" said Gloria.

"Oh, most definitely," Finter said. "If what your friend—your client?—told me was accurate, then this is most definitely a 'she.'"

"Care to explain that logic?"

"The unwavering stubborn determination alone suggests the presence of an entity of the feminine persuasion."

"That's awfully damn sexist."

"It's not meant to be offensive. It's not meant to be anything, really. It's actually quite complimentary, if you think about it in a certain way. All things considered."

"My client is currently sitting in jail on attempted murder charges," Gloria said. "At his house, he'd hidden this book inside a series of…I don't even know how to say it…wooden boxes? He thought some war was being waged between him and this book."

"Oh, don't be fooled," Finter said, readjusting his bifocals. "This is no book."

No wonder McElroy went off the deep end, she thought. *He came here looking for help and found this lunatic.*

"Then what is it?" she asked.

"First things first," Finter said. His eyebrows arched above the rims of his glasses. "Attempted murder charges, you said?"

"He tried to kill the man who wrote this book."

"Mistake number one," Finter said. He raised an index finger toward the ceiling. "The author of this book is incidental. Killing him would be like…" He fluttered his hand about. "Well, it would be like expelling posterior gas into the wind, if you'll pardon the expression, madam."

"What do you mean it's not actually a book?"

"Well, you see," Finter said, wrinkling up his face as he studied the Fish novel on his desk; he kept poking it with the ruler. "It's a container of sorts. A totem that only *looks* like a book. But in actuality, that is just the form it takes in our world."

"Okay, thank you," she said, and snatched the book off his desk. As she made her way to the door—

"Wait!" Finter cried out.

She turned, agitated.

"Your friend," Finter said. "Was he tasked with manipulating the book in any way?"

"How do you mean?"

"Manipulating," Finter articulated, peering at her from over the top of his bifocals. "In any way."

"He was adapting the book for a movie," she said.

Finter frowned, presumably failing to understand.

"He was writing a screenplay based on the book so that it could be made into a movie," she clarified.

Again, Finter's glistening button-eyes widened. Slowly, he began nodding his head. "Oh, yes," he intoned, his voice barely above a whisper. "Yes, indeed. That'll do it, all right."

"That'll do what?" she asked.

"Set things in motion. Do you happen to have this, uh, adaptation, uh, in your possession?"

Gloria took McElroy's screenplay from her purse and set it on Finter's desk. The pages were curled from being in her purse all morning.

Finter licked a finger then turned past the title page.

"I'm going to level with you, mister," she said. "Yesterday, there were seventy-nine pages of text in that document. Now there's only about a dozen or so pages. All the rest are blank. It wasn't that way when I first found it yesterday."

Finter's stare felt tangible, like he was poking her with something.

"What's it mean?" she asked him.

"You said your friend is currently in jail?"

"Yes."

"Then he's very lucky."

She laughed dryly.

"Listen here," he said. "This book—you must think of it like the shell of a mollusk. A *thing* lives inside it."

"A *female* thing," Gloria said.

Ross Finter gave her a shark's smile.

"Whatever lives inside this book," Finter said, "it wants to *remain*. That is its sole purpose, do you hear? *To remain*. She doesn't want to leave, and she certainly does not want to be *altered*. She does not want change. This…this product here," he said, tapping the screenplay with the ruler. "This *base thing* threatens her. It attempts to change her, to alter her. To do away with her. She won't have it."

"You mean because the story has to be changed to work for a film—"

"The story does not want to be changed," Finter said. "The entity that resides inside the story does not want it changed. You cannot alter the story."

"What are you telling me? That this book is possessed?"

"It's not the *book*, madam, but the *story*. Aren't you listening? There is nothing special about this particular *book*—its paper and cardboard and glue and ink. It's the *story* that doesn't want to be changed. It's really that simple."

"So what the hell happened to the screenplay?" Gloria asked him. "Where'd the pages go?"

"Quite simple," Finter said. "The book ate them."

Gloria sucked on her lower lip and stared at the little man.

"It does not want this version to exist," Finter went on. "It wants to remain as it has always been, and does not want to change. My suggestion to you, madam, is to *let it be*."

She turned to face the window, gazing out at the people weaving up and down the sidewalk. She turned and looked at the shelves of books, so many shelves, so many books. The place smelled like a tomb, stale and forgotten.

"So what do we do about this?" she said eventually.

"The simplest thing," Finter said, "is to give it what it wants."

He turned and waddled down the length of the shop, one index finger extended like a divining rod. Gloria noticed that he was not looking at books on the shelf, but at a series of metal safes stowed back there on the shelves. A whole collection of them.

Finter selected one, held it up to one ear, shook it.

"Empty," he determined, and carried the safe over to his desk. He set it down, fished a ball of keys from a retractable wire attached to his belt, and unlocked the safe. It was empty. Before doing anything, he looked back up at Gloria and said, "May I?"

"Go for it," she said.

He placed the paperback novel inside, then tucked McElroy's screenplay in after it. He locked the safe, let the keys retract, then placed the safe back on the shelf, among the others.

"I can't wrap my head around any of this," Gloria said. "This is a bad dream, right?"

"Whatever gets you through the night, madam," said Finter.

"That book," she said, and then said nothing.

"Yes?" said Finter, climbing back onto his stool.

"I think it ate my cat."

Ross Finter nodded, rubbing his chin. "Quite possible," he said. "Quite possible, indeed."

19

She was contemplating what to say to Jack Baer when Jack rang her cell phone. She was standing on the corner of Worth and Lafayette, fumbling the phone to her ear, still somewhat in a daze from all that Ross Finter had told her. She had a hand raised for a taxi, but slowly lowered it as Jack's voice filtered through the phone.

"Clear your schedule tonight," Jack said, forgoing salutation. "John Fish has invited us to his Park Avenue residence this evening."

"Fish? Me? What's going on, Jack?"

"I don't know, but I get the sense it's going to be a bombshell."

Why not? she thought.

"Gloria? You still there?"

"I'm here," she said.

"I've been avoiding the studio folks all afternoon. I was waiting to hear from you. What's the status of the screenplay? Can we get copies sent out or what?"

Her mind was reeling. "I've got a lot of balls in the air right now, Jack. I'll get back to you on the screenplay."

"And tonight?" he said. There was a pleading quality to his voice. "You'll come, won't you?"

"If John Fish says jump, we jump."

"That's the spirit," Jack said.

20

John Fish owned a penthouse apartment on Park Avenue, where he whiled away the months of autumn. His summers were spent on a horse and sheep ranch in Montana, and the rest of the year he could be found behind the security-enclosed gates of his Hollywood Hills home in Central L.A.

Gloria arrived at Fish's building five minutes earlier than the time Jack had told her. She gave her name to the security guard at the lobby desk, and he acknowledged that Mr. Fish was expecting her. He used a special key to allow the elevator to carry her to Fish's floor.

She knocked on the door and a woman with severe black eyebrows and a supermodel's emaciated figure bid her entrance. This woman led Gloria to an opulently decorated parlor, where Jack Baer stood cradling a gin and tonic while absently poking a key on the Steinway that stood in one corner of the room. The woman departed before Gloria could thank her.

"Something about this is making me uneasy," Jack said, transitioning from the piano to the wet bar. He appraised her.

"Glass of wine," she said.

"Red or white?"

"Whatever is in that decanter there."

He poured her a glass, handed it to her. Muttered a toast in Latin.

"So you still don't know what this is about?"

"No," said Jack. "For all I know, we're about to become party to whatever lawsuit he's getting ready to lodge against McElroy, Bertoli's, the City of Manhattan, and whatever else he can think of."

"I wouldn't worry about that, Jack."

"Or maybe it's about the deal," Jack said. "Maybe he wants to see this screenplay before we do anything else. I'm sure McElroy hasn't left him with the best taste in his mouth, given everything that's happened. Have you read it? The script?"

She smiled at him. "So, here's what I'm thinking," she said. "We own the media's account of what happened at Bertoli's, use it as publicity, as a promotional tool. We spin it that way to the studio, too, and have them hire another writer to come in and rewrite the screenplay from scratch. We trump up the story about what happened in the tabloids, get people talking about this project before they even start principal photography. A new screenwriter can add to the mystique of what happened; it can turn into its own self-propelled urban legend. We play it up and own it, Jack. We can spin this to our benefit."

Jack looked like someone had just threatened to kick him in the nuts.

"What, Jack?" she said.

"What's wrong with the screenplay as it is?" he asked.

It's gone, she thought. *It's disappeared right off the page. Eaten by a haunted entity trapped inside a story.*

Instead, she said, "It's crap, Jack. The screenplay is crap. We can't turn it in. So we need to spin this or we'll lose the deal."

"Lose the deal," he muttered, and stared down at his drink.

Someone cleared their throat. They turned and saw John Fish standing in the doorway. He was dressed in a crimson kimono, cinched at the waist, and startling white athletic socks. He trudged into the room and went straight for the wet bar. Without uttering a word, he motioned to the ornate sofa for Gloria and Jack to sit.

"How's your arm, John?" Jack asked, as he and Gloria claimed a seat at either end of the sofa.

"I'll live," Fish said, and poured himself about three fingers of Blue Label scotch into a crystal glass.

Gloria glanced at Jack, saw that he was sitting forward with his own drink clutched in both hands between his knees. Even in the dim museum lights of the parlor, she could see he was perspiring; the side of his face glistened with gently rolling spangles of sweat.

Fish carried his drink to a wingback chair piped with brass tacks and dropped himself into it. The *sound* that escaped his throat sounded like the tortured bleat of an oboe. His massive tree-trunk legs—fish-belly white and woven with dense black hair—poked out from beneath his kimono.

"I'm glad we could all get together like this," Jack jumped right in. "Gloria was just telling me this wonderful idea she's had for the film project. In a sense, we use what transpired at Bertoli's to our benefit, spin it so…well, Gloria can tell you better than I can…"

Gloria cleared her throat and opened her mouth to speak, but John Fish cut her off before she uttered a word.

"The project is dead," Fish said. "I'm pulling out of the deal."

Gloria only raised her eyebrows and closed her mouth.

Jack shifted uneasily in his seat. "Listen, John, I think we all realize we owe you an apology for what happened at that restaurant. Clearly, if either of us had any inkling that Davis McElroy was in any way a danger to you—"

I had an inkling, Gloria thought but didn't say. *In fact, it's probably fair to say I had* more *than an inkling.*

"—we would have never allowed that meeting to—"

"This isn't about Davis McElroy," Fish said. He turned his small, sparkling eyes on Gloria. "I spoke with the district attorney's office this afternoon, in fact, and told them I wouldn't be pressing any charges against your client. For whatever that's worth. I assume they can—and still may—prosecute, but I just wanted to make my position known for the record."

Gloria was surprised to hear this. She kept seeing the fear blazing across Fish's face as he squirmed on the floor of that restaurant while McElroy advanced on him like some crazed lunatic escaped from an asylum. "That's very kind of you," was all she could muster.

"And a note of gratitude to you," he said to Gloria. "What was that thing you were wielding like some medieval knight?"

"An expandable baton." And before she could catch herself, she added: "My girlfriend calls it her Penis-Be-Good stick."

Some facsimile of a grin creased the lower half of John Fish's face. "I like that," he said, and took a sip of his drink.

"John," Jack interrupted, "I don't think we should be too hasty about this. What exactly is the problem, if it's not Davis McElroy?"

"It's the book," Fish said, and Gloria felt a chill tremble down her spine. "I'm pulling it from the studio. *The Skin of Her Teeth* will not now, nor ever, become a motion picture."

Jack Baer shook his head. "I don't understand…"

"No, you wouldn't," Fish said. "Let me elucidate."

"Please," Jack said in a huff, and reclined into the sofa. He had his drink rested on one knee.

"This was not the first attempt at adapting my novel," Fish explained. "The book had gone through this process a number of times before—long before I transitioned over to your agency, Jack. You may have read about it in the trades at the time."

"I'm aware," Jack said, his tone flat.

"The first screenwriter was a man named Eddie Lustig. At the time, he was flying high after writing some tent-pole Hollywood blockbuster—aliens or superheroes or some such nonsense—and he thought he could punch his own meal ticket. He sought an option from me without the backing of a studio, figured he could write the damn script on spec and sell it at an auction. I don't believe Mr. Lustig was wrapped too tight and he indulged in his share of nose candy from time to time…although in retrospect, McElroy's actions at Bertoli's made Lustig look positively saintly."

Jack grunted and crossed his legs. The ice in his drink chimed against the glass.

"Lustig never completed the screenplay. He died in a car wreck somewhere in the Hollywood Hills. Police reports said he was swerving, speeding like a madman, and ultimately careened through a guardrail and rolled to the bottom of the canyon. I have it on good authority that Lustig was removed from the vehicle in two separate body bags. The steering wheel of his sports car, you see, bisected the poor fellow completely in half."

"Lord," Jack said, and he turned to look out the glass doors that led to the balcony.

"Sometime later," Fish went on, unperturbed, "an independent production company optioned the book and hired a duo of female screenwriters to write it. Their names elude me, but I *do* remember that they had been something of an item—romantically, I mean—living together somewhere in Arizona or New Mexico or someplace dry and orange. They actually *completed* a draft, but before they could work on any rewrites—you know how those studios are about giving notes, even the small independents—they died in a bizarre murder-suicide."

"I remember that," Gloria said, sitting straighter now in her seat. "One woman shot and killed the other and then she shot herself in the head."

"That's the *Reader's Digest* version, yes," said Fish, that serene grin reappearing on his face. "The one woman shot her lover and writing partner *thirty times* in the chest and face. The weapon was a Glock semiautomatic with a fifteen-round magazine, as I recall.

Only one magazine was found at the crime scene, which means she had to *reload* the damn thing in order to *unload* those additional fifteen rounds into her former lover and business partner. And then, of course, one more round in the chamber for herself after she'd completed the deed."

Gloria remembered seeing the images of the crime scene on the TV news. Fish was right—they'd lived someplace in the Midwest, in a single-story white stucco house with a pool out back. Gloria had been living in L.A. at the time, and talk of this lurid event had circulated at dinner parties and studio events.

"Then," Fish continued, "just a few scant years ago, a playwright named Genarro was adapting the book for a stage play. My contact with Mr. Genarro was practically nil, and I never heard much about him until some peculiar tragedy struck his family. His wife attempted suicide, slicing open both her wrists. There was something else, too—something about Genarro's daughter, I believe. Due to these circumstances, Genarro walked away from the project. And it had sat dormant until your client, Ms. Grossman, had the misfortune of stirring it back to life again."

"Oh," was all Gloria could say.

"You're telling us that you think there's—what? Some kind of curse on this book?" Jack said. "Like Shakespeare's *Macbeth*?"

"Not the book," Fish corrected. "The *adaptations*."

Jesus Christ, Gloria thought. She suddenly felt very cold.

"There have been too many tragedies associated with these attempted adaptations," Fish said. "Mr. McElroy is only a sad little pawn in some greater tapestry, if you'll forgive the mixed metaphor."

Gloria brought her wineglass to her mouth, but the smell of it suddenly made her ill, and she recoiled from the glass. In her head, she recalled the story about George Lee Poach, and how he'd needed to get out from that bad juju. This, too, was bad juju.

"Therefore, as of this moment," Fish proclaimed, "I will no longer allow that book to be adapted for any medium—film, stage, radio dramas, any of it."

"For Christ's sake, John," Jack said. "You can't really believe this."

Fish's stare said all there was to say.

Jack laughed, shook his head. "I mean, there's audio books, aren't there? Nobody's dying listening to audio books. And foreign translations!"

"The audio books are a verbatim reproduction of the text of the book," Fish said. "The foreign translations only *translate* the story. No one is *altering* it."

Altering, Gloria thought. It was the word Finter had used, too: *Whatever lives inside this book, it wants to* remain. *That is its sole purpose, do you hear?* To remain. *She doesn't want to leave, and she certainly does not want to be* altered. *She does not want change.*

"She," Gloria heard herself mumble. Fish's eyes swiveled in her direction, but Jack Baer didn't acknowledge her.

"This is preposterous," Jack said. "There's a lot of money on the line here, John. Moreover, do you have any idea what Gloria had to go through just to *get* the damn script from McElroy?"

"I suggest you destroy it, if you haven't already," Fish told her. That previous little grin was gone now; he looked as sober as a judge.

Jack dumped the rest of his drink down his throat then rose off the sofa. "I thought we were here to talk business. I thought we were here to come up with a goddamn battle plan on how to rescue this deal. Not to talk about curses and hocus pocus."

John Fish said nothing. He kept his gaze leveled on Gloria.

"I've spent a lot of time on this thing," Jack was saying. He strode over to the piano, set his empty glass atop it. "And let me be straight with you, John. Your numbers haven't been so great lately. How many units did *The Postman's Granddaughter* move?" When Fish did not reply, Jack said, "Not enough. That's how many. Sure, your first editions go for big money on the secondary market, but that doesn't mean shit for me."

"*The Postman's Granddaughter* has some wonderful descriptions of trees, if I do say so myself," Fish intoned, and Gloria couldn't help but smile. In that instant, she did not completely dislike John Fish, and she wondered if all the stories she'd heard about him over the years were, in fact, true.

"Yeah, great, descriptions of trees," Jack muttered. "That'll pay the bills."

"I'm of the opinion," Fish said, speaking to Jack without turning to look at him, "that perhaps a little fresh air would do you good." He acknowledged the balcony doors with a wave of his hand.

"You're goddamn right," Jack said, only he made his way across the room and toward the hallway. He paused at the door. "Are you coming, Gloria?"

"Actually, I think I might finish my drink," she said. She looked at Fish. "Is that okay?"

"By all means," Fish said.

Jack's lips thinned. His face had turned beet-red. He looked like he wanted to say something more—to shout something, perhaps—but in the end, he left that place without uttering another word.

"Refill?" Fish said.

"I've still got half a glass, thanks," she said.

"No, dear, I meant me." He held out his empty rocks glass for her.

Under ordinary circumstances, she would have followed Jack out into the hallway and out of the building, but something about Fish's presumption was almost endearing. Besides, there was more to Fish's story—she knew there was—and she wasn't going to leave until she heard the rest of it.

She refilled Fish's glass with scotch, handed it back to him, then reclaimed her seat opposite him on the sofa.

"What I'd like to know," she said, "is *why*."

One of Fish's bushy eyebrows leapt toward his receding hairline. "Why?" he said.

"Yes. As in, *why* do you think these adaptations have been cursed? Granted, everything you've said tonight—what happened to all those other writers—certainly paints an unusual picture. And what happened with Davis McElroy is like the icing on that strange little cake. But you were worried something was up even *before* McElroy planted that steak knife in your arm. That's why you agreed to meet with him. You wanted to meet with him just as much as he wanted to meet with you."

Fish tipped his head back against the chair. The pouch of flesh beneath his chin looked as pronounced as a goiter. He tasted his drink, then said, "I wanted to see it for myself. It would be unfair and rather tactless of me to call Davis McElroy something of a litmus test, but in all honesty, that was what he was."

"Because you'd heard of what happened to those other writers but you'd never *seen* it," Gloria finished his sentiment. "McElroy was missing in action for over a month, people were running around trying to find him, *I* was running around trying to see what the hell was going on, and here you were, waiting to see if another tragedy would unfold."

"It would have been the final confirmation for me. I'd started suspecting…well, *something*…but needed just one more bit of evidence to prove it to myself. I know it sounds crass, but please understand that had I been *certain* this would have ended poorly for Mr. McElroy—for any of us, really—then I wouldn't have gone through with this project from the very beginning. But I didn't *know*. I wasn't one hundred percent certain."

"But you are now," she said.

"When you found him alive," Fish said, "and you brought him back from whatever hole in the wall he'd hidden himself, I wanted to *see him with my own eyes*. I wanted to see if I could feel the curse emanating off him, if I could see some dark, irrevocable aura clinging to him like a funk. They say there are psychics who can see dark auras surrounding those who are soon to die. I wanted to *see it*, Ms. Grossman. To see if Davis McElroy *had* it."

"Did you see it?"

"That steak knife that McElroy had planted in my arm, as you so poetically put it, was proof enough for me."

I've seen the aura, she thought. *Back at the house—the Hole in the Wall—when McElroy had first come around from the back to see me standing there. He'd looked like some ghoul roused from a cemetery.*

"You haven't answered my question," Gloria said. "The *why* of it all. How did your story become cursed?"

"Well, now," he said, readjusting his girth between the armrests of the wingback chair. "I don't know if I have an answer for that particular question."

"Do you know a man named Ross Finter? He owns a used bookshop downtown."

"I do not."

"Some of your comments this evening have echoed similar statements Mr. Finter had made to me this afternoon."

"What statements would those be?"

"That the story does not want to be altered. He used that exact term—*altered*. He also said it wasn't the book itself that was cursed or haunted or whatever, but the story itself."

Fish leaned forward the slightest bit in his chair. The wooden legs creaked. "And how did this Mr. Finter become acquainted with our little situation here?"

"Well," Gloria said. "If I'm going to tell you and not convince myself I sound like a crazy person, I think I will take that second drink after all."

21

She began with her arrival at the Hole in the Wall, including how McElroy had looked when he'd come around the side of the house. A man possessed—or *obsessed*—with the haunted, hollowed-out eyes of a jack-o'-lantern. She relayed McElroy's story about the book first trying to escape from him but then attacking him, both physically— she mentioned the wounds she saw on his arms and shin—as well as his claim that the book was somehow ingratiating itself inside his head. She told him about the giant wooden crate in the middle of McElroy's parlor, and of the smaller crates inside. Gloria found this to be the easy part of the story to tell, mainly because it entailed her relaying the facts as she'd witnessed them, and Fish listened with genuine interest. It was the latter part of the story that took some summoning of courage on her part, for she feared that to speak aloud what had transpired once she'd gotten the book and the screenplay back to her apartment would confirm, at least in her own mind, a burgeoning madness that had somehow leapfrogged from McElroy to her.

She described how she found her lamp broken last night and how, come morning, she'd discovered the hole in her purse, and all of the purse's contents strewn about. She explained how the paperback edition of *The Skin of Her Teeth* had somehow relocated from her purse to her nightstand, and how it had intertwined its pages with those of the screenplay—a screenplay that now only had about a dozen pages of text, as opposed to the seventy-nine pages of text it had had the night before. The only part she didn't confess was how she'd found that mound of damp cat fur tacky with a gluey pink slime. (That part was just too much for her to rationalize, and she didn't feel comfortable speaking those words aloud.) When she'd finished, she looked down and found that her wineglass was empty.

"And this Finter fellow?" Fish asked. Throughout the telling, his expression had remained stoic. If he thought she was lying or crazy (or both), he did a good job hiding his emotions. "How does he fit in to all this?"

"McElroy mentioned Finter to me while we were up at the house. He said he'd gone to see him based on a recommendation, and that Finter was a sort of…I don't know…rare book guru?"

"Was he?"

"He was *something*," she confessed. "And like I said, some of the words he used mirrored what *you'd* said tonight."

"What else did he say?"

"That the book wasn't really a book, but a vessel. A container." She was missing something, and she racked her brain to remember what it was. Then she got it, and she nearly squealed as she said it: "She! That's what he said. Whatever was contained in that vessel wasn't an *it*, it was a *she*. He said it was female. And whoever she was, she didn't want the story to be *altered*."

A darkness fell over John Fish's face. So noticeable was this change that Gloria glanced behind her, expecting to see someone in the doorway casting a shadow over the man. But there was no one there, and the doors were still partially closed, just as Jack had left them.

"What?" she said, her voice barely above a whisper now. "What is it?"

Fish killed the rest of his scotch then held out the glass for her to refill again. As she got up from the sofa and took his glass, he said,

"Get some for yourself, too, my dear. No wine. We need the hard stuff. Listen, listen—open the cabinet beneath the bar."

She opened the cabinet beneath the bar. It looked empty inside, the shelf furry with dust. But then she bent down and saw a bottle back there. It had no label and it was capped by a greenish cork.

"What is this stuff?" she asked, taking the bottle from the cabinet.

"Unfathomably expensive, is what it is. A finger each should do the trick."

She uncorked the bottle and poured a measure into each glass. The smell of the stuff caused her eyes to water. She returned to the sofa, handed Fish his glass, then sat in the place Jack had been sitting earlier—a seat closer to Fish, so that they could speak in low voices. It seemed fitting.

"As you may or may not know," Fish began, "*The Skin of Her Teeth*, while my fifth published book, was the first novel I'd written. It still reads that way to me now, on the rare occasions I take it down from the shelf and skim the pages. Not in a juvenile or naive sense, as you might think—although every writer's first novel is arguably an exercise in juvenilia—but in its *passion*. That's the thing that often fades for a writer over time—the passion. *The Skin of Her Teeth* had it because I was still young and foolish and wide-eyed at the time I wrote it. My later stuff? Well, let's just say our good Mr. Baer wasn't exactly off the mark when he'd said my latest book wasn't exactly setting any fires."

Gloria was no John Fish connoisseur, having only read three of his novels, but she agreed that there was something *alive* in the language of *The Skin of Her Teeth* that hadn't been present in his other two novels. (Now, however, the idea that something in that book could be construed as *alive* chilled her to the bone.)

"I was in my early twenties when I wrote it. It took me a full year, although I could have written it much more quickly back then had

I wanted to. The thing is, Ms. Grossman, I didn't *want* to write it quickly. I needed to stretch it out, because the writing of that novel was a *balm* for me. A soothing distraction. A place I could lose myself. You see, Ms. Grossman, while I was writing that novel, my dear mother was in the same house with me, mostly unresponsive in the back bedroom, where she lay slowly dying from a cancer that was transforming her gray matter into tapioca."

Gloria thought she remembered reading an interview with Fish in *Rolling Stone* or some such publication where he talked about his mother, but the details surrounding her death were either left out of the article or hadn't resonated with her at the time.

"She hung on for an entire year in that state, never fully waking, she and I the only two occupants in that stuffy New Hampshire cottage with no air conditioning in the summer and a busted furnace in the winter. Because we had no money, I was her sole caretaker. I undertook all the tedious, stomach-churning, degrading tasks one would associate with such a foul occupation."

"I'm sorry to hear that."

"She was a monster, you know. She *refused* to die. She'd even say that from time to time, singsong it like a bullying chant, 'I'll never die, I'll never die.' It was getting so I was starting to believe her. I wrote *The Skin of Her Teeth* as an escape from her, carefully printing the whole thing out longhand in a series of composition books. The words would come to my mind and I would broadcast them to the pen, which, in turn, would commit them to the page. For me, it was like hypnosis."

He leaned closer to her in his chair, his pale legs covered in spidery hair inching farther out from beneath the hem of his silk kimono.

"A confession, Ms. Grossman—*I killed my mother*."

She leaned closer to him, too, closing the distance between them. She said nothing.

"When she was lucid, she was vile and degrading. She'd curse me, strike me, spit at me. She'd soil the bed in spite, knowing I'd not only have to change the sheets, but also have to lift her wasted frame from the bed and move her into *my* bed, where she would then proceed to soil *those* sheets. A spiteful witch, do you see?"

"Was it the cancer causing her to behave that way?" Gloria asked.

John Fish unleashed a garrulous howl of laughter. It lasted for nearly a minute, during which his small, sparkling eyes filled with tears. When the laughter subsided, he winced at the pain in his injured arm, then glanced down at the splotches of booze that had sloshed from his glass and darkened the fabric of his kimono.

"No, it wasn't the cancer. She was a righteous bitch her entire life," Fish said, thumbing the tears from his eyes. His face was red and his eyes gleamed. He looked like some celestial phenomenon. "It's the reason my father pulled a Houdini during the first year of my life, I have no doubt. That woman was *demonic*."

In her mind's eye, Gloria could see Ross Finter poking the book with his ruler, muttering, *This is her, all right. A naughty girl*.

"The only time she was calm was when I would read to her. She wanted to know what I was doing all night, awake at my desk. She said she could hear my pen scribbling, which I knew was impossible, yet she wasn't *wrong*. In hindsight, I think she must have seen the ink smears on my fingers each day and made the assumption, although another part of me insists she was too far gone to notice such a fine detail. I can't explain it."

I can't explain it, either, she thought, picturing those clumps of damp cat hair on her bedroom floor.

"So I would write at night and read what I had written aloud to her during the day. It seemed to calm her. She would behave. Often, she would lapse into unconsciousness, yet I would continue reading.

"This went on for about six or seven months. I grew tired of the chore, not to mention I needed to find work to keep the lights on and couldn't waste away along with her in that house. She grew irate once I'd stopped reading to her. I was back to changing soiled bed linens and suffering the weak thrusts of her physical assaults.

"One night I lost my temper. I leaned over her bed, gripped her about the shoulders, and shouted in her face, 'When will you die?' Do you know what she did, Ms. Grossman?"

Gloria shook her head.

"She *laughed*. She laughed at me, Ms. Grossman. The whole thing was a game to her. And then she spoke, and do you know what she said?"

Again, Gloria shook her head.

"She said, 'How can I die, John? I need to hear how it ends.' It was the novel I was writing, *The Skin of Her Teeth*, although I don't think I had the title at that point. She needed to hear how it was to end.

"My depression had caused me to forgo any further writing for at least another month or so, but upon hearing those words, I found myself inspired all over again. That night, I picked up the pen and continued with the story. The following day, I read to my mother all I had written. Like that old adage about music soothing the savage beast, so was it that my admittedly inexperienced prose was lulling the bed-ridden demon into a state of passivity. Of contentment, even."

Fish finished off his drink, winced, then peered down at the untouched drink in Gloria's hand. She could intuit his question without him having to ask, and so she handed him her glass. He took a sip, winced once more, then smacked his lips.

"I'm loosening myself to get to the end of this story, Ms. Grossman," he confided.

"You don't have to tell it if you don't want to," she said, although she could tell he was going to finish now no matter what. That was good; she wanted to hear the rest.

"We've come this far, haven't we, Ms. Grossman?"

"We have," she said.

He smiled rheumily at her, then reclined in his chair. His gaze trailed up to the vaulted ceiling, his eyes unfocused.

"As you can probably tell," he continued, "my mission became clear. My mother had never been someone to discharge rhetoric, so I took her at her word. If the only way I could get her to die was to finish the novel, then by God, I'd finish the fucking novel.

"It took me the rest of the year. As much as I'd wanted to rush through to the end and close the curtain on this waking nightmare that was my life, I had fallen in love with the story I'd been writing. I could not dismiss it for something so crude as matricide. The story had provided me solace, had kept me sane. I owed it to the story to finish it *properly*."

"I understand," Gloria said. "As desperate as you were, you wanted to see the story through to the end. The real, true end."

"Yes!" One sausage-like index finger sprung up from Fish's hand and jabbed at the air over his head. "Precisely!"

He spilled more booze on his kimono.

"By the end, to look at her, you would have thought she'd died months earlier. And do you know what? I think maybe she did, in a way. By the end, the only part of her hanging on—the only part somewhat alive—was the stubborn, angry, hateful monster that was hell-bent on hearing how that story ended. Her skin was so thin, her face was like a transparent mask through which you could see the network of blood vessels and muscles doing their thing. Her hands were hooked into arthritic claws, the nails curled and yellow as talons. She was having difficulty swallowing, so as she'd lay there, spit would pool in the corners of her withered mouth and drool in shimmery threads down the sides of her wasted face, dampening her pillow. It was closing on summer as we got near the end of the story, and flies had taken to buzzing above the bed. Sometimes they'd even land on her face and scurry across her lips, her forehead, even her gazing eyeball. The whole bedroom reeked of death."

A strong wind rattled the balcony doors. Gloria whipped her head around and watched them shake in their frames. It was probably a typical occurrence, because Fish didn't bat an eye in their direction. Either that, or he was already good and drunk.

"The night I finished the novel, I set my pen down and sat at my desk, staring at the last sentence I'd written. A giddy sort of relief washed over me. Suddenly, I felt like I could run a marathon, could do cartwheels in the street. My sentence was coming to an end.

"I hardly slept that night. When the sun poked through my partially shaded bedroom window, I got up, showered, then poked my head into my mother's room. I'm telling you, Ms. Grossman, you couldn't even hear her *breathing* anymore, couldn't discern the rise and fall of her chest as she took in air. I'll bet if I'd held a mirror up to her nose, the damn thing wouldn't have fogged up in the least. She was, for all intents and purposes, *dead*. But still hanging on."

"For the ending," Gloria said.

"For the ending," Fish answered. "So I gave it to her. I read those final pages, and she just lay there staring blindly at the flies that had collected on the ceiling, not breathing, those silvery threads of spittle slaloming down the creases and wrinkles and grooves around her mouth. Her pillowcase was brown with that dried spittle. Even the flies wouldn't go near it.

"When I was done, I closed the composition book and just sat there, staring at her. I'd read to her that entire year from a wooden folding chair near the side of her bed; the chair creaked now as I shifted my weight in it—I had never been a slim fellow—and the stressing of that wood caused her eyes to blink.

"'You've heard the ending, you old crone,' I said to her through gritted teeth. 'Now do what you're supposed to do and die already.'

"She hadn't moved in so long I thought she was incapable of it. But at the sound of my words, I watched as her eyes shifted slowly in my direction. They must have been so dry, those eyes, because they made a sound like crinkling cellophane as they moved in their sockets. A single black fly, big as a dime, landed dead center on her left eyeball. I recoiled in horror but my mother hadn't noticed.

"Her mouth drooped open. She had no teeth at this point, only a ridge of purple, diseased gums. Something alien floated between those gums, narrow and dry as a twig. It took me a moment to realize it was her tongue.

"'Never change a word of it,' she said to me. Her voice was barely a whisper, creaky as an old leather shoe, but I heard her clear as day. Even over the buzzing of all those flies, I heard her. 'Never change a word of it.' And I thought to myself right then and there, *I'll kill her myself. I'll choke her to death then kill myself, too. Anything to end this nightmare.* And I was out of my chair and halfway to her bedside, my hands extended and reaching for her neck, when she finally expired."

The story had exhausted him; he slumped back against the chair and took another sip of his potent alcohol.

"She was really dead?" Gloria asked him. "Like, *fully* dead?"

"That's good, I like that," Fish said, wagging a meaty finger at her. "Yes. She was *fully* dead. The flies descended en masse from the ceiling to claim her body. The single white sheet that had been drawn up to her frail collarbone collapsed inward. I stared at her, kept waiting for her to turn to dust, but that didn't happen. In the end, I just went downstairs and called for an ambulance.

"That fall, I got a job at a foundry, stayed on at the house, and just kept my head down until I could catch my bearings. I never went back in her bedroom—I'd dragged an old armoire in front of the door, partially to keep me from wandering in there while drunk, but also because I didn't want anything coming *out.*"

"What would come out?"

"Whatever," said Fish. "Whatever was left behind in that room. Some remnant, some particle? There's a novel called *Floating Staircase*, written by a fellow named Travis Glasgow. Are you familiar with it?"

Gloria shook her head.

"It's nothing to write home about, tell you the truth. In fact, the only thing that resonated with me was the opening paragraph. I remember that paragraph freezing me to my core. It's a bit of a play on Shirley Jackson's *Hill House* opening line, where this writer, Glasgow, posits that nothing in nature can disappear—that things change and evolve and become other things, but once you've existed, you can't *not* exist. I read that book years after my mother's death, but that paragraph struck me, because that was exactly what I'd been afraid of living in that house after she'd died. That some part of her— some 'formidable semblance,' I believe that Glasgow fellow termed it—was still with me in that house."

"No," Gloria said. "Not in the house. In the book."

Fish shook his head. "Not the *book*, Ms. Grossman."

"That's right," she said. "The *story*."

Fish winked at her. "And as you know, I kept writing. I'd stowed the manuscript for *The Skin of Her Teeth* away in a trunk and worked on something fresh. Four books later, I was enjoying time at the top of the bestseller list. Movies were made, awards were amassed, vacation homes were purchased. I was punching my *own* meal ticket by then, you could say.

"I still owned the house in New Hampshire, though I'd never gone back. But that year—the year after my fourth novel, *Shadowplay*, was published, I returned. Perhaps like Mr. Glasgow suggested in his book, I was being drawn back by whatever formidable presence still remained. When I got there, I raced straight up the stairs. The armoire was still standing in front of her closed bedroom door. I shoved it aside and opened the door.

"For all the world, I expected to find her lying in that bed, her body swarming with black flies, her pillow the color of tobacco from all the drool that had dribbled out of her mouth over the years. I expected this *so certainly* that I burst into maniacal laughter when I saw that she *wasn't* there. I was nearly incredulous!"

He laughed again, but there was no humor in it this time. The tears welling in his eyes weren't from laughter now, either.

"I needed to unload the house. I had a local realtor do whatever they needed to do. They sold it quickly for a pittance. I didn't care, and I certainly didn't need the money. I just wanted that part of my life *gone*.

"Before I left, I went to my old bedroom and found the composition books containing the handwritten manuscript for *The Skin of Her Teeth* in my old steamer trunk. Looking at those comp books in that trunk, Ms. Grossman…well, it was just about the equivalent of witnessing your own birth. I don't know how else to describe it.

"I dragged the trunk down the stairs and out to my car. Took those comp books home with me to Beverly Hills, where I was living at the time, then spent the next few months transcribing every word onto my word processor. *Every word*. Do you understand?"

"I do," Gloria said. "You did just as your mother told you. You never changed a word of it."

"Never a word," Fish said. "And when I turned it in to my publisher, that was the note I gave them—*do not change a word*. I was commanding big advances at the time, so no one was going to argue with me. The book was published eleven months later just as I'd written it—just as I'd written it at twenty-two years old, longhand, while my mother turned into a monster on her deathbed, alive for a time even in death."

Gloria reclined against the back of the sofa. "Have we reached a conclusion tonight, Mr. Fish? About your mother and the curse that clings to that story?"

John Fish seemed to consider this for a while. He pressed a wide index finger to his philtrum, rubbed the sweat-dappled flesh there. His big thighs had parted and Gloria realized he wasn't wearing any underwear beneath the kimono. She quickly averted her gaze.

"It means, Ms. Grossman, that my mother had been right all along. Her little singsong chant?" Fish leaned forward in his chair, and in an unexpectedly delicate voice, sang, "*I'll never die...I'll never die...*"

22

It was closing in on midnight by the time Gloria got up to leave. Drunk, Fish made a show of pretending to rise, but remained slouched in his chair, the hem of his kimono high enough to reveal more details about the great author than Gloria really wanted to know. She collected the glasses, placed them atop the wet bar, then told Fish that she would see herself out.

"Ms. Grossman?"

She turned toward him. "Yes?"

"Where's that screenplay now?"

"I gave it to Mr. Finter. Well, what was left of it. Along with the book. He put it in a little safe and locked it up."

"That's good, I suppose."

"I suppose," she said.

"Can I ask you another question?"

"Of course."

"I know you primarily handle screenwriters who dither away in the doldrums of that beastly machine known as the motion picture industry, but would you have any interest in adding an aged yet mostly reliable and certainly *commanding* novelist to your roster of clients?"

Gloria smiled. "That sounds like a good discussion for when we're both clearheaded and sober."

"I'm going to take that as a yes, dear," he said. He wasn't looking at her, but instead at his own tired reflection in the dark panel of glass that made up one half of the balcony doors.

"Mr. Fish?" she asked.

"Hmmmm?"

"What was your mother's name?"

He didn't answer at first, just kept gazing at his reflection in that dark sheet of glass. Then, his voice hoarse and barely a whisper, he said, "Zora. It's Slavic for 'dawn.' Perpetually risen, I suppose you could say."

"Goodnight, Mr. Fish."

His bleary reflection in the window raised a hand in farewell.

23

Three months later, Gloria moved back to Los Angeles, where she'd started her career. She'd fallen in love with Manhattan, but it was tougher to "dither away in the doldrums" of Hollywood, as John Fish had put it, while living on the East Coast. Besides, Manhattan had been an experiment necessitated by her relationship with Becca, a lifelong New Yorker, who refused to entertain the notion of living anywhere else. Midway through a somber dinner at their favorite Mediterranean restaurant, Gloria realized that Becca had invited her here to break up with her for good. She tried to mollify Becca with promises of more time spent together, more dedication to their relationship, more consideration for her as a partner. None of this seemed to resonate with Becca; she was too hurt and too tired and didn't want to do this anymore. "You've just burned me out, I guess, Gloria," was how she put it. Then Becca paid the bill, kissed Gloria on the cheek, and left.

24

As it turned out, she did not take John Fish on as a client. She had every intention of doing so that night as she left his Park Avenue apartment—he wasn't quite the monumental lout his reputation led her and everyone else to believe—but then they'd met for lunch later that week (at Bertoli's, because Fish had a morbid sense of humor) where Fish said he'd changed his mind.

"Has nothing to do with you, of course, Gloria," he told her. "This is a personal decision. I'm going to take a bit of a respite, maybe even get out of the city for a while. Clear my head, as the average bozos say. I've got a place in Montana, a ranch with some smelly animals there. I may even have some illegitimate kids living there, who can remember? Bottom line, I'm considering retiring from this whole sordid business."

"Novelists retire? I just thought they died."

"Of course they retire, dear. Hell, Stephen King retired twice. But for me, maybe once is good enough. Maybe it'll stick."

"Is it something you can give up, just like that? The writing, I mean."

"Who said I'm giving it up?" he said, his eyes twinkling. "Anyway, moving on to bigger and better things, I hear they've actually dropped all charges on your protégé McElroy."

"He's not my responsibility anymore," she said, holding up both hands to profess her innocence.

"You *do* realize that he isn't to blame for any of this, don't you? If we both agree to believe what it is I *think* we believe, then we must acknowledge McElroy's blameless. He was poisoned by her, just like the others."

She knew it, and she agreed with him on that score. Only problem was, she didn't want to have to see Davis McElroy again. She felt she was walking a tenuous rope as it was; the sight of McElroy—and the memory of his mad, blazing eyes—might be enough to cause her to lose her footing. She couldn't risk that.

"What will you do if he calls you?" Fish asked.

"I guess I'll cross that bridge when I come to it."

But it never came to that; Davis McElroy never called her again.

25

John Fish's retirement didn't stick. Two years later, she heard rumblings of a new Fish novel getting ready to pop on the market. Hollywood began sniffing around for the film rights (all except Paramount, who still had a bad taste in their collective mouths after Fish, without explanation, had killed their last deal). She looked up the deal and saw, with little surprise, that it had been brokered by Jack Baer. She called Jack to congratulate him. They hadn't spoken since she'd left Manhattan, but Jack was in a good mood and was happy about the deal, so their conversation was pleasant enough. Jack promised to send her an advance copy of the novel, but he never did.

A few months after that, she was having a business lunch at The Grove at Farmers Market. When the lunch was over, she stopped in the Barnes & Noble. Fish's newest novel was on a front-table display, a glossy hardback titled *More Than She Ever Knew*. Gloria picked up a copy, turned toward the register, but then paused. She headed deeper into the store, weaving in and out of aisles until she came upon the Fs. A whole shelf of John Fish novels, each one as dense and weighty as the author himself. She ran her finger across the spines until she found a reissued trade paperback edition of *The Skin of Her Teeth*. This new cover was stylized to match the dust jacket of *More Than She Ever Knew*, but Gloria still felt a strange twinge just holding the book.

She brought them both to the counter, paid the clerk, and slipped away like a thief.

26

Two nights later, she awoke screaming from a nightmare wherein a swarm of flies picked her body apart with miniature steak knives. There was a sound in the room with her, somewhere in the dark depths of her bedroom. The first thought to cross her mind was *Orville*, but then she remembered Orville was gone, *had* been gone for over two years now, and that she was alone.

Something was moving around in her closet.

She leaned over, switched on the bedside lamp, then rolled out of bed. The sound stopped. She stood there in silence, waiting for it. Nearly two full minutes passed. Then the sound started up again—a deliberative rustling sound, coming from the closet.

The closet door was partway open. She crossed the bedroom, still hearing that sound, still trying to place what it was. *What makes that sound? What is it?*

She pulled the closet door open the rest of the way. Once again, the sound stopped.

She'd been in this place for the better part of two years, yet she still had boxes and bags of old clothes wedged in here. She reached in, rolled some of the bags of clothes out of the closet, and peered around. At first, she couldn't see anything out of the ordinary…

But then she saw the fist-sized hole in the large cardboard box at the back of the closet. Curled bits of cardboard littered the floor below the hole, as if some rodent had chewed its way inside.

She bent down and opened the top flap of the box. Inside were stacks of papers, binders full of contracts, Rolodexes overflowing with ancient business cards. She reached inside the box, shifted some items around.

There, at the bottom, was the copy of *The Skin of Her Teeth* she had purchased two days earlier at the Barnes & Noble. She would have thought the sight of it would have sent her into hysterics, but she felt eerily calm. She lifted the binders and stacks of paperwork out of the box until all that was left inside was the book, and the thing that the book was stuck to, *glued* to, by a tacky membrane of pink slime: the yellow legal pad with her handwritten notes for the end of McElroy's screenplay.

There was no movement, no more strange sounds. Finally, Gloria said, "Go on, Zora. Do your thing."

The book's cover rose, its pages rippled. It inched closer to the legal pad, drawn closer to it by the slime that now began to pulse and undulate and spill across the handwritten pages of the legal pad. That strange sound started up again, pink bubbles of slime swelling from its pages, and Gloria realized there was really only one way to describe that sound: it was *digestive*.

Gloria sat cross-legged on the floor of the closet and watched the book leach the writing from the sheets of legal paper. She could smell menthol, could hear its digestion, could see its interior pages rippling in a flurry that looked almost orgasmic.

I'll never die…I'll never die…

Gloria let the woman have her feast.

THE DARK BROTHERS' LAST RIDE

1

The Dark Brothers, as they were sometimes known, were just finishing up a late-night meal at the Roadrunner Diner when a sleek silver Mercedes glided sharklike into the empty parking space beside the brothers' matte-black Monte Carlo. The Mercedes had those irritating LED headlights that were either piercing or noncommittal, depending on the angle, and phony Colorado plates. Danny Drake—also known as Danny Dark, depending on your purpose for knowing him—looked up from his mediocre corned beef sandwich and gazed out the diner's plate-glass window at the vehicle idling out there in the darkness. The Mercedes's windshield was smoked black glass, but that didn't matter, because it was too dark to see anything out there, anyway.

Danny wiped his hands on a paper napkin then tapped the screen of his phone, which sat on the placemat beside his dinner plate. He noted that it was precisely 10:30 p.m. Alec Rudenko was nothing if not punctual.

Truth was, the brothers weren't *both* finishing up their meals. Across the table, Tommy's food—French toast and fat gray fingers of sausage drowning in too much blueberry syrup—sat uneaten. Tommy's appetite this evening was of a different variety; he was across the diner right now, slouching against the countertop while attempting to charm the starched white apron off their waitress. Danny watched him for a moment, unobserved. Tommy was too brash, too careless, and constantly on the hunt for immediate gratification. He had spent the drive out here to this godforsaken place complaining that he was *fucking starving, man*, yet here he was, switching gears on a whim while his food got cold.

"Hey," Danny called to him. "Tommy."

Tommy was in the middle of telling their young (and admittedly attractive) waitress a joke, and he didn't want to be derailed. He held up one finger in Danny's direction, and didn't bother turning his head. The waitress had been reeled in, of course—Tommy Drake was good at reeling them in, just like their old man had been—and she listened to Tommy with her hands planted on her waist, her hips cocked. She was giving him the full view, all right, and since the place was otherwise empty, there was no one else around to vie for her attention. She looked to be maybe in her early twenties, Danny guessed, with a college-girl figure and a commendable rack beneath her faded Def Leppard T-shirt. Just the type of girl Tommy took great pleasure in bulldozing to the ground.

"Tommy," Danny said again, a bit more urgency in his voice this time.

"Fuck's sake, Dan." Tommy swiveled his head around on his neck to meet his brother's steely gaze, his dingy blond ponytail snaking off one shoulder. His jacket and T-shirt had ridden up just enough for Danny to catch a glimpse of the pistol in his brother's waistband. They were lucky the place was deserted. "Cool your jets. I'm just getting a refill." As if to prove this point, he held up his coffee mug, which the waitress promptly refilled.

"He's here," Danny said.

Tommy's expression changed. The lust fled from his piercing gray eyes, while the joviality drained from his face.

"Who's here?" the waitress wanted to know. She was peering past Tommy and at the Mercedes idling just beyond the wall of plate-glass windows.

"Don't worry about it," Tommy told her. He ran his fingers through his hair, readjusting his ponytail.

"Fix your shirt," Danny said. He could still see the butt of Tommy's pistol poking up from the waistband of his jeans. Tommy caught on, and quickly tugged his shirt down over the gun.

When the door to the diner opened, letting in a blast of cool desert wind and a scrim of gray sand, Tommy shifted his gaze from his brother to the two men now standing beneath the stark lighting in the diner's entranceway. The waitress did, too. Danny, on the other hand, did not turn to look at them; he could see their reflection clearly enough in the dented aluminum of the napkin dispenser on his table.

Alec Rudenko was in his late fifties, and possessed the hungry, analytical stare of a jungle cat. Tommy sometimes referred to him as the Ninja (though never to his face) because the man had a predilection for dressing all in black. Tonight was no different—coal-black turtleneck, midnight slacks with razor-sharp creases, and a suede jacket that called to mind the velvety black pelt of a puma. Rudenko's shoes looked like they'd been chiseled from chunks of obsidian. The man standing beside Rudenko was of no consequence, just one of a dozen henchmen on the payroll, with a shaved head and the dead, sterile eyes of a mule.

The two men made their way to Danny's booth. Danny rose, shook Rudenko's cool hand, then glanced down at the black leather briefcase the henchman carried. Across the diner, Tommy slunk away from the counter, his wallet chain swinging from one hip. A strand of loose blond hair wafted about his head looking like a part of his soul had come detached and was working on an escape.

"It is good to see you, Danny," Rudenko said. His time in Middle

America hadn't blunted his Eastern European accent. He eased himself into the booth, then prodded Tommy's uneaten meal off to the side with a look of passing disgust. Rudenko liked to operate in what Danny often thought of as his "sphere of influence," which meant nothing between him and the person to whom he was talking. Right now, that was Danny. Lately, it seemed like it was *always* Danny. "You have been well?"

"Yes, sir," Danny said. He looked up as Tommy approached, hovering just beyond the perfect right angle of the henchman's shoulder. His eyes were jittery in his head, which confirmed Danny's suspicion that Tommy and the waitress had snorted a line or two in the restroom no more than ten minutes ago. "I'm just glad we could make it out here for you on such short notice, Mr. Rudenko."

"This whole operation is being done on short notice, Danny."

Danny just nodded. He felt suddenly amphibious in his clothes, with a runner of perspiration peeling down the runway of flesh between his shoulder blades. He could feel his own gun knuckling him in the small of his back.

Rudenko waved a dismissive hand, and the henchman pivoted around Tommy and sat in the next booth over, positioned so he could keep an eye on the door and his boss. And Danny. The henchman set his black leather briefcase on the table.

"Hey, Mr. Rudenko," Tommy said. He slid into the booth beside Danny.

Alec Rudenko's eyes narrowed as he studied Danny's brother. "What happened to your face?"

Tommy blinked his eyes, but then recollection dawned on him. Almost instinctively, he brought a set of fingers to the greenish purple bruise capping the summit of his left cheekbone. The bruise was over a week old, yet he winced as he touched it, as if the injury still caused him pain. Maybe the memory of it did, Danny surmised.

"This? Hey, it's nothing. What do they say? You should see the other guy, right?" A nervous laugh creaked up out of Tommy's throat.

Rudenko's grin was humorless, and Danny caught the flash of condemnation behind his eyes. Alec Rudenko did not like Tommy Drake, but he put up with him because he trusted that Danny would keep him in check. He trusted *Danny*. Showing up to a meeting with a week-old shiner didn't help bolster much confidence, however, and it made Danny feel like he wasn't in control. Not for the first time today, he wondered if he shouldn't have left Tommy back in Grand Junction.

The waitress came over, filled a mug with coffee for Rudenko, then asked if he'd like to see a menu. The smile Danny's employer gave her was more genuine than the cold grimace he'd fashioned for Tommy; he even reached out and took one of the waitress's hands in both of his. An enormous ruby gleamed on Rudenko's smallest finger.

"I do wish I could stay," Rudenko said, patting the waitress's hand. "Least of all for the satisfaction of your company, my dear. But duty calls, as they say."

The waitress returned Rudenko's smile, somehow not put off by the edge of false flattery in his tone, then returned to her station behind the counter. She appeared to have the good sense not to ask anything of the henchman.

Rudenko cleared his throat and said, "The client is an anonymous gentleman who needs a package delivered to a man named Choptank. This man Choptank will be waiting for you at noon on Saturday at a motel called The Mesa, on the border of Oklahoma and Arkansas. The motel's location is not available on any GPS device, but I have been provided a map for your convenience. Once the package is delivered, the map should be destroyed. Those are the instructions."

One of Danny's eyebrows ticked toward his hairline.

"Yes, I know," Rudenko agreed. "All of it is very dramatic.

However, the anonymous client was insistent that we operate in such a fashion."

This must be some package, Danny thought. He glanced at his brother, with his bruised face and his eyes trembling wetly in their sockets, and wished he'd told him to wait in the car.

"You will be paid the usual transportation fee, along with an additional twenty percent from our client as gratitude for following his specific requests."

"That's generous. What are we transporting?"

"From what I am to understand," Rudenko said, "it is a book."

For a second, Danny thought he'd misunderstood him. "A book?"

"I am told it is very rare and quite special. My understanding is this man Choptank is a collector of rare antiquities, and that he is rather anxious to get his hands on this particular item. He has purchased it from our client—it is this anonymous seller through which I have procured the item on Choptank's behalf—and both men want it personally delivered by hand."

Before Danny could respond, Tommy slapped a hand on the table and snorted laughter. "A fucking *book*? Are you kidding me?"

Rudenko tilted his head back the slightest bit, as if to appraise Tommy from a different angle. Despite the crudity of Tommy's outburst, Danny had to agree that the whole thing sounded a bit ludicrous, considering the type of merchandise he and Tommy were used to transporting. Nonetheless, he gave Tommy a subtle jab to the ribs from underneath the table with his elbow.

"Our client's instructions were quite clear—that this book is to be considered precious cargo."

"Is it stolen?" Danny asked.

"I'm not aware one way or the other," Rudenko said.

"Sounds like the risk on this one's pretty low."

"Admittedly, I am not intimately familiar with the world of rare books, but I should think, yes, Danny, the transportation and delivery of such an item poses much less potential interference than our typical arrangements," Rudenko agreed. "There are a few stipulations that need to be followed, as relayed to me by the client, and I trust you will follow them, Danny."

"Of course."

"To begin with, the briefcase is locked and cannot be opened. Only the client and Choptank have keys to open it. That is how I received it from the client, and that is how you will deliver it to Choptank. I am aware that you operate with utmost professionalism, Danny, but I was asked to make this part very clear. *The briefcase is to remain locked and the item is not to be removed from it under any circumstances.*"

"Understood," Danny said.

"I was also instructed to tell you that the item inside the briefcase is particularly delicate. Under no conditions are you to touch it." Rudenko's gaze shifted over to Tommy. "Neither of you."

Tommy scratched at the beard stubble along his neck. He said, "If it's in a locked briefcase that we can't open, how're we gonna touch—"

"Understood," Danny repeated, cutting his brother off.

Rudenko's jungle-cat gaze hung on Tommy for a beat longer than Danny was comfortable with. "As I've mentioned," Rudenko continued, his eyes ticking back over to Danny, "I've been provided a map for your use. The route our client has requested you take has been outlined for you. No doubt you've already done the math in your head, Danny, on the timeline to get from here to the Arkansas border—"

"Should be about a twelve-hour drive, depending on conditions. Tonight's Thursday, so if this Choptank guy is meeting us at noon on Saturday, that leaves us plenty of time."

"Under normal circumstances, you'd be correct. You will find, however, that my client's specified route of travel is rather…circuitous.

There cannot be any deviations; it must be that route exactly. You'll need to leave this evening if you're to make it on time."

This evening? That made no sense to Danny, but he just nodded his head.

"Lastly, if anyone approaches you and asks about the book—to see it, to hold it, anything at all—your instructions are to ignore them. That was the word the client himself used—*ignore*. In most cases, he said that should work. He added, however, that if any of these individuals persist and make it difficult for you to complete your assignment—if they cause you any additional aggravation or trouble, in other words—the client has suggested it be best to use any force necessary to avoid complications or further dealings with these people."

Danny shook his head. "I don't understand. Who would we run into?"

"I do not know."

"Does anyone even know we're in possession of this thing? Other than this guy Choptank and this anonymous client?"

"Not to my knowledge," Rudenko said. "I am merely passing along the instructions as I have received them. My advice is that we operate to the letter and ask no questions."

"All right," Danny said.

"You will receive partial payment in cash upfront for your services, as per our usual agreement," Rudenko continued. "Once you deliver the item to this Mr. Choptank at The Mesa Motel, you and I, Danny, will reconvene so that you may receive the remainder of your fee."

"Including the twenty percent," Tommy said.

"In the event that you follow all of my client's stipulations to the letter, then yes, including your twenty percent, Thomas."

"We'll make it happen," Tommy assured him.

"I recognize that this is all a bit unorthodox, gentlemen, but these were our client's requests. Now, are there any more questions?"

"Just so I'm clear," Tommy said, and Danny felt a lead weight sink down into his guts. "If I gotta take a dump, I can't open this briefcase and thumb through the book while I'm sittin' on the throne, right?"

"He's joking," Danny said quickly. "I'm sorry, Mr. Rudenko. He's only joking."

"Only joking," Rudenko said. He leaned back in the booth, folding his hands across his chest. That large ruby sparkled. Rudenko's sharp little eyes kept volleying between Danny and Tommy, Danny and Tommy. Then he laughed—a startling whip-crack of a sound. Danny had never heard the man laugh before, and he couldn't tell if it was genuine or not. "That *is* funny. Now, aside from your humor, Thomas, do you feel there is some problem with our arrangement as I've explained it to you? Something further we need to discuss?"

"Well—"

"It's no problem at all," Danny interjected before his brother could finish.

"I just want to make sure we are all on the same page here," Rudenko said. His eyes were fixed on Danny's brother as he said this. So were the henchman's, sitting forward in the booth behind his boss. "Do you see my own joke, Thomas? The 'same page'?"

Tommy stared at Rudenko for several drawn-out seconds…and then he grinned. That loose bit of hair floated around his head. "Yeah. I get it. Good one. Ha."

The lower portion of Alec Rudenko's face stretched into a cadaverous grin. "You," he said, pointing at Tommy, "are a better comedian than a…a whatever it is you do for your brother."

"Thanks, I guess," Tommy said. He'd dug a pack of smokes from his jacket pocket and was packing them now, *thump thump thump*, against the heel of one hand.

Rudenko's gaze lingered a moment longer on Tommy before settling back on Danny. His face softened almost imperceptibly as he nodded his head. "I trust you, Danny."

"Thank you, sir."

Alec Rudenko stood from his seat, and the henchman in the booth behind him also rose. On their way to the door, Rudenko paused before the counter and muttered something to the waitress that made her smile and blush. A moment later, the silver Mercedes was receding across the Roadrunner Diner's parking lot, its LED headlights dwindling in the deepening darkness.

"What a fucking rodeo," Tommy said, popping a cigarette between his lips.

"I told you to keep your trap shut."

"I was just fucking around."

"This is my job, Tommy."

"Yeah, I know. It's my job, too, remember?"

"Slide out."

"What?"

"Slide out of the booth."

Tommy slapped a hand down on the tabletop hard enough to make the utensils jump. He rolled out of the booth then sauntered back over to the counter. The waitress was talking to the cook through a partition in the wall. Tommy grabbed a handful of mints from a ceramic bowl and emptied them in the pocket of his fleece-lined jean jacket while he waited to catch her eye again.

Danny went over to the briefcase that Rudenko's henchman had left on the table. Its brass clasps shined like gold nuggets. As promised, there was a roadmap folded up beside the briefcase along with an unmarked envelope that Danny knew contained the first portion of their payment for this gig.

He gathered the items off the table then turned around to find

2

Because he thought it was fucking hysterical, Tommy had stuck a BABY ON BOARD decal to the Monte Carlo's rear windshield. He claimed it was to keep the big black car under the radar, but in Danny's estimation it only increased their suspicion: two grown men motoring along on a series of desert highways encapsulated in a cloud of cigarette smoke and with what looked incriminatingly like bullet holes along the car's rear quarter panels. He knew better than to fight Tommy on the little things, however, because Tommy *was* volatile. There was often no way of knowing what might push him over the edge. Cut him off early at a bar and he'd go from yodeling along with the karaoke singers to wanting to slit someone's throat with a broken beer bottle; tell him to remove the stupid fucking BABY ON BOARD decal, and he might let loose with a few rounds into the windshield, *There ya go, problem solved, all gone*. So Danny had learned to choose his battles when it came to dealing with his brother.

It was that stupid decal that Danny was thinking about now as he drove through the night, Tommy beside him in the passenger seat with the black leather briefcase at his feet. *Precious cargo*, Rudenko had said of the thing in the briefcase. Wasn't that the term you used when you were transporting something alive? Something like a baby on board?

Tommy must have been thinking something similar. As he pulled a small bottle of bourbon from the inner pocket of his jacket, he said, "You remember hearing about that guy who was running illegals across the border in those big panel trucks? Got all fucked up and drove the truck into a ravine? This was years ago. All those Mexicans trapped in the back of that truck drowned like rats."

Danny said nothing. He'd heard the story, of course, but didn't want to dwell on it now. Anyway, that was like a million years ago.

Precious cargo, he thought.

"No way there's a book in there." Tommy thumped a motorcycle boot against the briefcase at his feet. "No way some asshole's paying us that kind of money to deliver a fuckin' book. I don't give a shit if it's an autographed copy of the fuckin' Bible."

"Doesn't matter what it is."

"Sure it matters. We're supposed to know what we're carrying."

"No, we're not."

"What if we get stopped?"

"We won't get stopped."

Tommy leaned his head back against the headrest. He took another swig from the bottle, then offered it to Danny, who declined. He stowed the bottle back in his jacket, then lit a joint. "Guns, drugs, whatever," he intoned after taking a strong pull on the joint. "I'd just like to know what's really in that fucking briefcase in case Deputy Dawg comes a-knocking."

"No one's stopping this car," Danny assured him.

Tommy side-eyed him. Threads of smoke were being drawn from his lips and sucked out the window into the night. "What if it's a dirty bomb?"

"What are you talking about?"

"They make 'em in suitcases and briefcases, you know. Like the kind that dude used to blow up that federal building in Oklahoma City."

"That was a truck full of fertilizer."

"Same difference."

"It's not a fucking bomb."

"You don't know that. Rudenko says it's a book, you take him at his word. Fuck that guy, fuck his anonymous client, and fuck this Choptank motherfucker, too."

"It's not a bomb, Tommy."

"Yeah, well, you keep on believing that. But mark my words, you hit one pothole out here and it's sayonara, brother bear."

"You need to rein it in, man."

"I'm just thinking out loud."

"I'm talking about what you said back at the diner. No one needs to hear your smartass mouth when we're doing business."

"You mean that shit I said to Rudenko? Fuck that. Everybody's so goddamn serious, they need to lighten up. You included. It was just a joke."

"Did he look like he was there to catch a comedy act? Just dial it down, is all I'm saying. And quit kicking that briefcase."

Tommy chuckled. "Because it's a bomb, right?"

"Get that map out," Danny told him. It was late, he was tired, and his temples were beginning to throb. There wasn't much more steam left in him. "See if you can figure out why this guy's got us driving halfway around the world instead of taking the straight shot."

They had looked briefly at the map back at the diner, perplexed to find that whoever had provided the map hadn't simply outlined an alternative route, but had drawn one of their own, then highlighted it with a neon yellow marker for good measure. This makeshift route had them dropping down into New Mexico, then cutting east through Texas and Oklahoma toward Arizona. It was unnecessarily convoluted. The quickest route to Arizona was to hop on I-70, but whoever this anonymous client was, the son of a bitch had them doing the hokey pokey like a couple of assholes.

Danny had questioned whether or not these ink-drawn roads even existed, but they had come across the first one soon after leaving the diner—a nameless, single-lane stretch of blacktop arcing deep into the desert—and they had taken it.

Tommy unfolded the map that Rudenko's henchman had left for them and smoothed it out across his lap now. Then he brought it up to his face to study it, so close Danny feared the tip of his joint might set it ablaze. "If you're asking me to be a mind reader, I'm not gonna have any answers for you. If I had to guess, whoever this clown is, he doesn't want us on any of the major highways. I mean, the road we're on right now isn't even on this map."

"That seems a bit paranoid."

"Not if it's a bomb in that briefcase."

Danny shook his head. Then he yawned. "We should find a place to crash for the night. I'm beat."

"I can drive for a bit."

"You're stoned."

Tommy said nothing. The Monte Carlo's radio was busted, so for a time the only sound was the steady growl of the car's V8 engine and the rumbling of the tires as they gobbled up the asphalt. Danny felt the hairs along the back of his neck begin to prickle. After a while, he glanced over at his brother.

Tommy sat staring at him from the passenger seat. He was mostly masked in darkness, though the parts of him that were visible in the glow of the car's dashboard lights looked disturbingly insubstantial. Like maybe he was a ghost.

"What's the matter with you?" Danny asked.

In a cold, quiet whisper, Tommy said, "I'm not fucking stoned."

Danny shot him another glance then quickly brought his eyes back onto the double yellow line of the highway. Christ, they hadn't passed another vehicle out here since they'd left the Roadrunner Diner, and Danny felt like he was road-tripping on the dark side of the moon. "All right, Tom. My mistake. I apologize."

"Don't." Tommy's voice: still that cold whisper. That thing in him having changed. That switch flipped. "Don't apologize if you don't mean it. You know I hate that."

"I know. I mean it. I'm sorry."

It suddenly felt like the interior of the car had dropped a handful of degrees.

I should have left him back in Grand Junction. He's been slipping again, and I can't keep doing this. He nearly got us both hemmed up last week in Williston. Next time, he won't be so lucky to walk away with just a black eye, if he even walks away at all. He'll fuck us both eventually. I shouldn't have brought him with me on this.

A sharp cackle bolted from Tommy's throat. The sound of it caused Danny's heart to lurch, and it was all he could do not to jerk the steering wheel. Still laughing, Tommy leaned over and clapped him on the shoulder, then settled back against the passenger seat once more. The roadmap rustled across his lap as he took another toke of the joint.

"I'm fucking with you, dickhead," Tommy said. Still chuckling.

No, Danny thought. *You weren't. You were slipping again.*

And just like that, the eerie wave of cold air dissipated, leaving in its wake nothing but a lingering sense of disquiet along the perimeter of Danny Drake's psyche.

3

They stopped at a crummy motel for a few hours' shuteye. The place was nearly deserted, which suited Danny just fine. Tommy stayed in the car while Danny went inside to the front desk and got a room. When Danny returned, Tommy was gone. Panic momentarily clutched at Danny's throat. He opened the passenger door and saw that while Tommy had vanished, the black leather briefcase was still there in the footwell. In the end, that was all that mattered, wasn't it? He grabbed the briefcase then popped the trunk and gathered up the duffel bag he kept in there for emergency overnights on the road—a change of clothes, fresh underwear, toiletries. There were also a few tabs of uppers in a foil sleeve, in case the job required he stay awake beyond the limit of what his body could handle. He carried everything into the motel room.

The room was supposed to have two single beds, but instead there was just a solitary queen in the center of the room. He considered going back to the lobby to request a room change—the parking lot was practically deserted, so surely there were vacancies—but in the end he decided to hell with it. He was too tired to argue with the goggle-eyed moron manning the check-in desk; he just wanted to close his eyes for a few hours before hitting the road again in the morning.

Also, where the hell was Tommy?

Danny tossed his duffel bag on the bed, then set the briefcase down a bit more judiciously beside it. He'd dismissed his brother's comment about a dirty bomb earlier, but if he was being honest with himself, he hadn't fully been able to forget about it. A book was certainly among the most unique things he'd ever been paid to transport, wasn't it? Anyway, what did he know about rare books? Just because it was unusual didn't mean Alec Rudenko hadn't been telling him the truth. Maybe there were some books out there worth more than a kilo of coke, that were more in demand than a briefcase full of counterfeit hundred-dollar bills. Danny Drake had learned of stranger things than that in all his thirty-four years.

Rudenko said that when he received the briefcase from the anonymous seller it was already locked. Which means even Alec Rudenko doesn't truly know what's inside.

He reached behind him and unclipped his in-the-pants holster. Once upon a time, the Glock had been his father's, a black-market job with the serial numbers filed off. The old bastard had no use for such an item now. He wasn't dead, but given the remaining years on his sentence at the federal penitentiary in Montana, he might as well be. In one of Danny's recurring nightmares, he and Tommy were stopped by a police roadblock, arrested, and thrown into a cell with their father. There, they would reenact Danny and Tommy's own miserable childhood for the remainder of their days, only this time in a six-by-eight-foot cage. The three of them, living like animals trapped behind bars, and feeding off each other's aggression and misery, until they tore each other apart.

Don't think about that, he told himself now, unzipping the duffel bag. He stowed the gun and its holster beneath a pair of folded white boxer shorts, then zipped the bag back up.

Came close in Williston, though, didn't you? a voice inside his head interjected. *No police roadblock, but one second later and you'd be sitting in a jail cell in North Dakota right now. All because of Tommy.*

Where *was* Tommy, anyway?

Danny dug his cell phone from his pocket and dialed Tommy's number. Of course, it went straight to voicemail. Either Tommy hadn't charged his phone or he'd deliberately turned it off and forgotten about it. Nothing new there.

He recalled seeing the neon lights of a cocktail lounge next door, as he'd pulled into the motel parking lot. His brother was nothing if not predictable, and the volatile, alcoholic apple tended not to fall far from the ugly, fermented tree. Normally, Danny wouldn't begrudge Tommy a few drinks after several hours on the road, but last week's incident in Williston was still fresh in his memory; the prospect of Tommy knocking back shots in a bar by himself set Danny on edge and made him consider the worst.

"You dumb motherfucker." He was unsure even as the words left his mouth whether he was referring to Tommy or himself.

I should have left him home.

Fair enough. But here they were. No use bitching about it now.

Nights in the desert were cold, and this night was no exception. Stepping outside the room, Danny hurried across the parking lot toward the lighted COCKTAILS sign above the lounge, his breath misting in the air. A neon martini glass blinked on and off above a set of smoked double doors. There were a few more cars here than there had been back at the motel, and the prospect of *too many people* made Danny uncomfortable.

He reached out to yank open one of the double doors, but then froze.

Tommy will be in there, shouting and drugged out of his mind, waving his gun around. I'll bet the cops are on their way right now.

He even paused to listen for sirens in the distance. But he was just spooking himself. The cops were not on their way.

The lounge had a languid atmosphere. Blue lighting made everyone look like ambulatory corpses, and the warbling country music coming from a wall-mounted jukebox didn't help matters any. Danny scanned the place until he saw Tommy seated at a table near the back of the bar. He was chatting with a waitress, his hands laced behind his head, his chair kicked back so that the front legs were off the floor. The waitress set a glass of whiskey on the table just as Danny approached.

Tommy looked up and seemed surprised to see him. It was as if they hadn't just driven all this way together.

"Hey, stranger," Tommy drawled, grinning.

"What do you think you're doing?"

"Shit, Dan, sorry to run off like that, but I suddenly realized I hadn't eaten back at that diner, and *fuck*, hombre, I'm *starving*."

"Kitchen's closed," the waitress informed them both. Despite the chill in the place, her forehead was pimpled with sweat.

"Ah, well, fuck." Grinning, Tommy lifted his drink and took a generous swallow.

The waitress turned to Danny. "Anything for you?"

"No, thanks."

"Come on, bro," Tommy insisted. "Have one with me."

"Tommy, I'm beat. You should get some rest, too."

"I'll rest when I'm dead. Get one for my brother," Tommy told the waitress, pointing to his own drink. "I'll have another one, too."

"Coming right up, fellas," the waitress said, and then she trod away through the blue-hued dimness of the lounge.

Danny sat at the table across from his brother. Exhaustion weighed on his shoulders, and the early stirrings of a headache that he had begun to feel during the drive out here were now in full effect. It felt like someone banging on a steel drum inside his skull.

"Hey," Tommy said. "Can I ask you something? Something serious?"

"What is it?"

"You ever do a job where you're transporting something that's worth so much fucking money that you think, screw it, I'll take it for myself?"

"Are you fucking crazy?"

"You never know, it might be worth the risk."

"It's not worth the risk. And I don't wanna sit here talking about this."

"Why? You think that Russian cocksucker's listening?"

"He's Ukrainian."

"You think he's got this crappy little bar in the middle of absolute nowhere bugged? That he's eavesdropping on this conversation right now?" Tommy rapped a fist on the table, then leaned down so that his breath sent a tumult of crumbs skittering toward Danny. "Hello? Mr. Rudenko? KGB? Tune in Tokyo!"

Danny leaned across the table. Lowering his voice, he said, "I think you should quit talking about this."

Tommy righted himself in his chair, his eyes bleary in his head. He knocked the rest of his drink back then set his empty glass on the table. Loud. "I love you, Danny, I really do, but do you know what your problem is?"

I sure do, Danny thought. *It's you.*

"Your problem," Tommy went on, "is that you're inherently risk averse."

Danny couldn't help it; he laughed.

"No, no, hear me out." Tommy held up his hands, ready to plead his case. A wrist full of hemp bracelets rolled up his arm. "No offense, man, but you're basically a glorified courier. A delivery boy. I don't mean that in a shitty way. I mean, if you get stopped by the cops, *you're* the one taking the heat for whatever you're carrying. Not that Russian asshole. Not the people you're carrying for. What I'm saying is, the money Alec Rudenko pays is good, but it ain't *that* good. It ain't *going to jail* good."

"If it's such a shitty gig, how come you're working right alongside me?"

"Well, that's simple," Tommy said. "I'm a fuckup. Eating your scraps is probably the best I'll ever do. I'm like one of those ugly fish that stick themselves to sharks' bellies. I'm not like you, Dan. I'm not smart like that."

Ever since they'd been kids, Tommy had a way of simultaneously insulting and complimenting his older brother. It had been a trend that had carried through to adulthood. Right now was no different. And despite the years of hearing similar platitudes, Danny never knew exactly how to feel or how to react. It wasn't just lip service; he knew Tommy really felt that way.

The waitress returned with their drinks. She set them on the table, laughed at some off-color joke Tommy laid on her, then slipped away again. She wasn't very attractive, but Tommy's eyes lingered on her caboose as she departed nonetheless.

"Listen," Tommy said. "I'm sorry about last week. I know I get... well, sometimes my head ain't always screwed on as tight as it should be. But really, that dude, he started it. I was just defending myself. I know it looked like I was off my rocker when you showed up, but that's the truth, man. Self-fucking-defense."

Danny knew his brother well enough to know that was bullshit. He didn't feel like getting into it now, however, so he stifled any comment by taking a drink of his whiskey. Maybe it was the exhaustion, but it tasted like shit.

"Anyway, I know you had my back. I do. Hell, man, you *always* have my back. I really think I would've killed that guy if you hadn't shown up and stopped me. You saved my ass, man."

Danny didn't know what to say. Tommy wasn't wrong about that part.

"It's why I'm bringing this up now," Tommy went on. "What I said about taking something for yourself, I mean. From Rudenko. Or whoever. I just want to see you do better than all this."

Danny set his glass on the table. "Tommy, do you have any idea what happens to people who rip off Alec Rudenko? They disappear. I'm not coming out a winner in that scenario."

"What if the payday was so huge you could take off and no one would ever find you?"

"I don't think a payday like that exists."

"What about whatever's in that briefcase?"

"It's a book, Tom."

"Is it, though?"

"As far as I'm concerned."

"If it's just a book, why are these two guys going through Rudenko to deliver it? Why hire guys like us when you could just ship it through FedEx or the fucking post office? Why give us a fucking *paper map* like it's goddamn 1985 so that we don't use GPS and risk being tracked? I'll tell you why—because it's *not* a book."

"That's right, I forgot. It's a bomb."

"It could be any fucking thing. I'm not saying I know exactly what it is, but I sure as shit know it's not a fucking copy of *Gone with the Wind*."

"Whatever it is, we're delivering it tomorrow. That's all there is."

"Christ, Danny. I just want the best for you."

"Then let's finish these drinks and get some rest. We've got a long day tomorrow."

"A long day tomorrow? Shit, you sound like Dad."

"Hey." Danny's voice was firm. "I told you not to bring him up."

"Yeah, right. Screw him. I don't want to talk about that shithead, either."

Danny finished off his own drink. "Come on. Let's go."

Tommy was gazing morosely down at his drink, running one finger along the rim. There was a tattoo of a dagger on the back of Tommy's hand, a red teardrop of blood dripping from the point of the blade. It was a shitty faded prison tat, something he'd had done by a cellmate during his stint up in Draper, but beneath the eerie blue lights of the lounge that drop of blood looked as black and stark as a portal to another dimension.

4

They arrived back at the motel room to find everything as it should be, except that the briefcase was now open. It was still on the bed next to Danny's duffel bag, just where he'd left it, yet the briefcase's lid was now up, its twin brass clasps gleaming beneath the naked bulb in the center of the ceiling.

Both brothers just stood there, staring at it.

Tommy spoke first: "You fucking asshole, you *opened* it." And then he laughed, like this was the punch line to some elaborate prank.

"I didn't open it."

Tommy went to the open briefcase, but Danny hurried into the bathroom, swept aside the plastic shower curtain, and then checked the linen closet, too. The motel room was empty. If someone had come in here and opened that briefcase in their absence, then they had already gone, and left no evidence behind. No evidence except that open briefcase.

"Jesus," Tommy said. He was peering down into the briefcase at whatever was inside.

For a moment, Danny worried that whatever had been inside that briefcase was no longer there. He saw an immediate future with him on the phone to Rudenko, telling him he'd been robbed, and then suffering whatever awful repercussions might come as a result of that call. But as he joined his brother at the foot of the bed, he could see that the briefcase did in fact contain what, in the very broadest sense of the term, might be considered a book.

It was about the size and shape of a photo album, and was bound in a material that at first appeared like a pale green silk. Yet on closer inspection, Danny saw that the book's covering bore the intricate network of veins and petioles that make up organic foliage. There were small divots in the material, like pores in flesh. It looked to him like the book had been bound in some strange plant matter. Vegetation.

"Well shit, I guess it *is* a book," Tommy said. "Sort of." He looked at Danny. "And if you didn't open it, who did?"

"I don't know."

"Maybe the briefcase is broken and it just popped open on its own."

Danny didn't buy that. Rudenko's anonymous client wouldn't insist on a series of precise and convoluted instructions for this thing's delivery just to toss it in a shoddy, busted briefcase. He went to the window, peered behind the drapes and out into the empty parking lot. The neon martini glass above the bar next door flashed above the highway and was reflected in puddles in the cracked asphalt.

"What a funky piece of shit," Tommy said.

Danny let the drapes sweep back into place. He looked over to find Tommy holding the book in his hands, turning it over, studying the texture of the binding the way he'd studied the roadmap back in the car.

"The hell are you doing? You're not supposed to touch it."

"You weren't supposed to open the case, either."

"I *didn't* open the case."

"What is it *made* out of?" Tommy ran a hand along the organic green sleeve covering the book. "It's like partially dehydrated leaves or something. I can *smell* it. Can you? Smells like a rainforest. Like…" He brought the book up to his nose and inhaled. "I don't know…"

Danny went to his duffel bag, unzipped it. His gun was still in there. If someone had broken in here to rob them, wouldn't they have searched his duffel bag and taken the Glock? More to the point, if someone had broken into this room to rob them, why wouldn't they have fled with the briefcase and duffel bag altogether? It didn't make sense.

No one broke in here. That motel room door was locked.

Which meant that whoever had come in here would have had a key.

Tommy sat on the edge of the bed, the book in his lap. He peeled open the cover and thumbed through a couple of pages. "Well this just gets weirder and weirder," he said.

"What?"

"It's empty."

"What do you mean?"

"The pages are blank."

"All of them?"

Tommy flipped through the pages—*fffip!* "All of them."

Danny peered over his brother's shoulder. The pages of the book *were* blank. The pages themselves looked strange, too—like they were sheets of old parchment, yellowed by time, and brittle as onion skin.

"Put it back," Danny said.

"Huh?"

"Put the fucking book back in the briefcase. Lock it up. Let's just forget this happened."

Tommy sighed. He took in another deep breath, then exhaled with his nostrils flared. "Christ, I wanna *smoke* the fucker. You don't smell that?"

"I don't wanna smell it. Put it away."

"You're such a fucking pussy, Dan."

Danny went back to his duffel bag, pulled out his gun. "Stay here," he told his brother, and then he was out the door and marshaling across the motel's parking lot. The lot was quiet and empty; even the sounds of the highway on the other side of the median were muted at this late hour. He had the gun down at his side, but his hand was itchy and he was grinding his teeth in mounting apprehension.

The Monte Carlo was the only car in the motel's parking lot. There were cars in the lot next door, in front of the cocktail lounge, so Danny went there. He was looking for someone suspicious, someone who might see him then bolt at the sight of the gun in his hand. But no one was out here. The only sound he heard was the faint hum coming from the lighted martini glass above the front doors—a feeling in the back of his teeth more than a sound in his ears, to be honest.

He tucked the gun into the rear waistband of his pants, crossed back over to the motel lot, then went into the lobby and to the front desk. The dipshit stoner with Coke-bottle glasses behind the desk looked up from his phone with all the zeal of a sleepwalker.

"Did someone go in my room?"

"Huh?" the dipshit stoner said.

"Someone's been in my room. You got housekeeping going around tonight?"

"Not until tomorrow."

Danny noticed the pegboard filigreed with spare keys behind the dipshit stoner's head. "Did *you* go in my room?"

"I didn't do shit, man. What's the matter? What's going on?"

Calm down, he warned himself. *You wanna start causing problems like your brother?*

"Forget it," he said, and turned to head out the door. Then he paused, turned around, and said, "There were supposed to be two beds in the room. There's only one."

The stoner's eyes fluttered repeatedly behind the thick lenses of his glasses. "You mean someone went into your room and took a *bed*?"

Fuck this noise, Danny thought, and stormed back out into the night.

Back in the room, he found Tommy splayed out on the bed, gazing sleepily at the TV. The book was back in the briefcase, although Tommy hadn't shut and latched it. Danny did so now, punching those brass clasps into place. It locked without incident. There. No one was getting into the goddamn thing now.

"I noticed you brought a change of clothes," Tommy said from atop the bed. His voice was muzzy with exhaustion, or maybe it was the marijuana. "That's my brother, always thinking two steps ahead. Hey, I used your toothbrush."

Danny grabbed his bag and vanished into the bathroom. He cranked on the shower, wanting nothing more than a couple of minutes beneath a hot pelt of water, but in the end he had to settle for a lukewarm trickle.

5

Danny was awakened at some point in the blackest hours of the morning not by some noise but by a subtle and inexpressible change in his surroundings. He was a light sleeper who was constantly aware, even on a subconscious level, of such things. A little of that had to do with his profession; more of it was a result of having grown up with a bipolar, alcoholic father who was in frequent jeopardy with the law. There'd been a lot of picking up and moving in the middle of the night back then, a lot of drunken blows to dodge. Whatever the reason, Danny had trained his body at an early age to respond to even the slightest alteration in his surroundings.

He sat up in bed, the room mineshaft-dark except for a silver beam cutting in through a slender part in the drapes. He was in the motel room with Tommy, he remembered, although Tommy was no longer sprawled out in the bed beside him.

A black shape shifted along the wall beside the covered window. A spectral hand breached the sliver of moonlight, parting the drapes ever so slightly.

"Tommy?" His voice was groggy with sleep.

It *was* Tommy—who else would it be?—standing by the window, peering out into the night. He was naked except for his briefs, his skin nearly luminous in the moonlight coming in through the window. He said something that Danny didn't quite catch.

"What?"

"I said it's the waitress." Tommy's voice was an urgent half-whisper. "I don't fucking believe it."

"What are you talking about? What waitress?" Danny's sleep-addled mind summoned the woman with the sweaty forehead from the cocktail lounge next door.

"Come see this," Tommy hissed.

Danny leaned over and felt around for his cell phone on the nightstand. It was 3:06 a.m. Danny's headache had receded, but like the aftereffects of a frat party, it had left the interior of his skull a mess.

He swung his legs out of bed then joined Tommy by the window. Tommy parted the drapes a bit farther, exposing a glistening, moonlit parking lot. The neon martini that overlooked the highway was now dark.

"She's right back there, watching us," Tommy said, his breath fogging up the glass. He pressed a finger to the glass and left a clear spot in the fog. "You see her? I don't understand what she's doing here."

It took Danny some searching, but then he *did* see her. She was standing at the far end of the motel's parking lot, spotlighted beneath the radiant glow of the three-quarter moon. As impossible as it might seem, it looked like she was staring right at them through the window.

Something about the woman didn't jibe with the word *waitress*. He was still envisioning the woman who'd brought them whiskey earlier at the lounge next door, but he couldn't reconcile his mental picture of that woman with the one standing out there right now in the parking lot.

"That's not her," Danny said.

"Like hell it's not. I had my tongue halfway down her throat, I ought to know."

That was when Danny realized his brother was talking about the *other* waitress, the one Tommy had been flirting with back at the Roadrunner Diner earlier that evening.

"It *can't* be her," Danny said, because that was really the only logical thing to say. They were over a hundred miles away and it was after three in the morning.

"Like hell," Tommy said. "She's still wearing her fucking apron."

Danny could say nothing to that. He just kept studying the woman who, in turn, appeared to be studying him right back. A tall hedgerow separated the motel's parking lot from the road, encircling the lot on two of its four sides. She stood in the lee of the hedgerow, nearly up against it from what Danny could tell at such a distance. Had the moon not been so bright, they might not have seen her at all.

"You think she followed us out here?" Tommy asked.

No, that didn't make sense. What *did* make sense—

Danny turned and squeezed his brother's forearm. "You didn't say anything to her about where we were headed, did you?"

"Of course n—"

"You sure?"

Tommy yanked his arm free. "I'm fucking positive! You think I told her to meet me out here for a three a.m. booty call? She's freaking me out, man." He turned back to the window. "What is she, *watching* us?"

"That's impossible."

"Yeah, but look at her. She's just fucking *staring*, man, like she can see us from all the way over—"

"This is ridiculous," Danny said, turning away from the window. He fumbled around in the dark, found his pants, tugged them on.

"You're going out there?"

Danny ignored the question. He debated whether or not he should grab his gun from the duffel bag, but decided that might be overkill. He shoved his feet into his shoes, then stepped outside into the parking lot.

Frigid desert air caused the sweat that had sprung out along Danny's bare chest to cool. His respiration plumed in the air in front of his face as he walked alongside the Monte Carlo toward the center of the parking lot.

It's her, all right. It was an impossible admission, void of logic, but goddamn if he could refute it. She was *right there*, watching *him* now: he recognized her face, the tatty Def Leppard T-shirt, the white sash of her apron still slung across her hips. *How in the world did she find us out here?* And on the heels of that thought: *What does she want?*

Something in the way she was standing there motionless in the dark, watching him, caused Danny to freeze halfway across the parking lot.

Or maybe I'm still asleep and dreaming…

He cleared his throat and said, "You're the girl from the diner. The waitress." These were not questions, but statements of fact. His voice sounded flat and toneless in the cold desert air.

The waitress said nothing in return. One corner of her apron billowed out as a gust of cool wind came through.

"Someone send you here to find us?" He glanced around the parking lot, realizing that there were no other cars in the vicinity except their Monte Carlo. "How'd you get here?"

Only response was the *sssssss* of highway grit skirling across the surface of the blacktop.

"How'd you know we were here? Did Tommy say something to you?"

"I didn't say shit."

Startled by his brother's voice, Danny turned and saw Tommy creeping out of the motel room behind him, his bare feet crunching on the tiny granules of sand scattered about the pavement. Danny held up one hand to halt his brother's progress and to keep him a couple of paces back, but Tommy either ignored the gesture or didn't understand. He came up beside Danny, a contrail of vapor unspooling from his lips.

"What's her name?"

"Uh…"

"Christ, Tom."

Tommy raised a hand, waved to her. "Heya! Hi! Whatcha doin' out here?"

I don't like this, Danny thought. *Something's off. It's not just the fact that she's here, but something about her is out of whack. Something…*

He tried to grasp what it was but it kept evading him.

I should have brought the gun.

"I'll go talk to her," Tommy said, and took a step forward.

Danny grabbed him around the arm and tugged him back. "No. I don't like this. Where's her car? How'd she get here?"

Tommy was scanning the parking lot now, coming to the same conclusion.

"It's not some kid waitress I'm worried about," Danny told him, lowering his voice further. "It's whoever else is out there with her."

"Shit," Tommy said. He sucked in a lungful of air through clenched teeth.

The waitress began walking toward them. She moved with the slow, calculated gait of someone negotiating a minefield.

"Who's with you?" Danny called to her.

She stopped maybe fifteen feet from them.

"How did you—"

When she spoke, her voice possessed an eerie singsong quality that hadn't been present when she'd taken their orders back at the Roadrunner Diner: "Do you have it?"

Tommy took a step back. He glanced over at Danny. "Have what?" he asked, still staring at Danny.

"Can I see it?" she asked. "Can I *touch* it?"

"The fuck are you talking about?" Tommy said, his voice rising a notch.

"Can I *hold* it? May I *see* it? Will you bring it *out* to me?"

Tommy said, "Bring *what* out, you crazy bitch?"

"The...*book*..." she said. Her words seemed to crystallize in the air between them.

"Sweetheart, you're out of your fuck—" Tommy began.

"Stop." Danny's voice was calm. "I know what's going on here. Let's get back in the room."

"Danny, you think this—"

Danny squeezed his brother's shoulder. Leaning close to Tommy's ear, he said, "Right now, Tommy. Right now."

Tommy just stared at him, eyes like fishbowls. "Whuh...?"

"Come on," he said, and turned back toward the motel room.

Tommy lingered in the parking lot a moment longer. He gazed at Danny then looked back out toward the waitress. She had taken another step toward him, closing the distance between them.

Come on, Tommy, you asshole...

Tommy snapped from his stupor and followed his brother back into the motel room.

6

"It's a test," Danny said once they were back inside the motel room. For good measure, Tommy had engaged the chain lock on the door, then scurried over to the window to peer back out into the parking lot. The waitress from the Roadrunner Diner was still out there, staring at their room. Closer now than she had been before.

"She's still there," Tommy said. He glanced over at Danny. "What do you mean it's a test?"

"We're being tested to make sure we follow the rules," Danny said. "It's the only thing that makes any sense."

"What fucking rules, man?"

"The instructions Rudenko's client gave him. The instructions he gave to us. Not to touch the book, not to deal with anyone who comes around asking about the book. *Those* fucking rules."

Danny waited while his brother soaked this in. He could see through the part in the drapes that the waitress was indeed still there; the moon at her back, her shadow stretched like sackcloth across the passenger side of their car.

"Why would someone do that?" Tommy said.

"To answer that, you first gotta know who's doing the testing."

"You mean that Choptank guy?"

No, Danny didn't think it was Choptank.

"If this book is so important to this Choptank motherfucker, why's he playing games?" Tommy said. "If he's out there right now, let's give him what he's paying us for."

Danny shook his head. "It's not Choptank."

"Who, then? Mr. Anonymous Client Motherfucker?"

Danny said, "It's Rudenko."

"*What?* The fuck sense does that make?"

All the sense in the world, Tommy, if you have half a brain and can read a room, Danny thought.

Tommy shook his head. He let the drapes close, dousing them once again in complete darkness. Neither one of them made a move to turn on the light. "I don't understand."

"You remember Robert Benzo? Guy who used to run the East Coast corridor a few years back?"

"Dude, I was in prison a few years back. Who the fuck is Robert Benzo?"

"A moron with a death wish, that's who," Danny said. "He was one of Rudenko's trusted guys, but he got a bug up his ass at some point. Starting pilfering from every package he was transporting. Drugs, money, whatever. Didn't matter. When the clients complained, Benzo said they were full of shit, that he delivered every package in full, just the way he'd received them. Rudenko got wise, but he wasn't one hundred percent sure who to believe. So he set Benzo up. Gave him a phony package. Benzo took the bait, and Rudenko knew he had a thief and a liar on his bankroll."

"What happened to the guy?"

"Rudenko had him killed."

"And what's this got to do with us and a fucking waitress standing out there in the parking lot?"

"Same scenario as Benzo's. Only you and me, we're not thieves."

"Then what are we?"

Danny considered how to say it. "A liability."

"What's that mean? How're we a liability?"

Not "we," Tommy, he thought. *Just you. My sin is in the blood—in being your older brother. My sin is bringing your ass into the fold.*

But he couldn't say those things to Tommy. The asshole might spiral again. Might *slip*. And that was the last thing Danny needed right now.

Instead, he asked Tommy if he'd told anyone about what had happened last week in Williston, North Dakota.

"Are you kidding me? I didn't say a word to nobody."

"I know how it is," Danny told him. "Guys go out, have a few drinks. Stories start flowing. Maybe shit you shouldn't tell nobody…"

Throughout the entirety of their conversation, Tommy had been crouched on his haunches beside the window, where he would occasionally peer out. He stood now and took a step in Danny's direction.

Easy, Danny thought. *Take it easy.*

"That's not what fucking happened." Tommy's voice had that familiar edge to it, just like he'd had back in the car when Danny had accused him of being stoned. "I never told anybody about what happened. You're the only one who knows."

Even if that was true—even if Rudenko hadn't caught wind of the incident in Williston—Danny's boss had never trusted Tommy. If Rudenko had wanted to set them up as a way of shaking out a bad apple—Tommy being that apple—it wouldn't surprise Danny. This particular scenario, however, didn't *smell* like something Rudenko would do. This wasn't Alec Rudenko's style.

"You know," Tommy said, and there was the old calmness in his voice now. "He said something to that waitress just before he left the diner. You remember that?"

Danny made a noise that approximated a yes.

"I didn't hear what it was," Tommy continued, "but he could have told her to follow us."

That sounded like bullshit to Danny, but he wasn't going to say it.

"He could've sent his knuckle-draggers out here, too." Tommy was talking more to himself than to Danny now, it sounded like. Danny just let him go. "That baldheaded son of a bitch from the diner could've come in here while we were at the lounge and opened up that briefcase. And—and *shit*, Danny, *I picked up the fucking book.* Just like we were told not to do."

That you did, Danny thought. His eyes had acclimated to the darkness of the room—neither one of them had made a move to turn the light on—and he could see Tommy's shoulders begin to sag. It brought him some satisfaction to see his brother have an attack of self-awareness for once.

Tommy lowered himself down on the edge of the bed; the mattress springs groaned beneath his weight. "Goddamn it, Danny, I fucked up."

"No one knows you touched the book but me."

"My fingerprints will be on it. He's gonna do me like he did that Benzo guy."

"That's not gonna happen. Just let me think for a minute."

By thinking, he meant he had to take a leak. He went into the bathroom and took a piss in the dark. When he came back out into the room, Tommy was still sitting there on the edge of the bed, his body a bleak, amorphous shape in the lightlessness of the motel room.

In his mind's eye, he was back in Williston, North Dakota. Tommy wasn't supposed to be with him on that particular gig—the client had explicitly requested one courier only—but Tommy needed the cash. Danny had grown tired of forking over wads of bills to his brother whenever he ran dry, so he said he'd pay him but he was going to put him to work. He had Tommy do the bulk of the driving, but when it came time to deliver the package, Danny had dropped Tommy off at a roadhouse on the outskirts of Williston. Danny was gone for no more than two hours. It was close to midnight when he steered the Monte Carlo into the rear parking lot of the roadhouse. The Monte Carlo's headlights fell upon the quaking, furious visage of Tommy pointing his gun at a man sprawled out on the pavement. Danny hopped from the car and talked Tommy down, until Tommy eventually lowered the gun. The man on the ground had already taken quite a beating—his face looked like ground beef and the fingers of his left hand were all bent at unnatural angles. Danny ushered Tommy into the car and they got the hell out of there as fast as they could. Tommy's sole statement, like a child defending himself against some injustice on the school playground: *He started it*.

Had Danny arrived a second later, Tommy would have pulled that trigger. The course of their lives might have been altered from that moment forward. In the days that followed, Danny couldn't shake that nightmare of being trapped in a cell with his erratic brother and his raging, lunatic father.

Danny went to the window, peeled back the drape, and looked outside. "She's gone," he said.

Tommy said, "Are you sure?"

"I don't see her."

"Goddamn it. I'm sorry, Dan. I fucked up."

He let the drape fall back into place. "Maybe no one's gotta know."

The mattress springs squealed as Tommy rose from the bed. "I'm gonna catch a shower."

Tommy's dark shape negotiated around the bed and slipped into the bathroom. The doorway blazed with a pale yellow light, and then the door was shut. A moment later, Danny heard the pipes clang and a rush of water spatter into the tub.

Whatever had happened here tonight, it was too clumsy of an operation for Alec Rudenko. Having that chick show up here at three in the morning? The bizarre way she'd asked to see the book?

Can I hold it? May I see it? Will you bring it out to me?

It was all too on-the-nose to be a setup.

Something else, too…something…

Something was off.

Something was out of whack.

Another image popped unbidden into his head, this one much older than the week-old incident in Williston. A man enraged, tearing his boys from their sleep, from the bed that they shared, a lumpy mattress on the floor of a roach-infested apartment, terror in those boys' eyes as the man—their father—shrieked and raged and grabbed items and stuffed those items into a nylon bag, *come on fuckers get up*, grabbed drugs, grabbed a semiautomatic handgun from the top drawer of a dresser, *get fucking dressed*, piss stains on the man's gray sweatpants, booze and sweat clinging to his flesh, *move move move you little fuckers*, a cavalcade of feet down the apartment's steps, the boys silently weeping, an orange plastic tube of pills cartwheeling down the stairs, *move you fuckers or I'm a dead man*, and then into a car, the jolt as the car sideswipes something parked in the street, a maniacal shriek from behind the steering wheel, the hairs on their father's head like bent spokes in a wheel, all of it a wheel, *they want me dead you boys won't be happy until your old man is dead*, and there, speeding off into the center of night—

Danny shook the memory from his head. It was one of a million he had buried in there, deep as pirate treasure. He focused on the sound of the running shower, and found that—

(move move move you little fuckers)

—it soothed him.

What the fuck had happened here tonight?

He remembered Tommy coming out of their motel room and joining him out there in the parking lot to confront the waitress. *Someone send you here to find us? How'd you get here?* Tommy had left the motel room door open, hadn't he? Left it open for someone else to slip in.

Had the waitress been a diversion?

He went to the dresser and saw that the briefcase was still there. It was locked once more, but he lifted it and could feel the weight of that strange book sliding around inside. This brought him some measure of relief. Whatever had happened here tonight, perhaps they'd acted appropriately. Perhaps—

(move you fuckers or I'm a dead man)

A dead man.

And it was then that he realized what had been troubling him when he and Tommy had gone out there to confront the waitress. The needling *something*, the *wrongness*, that had evaded him until now. It had been cold out there, and both he and Tommy, in their trepidation, had been standing out there filling the air with shuddery clouds of vapor.

The waitress outside in the parking lot had not.

No breath.

No breathing.

No vapor.

He went back to the window and swept the drapes apart. The parking lot was empty. Was she hiding in the shadows somewhere out there? Stowed away in the backseat of their car, maybe?

He could see nothing.

No breath...no vapor...

You're remembering it wrong, said the practical side of his brain.

"Go fuck yourself," he told it. And then he stripped off his pants, climbed into bed, and tried to get some sleep.

7

Where's your daddy, Danny Drake?
Gone to jail with a prison shank!
Where's your mommy, Tommy Drake?
Dead in the ground, that dirty—

8

The remnants of some disremembered nightmare raking its claws across his gray matter, Danny Drake bolted awake in an empty motel room. Daylight streamed through the space between the drapes; it carved a sizzling passage down the center of the otherwise gloomy room, and seemed to highlight the fact that Tommy was not here.

"Tommy?"

Danny climbed out of bed and staggered to the bathroom. It was empty; Tommy was not there. He took a piss, examined his burgeoning beard stubble in the cracked mirror above the sink, then schlepped back into the room. The black leather briefcase was still on the dresser, just where he'd left it. He went to the window and pulled the drapes farther apart, so that he stood, half naked, in a column of sunlight. The warmth felt good on his tired flesh.

Their car was gone.

He dressed quickly then hurried out the door into harsh daylight. He was thinking of the waitress from the night before—how she stood out here watching their room, and then how she'd vanished. In the light of a new day, the events of the previous evening—really, just a handful of hours ago—struck him as preposterous. He knew it had happened; he just felt detached enough from it now to wonder if he'd misinterpreted something in all of it.

Def Leppard T-shirts don't lie, said the pragmatic part of his brain. She'd been here. She'd tried to get them to—

Where the fuck is the car? Where the fuck is Tommy?

Before he knew what he was doing, he was charging across the parking lot toward the road. Next door, the cocktail lounge was an empty shell: lights off, all previous forms of life dispatched to the far reaches of the galaxy. The sight of that unlit martini glass made something clench in Danny's throat.

Where the fuck is—

A car came careening around the side of the hedgerow, thundering over a rumble strip and belching coal-black clouds of exhaust into the air. The brakes squealed as it rocked to a stop mere inches from him. The goddamn Monte Carlo. He planted his palms on the steaming hood of the car while his heart threatened to crawl up his throat.

The driver's side window cranked down and Tommy's face

appeared. "You look like shit, Danny." Then he gave Danny one of his patented Tommy Drake grins, and held a greasy paper pouch out the window. "Got us some breakfast!"

9

"So what's the logic here?" Tommy asked. He was drinking a beer and smoking a joint in the passenger seat while Danny drove. The day was mild, but they kept the windows down to circulate some fresh air into the car. "If Rudenko's setting us up—like, if it's all bullshit—then why are we even going through with this?"

After a few hours' sleep, Danny wasn't sure what he believed. Had Rudenko tried to test them last night? It didn't seem likely, particularly in the way it had happened, yet it was the only logical thing Danny could come up with. And what about that book? No text, just blank pages? It all kept coming back to Alec Rudenko—a test to weed Tommy out of the picture—but all the pieces didn't seem to fit together the more Danny labored over it. It just wasn't Rudenko's *style*.

"Even if it's a game, we're gonna play it," Danny told him. "We do our job. That's it."

"You know, we did some fucking blow in the bathroom."

"Who?"

"Me and that waitress. Back at the diner. Told her I had a bag on me. Was trying to get in her pants. We did a couple lines off the toilet tank. Romantic as hell."

"You don't remember anything about her? A name? Anything she might have said that might make sense to us now?"

"Dude, she didn't say shit. She was just some bumfuck waitress pulling an all-nighter at a dive joint. What's she gonna tell me, her Social Security number? Can't you call Rudenko and clear this shit up?"

He didn't have a phone number for Alec Rudenko, nor had he ever had to call the man. Danny had a burner phone, on which Rudenko could reach him whenever he desired, but that was about it.

The car crested a hill, revealing a landscape ablaze in warm desert colors. The terrain beyond the hill was flat, with tufts of gray sagebrush poking through cracks in the arid soil. Tommy glanced up at the horizon with only a passing interest, then finished off his beer. He crunched the empty can then sent it sailing out the window.

"Come on," Danny said. "Are you looking for more problems?"

Tommy laughed. "What are you talking about? Problems from who? Cops? There's no cops out here. Hell, we haven't seen another car all day."

That was true. Danny had noted that himself a few hours earlier, but hearing Tommy say it only confirmed his unease on the subject. "Check the map, will you? Make sure we haven't gone off course."

"Our course *is* off course," Tommy commented as he popped open the glove compartment and tugged out the map. He started to unfold it, rolled up his window, then unfolded it some more. "I mean, we're on the right road, far as I can tell. What's bothering you?"

"Just what you said. I've been noticing the same thing. That we're the only idiots out here. And that we seem to be taking two and a half days to do something that could have been done in twelve hours."

"I love you."

Danny looked at him. "What?"

Again, Tommy laughed. "You're so high strung, I love it. What are you worried about? If there's too many cars on the road, you get hinky. Now, we've got *no* cars, and you're all suspicious and shit."

Danny readjusted the rearview mirror. The black leather briefcase was back there, vibrating on the back seat.

Tommy said, "You ever wonder what'll happen when Dad gets out of prison?"

A knot tightened in Danny's chest.

"He'll be an old man. Like what's-his-name in that *Shawshank Redemption* movie. The old guy who hangs himself from a ceiling rafter."

"I don't wanna talk about Dad."

Tommy cracked another beer—he had a case of Milwaukee's Best at his feet—and took a noisy slurp. He held the joint aloft in his other hand, the thing no bigger than a hangnail now. "You think you'd be doing something different with your life if he'd been a different kind of guy? Dad, I mean."

Danny didn't respond. He'd told Tommy a million times not to bring up their father. Yet here he was. No wonder someone was out there fucking with them now.

"You know what I'd like to be? A movie star." Tommy spread his arms wide. "My name on the big screen. Only I'd go with Tom Dark, because, fuck, that just sounds so killer. Do a bunch of action hero movies or whatever. A love scene or two. Real steamy. You think they really fuck when they're doing love scenes?"

"No."

"Well, maybe I'll make that a point in my contract. 'Gotta do real fucking.' Hey, who's the hottest actress out there now?"

"I don't know."

"You ever seen that Kirsten Dunst? She's all right, I guess. Seems totally getable. Like, if I saw her in a bar, I could probably chat her up and fuck her. Some actresses look like that. Makes 'em hotter, I think, because you think you really got a shot. Same with that one blonde chick who's always in those movies fucking black dudes. She always looks like she's hungry to get down on some dick."

"I have no idea what the fuck you're talking about."

"Never mind. Who's the chick that was in *Speed*?"

"I don't know."

"She was in that *Bird Box* movie, too. She looks totally getable."

"Did you see that?"

"What? *Bird Box*?"

"That speed limit sign we just passed."

"What about it?"

Danny looked over his shoulder, as if he'd be able to read that sign from the back. It was already a dwindling piece of metal on the side of the road.

"Said the speed limit was one hundred miles an hour."

Tommy turned around in his seat, too. He stayed like that for a while. Ultimately, he said, "Don't fuck with me."

"I'm not fucking with you. That's what it said."

Tommy sat back around. "There is no place in America where the speed limit is a hundred miles an hour."

"That's what the sign said, Tom. Swear to God."

"Then it was a fake sign. Someone playing a prank."

Danny shot him a look. "How many pranks are people gonna play on us?"

"I'm talking about teenagers spray-painting signs."

"Out here?" Danny said. He raised a hand to the windshield to acknowledge the vast emptiness of their surroundings.

Tommy's eyes narrowed. Danny could tell the wheels were working inside his brother's head now. Tommy took another sip of his beer, then yanked his cell phone from the pocket of his jean jacket. "I'll look it up, see what the interwebs has to say about it. But I'll bet you a hundred *bucks* that there are no speed limits at a hundred *miles* an hour…"

And then he was quiet for a while.

"What is it?" Danny said, worried that Tommy might have slipped again.

The Monte Carlo went *brrrr-brrrr*.

"No cell phone service." Tommy glanced up through the windshield, as if that tequila-colored horizon had some words of wisdom for him. "Have you even seen any towers out here? Or telephone lines, for that matter?"

No, Danny hadn't seen a goddamn thing.

"Billboards? Signs for rest stops? *Anything?*"

No, Danny hadn't. For hours, it had been nothing but him, Tommy, and whatever that fucked up book was in that briefcase.

The Monte Carlo went *brrrr-brrrr*.

"No birds, no wildlife, no bugs splooshing against the windshield." Tommy chugged his beer, then tossed the empty can out the window. This time, Danny didn't say anything about it. "We are traversing the desolate wastelands of this great nation. This route that our generous benefactor, the anonymous client, has chosen for us is really a window into another dimension. Do you feel it? Do you sense how we've drifted slightly left of center?"

"Quit smoking that shit," Danny said.

Tommy took one final toke of the joint, cracked the window, cast it out. "I'm getting hungry."

That was something else Danny hadn't seen since they'd hit the road that morning—not a single restaurant or even a *sign* for a restaurant during the whole drive. It was possible they'd passed some earlier at the start of the trip, when they hadn't been looking for them, but Danny couldn't be certain. What if whoever had sent that waitress to their motel last night had also fashioned them a map that would send them careening off into the middle of fucking nowhere? The only sign of humanity out here was the road itself. And not just *humanity*, but life itself. Not a bird in the sky, not a single string of power lines on the horizon. Where the fuck *were* they?

"Look at that," Tommy said. He sat upright in the passenger seat and pointed directly out the windshield. "There! There!"

Danny looked, saw nothing at first, but then slowed the car

down. For the past hour, they'd been driving through a wide expanse of desolate scrubland, where the horizon unfurled forever in every direction. The only indication of a changing landscape was the distant tufts of greenery sprouting from a bedrock of taupe sandstone. Now, they were shuttling through a canyon of sorts, great rocky formations rising up on either side of the roadway. The formations weren't high, but they were doing a good job blocking out the sun, and they had seemingly come out of nowhere. Danny felt claustrophobic just driving through them.

It wasn't the formations that Tommy was pointing at. Rather, it was something *atop* one of the formations, a stark yet blurry image, there for a moment then gone the next, fleeing against the sudden shift in horizon. A thing that, in the quick glimpse Danny caught of it, looked like a black goat with an impressive headdress of spiraling horns.

Tommy sat forward in his seat. "Did you see it? Did you see it? What a fucking ugly thing! What *was* that?"

"It looked like some kind of mountain goat."

"It looked more like the devil incarnate," Tommy said. "It looked like Saint Peter took a shit on a hillside and it came to life. Did you *see* it?"

"Just a glimpse," Danny confessed. He'd watched as *something* bounded across the top of the mesa and vanished down the other side.

"It had wings," Tommy said.

10

Twenty minutes later, they came upon a sign that read:

COAL DUST
Population: -11

"Take the exit," Tommy said. "I'm starving to death."

"Negative eleven?"

"Take it, take it, take it!"

Danny took it, and coasted down a slalom of narrow, sun-bleached pavement with no real end in sight. It was late in the afternoon, the sun having repositioned itself somewhere behind them (and occasionally hiding behind a bank of sooty clouds), and the car was getting low on gas. Wherever the fuck they were, they all needed some fuel.

After a mile, the paved roadway turned to gravel. After another half a mile, it vanished completely into the sand. Danny slowed the car to a crawl, uncertain if they should continue in this direction or not. No buildings, no billboards, no telephone poles. Just a straightaway ribbon of sand cutting through a channel of mesas at the darkening horizon.

Tommy sat up in his seat. "You took the right exit, didn't you?"

"Did you see any other exit?"

Tommy took out the map, studied it while beads of sweat cropped up along his forehead. "There's no town called Coal Dust anywhere on here."

Up over a crest, down a ravine, some Joshua trees reaching out of the sandy earth toward the deepening sky.

"Does this count as us veering off the route?" Tommy said. "Like, are we breaking another one of the rules?"

Danny didn't have the patience to consider unanswerable questions. He kept looking at the Joshua trees. They were bugging him.

"What?" Tommy said, sensing his unease.

"Those trees shouldn't be here. They should be much farther west."

"How far west?"

"California. Arizona. Utah."

"You sure? What do you know about trees?"

It wasn't that he knew about trees; it was that he'd spent over a decade traversing the desert byways of the United States and had become familiar with even the subtlest differences in geographic topography.

"Hey," Tommy said. "Wouldn't it be funny if we've actually been heading in the opposite direction this whole time?"

"Yeah. That'd be a fucking riot." Danny chewed on his lower lip for a couple of seconds. "Turn on your phone's GPS," he said.

"Rule breaker," Tommy said, but that didn't stop him from firing up his cell phone. Tap-tap-tap on the screen. Then: "Still no signal."

"This is insanity."

"Listen, can we pull over? I need to clear my head for a minute. The smell of that book is making me sick."

"What smell?"

Tommy glared at him. There was too much moisture in his eyes. "You haven't been smelling that? It's seeping out of that briefcase like poisonous gas. It's been making me sick for hours."

"I don't smell anything."

"Bullshit."

"I'm serious."

"Well, it's killing me. Pull over so we can toss it in the trunk, will ya?"

Danny eased the Monte Carlo to a dead stop in the middle of the road—or the place where the middle of the road would have been, had there *been* a road. He got out and popped the trunk. The air was odorless, the temperature mild. The scrim of sand covering his leather boots looked like salt.

Tommy climbed out of the car and carried the briefcase over. He dumped it in the Monte Carlo's trunk along with the spare tire, the jack, and a Medusa tangle of jumper cables.

"I only slept for a couple of hours last night," Tommy said, "but I had this dream that Dad turned into a weird fish-type thing and slipped through the bars of his cell. 'I'm coming for ya, kiddo,' he said. 'I'm coming for ya.' I know it was a dream, but it felt real as fuck."

Why are you telling me this? Danny wondered.

"I still smell it on me," Tommy said. "The book, I mean." He was staring at the palms of his hands. They appeared to tremble.

Danny slammed the trunk shut.

11

An inexplicable thing happened soon after they decided to turn around and head back to the service road. Danny was leaning forward over the steering wheel, squinting through the accumulation of highway grit on the windshield for signs of the road that would take them back on route, when a small cluster of buildings materialized through the haze off to his left. Their arrival bore all the telltale signs of a mirage, right down to the way they appeared to undulate behind a curtain of rising heat, making them look insubstantial. Something out of a dream.

Tommy saw them, too. "Is that the town? Coal Dust?" There was an uncharacteristic touch of awe in his voice. "How'd we miss it on the first pass?"

"Beats me."

"How do we get there? There's no road."

Fuck it, Danny thought, and spun the wheel. The car bounded in the direction of the town, tires tearing up the desert floor and casting a rooster tail of dust in their wake. It was nothing the car couldn't handle—the Monte Carlo was outfitted in heavy-duty tires—yet Danny lowered the speed nonetheless, just to be safe.

"I'm gonna kiss the first person I see right on the mouth," Tommy said.

"Wonderful. Maybe they'll show up at our motel room tonight, too."

He expected a chuckle or even a smartass retort from Tommy, but nothing came. Only silence. Then came the strange prickling in the air between them followed by a chilly wave of disquiet. Danny glanced at his brother from the side of his eye and saw that Tommy was staring at him, his face hard. The muscles in Tommy's jaw kept clenching.

"It was just a joke," Danny told him.

"You blame me." It came out in a whisper, barely audible over the growl of the Monte Carlo's engine.

"No, Tom. Whatever happened last night, that was someone messing with—"

"Because of me." Still whispering. His eyes boring into the side of Danny's face.

A part of Danny wanted to stop the car, drag his brother out, and beat the shit out of him. Another part of Danny wanted to make quick amends, finish this gig, then never deal with his brother again. Did he love Tommy? He couldn't really say anymore; time and wear had blunted any sort of emotion akin to love. What he felt—what he'd *always* felt—was a responsibility toward his brother. That was what happened when your mother died young and you had a petty shithead criminal for a father. It was this sense of stewardship that had bound them together this far.

As they drew closer to the town, Danny said, "Ignore me all you want. I actually appreciate the silence."

This statement could have pushed Tommy completely over the edge—he could have smashed a window, kicked a dent in the dash. He could have done anything, really. Instead, his whole body began to tremble. His face remained hard, those muscles in his jaw flexing… but then his whole expression changed. Laughter erupted from his throat, shrill but genuine. Tears flooded his eyes. Clutching his stomach while still laughing, he repositioned himself in the passenger seat, his head ratcheting back against the headrest.

"That," Tommy said, once his laughter had begun to subside, "was a good one."

He's crazy like Dad, said that niggling little voice inside his head.

Tommy sighed. He was breathing with such intensity, a crooked grin on his face as he gazed out the windshield, that Danny could hear it over the sounds of the tiny stones plinking off the car's exterior.

They drove past blood-red letters painted on a large stone:

WELCOME TO COAL DUST
POP. -9

"Hey, that's good news," Tommy said, wiping the tears from his eyes. "Population's creeping back up."

A gust of wind swept a curtain of sand from a strip of asphalt, revealing the road through town. Danny took it. The road cut down the center of the town, although by this point, Danny was beginning to consider the term "town" to be more than generous. "Ghost town," more like it.

Tommy looked around, stating the obvious: "There's no one here. Place is deserted."

They passed through a wedge of crumbling one-story buildings. Windows boarded up, business signs missing letters, a blanket of white dust covering everything. It looked like one of those phony towns constructed in the middle of the desert for bomb testing. There were some abandoned vehicles perched cockeyed on mounds of sand, their bodies rusted and all their windows blown out.

A plot of land off to the right, where a series of ancient tombstones protruded from the hard earth at crooked angles behind a low iron fence.

Danny slowed the car to a crawl as they drove past a cluster of palm trees, some of them three stories high, sprouting from the earth. Scattered about the base of the trees were the wiry brown skulls of coconuts, half buried in the ground.

"Those can't be real," Tommy said.

Yet as strange as all this was, stranger still was what waited for them at the end of the road.

It was a gas station and convenience store—and it appeared fully operational.

"Well, shit," Tommy said.

The place was filthy and gone to pot, but the sign above the pumps, GAS AND GULP, was illuminated. Which meant someone was out here paying the electric bills.

Danny edged the car alongside one of the pumps, then shut it down. He told Tommy to gas it up, then climbed out of the car.

The day had turned warm, the air still. There wasn't a cloud in the sky. Not a single bird, either. Or any airplanes, for that matter.

As he approached the store, Danny paused as his gaze fell upon a sign behind the cruddy, smoked glass of the door—ALL SHOPLIFTERS WILL BE PROSTRATED AND PERSECUTED. He tried to find some humor in it but couldn't.

He stepped into the convenience store to find the lights on, a fresh pot of coffee sitting on a hot plate, and Muzak trickling from hidden speakers. The shelves were fully stocked and the bananas in the produce section were still green. It was the sheer *ordinariness* of what he was seeing that served to increase his discomfort. How could this place function all the way out here, at the ass end of a ghost town in the middle of nowhere? It wasn't even off the main road for travelers to find…not that there had been any other travelers on that road all day, as far as Danny was aware.

The whole thing made him nervous.

"Hello?"

There was no one behind the counter. At the back of the store were two doors, one for a unisex bathroom, the other with an EMPLOYEES ONLY sign on it. Danny went to the bathroom door, opened it…then recoiled at the punishing smell. There was no toilet, only an open drain in the floor. Rusty brown streaks had dried on the walls—streaks that could have been blood or shit or both. There was no sink, either—just a prong of naked pipes jutting from the wall— and where the mirror should have been, someone had used a thick black marker to draw a smiley face. Above Mr. Smiley, someone had written this phrase in a child's shaky handwriting:

this is how i learned to swallow faces

The restroom should have been electric with flies and all manner of creeping insects, but it wasn't. There wasn't a single gnat floating in the air.

Danny shut the door, then went to the one for employees only. He twisted the knob, but it was locked. He rapped his knuckles on the door, called out to whoever might be in there, then waited for several seconds. No one responded. It was as if the place had been recently evacuated.

When he turned, the sight of Tommy standing in the aisle startled him. He hadn't heard him come in.

"This place can't actually *exist*, can it?" Tommy said, looking around. He spied a security camera in the ceiling and flipped it off. "I mean, where *is* everybody?"

"I don't know. Let's just take some of this stuff and get out of here."

There were canvas tote bags hanging on a rack. Danny took one down and began loading it up with protein, carbs, aspirin, bottles of water. Tommy went directly behind the checkout counter and started yanking down cartons of cigarettes from the shelves.

"Check the phone while you're back there," Danny called to him.

"Good idea." He looked around, dipped beneath the counter for a moment, then popped back up. "There's no phone."

Danny wasn't surprised, though it certainly didn't help settle his nerves any.

Tommy snatched a handful of scratch-offs, then carried them and several cartons of cigarettes outside. When he returned, he went directly to the refrigerated doors at the far side of the store, then crowed in vindication when he discovered cold beer in the fridge. He hauled two cases of Budweiser, one under each arm, out to the car.

Midway through filling up the tote, Danny realized that none of the food in this place was name brand. Every label, every package, bore some generic name he had never heard before. The potato chips were called Crispy Crunchers, the bags of beef jerky were labeled as Gentleman's Jerk, and the liter bottles of imitation Pepsi and Coca-Cola were called PopSuds and Caro-Mello, respectively. They reminded Danny of the type of fake products used in TV shows.

He went over to a rack of magazines. To his surprise, there was nothing but porn on the rack, each magazine sealed in a plastic bag. But even the names of these magazines were unfamiliar to him—*Jubbers* and *Swing Time* and *Lickety Split*. One was even called *Gentleman's Jerk*, and bore the exact same logo that was on the bag of beef jerky, right down to the font.

A giddy sort of madness was beginning to filter into his brain.

Let's just get the fuck out of here.

He hurried back to the car, the tote bag heavy in his grasp. Tommy had left the passenger door open, so Danny leaned in and dumped the food in the backseat, right next to the two cases of beer Tommy had hustled out of the store. When he'd watched Tommy carry them out, he had mistakenly thought they were two cases of Bud. Fair enough, because the packaging looked very much the same. But in actuality, Tommy had carried out two cases of Budscheisse. Whatever the hell that was.

The pump clicked, and that was when Danny realized Tommy was not here. He climbed back out of the car, replaced the pump nozzle, and then scanned his surroundings for his brother.

He spotted Tommy roving up the center of the road toward one of the dilapidated buildings. The doors at the front of the building were glass, soaped over and furry with bone-colored dust. A sign over the doors read FIRST CHURCH OF CHRIST & LAUNDROMAT.

"Tommy! Hey!"

Tommy didn't turn around. Instead, he pulled open one of the doors and went inside.

Danny headed in Tommy's direction, then paused and returned to the car. He popped the trunk, slid aside the briefcase containing the strange book, and dug around in his duffel bag until he found his gun. Then he hurried down the street in the direction of the church and Laundromat combo.

"Tommy?" he said, poking his head inside.

The place was musty, with only the palest shimmer of daylight able to penetrate the heavily soaped windows. As preposterous as it was, the sign outside had been accurate—one wall was lined with coin-op washers and dryers while the several rows of wooden church pews stood in the center of the room. The pews faced a pulpit that looked like it was cobbled from vegetable crates and soapboxes. The cross that hung from a dust-caked ceiling fan had been clearly fashioned out of two broom handles.

Praise Jesus and don't over-starch the whites.

Tommy was standing back there, beyond the pulpit, staring off into a darkened corner. As Danny's eyes acclimated to the dimness of his surroundings, he saw that someone had painted a rather disconcerting phrase on the wall beyond the broomstick cross, in the same blood-red paint that had been used on the large rock at the entrance to town:

ALL HAIL THE CLEANER
HE CAME THROUGH

Those two phrases unsettled him. Who exactly was the Cleaner and what exactly had he come through? *Maybe that was the name of the guy who used to work in the Laundromat section of this joint,* Danny thought, attempting some levity, even if it was just for his own benefit.

Tommy took a step deeper into the darkness at the back of the room.

"Tommy?" Danny crossed down the aisle of pews, his gun at a low ready beside his right hip, muzzle scanning the room. "What are you doing?"

"I heard something." Tommy's voice was thin and shaky. Not his own. His back was toward Danny as he peered intently into the darkness. "Children."

"You heard children in here?"

"They were singing. Or…more like…*chanting*. No, wait. Not chanting. They were…were…"

"There's no one in here. There's no one *anywhere*."

"Teasing," Tommy said. "That's what they were doing. Not chanting. They were teasing me."

"Tom—"

Tommy took a step farther into that darkness. The shadows were swallowing him up. To Danny, that darkness seemed impossibly dense.

He was suddenly overcome with the irrational fear that if his brother took one more step, he'd fall *into* that darkness and be lost forever.

"Goddamn it, Tommy," and wanted to add, *Don't go in there*, but couldn't bring himself to do it.

Tommy vanished into the dark.

Danny stood there, holding his breath. Holding his gun.

All hail the Cleaner, he thought. *He came through*.

Then Tommy reemerged. His face was pale, and he looked confused. Something had rattled him pretty badly.

"You're hearing things," Danny assured him. "No one's here."

That numb look still on his face, Tommy nodded.

"Come on," Danny said, and jerked his head toward the door.

They exited the place together, back out into the bright sunshine. For one fleeting moment, Danny had a vision of them arriving back at the gas station to find their car gone, but that wasn't the case. It was right where they'd left it beside the gas pump. Even the car's trunk was still open from when Danny had—

Shit.

He raced over to the car, certain he'd find the briefcase missing from the trunk. Certain that whatever noise Tommy had thought he'd heard had been real, and had been a deliberate distraction. That they'd been played for fools.

But the briefcase was still there.

I'm growing paranoid. I'm starting to lose it. There's no one out here to steal shit. And who would?

The Cleaner, of course, whispered a small, unhelpful voice in the far recesses of his head. *He came through, remember?*

Tommy approached the car, shuffling his feet across the sand-covered concrete in a daze. His body moved as if his muscles ached. He kept glancing over his shoulder at the Laundromat church. The building looked deceptively benign out here in the daylight.

Danny opened the driver's door. "This place is getting in our heads. Let's split."

"Yeah, okay," Tommy muttered, then ambled around the front of the car toward the passenger side. He was still peering over his shoulder at the building across the street. He looked as though—

Something came whistling out of the sky and detonated off the hood of the Monte Carlo. Danny saw it bounce back into the air, strike the ground, then roll several feet across the dusty ground. Danny glanced over, saw that whatever had struck the car had either been pretty heavy or had come from some great height, because it had left a fist-sized dent in the hood.

"Jeez," Tommy uttered. Then he snapped from his stupor and ambled over to the item.

"What is it?" Danny called.

Tommy bent down and picked it up. Then he glanced skyward, in an attempt to reconcile where the item had come from. He was still staring down at it when he ambled back over to Danny.

"What *is* it?" Danny repeated.

"A baseball." Tommy tossed it over to Danny.

Danny didn't want to touch it, but his reflexes snatched it up. He looked down at it and saw that, yes, it was just a regular old baseball. Scuffed up and dirty, too. He turned it over, saw a word printed on it in black marker. He didn't know what it meant. It said: JOYA.

"Where the fuck you think that came from?" Tommy was gazing back up into the sky again. "A passing airplane?"

Danny tossed the ball on the ground, then wiped his palm down the thigh of his pants. "I don't know, but it doesn't make me feel all warm and fuzzy. You ready to get the fuck outta here?"

Tommy was nodding his head, though still gazing at the sky.

Danny climbed behind the wheel and cranked the ignition. In the split second before the motor engaged, he was certain that the car wouldn't start—that whatever gasoline had been in that gas pump would have the opposite effect of fueling it up. They'd be stranded here in Coal Dust. Population negative nine.

But the car *did* start—and with a robust roar beneath the hood. It seemed just as eager to blow this joint as they were.

"Get in!" Danny shouted, and Tommy jumped into the passenger seat.

Danny geared the car into drive and the Monte Carlo lurched forward. He kept his foot heavy on the accelerator until they'd burned down the center of the street and crossed back through the desert, until the creepy, abandoned town with the peculiar name was left in its own titular dust.

12

Don't do it, Danny.
Don't do it, Danny.
Don't do it, Danny.
Don't do it, Danny.

13

Danny was catching some z's in the passenger seat when Tommy jostled him awake and said, "Hey. Look at that."

Danny unstuck his eyelids then winced at the glare from the sun across the windshield. He felt queasy. After hightailing it out of that creepy-ass town and before swapping seats, they'd eaten some of the food they'd taken from the Gas and Gulp, ravenous to fill their bellies. But the food had been tasteless, the jerky like strips of burlap, and the bottled water had had a queer metallic tang to it. Even the beer that Tommy had absconded with tasted flat and curiously bitter, but Tommy powered through a couple of cans nevertheless.

Thinking of that food now only made his queasiness more pronounced. Danny wriggled up straighter in his seat while Tommy pointed at something on the right-hand shoulder of the road. It took Danny's eyes a moment to adjust and to see the thing with any clarity.

It was a motor home, parked on the side of the road. It boasted a two-tone paintjob and an airbrushed mural of wolves on the back. The vehicle didn't look old or in poor shape, but there was a film of dust clinging to the whole thing, which suggested it had been here for some time. As they approached, Danny could see it bore California plates.

Tommy eased off the accelerator as they drove past it, giving them both a good look at it. The windows along the side were tinted, making it impossible to see inside. But the cab of the vehicle appeared empty.

"Hold on," Danny said. "Stop. Go back."

Tommy executed a U-turn in the middle of the road and headed back toward the motor home. He pulled up nose-to-nose with the recreational vehicle, then shut the car down. A curtain of dust swept over the hood and windshield of the Monte Carlo. As it dissipated, and from this angle, Danny could see that the door on the side of the motor home stood open; it waved gingerly in the breeze coming off the roadway.

The brothers got out of the car and approached the vehicle. Danny tried the passenger door of the cab, but it was locked. He peered inside, confirming that the cab was in fact empty, but the windows and windscreen were too grimy for him to make out much more beyond that.

Tommy stood before the open camper door. He was peering into the motor home with a look of unobstructed apprehension on his face. His blond ponytail shone like sheet metal in the midday sun. He cupped both hands around his mouth and shouted into the open doorway of the camper: "Hello! Anybody in there?"

Danny looked around for signs that someone might have fled the vehicle on foot, but he couldn't see anything—no footprints or tire tracks from a bike or anything. Coming up beside Tommy, he saw a section of extension cord hanging over the side of the camper, its end fashioned into a loop.

No, not a loop, Danny realized. *A noose.*

He stepped in front of Tommy and peered through the doorway into the gloomy interior of the recreational vehicle. "Anybody need any help in there?" he called, then knocked on the side of the camper.

No one answered.

Tommy reached out, made as if to touch the noose hanging down the side of the motor home, but then drew his hand back at the last second.

Danny climbed inside.

The interior of the motor home reeked of booze. In fact, he hadn't taken more than two steps inside the camper when his foot struck a handle of liquor; he sent it rolling in a semicircle across the cluttered floor, the trickle of amber liquid inside the bottle sparkling. There were clothes strewn about, and loose papers and books scattered underfoot. Danny wondered if someone had ransacked the place, or if this was just the status quo of whoever had been holing up in here.

He took another step, ducking beneath a constellation of dreamcatchers hanging from the ceiling by catgut. Unwashed dishes were piled in the sink, and an entire regiment of canned food—various soups and beans and vegetables—were huddled on the counter. (It was with unmasked relief that Danny noted the soups were Progresso, the vegetables Green Giant—brands that were comfortably familiar to him.) An ironing board protruded from one wall like the arm of a tollbooth; the iron sat below it on case of Ragged Branch bourbon, its cord snaked around its body.

The only spot that was kept remotely neat was the small table beside a window. On it was an old manual typewriter, and a stack of blank paper beside it. Serving as a paperweight atop the stack was a golden statuette depicting a figure with lightning-bolt wings holding a wire sphere above its head. Danny Drake was not one to embrace popular culture, but he recognized the thing as an Emmy. He picked it up and saw, via the name inscribed around its base, that it had been awarded to someone named George Lee Poach. There was a second Emmy on the windowsill, amid a clutter of empty beer bottles and rocks glasses. The same name was etched along the base of that one, too.

Danny peered down at the typewriter. A sheet of paper stood in the roller. It sported a few enigmatic words:

```
myself asks
am i here?
i've lost myself
i fear
```

Tommy shuddered in through the doorway. He looked around, then sucked down a deep breath. His gusty exhalation set the collection of dreamcatchers a-twirl. "Smells like a distillery in here."

True, the stink of alcohol was potent enough in here to draw tears from Danny's eyes, but given the unsettling lack of odor back in Coal Dust, he welcomed it. Despite the fact that this vehicle looked like it had been abandoned in a hurry, there was still a reassuring sense of familiarity to it. A *realness* that had been eluding them since they'd been on the road—a fact Danny had missed up until now, standing here, his senses once again accepting dispatches from the real world. There was no other way to explain it.

But still…what had happened here?

Tommy ducked down below the dreamcatchers and hooked a right toward the cockpit. His boot struck the same bottle of booze Danny had, sending it rolling across the floor again.

Danny looked up from the cryptic little poem—if that's what it was—percolating in the typewriter. There was an accordion door at the rear of the motor home, partway open. Too dark to see anything in that sliver of space from where he stood.

He stepped around a broken lamp and a jumble of unwashed clothes—the sleeve of a checked flannel shirt attempted to snare his ankle—on his way to the door. The thing was stuck in its track, but he managed to finagle it open far enough to slip inside.

A messy bed was framed in a rectangle of bourbon-colored light that spilled down from a skylight. More books and clothes were tossed about in here, plus a contingent of tiny desert plants in shot glasses on a ledge below a porthole window. Additional dreamcatchers dangled from the ceiling; more bottles of booze everywhere.

He jostled open another, smaller accordion door and found himself staring at a small toilet and shower stall. A bar of soap lay crusted to the sink, beside a disposable razor whose head bristled with black, wiry quills.

The mirror above the sink was busted, the sink basin itself shining with about a thousand shards of broken glass. There was a disconcerting amount of blood in the sink, too.

This made him think of the town of Coal Dust, and how off-putting that whole place had been, from its Laundromat-church combo and the dried russet stains on the restroom walls back at the Gas and Gulp. Somehow, since they'd fled that place, he'd managed to convince himself that it hadn't been all *that* unusual. Most likely his sleep-deprived mind had overhyped the situation. Even as he thought about it now, what they'd experienced in Coal Dust held the same dreamlike quality in his mind that the visit from the waitress had the night before. Not enough to think he'd imagined it, of course, but enough to make him second-guess just how *off* that place had been.

He peered down at a million variations of his reflection gazing up at him from that bloodied sink.

Don't downplay how bizarre things have been, he told himself. *Don't laugh it off as your overworked imagination. Because next thing you know, an hour from now you'll be downplaying how fucking off this stranded motor home is, too.*

Right. Good advice. Downplaying it was eerily tempting, but it also possessed an anesthetizing quality that numbed his mind. It was as if something kept trying to dull his memory of just how unsettling things had been since he and Tommy had hit the road.

It's like something is trying to get you to forget about it, the little voice in his head suggested.

He exited back into the main room of the motor home just as Tommy returned from the cockpit. "George Lee Poach," he said. He was reading the name off a license from a wallet he'd found. "From San Luis Obispo, California."

"That's the same name on those Emmys over there." He nodded toward the typewriter table.

"Emmys?"

Danny took the wallet from his brother. The man in the driver's license photo looked about sixty, with an alkie's bulbous nose and a scrim of wild hair along the sides of his head above his ears.

"Keys were still in the ignition but the thing won't start," Tommy was saying. "Battery's probably dead."

Why would someone walk away and leave their keys and wallet behind?

Maybe no one walked away at all, offered that same voice in Danny's head. *That makeshift noose dangling over the side of the RV out there? That broken mirror and all that blood in the sink? What if the old Emmy-winner killed himself in here?*

But no, not in here. There'd be a body.

Out there, then?

Danny's eyes flitted to the open door. Through it, he could see a perfect rectangle of the unforgiving desert that surrounded them.

And if our good friend the Emmy-winner did in fact kill himself, was it because he found himself trapped in this desert with no way of getting out, without another sign of life anywhere, and where the water tastes like metal and the food tastes like pillow stuffing, and where coyotes could've dragged the poor bastard's body deep into the desert if in fact he had—

He had to stop thinking like this. It wasn't like him, and it was only making him feel worse.

Tommy was rubbing his left arm as if it pained him. He was looking at the paperweight Emmy, too, perhaps calculating what something like that might fetch on the black market. But even Tommy's penchant for greed was overridden by the sheer strangeness of this place, and whatever had happened here. Danny could read the concern in his brother's eyes, and feared he had a similar look in his own.

They climbed out of the motor home, got back in their car, and drove off. Tommy didn't even bother snaking any of the booze.

14

Tommy said:

"Remember me telling you about that dream I had, the one where Dad turned into a fish and slipped through the bars of his cell? How he kept saying he was coming for me? Well, that wasn't all.

"See, he chased me down this long hallway. I guess it was a hallway in the prison, because that's where he was—that's where he *is*—but also because the walls were cinderblock and there were the shadows of barred windows going back and forth across the floor as I ran.

"But then at some point, it changed. We weren't in a prison anymore. I was outside, running straight down the center of a highway. It was the middle of the night and there were like a gazillion stars. I was in the desert someplace—the middle of nowhere, just like here—and I was all alone. Except that he was somewhere in the darkness behind me, still coming after me. Not a fish anymore—I couldn't see him, but I got this sense; you know how it is in dreams—but something else. Something black, with horns and wings. I'm not really sure.

"All I knew was that he was still coming, and I had to run faster and faster just so he wouldn't catch me. But I kept slowing down. I mean, something was there, slowing me down. It felt like my body was growing heavier and I was being pulled into the earth. I looked down to see if my feet were getting stuck in tar or something, because that's what it felt like. I didn't see any tar, but I *did* see these weird plants growing straight up out of the highway. I looked up and saw a bunch more cropping up through the blacktop ahead of me. These weird, furry plants.

"Only they weren't plants. They were the tops of people's heads—people who couldn't outrun whatever was chasing me, and were sucked down into the earth. Only their scalps were showing.

"And then, in this dream, I came to a dead stop right there in the middle of the road. I guess maybe I realized running was futile, but who really knows? I mean, it was a dream, right? *Who knows?* All I know is I looked down at my arms, and it was like they were glowing beneath the light of all those stars.

"They were covered in bruises. My arms. And then I saw myself—like how you do in dreams—and I was covered in bruises from head to toe. Only they weren't normal bruises. It was like someone had dipped a finger in an ashtray and then used that finger to mark up my flesh."

Tommy tugged his left arm out of his jacket and showed the bruises to Danny.

"I don't know where they came from," he said, his voice paper-thin, "and I'm starting to feel really weird."

15

They came upon a town just as a belt of darkness crept in from the east and the western horizon lay hacked into slats of bleeding sunlight.

Tommy howled from the passenger seat: "Praise Jesus, hallelujah, hocus pocus, amen!"

Danny felt a giddy sort of elation quiver inside him as well. His eyes scanned the approaching town, taking in a collection of mom-and-pop shops, a movie theater, a restaurant called The Roost (it had a plaster chicken the size of a Buick on the roof), and—thank you, Jesus!—a motel. The motel's marquee demanded, quite succinctly, COME INN.

A maniacal laugh shrilled up out of Tommy's throat. As Danny pulled into the motel's lot, Tommy slapped his hands together and hollered, "Yes, sir! A hot meal and a couple warm beds with our names on it. Maybe we can even catch a movie."

An old man in a cowboy duster smoking a cheroot stood on the curb outside the motel. He watched them rumble into the lot and slide into a parking space next to a glowing OFFICE sign. There were several other cars in the lot, something that would have ordinarily deterred Danny from staying here. The sight of them now had the opposite effect on him; he was actually relieved to see not only those cars, but the old cowboy out here giving them the stink eye.

Danny shut down the car. "Let's get a room, then we can grab something to eat."

Tommy shot from the car, his boot heels spring-loaded. He shouted a hello to the cowboy, whose expression of mild discontentment didn't alter in the slightest.

"Wait out here with the car," Danny told him.

"Why?"

"Did you forget about the thing in the trunk?"

Tommy didn't need to reply; Danny could tell by his expression that he *had* forgotten all about it. Danny could hardly blame him. Given all that had happened in the past twenty-four hours, that book now seemed no stranger than a pack of smokes.

The motel's lobby was furnished in dark blue shag carpeting, mood lighting, and lush velvet chairs. It looked like the set of a 1970s porno, except for the two dozen birdcages hanging from an assortment of shepherd's hooks and eyelets in the exposed rafters in the ceiling.

A woman with immense glasses poking through a nest of frizzy black hair smiled up at him from behind the desk. "Howdy, stranger!" Her voice was ebullient. "Looks like you've had a long drive."

"Longest of my life. Can I get a room?"

"Abso-surely."

She set something down on the counter in front of him, and he did a double take before taking a step back. It was an ink-black raven, its jeweled black eyes glittering.

The woman giggled. "Oh, that's Hector. He won't snap at you. Pet him, if you'd like."

The bird fell over on its side, and Danny took another step back from it.

"Lord, I tell you, the legs are the toughest part," said the woman.

She picked up the bird and stood it upright once more. Then she cleared her throat with an aggressive *guhh!* "One leg's always shorter than the other. That's why I prefer to wire them to the perches."

"Oh," Danny said. "It's fake."

"No, not fake. Stuffed. It *used* to be alive. Once upon a time. Or, as my grandpa used to say, *oonce upoonce a toonce*." Another giggle, followed by another throat clearing.

Danny turned and peered into the nearest cage—a bell-shaped metal contraption hanging from one of the shepherd's hooks. Two lovebirds sat together on a wooden swing. They were every bit alive as Danny's boots. He glanced around at the rest of the cages. "Did you stuff all these birds yourself?"

"Abso-surely."

"Where'd you get them all?"

"Oh," said the woman. She was consulting a ledger. "They come."

"Where exactly am I?"

"You're at the Come Inn, in Tall City, Oklahoma."

"Tall City," he repeated.

"Where you can reach up and touch the stars!" She said this with a smile, eyeing him from over the lenses of her big glasses. Then she startled him with another *guhh* from the back of her throat. "That's our motto 'round here, in case you didn't see it on the sign."

"I never saw a sign."

She'd been running a finger down the margin of her ledger, but now she stopped. Froze, more like it. "Oh," she said, her voice small.

"How far are we from the Arkansas border?"

She didn't answer at first, only stared down at the ledger. Danny listened to the ticking of a clock from somewhere, trying not to lose his patience. Then she went *guhh*, and said, brightly, "Oh, Lord. Maybe three hours' drive? Bit quicker if you're lead-footed, as my grandpa used to say."

"That restaurant with the chicken on the roof any good?"

Her face brightened. "Best chicken in town! Wait, wait…"

She dropped down behind the desk, then popped back up with an old shoebox. Danny glimpsed a purple rabbit's foot and a switchblade in there, among other assorted junk. She took a card from the box and handed it to Danny. There was a cartoon chicken on it, and some small typeface that read:

CLUCKY demands you PIG OUT at THE ROOST!

This card is good for one half-priced entree,
so go HOG WILD!

OINK OINK OINK!

"What's with the pig references? I thought it was a chicken joint."

Once again, the woman's hand froze midway down the ledger. The fingernail on her index finger had been gnawed down to the quick, and there was dried blood beneath what remained of the nail. Danny had time to wonder why she was using a ledger at all, and not a computer. On the desk, the dead raven stared at him with its ink-spot eyes.

As if jolted by a surge of electric current, the woman's whole body flinched. She shook her head, cleared her throat repeatedly—*guhh! guhh! guhh!*—then looked up at him again. This time, she didn't offer him a smile. There was a fingerprint on one of the lenses of her glasses.

She placed the ledger on the counter, along with a brass key affixed to a plastic fob in the shape of a little man. The man held his hands together in prayer. He had no face.

With a chill, Danny thought, *All hail the Cleaner. He came through.*

"I've got you in Room Six," she said. All previous ebullience was gone from her voice now. She sounded like someone teetering on the precipice of depression.

Danny signed a fake name to the ledger, then said, "I'm sorry, I forgot to mention. I need a room with two beds."

"Someone else with you?" She peered around him and out into the parking lot, a glum expression on her face.

"My brother."

"All our rooms have two beds." She turned her head and *guhh*'d off to one side. "I suppose you'll want another half-price coupon, as well." She rooted around in the shoebox again. Then, quite morosely, she said, "Shit. I'm sorry. I'm all out."

Danny forced a smile. "No problem."

"It's cash up front. Hope you don't mind paying cash."

It was the only way Danny ever paid.

He dug a handful of bills from his wallet and handed them across the desk to the woman. When she reached out and took them from him, he was careful not to have his fingers touch hers.

16

Danny came back out to the parking lot to find Tommy leaning against the car, smoking a cigarette and examining the bruises on his arms. Tommy had spooked himself with that story about his nightmare, and he was looking down at those bruises now with unwarranted gravitas.

Danny handed him the room key and told him to go clean up. Tommy took the key without a word, found the door to the correct room—like the motel the night before, all these rooms opened directly onto the parking lot—and then he vanished inside. The pep was gone from his step.

Danny went around to the rear of the car and popped the trunk.

He glanced around, and noted that the guy in the duster was gone. A group of young kids were throwing rocks at a tin can in an alcove between the motel and a fenced-in swimming pool. The sign on the fence's gate said FOR MOTEL GUESTS ONLY, and was locked tight with a heavy-duty chain. A man in a denim jumpsuit sat in a chair on the other side of that fence, facing the swimming pool. If there was any water in the pool, Danny couldn't tell; it appeared filled with dead leaves and all manner of garbage.

Danny lifted the briefcase and his duffel bag from the trunk, then slammed the trunk shut. The sound was loud as a gunshot, and the kids throwing rocks in the alcove looked up, startled. There were three of them—two boys and a girl—and they were maybe eight or nine years old. Danny afforded them nothing more than a passing glance on his way to his room. When one of them spoke up, he hardly paid any attention. It wasn't until they all joined in together with their reedy, singsong taunt, that Danny froze on the spot:

> *Where's your daddy, Danny Drake?*
> *Gone to jail with a prison shank!*

Danny turned and faced the children.

They stood in the alcove, staring at him, their fists loaded with rocks.

He took a step in their direction. "What'd you just say to me?"

They said nothing. Only stared at him. If they were fearful of him as he approached, they didn't express it.

"Where did you hear that?" he demanded, closing the distance now. "Who the hell are you kids, any—"

The girl chucked a rock at his head. Danny hardly knew what had happened until the thing had already whizzed past his ear. The boys began throwing their rocks at him, too, until Danny was dodging and sidestepping the barrage. One struck him in the shin, another rebounded off his elbow. Pain surged up his funny bone.

The children chanted:

> *Where's your daddy, Danny Drake?*
> *Gone to jail with a prison shank!*
> *Where's your mommy, Tommy Drake?*
> *Dead in the ground, that dirty skank!*

"Hey!"

Their ammo expended, the three children took off running. Danny chased after them, his duffel bag and briefcase in tow. But by the time he turned down the alcove that ran between the motel and the pool, the kids were gone.

Where's your daddy, Danny Drake?

An impossible thing for these children to chant, because the *real* children who had chanted these things were from Danny's youth, in a wholly different time and place. Schoolyard bullies who had sensed a target in Danny and his brother. Cruel children who took dark pleasure in hurting them because their father was a drunk and a criminal, and because their mother had died an addict with a sordid past.

Where's your daddy, Danny Drake?

Danny looked down at the tin can at his feet. The children, he realized, hadn't been throwing rocks at the can; they'd been throwing rocks at a bird that someone had tied to the can. It was a sparrow, with a frayed bit of string tied around one of its sticklike yellow—

(legs are the toughest part)

—legs. Blood frothed from its open beak.

Danny assumed it was dead, but then one wing jerked open. It strummed the air then went still again.

17

The motel room had the same swanky seventies vibe that the lobby had, and there were even coin-operated boxes beside both beds that, for a buck, would make the mattress vibrate. Danny heard the shower running, so he assumed that Tommy was in there scrubbing the day's misery from his flesh. But when Danny opened the bathroom door, he saw Tommy standing naked before the mirror, staring in horror at his black-and-blue reflection.

The sight of all those bruises caused Danny to break out in a sweat.

"This ain't right," Tommy said, his voice quaking. He met Danny's eyes in the mirror. "The fuck's happening to me, Dan?"

It looked like someone had taken a crowbar to Tommy's arms, legs, and torso. The bruising was so prominent and complete, it was impossible to think that this had all occurred over a period of a few hours.

"Does it hurt?"

Tommy shook his head. He raised his right arm, exposing a flank covered in eggplant hematomas. When he rotated his arm at the shoulder, his tendons clicked audibly.

"It's the book," Tommy said. He brought his right hand to his face and sniffed the bruised flesh on the back of his hand. The dagger tattoo on the back of his hand was lost among all that discoloration. "I smell just like it, Dan. It's like it got into my skin somehow. Into my *blood*. It poisoned me."

"I don't smell anything."

Tommy extended his hand, and although Danny's instinct was to recoil from him, he didn't. Instead, he took a breath. But he could smell nothing other than the moldy bathroom. He said as much.

Defeated, Tommy dropped his arm at his side. "Maybe you gotta be poisoned with it to smell it."

"You're not poisoned."

"We gotta get rid of that fucking book, Dan. We gotta *destroy* it."

"Tommy, listen to me. We're gonna deliver this thing tomorrow at noon. And then we'll be done with it. We'll leave this whole strange trip behind us."

"What about me, man? Something's happening to me."

"Maybe it was something we ate from that gas station back in Coal Dust. The food was off. You drank a few of those weird, shitty beers. Smoked those cigarettes."

"Ah, Christ." Tommy leaned forward, his mottled elbows on the sink top, his face in his hands. His back was just as bad as the rest of him, the ridge of his backbone a shiny purple crest. "What if this thing kills me?"

"Nothing's gonna kill you. Listen to me, Tommy. The second we drop this book off tomorrow, I'll take you to a hospital. You hear me? Tommy?"

"Yeah, yeah, okay." His voice was muffled as he spoke into the palms of his hands.

"Meantime, you gotta just chill out. You said it doesn't hurt, right?"

"Doesn't hurt," Tommy muttered.

"So take a shower, clean yourself up. I'll go walk down to that restaurant and get us something to eat."

"I don't know if I can eat anything."

"You will. You'll see. Just relax, okay? Take a shower and chill out."

Tommy was nodding, his face still buried in his hands.

"I'll be back soon," Danny said, and left.

18

It was fully dark when Danny stepped back outside. The temperature had dropped, leaving a chill in the air. Head down, he walked along the strip of shops toward the restaurant with the giant chicken on the roof. The shops had already closed for the evening, and there was no one out walking the street. The only place that still looked open across the road was the movie theater. Danny glanced at the marquee, and saw that the only movie playing there was *Xanadu*.

The exterior of The Roost was lit up like a nightclub, but it was dark when he went inside. It was one of those Texas-style roadhouses, with red-and-white checked tablecloths and cowboy paraphernalia on the walls. Big wagon-wheel chandeliers hung from chains in the ceiling, but very few of the light bulbs were in working order. The dimness gave the whole place a dungeon-like quality.

Also, the restaurant was completely empty.

Danny stood in the middle of the restaurant, looking around at all the empty tables. There was a bar toward the back, with drink specials listed on a chalkboard, but there was no one tending the bar, no patrons seated on the barstools.

He cupped his hands around his mouth and shouted, "Hey! Hello! Anybody here?"

His voice echoed through the cavernous space.

He spent the next five minutes searching the place, only to arrive at the same conclusion: that he was alone. Moreover, the kitchen was spotless and sterile; the stainless steel appliances looked as though they'd never been used. He pulled open the door of a walk-in freezer and found the shelves empty.

This is crazy, he thought, panic tightening around his throat as he backed out of the restaurant. *We must be in hell. We must be dead and in hell and don't know it.*

Back outside, he ran across the street toward the movie theater. The lights were still on, but there was no one selling tickets at the ticket window. The doors were unlocked, so Danny hurried inside. The lobby was well-lit, but just like the empty ticket window, there was no one manning the snack counter. Nobody stood at the entrance to the theaters to tear tickets. Show times scrolled across a screen above the concession stand:

XANADU: 11:11, 2:18, 3:11, 5:13, 7:07, 9:46, Midnight, 13:13

Danny went down a darkened corridor, where theater doors stood in recessed alcoves on either side of him. He passed through one set of doors and entered a darkened theater. *Xanadu* was playing on the screen, but to an empty theater. Danny looked up at the square window of the projection booth, where the white light flickered. Someone had to be up there running the projector, right?

He went up the aisle and found a door hidden among the wall at the back of the theater. It said EMPLOYEES ONLY on it, so he thought it might be locked just like the one back at the Gas and Gulp in Coal Dust, but it wasn't. He turned the knob and eased the door open on silent hinges.

A set of stairs climbed to the projection room.

Danny took the stairs to the top. There was another door here, unmarked. White light flickered beneath the door. He could hear the projector running in there, could hear the muffled soundtrack of the movie.

He grabbed the knob, once more expecting to find it locked, but it turned in his grasp.

He pushed open the door to reveal an empty projection room.

There was a chair with a nylon jacket draped over the back, a steaming cup of coffee and a folded newspaper on a table, but the room was empty. The projector whirred and fired its bolts of white light through the square panel of glass.

Danny went to the window and peered down into the theater. Below, a portion of the screen went black as Danny's head blocked out some of the light.

There were people down there in the seats now.

Son of a bitch!

Danny turned and bolted back down the stairs, bursting through the door at the bottom and back out into the theater.

The film's audio stretched like taffy and then died just as the screen went black. Danny was doused in complete and utter darkness.

He stood there for a moment, feeling the darkness close in around him. At first, all he heard was the sound of his own ragged respiration…but then other sounds began filtering to him through that sightless void. People—some very close to him—moving around in the darkness. He backed up against the wall and listened as those furtive movements advanced in his direction. He could hear more than just his own respiration now, coupled with the shush of a multitude of feet advancing in his direction.

Danny craned his neck and saw a lighted EXIT sign down by the screen. He could make a break for it…although the thought of running blind into whatever mob was slowly closing in around him kept him rooted to the spot.

Come on, Danny. Come on, boy.

He bolted for it, hands swiping at the ink-black darkness ahead of him, certain that fingers were grazing his face and tangling in his hair, were groping for his arms, were trying to grab him, snare him, claw at him, or maybe that was all in his head…

He exploded through the fire exit onto a cool patch of sidewalk.

A single streetlight hung above his head, casting him in a cone of bleary light.

He didn't wait around to see if anyone would pursue him through that fire exit.

He ran back in the direction of the inn.

19

The parking lot of the Come Inn was dark when he arrived. The Monte Carlo was still parked out front, but all of the other cars from earlier were gone. The windows in all the rooms were dark, too, with the exception of Room Six: a bright yellow light pulsed around the edges of the blinds.

He was halfway across the lot, his breath rasping from his throat and his body greasy with sweat, when he heard a shrill *reeeeet* echo through the night. He froze in mid-step and looked around. Nothing at first…but then he noticed that the gate in the fence surrounding the pool stood open. It had been locked with a chain earlier.

He didn't hang around to see who—or what—had opened it. He hurried to the door of Room Six, digging the key fob of the faceless man from his pocket, and jammed the key into the lock.

The room was empty. The ceramic lamp that had been on the nightstand was now lying shattered on the carpet between the two beds; the lampshade had rolled away, but the bare bulb was somehow still functional, casting a spotlight onto the ceiling. Danny's duffel bag was still on the bed, Tommy's pistol on the dresser, but the briefcase was missing.

The bathroom light was on, the door partially closed. Danny saw movement in the lighted space, followed by what sounded like a sharp intake of breath. He called out for his brother, but his throat was too constricted to put any real force behind it. It was nothing but hot air hissing out of a teakettle.

He went to the bathroom door and pushed it open.

Tommy was kneeling on the floor in front of the bathtub. He was still naked, and Danny could see that in his brief absence, his brother's condition had worsened exponentially. The entirety of Tommy's back was a swollen, purpled trunk of flesh. The bruising had crept up his spine and blossomed across each of his shoulder blades in an intricate, almost floral pattern. The way Tommy was kneeling, Danny could see greenish purple whorls on the soles of his feet.

The briefcase was on fire in the bathtub.

"Goddamn it, Tommy!"

Danny shoved his brother aside, then dropped to his own knees before the bathtub. The heat from the fire drew tears from his eyes as he twisted on both the cold and hot taps. Water belched from the spigot and then burst from the showerhead above. Danny grabbed a towel off the sink and smothered the flames while the water doused the whole affair.

Tommy watched him with a mixture of contempt and pity. He sat right where Danny had shoved him, his back against the wall, his battered arms propped up on his knees. The elastic band keeping his ponytail in place had snapped, heaping ringlets of damp, golden hair atop his discolored shoulders.

"You're making a mistake, man," Tommy said. Given his overall appearance and what he'd been trying to do when Danny had burst in here, his voice was unnervingly calm. He was still clutching a silver Zippo in one eggplant-colored hand. The bottle of bourbon he'd been hauling around in his coat sat on the tiled floor beside him—what he'd most likely used for accelerant. "You should've let it burn."

Danny peered over the side of the tub. The water still running, he peeled the wet towel from the briefcase. The fire had eaten straight through the leather, but it hadn't been able to do much to the stainless steel frame beneath it. He lifted the briefcase out of the tub by its handle, trailing a stream of water and loose flaps of leather as he set it upright on the floor beside the toilet.

"Look what it's doing to me." Tommy held his arms out toward Danny in a parody of supplication. There were bruises along his inner arms the color of cigarette ash. "It's killing me, man."

In the tub, the water still ran. The pipes chugged and clanged behind the wall.

"I'm scared, Dan. You're scared, too. I can see it in your eyes. That same look from when we were kids. Always scared. I know you too well for you to hide it." He leaned forward, his damp back peeling audibly off the bathroom wall. He was gazing deep into Danny's eyes. Reading his mind. Reading his soul. They were brothers, after all. "What just happened to you out there?"

"I don't know," Danny said. His throat felt thick and it was difficult pushing the words out. But they were true enough. "I can't explain it. This whole trip has been…"

Neither of them completed the thought.

"A proposition," Tommy said. "We pick up our shit and we leave this place right now. No looking back. We leave the briefcase with that book behind, too. We forget this whole thing ever happened."

"I agree that we gotta get out of here," Danny said, "but I need to finish the job. We're almost to the end."

Tommy laughed, hung his head. Spidery tendrils of wet hair hung between his knees. Danny stared at his brother's hands, dangling from his discolored knees. It looked like someone had cut off the circulation to Tommy's fingers. The only remnant of the old Tommy was the dagger tattoo on the back of his right hand, floating now in a turbulent black-blue sea of hematomas.

"It's not the book, Tommy."

"I *touched* it, man."

"You also ate all that weird shit from the gas station back in that ghost town. Drank half a case of that beer."

"You ate some of that stuff, too. Your skin ain't turning black."

"It's not about that book, Tommy. Something's been off since we left Colorado. It's like someone's been playing us, although I can't figure out for the life of me how the *hell* they're doing it."

"If it's not the book, then why are you whispering right now? It's like you don't want it to hear you."

Danny exhaled a shaky breath. He leaned his head back against the wall. The drain in the tub must have been clogged because the water was filling up. He let it keep running.

"Just walk away from it," Tommy said.

"I can't."

"You're pushing us both off a cliff, Dan, and you're too stubborn to see it."

"You don't know how it is."

"It's however you want it to be."

They sat like that for a full minute, listening to the bathtub fill up. Whenever Tommy met his eyes, Danny held his stare for a short time before looking away. After a time, he leaned forward and picked up the bottle of bourbon that sat on the floor next to Tommy and unscrewed the cap. He took a strong pull, letting the liquor singe a passage down his parched throat.

Tommy smiled ruefully as Danny handed him the bottle. He knocked back a mouthful, his lips gleaming. The skin beneath his eyes looked dry and scaly.

"Listen," Danny said. "I'll check the map and see where the nearest city is. I'll take you there tonight, get you to a hospital. Tomorrow morning, I'll deliver the package to this Choptank guy on my own, then come back and get you."

Tommy had been gazing down at the bottle in his hands. He looked up now and met Danny's eyes. Danny expected to see conflict there, but his brother's gaze was steadfast. "We're a team, Dan. The Dark Brothers. If you go, I go. That's just how it is."

It was Danny who was conflicted. Tommy looked severely ill, and those bruises had come on quickly. He probably *should* go to a hospital. But Danny knew his brother well enough to know that he wouldn't let Danny go the rest of the way on his own. Chalk one up for Tommy in that regard.

"All right," he said. He climbed to his feet and picked up the briefcase by the handle. Water dripped from it and pattered to the cracked linoleum tiles. "Get dressed so we can blow this shithole."

20

Danny tucked his father's Glock in the waistband of his jeans, then grabbed Tommy's pistol off the dresser. He was about to stuff it into his duffel bag when Tommy came out of the bathroom with a towel around his waist and said, "No. I want it with me."

Danny appraised his brother for perhaps three seconds. Then he tossed the pistol onto the bed in front of his brother. Tommy got dressed, then took the gun and stowed it away beneath his jean jacket.

"You gonna tell me what spooked you so bad while you were gone?" Tommy asked, retying his ponytail.

How could he say it without sounding like a madman?

"You know what," Danny said, "I don't think I am."

Tommy stared at him for the length of a single heartbeat, and then he burst out laughing. It cracked the tension wide open, and Danny couldn't help it—he started laughing right along with him.

21

Danny and Tommy Drake hadn't seen their father in well over seven years, ever since the bastard had been put away on his latest felony charge, but they both immediately recognized the man standing in the parking lot as they stepped out of the motel room. Still dressed in his prison jumpsuit, Bill Drake gazed at his two sons from beneath the furrowed ridge of a downturned brow. His shaved head shone beneath the spotlights of a thousand stars. He was standing beside the Monte Carlo, one hand on the car's roof. As if to claim it as his property.

"There's my boys," Bill Drake said.

The Drake brothers just stood there.

"I hear you boys have had a time of it out here. You in particular look like shit warmed over, Tom."

Tommy took a step toward him.

"Tommy," Danny said. He dropped his duffel bag and grabbed the fleece-lined collar of his brother's jean jacket. "Don't."

Bill Drake settled his gaze on Danny. "You the leader of this wolf pack, boy?"

"Get away from the car," Danny told him.

His father laughed. "I guess you been playing big boss hot sauce while I been tucked away behind bars. How come you boys don't come to see your daddy?"

"What are you…what are you *doing* here?" Tommy said.

"Come to see my fellas. Come to finish the job your brother here done fucked up."

"Get away from the car," Danny said again.

Bill Drake did not get away from the car. Instead, he folded his arms and leaned against the driver's door. "Tell you what," he said. "I'm feeling generous, so I'll do you both a solid. Give me that briefcase and I'll finish the job for you. I don't even want any money."

Tommy knocked Danny's hand off his jacket collar then took another step toward Bill Drake. "How the fuck are you out of prison?" Tommy demanded.

"You're not hearing me, boy. I got a reputation, and I can't have my dickhead sons fucking things up for me." Their father held out one hand, palm up. Pumped his fingers in a *gimme* gesture. "Hand over the briefcase so I can finish the job. Looks to me like you need a doctor, anyway, Tom. You and Danny can head to the nearest hospital while I clean up this mess you've made."

Something in their father's words gave Tommy pause.

"You lick his fuckin' boot heels, boy, and what do you get for it? He's *poisoned* your ass! You'll be dead by tomorrow, and he'll get the payday. Is that what you want? Because it sounds like a raw goddamn deal to me, Tom."

Tommy glanced over his shoulder at Danny.

"Ignore him, Tommy," Danny said.

Bill Drake laughed. "Boy, that's rich! *Ignore* me? Never had much luck with that, did you, Big Dan? Back when you would cry like a little bitch? Back when you'd hide in a corner and piss your pants? I spent my best years trying to raise you two pussies to be *men*, and just look at this sad display. What a couple of fucking disappointments you both turned out to be—"

What happened next happened so fast, Danny wasn't able to register any of it until it was all over.

Tommy pulled the pistol out from his jacket and fired a single round to the center of Bill Drake's chest. The gunshot echoed out across the parking lot and far beyond the distant canyons. Bill Drake glanced down at the small hole in the middle of his chest just as a dark stain appeared and spread outward.

Tommy marched toward him, the gun still zeroed in, and fired several more rounds. Each pop rolled like thunder. By the time Tommy had finished, and before Danny knew what the hell had happened, Bill Drake was lying dead on the asphalt. His bloodstained prison jumpsuit was riddled with bullet holes, a section of his skull had been sheared away, and a solitary round had tunneled straight through his left eye socket and out the back of his head.

The silence that followed the gunfire was thick and cottony.

22

They drove east under cover of darkness for an unknowable amount of time. Neither of them spoke for a while, until Danny, unprompted, told him what had happened when he'd gone into town to bring back some food. When he ended his story with him fleeing through a fire exit of the movie theater, the silence that fell between them seemed even greater than it had been just moments ago.

"Maybe," Tommy began, once the silence had become too overbearing, "maybe we've been driving through one of those old nuclear test sites. Maybe we've both got radiation sickness and it's messing with our heads." He turned and stared at Danny's profile, both their faces goblin-green in the glow of the dashboard lights. "Was that really Dad back there at the motel?"

Danny didn't know how to answer that, so he didn't. He just kept driving.

Tommy took the bottle of booze from his jacket, unscrewed the cap, and downed a healthy swallow. He wiped his mouth on the sleeve of his jacket then offered the bottle to Danny, who declined. Tommy just nodded, as if he'd expected as much, and proceeded to finish the bottle himself.

23

Tommy was passed out in the passenger seat when Danny spotted a billboard on the shoulder of the road. The billboard depicted a man in white overalls and what looked like an engineer's cap hoisting a squeegee above his head. What this billboard was advertising, Danny could not fathom. The missive read:

WHEN THE GOING GETS TOUGH
THE TOUGH *GET IT!!!*

All hail the Cleaner, Danny thought as he steered the car off the road and pulled up behind the billboard. *All hail the Cleaner. He came through.*

He shut down the engine and the brothers got a few hours' shuteye.

24

Don't do it, Danny.
Don't do it, Danny.
Don't do it, Danny.
Don't do it, D—

25

Tommy looked worse in the morning.

Not just worse—*strange*.

Something inexplicable had happened to him in the night.

Danny awoke to the finger of God blazing in the east, searing his retinas and coaxing sweat from his tired body. Tommy was slumped in the passenger seat, still asleep. He thought Tommy might wake up when he started the Monte Carlo's kick-you-in-the-face V8 engine, but he didn't. Danny dug the roadmap out from between the seats, splayed it out across his lap, and let his brother sleep while he drove.

Tommy had stripped off his jacket in the night, which was odd, because it had been freezing out here in the desert. He lay asleep in the passenger seat now in nothing but a ratty old Metallica T-shirt and his faded jeans. Danny glanced down at his brother's left arm and saw that the bruises had changed in the night. In fact, they were no longer bruises at all. It looked like Tommy had been tattooed while he slept: the entirety of his left arm was covered in a tapestry of intricate black symbols. To Danny, they looked like characters from an ancient Egyptian language.

Don't wake him up, said that small voice in Danny's head. *If he sees what's happened to him, he'll freak. With any luck, he'll sleep until you arrive at The Mesa to meet this Choptank asshole. If for some reason Tommy was right, and this is all because of that book in the trunk, then maybe Choptank will know how to fix it.*

It was the first time he allowed himself to consider the book might be the problem.

26

It was 11:11 a.m., according to the clock on the dashboard, when The Mesa appeared in the car's windshield. It crested like an ancient god above the horizon, backlit by a crown of sunlight—a fever-dream oasis. Danny hadn't even seen a sign welcoming them to Arkansas, let alone a sign telling them they'd arrived at their destination, but by now, that was par for the course. Anyway, the landscape looked more like the Mojave than it did western Arkansas. Where were they *really*?

Beside him in the passenger seat, Tommy lay slumped and unconscious. His forehead was pressed against the passenger window, the left side of his face crawling with those inexplicable cuneiform hieroglyphics. He hadn't woken for the entirety of the drive that morning, and while that caused Danny some concern (though he could see that his brother was still breathing), it had made for a quiet and uneventful few hours.

What is this place? he thought, drawing closer to their destination.

The Mesa looked less like a motel and more like a post-apocalyptic Vegas wedding chapel. Spanish tile on the roof and stained glass in the windows. It even had a bell tower, although there was no bell. Danny didn't even realize this was the place until he saw a man holding a wooden sign above his head, the word MESA spelled out on it in Christmas lights. There was a young boy, perhaps seven or eight, standing beside him; he wore a gauzy towel wrapped around his head so that only one moist brown eye peered out from between the folds. The boy was holding one end of a frayed rope, the other end tied around the neck of a haggard-looking goat.

Danny slowed the car to a stop and rolled down his window. The man with the sign approached the car, grinning like an imbecile. He wore a 49ers jersey and a Beretta on his hip. When Danny opened his mouth to speak, the man—still grinning—waved a hand at him, which Danny took to mean shut up. The man pointed to a ball of cotton poking from his right ear, then he indicated that Danny should drive around to the rear of The Mesa.

There were people back here. A group of children chased after a chicken while two women in flowing cotton dresses carried trays of food and pitchers of juice over to a picnic table. A group of dark-skinned men sat on beach chairs watching the children play while others were in the process of erecting a volleyball net. There was a man in an apron and knee-high tube socks attending to a charcoal grill.

They all turned and stared as Danny pulled the car around back.

He shut down the engine, then turned toward his brother. "Tommy, wake up." He shook his brother's shoulder, but Tommy would not wake up. "Tommy. Hey."

Danny glanced back out the windshield. The man in the apron had set down his spatula and was marching over to the car. A few of the men had got up from their beach chairs and were following close behind him. These men carried assault rifles.

Danny got out of the car. He couldn't remember the last time he'd had a proper meal, and the smell of whatever was cooking on that grill caused his stomach to knot into a fist.

"You must be Danny Dark," said the man in the apron.

"Are you Choptank?"

The man pointed to the name embroidered on his apron—CHOPTANK. Then he untied the apron and slung it over the shoulder of the nearest rifleman. The rifleman didn't even blink.

Danny had been on Alec Rudenko's payroll for the better part of a decade. In that time, there had been no breed of criminal—from petty thugs and straphangers to mafia capos and hit men—that he hadn't dealt with. Movies about the underbelly of society were typically fraught with clichés because the people who populated that world were, themselves, clichés.

Choptank was not a cliché. He reminded Danny of a middle school history teacher, with his short stature, fussily combed hair, and trim mustache. He wasn't fat, but his face was round and jowly, and there was a nonspecific stockiness to him. He was maybe in his fifties, if Danny had to guess, and the only white guy (as far as Danny could tell) among a crew of dark-skinned men, women, and children. Also, the guy possessed a limp, noncommittal handshake.

"I got your book," Danny said, and Choptank followed him around to the trunk of the car. The men with the guns followed, too. A dog trotted over to them, barked twice, then cocked its head as a cloud of dust settled down upon its mangy fur. There was a craggy hornlike growth, pistachio-green and big as a sausage, corkscrewing from the top of the dog's head.

Danny opened the trunk, took out the briefcase, and handed it to Choptank. He didn't bother with an explanation for the condition of the briefcase, and Choptank didn't seem to care. Once Danny closed the trunk, Choptank set the briefcase on it, then produced a tiny silver key from the pocket of his safari shorts.

Something not wholly pleasant lit up behind the bulwark of Choptank's round, sunburned face as he opened the briefcase and gazed down at the book inside.

"She's beautiful, isn't she?" Choptank whispered, his voice filled with awe.

"What is it?"

"A very special item. One that I have been waiting to have in my possession for a very long time."

He closed the case with a loud snap, then relocked it.

"My brother's with me. He's in the car, and he's sick. He thinks your book is the reason."

Choptank shifted his gaze so he could peer past Danny and through the rear windshield of the car, at Tommy slumped in the passenger seat. If he noticed the incongruity of the BABY ON BOARD decal in the window, he made no mention of it.

Choptank turned to his men with the rifles and barked something at them in Spanish. The dog, too, barked.

The men went around to the passenger door. One of them pulled it open, and Tommy—still unconscious—spilled out. The guy halted Tommy's fall with his hip while a second guy repositioned Tommy back in the seat. The first guy—the one who'd caught Tommy with his hip—said something to Choptank in Spanish. Danny couldn't speak the language fluidly, but he knew the word *libro* meant *book*.

Choptank's men parted as the man approached the open passenger door. He crouched down and studied Tommy—more specifically, studied the intricate markings that covered Tommy's flesh.

"What's wrong with him?" Danny asked. "Do you know?"

Choptank looked up at him. He had one eye closed, wincing against the midday sun. Sweat sparkled on his brow. "You were given instructions not to touch the book." It wasn't a question.

"Is he gonna be okay?" Danny asked.

Choptank turned back to Tommy. He touched Tommy's forehead, which was the only part of him that wasn't discolored or marred by those strange symbols inked in his flesh. His voice much lower now, Choptank turned to one of his gunmen and spoke in a language that was not Spanish. It sounded like no language Danny had ever heard before in his life.

Two of the riflemen slung their weapons over their backs. They bent down and collected Tommy from the car, one of them grabbing his ankles, the other hoisting him beneath his armpits. Tommy's pistol fell from his pants and thumped to the sand.

Danny took a step toward them. "What are you doing? Where are you taking him?"

"We are going to try to salvage this situation," Choptank said as the two men carried Tommy across the stretch of desert and toward The Mesa. One of the women in the cotton dresses hurried to a pair of wooden doors and shoved her weight against it until it opened. She wore a diaphanous silk scarf covering the lower portion of her face.

"What do you mean, salvage the situation? What's the matter with him?" Danny asked.

Choptank watched the men carry Tommy into The Mesa. Then

he took a handkerchief from the back pocket of his safari shorts and blotted his glistening brow. "I had thought the instructions were quite clear. We'll do what we can for him now." Using the handkerchief, he crouched down and picked up Tommy's pistol from the ground. Then he stood and looked over at Danny. "Are you or your brother affiliated with any formal religious organizations?"

Danny said, "*What?*"

27

In a surreal turn of events, Danny was led to the picnic table at the rear of the compound to join Choptank and his companions for lunch. Most everyone spoke Spanish throughout the meal, so he knew little of what they talked about while they ate. Danny didn't care; he filled his belly with two cheeseburgers, some potato salad, and a tall glass of ice-cold lemonade. Midway through his meal, a young boy crawled onto his lap to show him the very large beetle he'd caught. Danny shifted uncomfortably until the child looked up at him, his nostrils flaring and his hot breath in Danny's face. The boy's left eye was nothing but a milky white orb.

In the middle of the meal, Choptank stood from the head of the table and addressed his companions—or were they his family?—in Spanish. Promptly, everyone grabbed their plates and filed into the building, leaving Choptank and Danny alone.

Choptank filled a glass with red wine then came and sat opposite Danny at the picnic table.

"What's going on with my brother?"

"My friends are trying to heal him. But you must understand, he's in a tenuous way."

"From what? Touching that book?"

Choptank's small eyes shifted to his wineglass. "It's not just a book, you know. It *breathes*."

"The hell does that mean?"

"It means that it restores things back to what they once were. It's one of many books, each imbued with their own distinct property. Their own reason for being. I have collected several of them over the years. This book in particular will fix some of the wrongs created by...well, the misuse of other books. Books on the other side that I haven't yet gotten in my control."

"The other side of what?"

"The other side of *here*," Choptank said. "Where you come from."

"Who are all these people?" He looked around at the assembled volleyball net and at a man standing beneath the shade of a yew tree with a rifle slung across his chest, watching them. Farther in the distance, the boy in the headscarf was dragging his goat across a dusty field. "What do you do here?"

"These people are my friends. They believe in my purpose, so we do right by each other."

"What's your purpose?"

"As I've said, I'm a collector. A collector's purpose is to collect."

"A book collector..."

"As I've *also* said, they are not just *books*. It is more akin to reaching up into the far reaches of space and grabbing yourself a piece of the universe. A piece that creates life? A piece that brings about chaos? A piece to turn back time? Is a dusty old stone really just a stone, or is it one tiny piece of a much greater whole?"

"What's with the riddles? Just tell me what's going on."

"I *am* telling. Are you listening?"

"What do you do with these books?"

"I hold on to them. I make sure they're safe. Many people want them, for all sorts of purposes. Some good, some bad. They come this way all too often seeking them out, I'm sorry to say. They can be dangerous in the wrong hands, even if those hands don't mean to cause harm."

"How can a book be dangerous?"

"Because they contain all the powers of the universe."

Danny chuckled, turned away. "People come *here* for these books?"

"Sometimes," Choptank said.

"Where *is* here?" Danny dug the roadmap from his jacket. He unfolded it across the table, smoothing it out with one hand. He pointed to the hand-drawn route that he and Tommy had been instructed to take. "Where in the actual fuck *are* we?"

Choptank offered him a thin-lipped smile. "You're on the other side of things, as we like to say around here. *Otro lado.* I apologize if the directions you were given proved...well, taxing to your sensibilities. But I assure you it was one hundred percent necessary that you followed them exactly as given. Your brother's current predicament is a good example of why it's dangerous to play fast and loose with the rules."

"Explain it to me in plain English."

Choptank took a sip of red wine. His teeth were stained with it. "The world as you know it isn't exactly *as you know it*. There are sides. Layers. Things upon things within things."

"Get down to it," Danny told him.

Choptank coughed demurely into a fist, then said, "Somehow, over the years, that particular book found its way to *your* side of things. Your world or your plane of existence, however you prefer to think of it. A place different from here. The book shouldn't have been there. It's downright *dangerous* for it to be there. I purchased it from a rare bookseller in your world, a man named Finter, and I required it *here*. On *my* side of things, with me, for my collection, where it's safe. You were hired as courier to bring the book from *your* side to *my* side. You've spent the past twenty-four hours, give or take, Mr. Dark, traveling through a sort of corridor that does not precisely exist in either world. It's a *connecting place*, you might say. A bit of metaphysical connective tissue that joins *your* side of things with *my* side of things. And many other sides, as well."

"The fuck are you talking about?"

"You don't understand it because your mind won't let you. But that doesn't matter. We're almost finished here."

Danny laughed. "You're crazy. You're fucking with me."

Choptank tasted his wine.

"Why didn't you just go and pick up the book yourself?" Danny said. "Or send one of your armed goons to get it?"

"We don't travel to your side," Choptank said. "Too dangerous."

"So you just dragged my ass out here? Me and my brother?"

One of Choptank's eyebrows arched slightly. "You're being paid handsomely, are you not? Besides, it's not dangerous for *you*, unless you don't follow the instructions. Most of the time, things work out just fine. Other times…well, somehow or another, some fool inadvertently finds himself inside the corridor. People without maps, people who have no concept of where they are or what rules apply. To be honest, I'm not one hundred percent sure how some of these people find their way in to begin with. I suppose the veil is thin in places."

"You're talking about some alternate fucking realm or something?"

"That's a fair assessment."

"Goddamn it." Danny laughed, though his throat felt tight and his nerves were wound. "So what happens to these people who find themselves…well, *here*?"

"Unpleasant things, I would suspect."

An image of that abandoned motor home surfaced in Danny's

head. The extension cord fashioned into a noose and a bloody sink full of broken mirror shards.

"The worlds are dangerous places," Choptank said.

Danny looked out toward the horizon. Cacti stood like scarecrows along the plateau. The boy was shouting at the goat while the goat bleated. Back at The Mesa, a dark plume of smoke had begun unspooling from a stone chimney, thick as bile. Danny could smell its acrid stench from where he sat.

"My old man showed up last night outside our motel," he said. "He wanted the book. Tommy blew his fucking head off."

"That happens from time to time."

"Does it?"

"That man wasn't your father. The thing wasn't even human. Neither was the woman who came the night before."

Danny felt like he was floating through a nightmare. "How do you know about…?"

"From the scuttlebutt I've heard," Choptank said, "you and your brother had attracted a comeforth."

"A what?"

"A shambling comeforth. They dwell in the corridors between worlds. They're hungry for power—in this case, the power that the book holds. But they'll take whatever sad morsels they can scrounge up. They will try to trick or coerce you by adopting forms that might connive or intimidate you, but they're essentially harmless. They're quite pathetic, in fact. They can't *hurt* you, unless you let them. Just like they couldn't take the book from you unless you handed it to them. Trickery is really their only weapon. Which is why your instructions were explicitly to *ignore* anyone who might come asking about the book, and to *follow the rules*."

Behind Choptank, a group of women filed out of the building. They all wore plain white cotton dresses, silk scarves covering the lower portions of their face, and they each had flowers in their hair. Their feet were bare. Danny watched as they made their way to his car. They kept glancing over at him and giggling like children. Then they opened the doors and began routing around inside the car.

"What are they doing to my car?"

Choptank didn't bother to look over at them. "Making sure there's no carryover. For when you go back."

Danny watched as the women took the tote bag full of food from the back seat, along with Tommy's cases of that no-brand beer. The cartons of cigarettes, too. All the shit they'd pilfered from the gas station back at that creepy town.

"Level with me," Danny said. "Am I dead and in hell? Or have I just lost my frigging mind?"

It was Choptank's turn to laugh. His thick jowls shook, and the sound of his laughter brought the mangy dog with the horn on his skull to the head of their table. Once Choptank's laughter subsided, he removed his handkerchief and wiped the tears from his eyes.

"I'm sure," Choptank said, "that you have witnessed some strange occurrences on this journey. I've got it on good authority, in fact, that you and your brother took a detour to the old town of Coal Dust. Is that right?"

"How the fuck do you know that?"

"I was informed by one of my watchers."

"Watchers, huh? My brother said he heard some kids singing or something in that town. He followed them into an old building that looked like a church. Or half a church." He paused, then added, "I think I saw them last night, too."

"My watchers are not children," Choptank assured him. He turned and called out to the rifleman who stood beneath the shade of the yew tree. The rifleman came over and rolled up his sleeve, so that Danny could see the tattoo on his bicep.

It was a black goat with wings.

"I don't understand," Danny said. He turned back to the women removing all that stuff from his car. He watched as they carried it into the compound. They left the car doors open.

"It doesn't matter if you do or don't," Choptank said. "You'll forget all about this trip in time."

"I doubt that."

Despite the dry heat, the smile Choptank gave him caused a chill to ripple up his spine.

"What happened to that town?" Danny asked. "Coal Dust."

Choptank said something to the rifleman in the language Danny could not place, then dismissed him with a wave of his hand. The rifleman went over to the boy with the goat, spoke something to him, then returned to his post beside the tree. The boy just stood in the field, his toweled head turned in Danny's direction.

"Things get dangerous the more you stray from the route," Choptank said.

"That's not an explanation."

"No," Choptank said, after a moment of consideration. "I suppose it's not. The corridor is a construct. It is safe, but once you stray, the worlds blur and merge. There is what we call 'bleed over.' In some places it's due to the thinness of the veil between worlds, and it cannot be helped. In other places—places such as Coal Dust—it's because there is another book out there in your world creating a doorway. Creating *problems*."

"Jesus Christ, man, I'm tired of the charades. What does that mean? What the fuck happened in that town? Who's the Cleaner?"

To Danny's surprise, Choptank's eyes sparkled. A lupine grin slowly worked its way across the man's thin, wine-stained lips. "Why," he said, "that's *me*."

28

"I've been a collector all my life," Choptank said. He had refilled his wineglass and was gazing absently at a pair of black flies as they tangoed above the rim of his glass. "The rarer an item, the more power it imbues. When you go deep into certain circles, you learn about items that most people have no idea about. These books I collect—they're the holy grail, my friend. And they're not just trophies. They don't just sit on a bookshelf for my personal admiration, collecting dust. Books have *power*. All books, yes, but the ones I collect in particular.

"It's how I ultimately came to this place. This side of things, you might say. Right from your world to this one. I used a book to pass through, easy as pie. The book was a key that made a doorway, and I just walked on through. It was the first book I collected, and I haven't stopped since. After a while, I no longer felt the need to go back to that other side; by the time I came through Coal Dust, I had decided I would stay."

All hail the Cleaner, Danny thought. *He came through.*

"There was much damage being done in Coal Dust by the time I arrived. The bleed over was bad. The merging of worlds had corrupted the landscape as well as the people. Stranger and stranger things took place. Palm trees sprouted from the desert soil. Buildings merged. People and animals alike began sprouting hornlike protuberances. Then a corpse in denim overalls fell from the sky and people began to swallow faces."

Danny was just about to ask what this meant when the boy in the headscarf arrived at their table, the goat trailing on its leash. Choptank said something in a foreign tongue to the boy, and the boy slowly began unwrapping the sun-bleached cloth from his face. His single eye held Danny in its gaze as he unwound the cloth, until finally the headscarf fell away, revealing a featureless bulb of flesh across the boy's face with only that solitary eye staring out. It was as though the rest of his features had been deleted by magic.

"A consequence of the bleed over," Choptank said. He reached out and gave the boy's shoulder a compassionate squeeze. Then he flapped a hand at the child, and the boy bounded off with his goat, the ends of his unwrapped headdress flapping behind him in the breeze.

"Jesus," Danny breathed. "Jesus Christ…"

"I rescued what people I could and brought them here, where we built this compound," Choptank explained. "Coal Dust remains unstable, as do many other parts of this world, many other towns and cities. Whatever books still exist out there in your plane of existence, Mr. Dark, they wreak havoc over here. I do not know what particular book is causing all the trouble in Coal Dust, nor do I know who has it. Perhaps one day I will get my hands on it. Until then, the book you have brought me today will go a long way in righting the wrongs brought down upon Coal Dust and its people, as well as some of the other thin places in our world. The book *fixes*. It *breathes*. Perhaps for that young child, we can even learn to *unswallow* faces."

Danny had had enough. "What's wrong with my brother?" he demanded.

Choptank's face was stoic. "Let's wait and find out," he said.

29

Just as Choptank was finishing his glass of wine, a procession of men, women, and children came out in single file from the open doors of The Mesa. At the head of the line was a young girl, no more than six years old. She, too, wore a plain cotton dress and a wreath of daisies in her hair. She carried an unmarked shoebox against her chest, and wore a tender smile on her face. Danny watched them come, feeling as though he were in a dream.

The girl led the line of people to the table. She came up beside Danny and placed the shoebox in front of him. Then, to his surprise, she kissed the side of his face before scampering away.

"What is this?" Danny asked Choptank.

"I'm sorry," Choptank said. "I truly am. I wish he'd followed the rules."

The shoebox was wrapped in masking tape so that the lid stayed on. Danny just stared at it. There was a sinking feeling in his gut.

Choptank got up from the table. He picked up the roadmap and handed it to one of the women in line. She held the map aloft while she produced a lighter from one of the folds of her dress—it was Tommy's silver Zippo, Danny saw—and ignited one corner of the map. She held onto it while it burned. When a soft breeze came and shifted the silk mask from her face, Danny saw that there was no mouth beneath it.

Danny looked back down at the shoebox. Then he stared at Choptank.

"What the fuck did you do?"

"Those," Choptank said, nodding toward the shoebox, "are your brother's ashes. We did the best we could, but he was too far gone. Practically dead when you arrived, in fact."

Danny's mind went: *what? what? what? what? what?*

He bolted up from the table.

"I want to see my brother!"

Choptank's eyes settled on the shoebox. So did the eyes of everyone standing in line before the table.

"No! No! What the fuck did you *do*?"

Another child ran up to the table, this one carrying the burned briefcase. It was the boy with the milky eye. He set the briefcase down and then backed away.

Choptank was tugging on a pair of latex gloves. Next, he produced the tiny silver key from his pocket. He unlocked the briefcase, opened it, and lifted the book up above his head.

Everyone dropped to their knees. Even the riflemen.

Danny staggered a few steps back from the table. Yet his eyes were locked on Choptank and that awful book he held above his head.

Choptank met his gaze. His face did not look unkind. He lowered the book in front of his chest, then peeled open the cover. Those strange onion-skin pages, previously blank, were now covered in a semitransparent membrane that was crowded with text. Not words—not to Danny, anyway—but symbols. Choptank turned each page, revealing more and more symbols, more and more cryptic text, the exact same sigils that had appeared all over Tommy's flesh, until one corner of the final page revealed the tattoo of a dagger with a teardrop of blood dripping from the blade—

Danny screamed.

All of those kneeling in the sand looked up at him.

He pulled the gun from the waistband of his pants. Raised it toward—

Gunfire exploded at his feet. Bullets whizzed past his face. He felt the shockwave of a million angry hornets needle past his flesh.

Danny dropped his father's gun and fell to the ground.

30

Choptank came around the side of the picnic table and peered down at him. "You haven't been shot, you know," he told Danny. "You can get up."

Danny sat up. His heart was beating so fast it pained him. He looked around at all the spent shell casings twinkling in the sand,

and at the riflemen with their weapons pointed at him. Even the boy with the milky eye was pointing the muzzle of a .38 Special in his direction.

Danny picked himself up off the ground. He glanced down at his chest, certain he'd see the spreading inkblots of blood on his shirt, but Choptank hadn't been lying. He hadn't been shot.

When Danny glanced down at his father's gun lying there in the sand, Choptank said, "Go on and pick it up. However, if you try a stunt like that again, my friends won't be so forgiving a second time."

Danny picked up the Glock and stuffed it in the waistband of his jeans. His gaze was drawn back to the shoebox on the picnic table, then to the book that Choptank still clutched in his gloved hands.

"The books require sacrifice," Choptank said. "As you and your brother no doubt saw, the pages of this book had yet to be written upon. Your brother's touch of it helped that process along. The book has been rebound to include your brother's...contribution."

"Contribution," Danny heard himself mutter. He sounded far away from himself. "That's his *skin*..."

"We're so very sorry for your loss," Choptank said.

31

He was told that if he headed back in the direction he had come, he'd see an exit for I-70 West. This would take him back to *his* side of things. *Otro lado.* This seemed impossible, of course, since he and Tommy hadn't crossed over a single interstate throughout their entire journey, but he had no choice except to take Choptank at his word.

He carried the shoebox containing Tommy's ashes to the car in a partial daze. Choptank and his people followed him, like family members bidding him safe travels. Some of the kids even hugged him. They all wished him well as he climbed behind the wheel of the car. They were all framed in the rearview mirror, waving with much enthusiasm, even the boy with most of his face missing, as Danny drove away with Tommy's ashes in the passenger seat.

His mind still snared in a fog, he drove as if on autopilot. Even though he didn't believe it, he kept an eye out for the exit ramp to the highway.

At some point, a figure standing in the middle of the road caught his attention. It was a man, and he was observing Danny's approach with the haunted, slack-jawed countenance of a lobotomy patient. Danny slowed down enough to swerve around the man, then slowed even more to get a better look at the man's skull-white face streaked with dark red streamers of blood. At the sight of him, Danny's entire body went cold. In his head, he could still hear this man pleading for his life, just as he'd done all those years ago in the *otro lado*—

(*don't do it danny don't do it danny don't do it danny don't do it d—*)

—as Danny pressed the barrel of his Glock to the man's forehead and then pulled the trigger. All of it, at the behest of his employer, Alec Rudenko.

The man in the road was Robert Benzo, and he still bore that bullet wound in the center of his forehead.

Danny punched the accelerator to the floor and didn't let up until the man was nothing more than a figment of his imagination—or was he?—in the rearview mirror of the car.

A little farther along, and he looked down at the shoebox in the seat next to him.

Precious cargo, he thought.

And when he came upon the exit to the highway, he took it.

32

No story has a true beginning or ending. All stories are part of a grand and mysterious tapestry—of all that has come before, and of all that will come in the future. Danny and Tommy Drake's story could have just as well ended with Tommy's ashes in a shoebox and Danny taking an exit to a highway that would take him back to his own world. The grand and mysterious tapestry would be okay with that.

However…

33

It was closing on midnight when a matte-black Chevrolet Monte Carlo pulled into the otherwise deserted parking lot of the Roadrunner Diner. Had anyone else been within view, they might have noticed how the driver—a guy in his early thirties with an expressionless face and dark, shifty eyes—seemed to be talking to someone in the car with him, even though he was alone.

Danny Drake got out of the car. He listened to the growl of an approaching storm while feeling the wind pick up all around him. Bits of grit needled his face, but he didn't mind. He stayed out there a moment longer, then went into the diner.

The place was empty, with only one waitress working the floor. She was barely more than a kid. Danny glanced at her T-shirt and saw that she'd traded in Def Leppard for Mötley Crüe.

He went to the counter and claimed a stool.

The waitress came over and gave him an exhausted smile. But then she recognized him, and she perked up.

"Hey," she said. "It's you. Where's your brother?"

He didn't want to tell her, so he said, "He's busy tonight."

"Oh, I'll just bet." The waitress winked at him. "He's something, all right." Then she slid a menu in front of him.

He slid the menu back in her direction. He was staring at her intently, as if to see if she was really who she was supposed to be. "I'll just have some coffee. I won't be here long."

"One coffee, coming right up." She filled a mug then set it down in front of him. "What's that?"

"This?" he said, looking at the empty beer can in his hand.

The waitress took it from him. She read the label aloud: "Budscheisse?" She frowned. "Never heard of it."

"It's not from around here," Danny said.

She handed him back the empty can. "*Scheisse* means 'shit' in German, you know."

"Does it?"

"Why are you carrying around an empty beer can?"

So I don't forget, was what he wanted to say. *It's the only thing that keeps me tethered to what happened. It's the reason those women cleaned out my car before I left—so I wouldn't come back here with totems that pulsed with the memory of that place.*

Without this empty beer can, the second-guessing would start. The forgetting. Those women had been thorough, but they hadn't checked under the passenger seat for any empty cans.

When he realized he hadn't answered the waitress's question, he said, "I guess I'm just sentimental."

Her smile faltered. Was he creeping her out? Well, he wouldn't be here much longer.

It was then that a pair of headlights turned into the diner's parking lot. A moment later, Alec Rudenko entered the diner with his bald-headed henchman in tow. Rudenko met Danny's eyes, then claimed a booth at the far end of the diner. His henchman took up a table nearby.

"Excuse me," Danny said to the waitress as he got up from his stool. He took his coffee over to Rudenko's table and sat down opposite his employer.

"I am sorry to hear about your brother," Rudenko said. "He had been ill for a while?"

"No," Danny said. "Actually, it was quite sudden."

"Ahh," Rudenko said, and a faint vertical crease appeared between his steel wool eyebrows. He withdrew an envelope from inside his black suede jacket and slid it across the table to Danny. "The remainder of your payment. Plus twenty percent."

Danny chuckled humorlessly, shaking his head. He tucked the envelope inside his own jacket pocket without bothering to count the money inside.

"I've got another package that requires delivery by next week," Rudenko said. "West Coast this time. Good weather, I hear."

"I think I need to take some time off."

"Ahh, yes. You are in mourning. How crass of me. Certainly—take whatever time you need."

Danny nodded his head. He took another sip of his coffee, cast a final glance at the henchman at the neighboring table, then got up. On his way to the door, he nodded at the waitress, and she beamed a smile right back at him.

The night was cold, and there was a storm rolling in; thunder rumbled and the low-hanging storm clouds pulsed with lightning. His hands in his pockets and his head down, Danny walked briskly toward his car. Rudenko's Mercedes sat next to it in the lot, the engine running. Danny glanced over at the driver, who had the window down and the radio playing softly. He was smoking a cigarette, and had his left hand hanging out the window. The hand was dressed in a splint.

The driver looked up and they exchanged a passing glance as

Danny continued to his car. There was a piece of medical tape across the bridge of the man's nose, and a fading bruise along the left side of his face.

They both turned and looked at each other again.

"Shit," said the driver, and he began fumbling with something in his lap.

Danny pulled his father's Glock from his pants, walked right up to the open window, and shot the driver in the face. The boom of thunder masked the sound.

Blood splashed across the Mercedes's windshield as the driver slumped over, dead. The radio still played, as if nothing had happened. Conway Twitty singing "After All the Good Is Gone."

Gun still out, Danny turned around and headed back toward the diner. When he entered, the waitress was taking Rudenko's order while the henchman grinned oafishly at something on his cell phone. Danny went directly to the henchman's table, raised the gun, and unloaded two rounds in his chest then one in the center of his forehead—*blam! blam! blam!*

The waitress whirled around, her face frozen in a rictus of shock.

Danny stepped around her and advanced on Rudenko, who sat wide-eyed and unmoving in his corner booth. He pointed the gun at him.

"You sent someone to kill my brother," Danny said. His hand holding the gun shook and his voice trembled, but he kept his gaze leveled on his employer. "Last week in Williston, North Dakota. I thought it was just a bar fight, Tommy shooting his mouth off. He said it was self-defense, that some guy was trying to kill him, but I didn't believe him. I *saw* the guy, lying on the ground behind the bar. His hand broken, his face busted up." Danny nodded toward the diner's parking lot. "That guy drove you here tonight. But he won't be driving you home."

Alec Rudenko raised his hands. His head shook the slightest bit. "Danny, that's not what hap—"

Danny unloaded the rest of his rounds into Alec Rudenko's body.

When the gun was empty, he turned and met the waitress's blank stare. She was still holding her pen to her order pad—a snapshot frozen in time.

But then she blinked her eyes and lowered her arms. With surprising authority, she said, "Go. Now."

Danny fled back out into the night, hurrying past the Mercedes that was still pumping exhaust into the air. Sporadic raindrops had already begun to fall.

His hand on the driver's side door handle, Danny paused. He looked over at the Mercedes idling next to him, just as lightning detonated directly above the Roadrunner Diner.

Danny went over to the open window of the Mercedes. The driver was slumped across the passenger seat, a pistol in the footwell. Marty Robbins was rolling through "Big Iron" on the radio now. Danny reached into the car and hit the trunk release. The rear of the Mercedes yawned opened.

Inside was a briefcase. Rudenko's payout money. Danny had seen it in here countless times in the past, and he knew what was inside it. Still, he flipped the latches, opened the briefcase, and gazed down at neatly filed stacks of banded hundred-dollar bills.

I just want to see you do better than all this, said the little voice in Danny's head. It sounded conspicuously like Tommy now.

Danny took the briefcase, threw it in the trunk of the Monte Carlo, then jumped behind the steering wheel. As he cranked the ignition, he realized he'd left the empty beer can back in the diner. He thought about going back, but then thought better of it.

In the boom of thunder and a flash of lightning, Danny Drake pulled onto the highway. Beside him in the passenger seat sat a shoebox with a BABY ON BOARD decal stuck to the lid. Danny flipped on the Monte Carlo's headlights, illuminating the endless ribbon of asphalt that lay before him.

He gunned the engine, and the Dark Brothers sped off into the darkness.

THIS BOOK
BELONGS TO OLO

ONE:

INVITATIONS

1

The boy stood at the cusp of the park, not moving. It was the middle of July, with a sky the color of faded blue jeans, yet he wore a plastic dime-store clown mask as though it were Halloween. The boy's eyes ticked back and forth behind the eyeholes of the mask as he watched the other children play. He held something red in his hands.

After a while, the children on the playground became attuned to his presence. They did not notice him all at once, but piecemeal—a boy at the top of the jungle gym glanced over at him just before rocketing down the slide; a girl hoisted into the air on one end of a seesaw was alerted to the abrupt sense of eyes on her, and turned; another child digging furiously in the dirt felt a twinge at the base of his spine only to look up and see the strange boy standing on the far side of the park, staring back behind the countenance of a plastic clown-face.

Had any parents been present, they might have observed the

boy with a sense of pity at first. He looked friendless and desperate, that creepy mask a misguided attempt at engaging with the other children on the playground. But that pity would then shift toward apprehension, as these parents—had there been any—noticed the boy's rigid posture and the overall motionlessness of his stance. They'd perceive the intensity of his gaze through the eyeholes of that mask, causing them to think of school shooters and all breeds of peculiar young boys who do queer and disturbing things when no one was looking.

The children were looking.

"There!"

"See him?"

"Who *is* that?"

A group of slightly older boys riding skateboards noticed him standing there, too. An eleven-year-old with long, feathered hair and an old-school Thrasher T-shirt pointed at him, laughing. More heads turned. Children perched like vultures along a split rail fence dropped to the ground on grubby sneakers, their collective attention abruptly rerouted by the appearance of the strange boy in the clown mask clutching something red to his chest.

Seen from the sky—if such a thing were possible—one might discern the calculated, predatory approach of the children on the playground as, in little groups, they graduated toward the boy in the mask. From such a height here in the sharp green sting of summer, a smoke-white sun burning through the lilac-scented atmosphere, the distant drone of automobiles out along the highway, the faint whoosh of lawn sprinklers punctuated by the occasional bark of a dog, with cement sidewalks swathed in hopscotch grids and discarded chewing-gum tumors, a baseball game broadcast on a radio thrumming from someone's open garage—from such a height, we might assume an assault of sorts was about to take place.

"Hey, weirdo, what's with the mask?"

"Is your face ugly under there?"

"Look at his clothes."

Despite the heat of midday, the boy in the clown mask was dressed in gray slacks and a short-sleeved button-down shirt, white as toothpaste. On his feet he wore cordovan loafers with shiny brass buckles. The clothes were neatly pressed and the shoes were buffed to a shine, but these boys in their skating T-shirts and chunky sneakers, and the girls in their frayed denim shorts whose pockets bulged with tubes of lip gloss and the occasional cell phone, saw only a target before them. One smallish boy in a Minecraft shirt even snatched up a rock and—perhaps to impress the older kids—chucked it in the direction of the strange kid who had dared to stand here among them. The rock came close to striking the shin of the boy in the mask, but he never once flinched.

Those dark little eyes kept swishing back and forth, back and forth, taking them all in.

"Wait a minute," said one of the girls in the group. She was only ten, but wore an off-the-shoulder T-shirt that was cropped enough to expose a tanned panel of midriff. Each of her wrists was adorned with a confusion of jangly bracelets. "I know who you are. You're the kid who lives in that big house on the hill."

"Yeah!" shouted another girl, her eyes bright. Earlier in the day, she'd applied some glitter high up on her cheekbones, causing her face to sparkle like a disco ball whenever it caught the sun at a certain angle. She was also ten years old. "You're the creepy kid who's not allowed in school."

"Too *weird* for school, is more like it," said the kid in the Minecraft shirt.

"Can I get a hoya?" sang one of the girls.

"Hoya!" caroled the others.

"Is that who you are?" asked the boy in the Thrasher T-shirt. He had his skateboard tucked under one skinny arm. His elbow wore a crisp brown scab. "You're the kid who lives in that weird house?"

The boy slid the clown mask up, revealing a round, heat-blotchy face and dark pewter eyes. A mustache of sweat glistened on his upper lip. "I am!" he said, smiling. His voice was ebullient. "My name's Bartholomew Tiptree. But you can call me Olo."

"Olo," mimicked the rock-thrower in the Minecraft shirt, smirking.

"We can call you weirdo," Thrasher suggested, and the other kids laughed.

Olo kept smiling.

"Why are you wearing that sus mask?" the girl with glitter on her cheeks asked.

"For fun!" said Olo. The clown mask was propped up on the top of his head now, and there were indentations just above his ears where the elastic band had been too tight.

"Is your house haunted?" the girl in the cropped T-shirt asked.

"Nope!"

"Are you retarded?" Minecraft asked, sniggering.

"I test out at genius levels," Olo assured him.

Minecraft spat laughter. "Holy *shit*, this kid…"

"What do you got there?" Thrasher asked. He was looking at the small red stack of whatever was clutched tightly in both of Olo's sweaty hands.

"Invitations!" Olo's steely eyes gleamed. "You're all invited to my tenth birthday party."

An ugly sort of noise rolled collectively through the group. It wasn't so much a laugh or a snort or even a gasp of surprise, but rather a combination of all those things twisted together. The sound bore a derisive quality, which tends to be the factory setting for ten- and eleven-year-old children.

"Here you go," Olo said, peeling an invitation off the stack and holding it out to Thrasher.

It was a bright red square of construction paper, folded in half. Drawn on it in black crayon was a smiley face, and there were dark, damp circles on the paper from Olo's fingers. Thrasher gazed at it with unmasked disdain, his otherwise pale face cratered with startling red pimples. He didn't touch it.

"Don't be shy," Olo said cheerily. "It's for you."

Thrasher flipped Olo the bird.

This didn't fluster Olo; he kept smiling while beads of sweat peeled down the heat-reddened sides of his face, his arm extended, the smiley face on that folded piece of red construction paper appearing to survey the crowd.

The girl with the glitter on her cheeks snatched it from him. She unfolded it, and a paper house decorated with glitter of its own sprung up from within. Startled, she said, "Whoa…"

Some of the other kids gathered around her to observe the paper house and to read what Olo had, quite painstakingly, printed on the inside of the card:

Once upon a time, Bartholomew "Olo"
Higgins Tiptree III was born!
Now he is turning 10!

You are invited to celebrate with him at
his home on Saturday at 3:00 PM!

There will be cake and ice cream and
games and prizes and surprises!
(You do not have to bring a present.)

As if she smelled something foul, the girl with the glitter on her face wrinkled her nose and shook her head. She pinched the invitation between her thumb and forefinger and held it aloft, perhaps hoping someone might pluck it from her. She held it the way someone might hold a dead rat by the tail.

"For you," Olo said to no one in particular, continuing to thrust invitations toward any child within his vicinity. The smile never faltered from his round, sweat-drippy face. "For you. One for you. It's my birthday."

Some took theirs with feigned disinterest, while others projected the appearance that they were merely playing along with a silly game meant for children even younger than themselves. A few of the older kids altogether refused to take their invitations, much as Thrasher had, and those folded slips of red construction paper seesawed to the ground at their feet.

A girl in a ball cap with a baseball glove propped under one arm came through the woods on the far side of the park. The number stitched on the back of her unbuttoned Bristol Bangers baseball jersey was 11 and the name above it said JOYA. She saw the mob of children standing at the edge of the playground, so she steered in that direction, snapping her gum and kicking at stray woodchips with the toe of her sneaker. When she arrived, Olo extended his final invitation to her. She opened it, read it, then looked up at him. "What kind of prizes will there be?"

"Really good ones," Olo said, his eyes growing wide. It was as if he could see the prizes right now, in his mind, and was astounded by their stupendous nature. "The games will be really fun, too! I promise they will. And whoever wins at hide and seek will get the best surprise of the whole day."

Thrasher and his friends laughed.

The girl with the glittered face said, "Bro, are you for real?"

Another girl said, "Hide and *what now*?"

"Hide and seek," Olo reiterated. "It's my favorite game. Do you know how to play?"

The boy in the Minecraft shirt who had chucked the rock at him was reading the invitation aloud, affecting a deliberate baby lisp that speckled the red construction paper with dark blotches of spittle. Some of the girls laughed.

"Hope you all can come!" Olo said cheerfully.

Thrasher *whooped* then dropped his skateboard to the ground. He hopped on it, executed some sort of flip kick overtop the discarded invitations, then rolled back in the direction of the playground. Thrasher's buddies followed, their stringy hair streaming behind them, their grimy sneakers with the floppy laces pedaling along the blacktop.

The rest of the crowd began to disperse.

Olo smiled at the girl in the baseball hat, who still stood before him with the homemade invitation opened in her hands. There was a bright red letter B on the front of her hat. Olo liked the color red—it was his favorite.

"Do you?" he asked her.

"Do I what?"

"Know how to play hide and seek."

"Well, everybody knows how to play hide and seek, I think," said the girl. "It's just that, it's kind of a baby game."

"Not the way I play," he said, then tugged the clown mask back down over his face. He stood there a moment longer, surveying her from behind the barricade of that cheap plastic, his armpits and the backs of his knees perspiring, his shirt clinging damply to his round little body.

Then he turned around and walked home.

Less than a minute later, the playground was deserted. Swings swayed lazily in the air while the seesaws sat frozen at acute angles.

Shouts and laughter could still be heard, but those sounds were distant now and fading fast, as the young denizens of that neighborhood, quick to lose interest, tromped off for richer territory. If not for the folded squares of red construction paper that littered the pavement, some with their black smiley faces grinning toward the sky, it was as if no one had ever been there at all.

2

It was called Helix House due to the repetition of corkscrew-shaped architecture throughout the home. There were two sculptures that served as supports for the awning above the house's front entranceway—wrought iron spirals that looked like springs from some mechanized beast on an alien planet—and the exterior brickwork was laid in a deliberate concentric pattern of alternating white and brown stones that gave the illusion of a monochromatic barbershop pole. Even the shrubs, though overgrown now since there was no one around to care for them, still retained the vestiges of their corkscrew shape.

Olo had spent the entirety of his nearly ten years living in this house. It had once belonged to the grandfather on his mother's side—a man Olo had never met, though his turgid, mustachioed countenance held court from the depths of an oil painting in the house's parlor. Olo had been named after this man (as well as his Uncle Bart, presumably, though he had died young), yet the boy failed to see any familial resemblance. Where the man in the oil painting looked formidable and intimidating, Olo was what his stepfather Roger sometimes called "mushy." He was short and overweight—pudgy, but edging toward fat, as Mother was quick to remind him—and the fact that he'd been reluctant to give up last year's clothes didn't help matters in that department.

Both Olo's mother and stepfather were writers. His mother was the renowned Maribel Sinclair. She authored a series of thrillers that followed the exploits of a homicide detective named Lucy Betancourt. Hardcover first editions of every Lucy Betancourt novel lined two whole bookshelves in the library of Helix House, his mother's name stamped in foil along the thick, glossy spines of each dust jacket. (Olo had read every single book.) The author photo on the back of each book was the same no matter which volume you picked up—a black-and-white headshot of a woman whose innate beauty was rivaled only by the sheer intensity of her intellect.

Maribel Sinclair was once Mary Tiptree. She possessed the same calculating stare and air of self-importance as Grandfather Tiptree's portrait. At some point in her writing career, Maribel had eschewed her ancestral surname and had hers legally changed to her pseudonym. She'd said in a few early interviews (which Olo had read in old magazines) that she'd never truly *felt* like a Tiptree, and was more at home inhabiting the body of the authoress Maribel Sinclair. A thing—a *woman*—of her own creation.

When his mother was working on a novel, she wrote every day in her office on the second floor of Helix House, where no one was permitted to bother her. The office walls were lined with various industry awards, framed magazine articles and favorable book reviews, and shelves bearing small potted plants in tidy rows. A carafe of coffee sat on a hotplate beside her desk. Sometimes, Olo would creep up to her closed door while she worked and listen to the whispery tap of her fingers on the keyboard of her laptop. She wrote in *spells*, a term she used not to indicate specific periods of time set aside for her writing, but rather the single-minded focus that overcame her when entrenched in a new book. She never took a break during these spells—not even a pause between sentences to let fresh thoughts filter into her brain, or to even use the bathroom. Not as far as Olo could tell, anyway. When writing, Maribel Sinclair was like something plugged into a wall, a thing that did not stop until the cord was pulled from the outlet.

Whenever she would finish with the day's output, which was promptly at six o'clock every evening, she'd drink a single glass of red wine, sit down to her dinner (whatever the housekeeper or, more recently, Roger had prepared), then vanish to the study again to review all that she had written throughout the day. Olo rarely saw his mother when she was working on a new book.

His stepfather, Roger Smalls, was quite a different breed of novelist, if he could even be called such a thing. Whereas Maribel Sinclair was loyal to her regimen and remained steadfast to the tribulations of Detective Lucy Betancourt, never straying from that character and the goings-on in her fictional Midwestern police department, Olo's stepfather was a self-proclaimed "literary prostitute." (He said this often enough and with such jocularity that Olo assumed this was a source of pride for the man.) Roger wrote in all genres, whenever the spirit struck, and took great pleasure in announcing this whenever the opportunity presented itself (which was usually when he was a few gin and tonics in the tank).

He was a man who was mostly tall and sinewy except for the ponderous thrust of a belly that would have looked less pronounced on a more redoubtable man's body. Roger Smalls possessed neither the intimidating stature of his wife nor the "mushy" physique of his stepson. He existed, instead, somewhere between both worlds—a man who may have been built for greatness but whose capacity for achieving it was limited by crippling self-doubt.

When they used to throw parties at Helix House, Roger could be heard whispering too loudly into someone's ear that it was certainly *nice* that Maribel got those big advances, went on book tours, and had bookshelves filled with her life's work, but really, he would find it *so creatively stifling*. There was Roger, drink in hand, propped against the fireplace mantel in the dining room, or maybe perched in one of the velvet wingback chairs in the library, watching his guests as they admired Maribel Sinclair's bookshelves. A fickle grimace curling one corner of his thin, moist lips, his small eyes red and bleary with drink, something dark and twisted beneath the well-groomed veneer of his face. Or perhaps he'd dwell in the parlor, reading passages aloud to some of his guests from a stack of damp pages excreted from his noisy typewriter—Roger always wrote his first drafts on a typewriter—forcing laughter at the funny parts so that his guests would know when to laugh, and spilling wine on the carpet.

His stepfather wrote—or attempted to write—in a cramped little room on the first floor of the house, a fair distance from the novel-writing juggernaut that was his wife. The bookshelves in this room were burdened with the accumulation of Roger's published work—slim literary journals and poorly formatted genre magazines, computer printouts of stories published online (for free), a few self-published chapbooks. There was the occasional anthology that had grudgingly paid him industry rates for one of his stories provided Maribel consented to having a portion of a previously published chapter reprinted in the very same volume. There were also several unfinished novel manuscripts stacked among these publications—great reams of crinkled, coffee-stained, cigarette-smelling pages. The typewriter ink was smudgy, and there were a lot of cross-outs and notes scribbled in pen on nearly every page. Much as he'd read all of his mother's Lucy Betancourt novels, Olo had attempted to read one of his stepfather's manuscripts, but he'd found them boorish and confusing. Also, they hurt Olo's head. (When Roger had asked him what he thought, Olo just grinned and gave him two thumbs up.)

His stepfather's writing room possessed a desk at its center—a great mahogany boxcar with pitted brass handles and gouges in the wood—and on that desk sat Roger's old manual typewriter. To Olo, the typewriter looked about as weighty as an engine block, and equally as cumbersome. Unlike the soft, musical tapping that whispered beneath the door of his mother's study when she wrote, Olo's stepfather assaulted the heavy keys of his typewriter with an aggression that often set Olo's sensibilities on edge. Whenever Roger was in one of his MOODS, Olo would hear those firecracker detonations echoing incessantly throughout Helix House, often underscored by a string of curse words in Roger's creaky baritone.

Olo had never known his birth father, a man whom Maribel had refused to marry despite falling pregnant, and who'd hanged himself from the wrought iron spiral staircase in the front hall of Helix House when Olo was only two years old. He'd been a writer as well, though nowhere near as successful as Olo's mother. In the dim and hazy years that bridged the gap between Olo's father's suicide and Maribel Sinclair's marriage to Roger Smalls, Helix House had entertained a number of other suitors. Olo remembered their names and occupations more than their faces—Lemieux the painter, Poach the screenwriter, Alexandross the concert pianist. Artists, all of them.

On this day, Olo walked up the long gravel driveway toward Helix House, the fingers of his right hand grazing the prickly foliage of the overgrown corkscrew topiaries, his face sweaty within the confines of his clown mask, humming "Happy Birthday" to himself. He waved hello to headless Mr. Tooms who stood between two shrubs with one hand raised in salutation. Farther ahead was Mrs. Keeley, clutching a large pair of pruning shears and tending to a mound of purple foxglove and thistle, the air around her speckled with bees. Lulu the Dancer pirouetted despite the marionette tangle of vines that twined around her peeling limbs and torso. Finally, there was Mr. Keeley—Mrs. Keeley's husband, of course—grasping his rake as usual, his sun-bleached, expressionless face reaching out to Olo from beneath the brim of a straw cowboy hat.

Olo said hello to each of them in turn, just as he always did upon arriving home, and then he paused as he noticed an unfamiliar vehicle parked in front of the house. It was a dusty brown sedan whose chrome bumpers blazed in the afternoon sun. The car's tires were dusted in white powder from the gravel driveway.

A curious kid by nature, Olo went up to the car. He set his clown mask atop his head, bracketed his hands around his eyes, and pressed his sweaty nose to the driver's side window of the sedan. His small, iron-colored eyes took in the clear plastic travel mug partway filled with coffee in a cup holder on the console, a pack of cigarettes above the dash, a cluster of tree-shaped air fresheners dangling from the smudgy rearview mirror. There were some books and a bag of sunflower seeds spread across the backseat, and a thick manila folder bristling with multicolored papers on the floor back there, small colored tabs stuck to some of the pages. Olo peered through the rear window and saw a pair of binoculars back there, too.

He moved around to the front of the car, his gaze trailing along the crack in the car's front windshield. The crack shimmered like liquid mercury in the sun. There was a bar of LED lights suctioned to the inside of the windshield, partially hidden behind the passenger-side visor.

Olo went around to each of the four doors, tugging on the handles. Each door was locked. He peered back inside the car again, this time from the vantage of the passenger side, to see if there was something interesting he might have missed. Other than an empty plastic soda bottle in the footwell of the passenger seat, there was nothing.

COP CAR, Olo thought, the words coming through his head in all capitals. A brain-shout, as he sometimes thought of it. *COP. CAR.*

A vein of giddy excitement pulsing through Olo's body, he wondered if Detective Lewis had come back to visit. This summoned a broad smile to the boy's lips…but then some other thought, another brain-shout, intervened—

(BEWARE)

—and this thought caused his smile to falter. That pulse of excitement drained from his body just as quickly as it had arrived.

Had someone been watching him from a window of the house—Maribel Sinclair, perhaps, taking an unheard-of break to peer out the window of her study to the unkempt grounds below—they would have observed a child standing motionless beside the car for several minutes. The back of the boy's shirt see-through with sweat, that odd little dime-store mask perched atop the nest of blond curls on his head, the boy's pudgy, heat-reddened hands down at his sides. The only thing not visible from such a perspective would be the boy's face—or, more accurately, the queer calculations that might appear to be taking place behind the placid gray discs of his eyes.

This person might watch, wondering what this child was up to, while their own breath cast foggy rose blossoms upon the windowpane. What was that child thinking? What kept him rooted motionless to that spot beneath the hot summer sun? Why didn't he flinch when a sizable bumblebee trundled past his face? These questions might have even lingered once the boy appeared to snap from his trance and whirl around, a smile once again planted firmly on his face as he raced up the wide staircase that led to the pair of hand-carved oak doors at the top of the porch. But surely not for long.

Boys like Olo Tiptree had a talent for not lingering in people's memories.

3

A spiral staircase stood in the center of the foyer, an intricate monstrosity that climbed to the shadowed, cobwebbed corners of the house's second story. Shafts of milky daylight seeped in through the high windows and crisscrossed the staircase, like something on a stage lit by various spotlights. Olo often wondered what it had looked like with his birth father's body hanging from that staircase by a length of rope, eyes bulging, face purpled, perhaps a dark wet stain on the front of his pants.

A man's voice—not his stepfather's—filtered down the corridor toward him. Olo stood there, listening as his excitement grew, but he could discern nothing but its low frequency. He passed down the corridor, through a maze of oil paintings and soft museum lights, until he was standing, unobserved, in the entryway of the parlor.

Roger Smalls was sitting forward on the sofa, his hands clasped in a pale ball between his pointy knees. He was dressed in a shirt and tie, but the tie was crooked and his hair was disheveled. He wore no shoes, just a pair of dark socks that had collected balls of white dust with all the force of a magnetic charge. Two or three days' growth was spread in the shape of batwings along the lower portion of his jaw.

It *was* Detective Lewis who sat opposite Olo's stepfather in a wingback chair, speaking in his low, dulcet voice. The detective's posture was less rigid than Roger's. He wore a tan suit and a maroon necktie on this occasion, as opposed to the dull black suit and tie he'd worn on his first visit to Helix House a month earlier. Detective Lewis's hair was short and the color of fireplace ash. He had a small notepad balanced on one thigh, and a ballpoint pen poised at the ready. When he sensed Olo watching him from the doorway, he turned and smiled.

"Well, hello, Olo," said Detective Lewis. "Good to see you again."

"Hello!" Olo beamed. He lifted a hand and waved enthusiastically at the detective.

Roger twisted his head around to see his stepson standing in the doorway. Roger's face looked constipated with thought. "Oh," he said, the word creaking out of him. He looked startled, as if he'd forgotten he had a stepson. "Detective Lewis and I were just talking about you, Olo. Where've you been all afternoon?"

"I went down to the park to play."

"Did you?" Roger's expression suggested he found this odd. He cleared his throat and said, "You should let me know when you leave the house. So I don't worry."

"I did," Olo said. "I told you at lunch."

"At lunch," Roger muttered, cutting his eyes back to Detective Lewis. "That's right, I remember now…"

Olo had eaten a peanut butter and marshmallow sandwich for lunch. Roger had finished half a bottle of wine.

"I see your friends are still out front, Olo," Detective Lewis said. He was still smiling, which made Olo happy.

"Yes, sir," Olo said. Then, trying for a joke that maybe really wasn't a joke: "They're always hanging around."

"Remind me of their names again?"

"They're Mr. Tooms, Mr. and Mrs. Keeley, and Lulu the Dancer," Olo said. "Mr. and Mrs. Keeley are married."

Roger coughed into a fist. "Olo is a creative young man. His mother and I are, uh, very proud of him."

"Which one wears that old cowboy hat?" Detective Lewis asked, paying no attention to Olo's stepfather.

"That's Mr. Keeley," Olo said. "He tends to the grounds. It used to be Mr. Cooper who tended to the grounds, but he got sick and had to leave us."

"Oh," Detective Lewis said, his smile faltering.

"Mr. Cooper was our groundskeeper," Roger explained to the detective. "He was a real person. He left us last year when he went into a hospice." He lowered his voice to a gruff whisper and said, "Stomach cancer."

"I see," Detective Lewis said, nodding. To Olo, he said, "Anyway,

I thought old Mr. Keeley might appreciate an upgrade in fashion." He leaned over the side of the chair and picked up something off the floor. It was a straw cowboy hat, just like the one Mr. Keeley was currently wearing, only it looked brand new. "I kept thinking about the condition of poor Mr. Keeley's hat since my last visit. I happened to have this one in my bedroom closet. Got it on a trip I took to San Antonio years ago, but I've never worn it. Would you like it?"

Olo considered the proposition. "I'll have to talk to Mr. Keeley and see what he thinks," he said, then immediately felt as though he'd said the wrong thing. His mother was constantly chiding him about saying WEIRD THINGS, and he thought this might have been one of those WEIRD THINGS. He quickly added, "I'm just playing pretend, you know."

Detective Lewis laughed. It was a soft and melodious laugh, unlike the sharp, nervous barks Roger sometimes dispatched with little regard into the ether. The detective set the hat back on the floor beside his chair. "I'd like to talk to you again about Iris, if you don't mind, Olo. Would that be all right?"

"May I change my clothes first?" Olo asked.

"Do you see that?" Roger Smalls said to the detective, his voice a bit too loud. His Adam's apple ticked up and down along the stubbly screen of his throat. "He's impossibly conscientious, that kid. He gets that from his mother, you know."

Detective Lewis gave Roger a sideways glance, then that smile was headed back in Olo's direction. "Sure, son," Detective Lewis told him. "I'll be right here waiting. Take your time."

Olo turned and wandered back down the hall, listening to his stepfather stammer through what sounded like some convoluted form of an apology for some reason: "He's a very bright kid, tested on the genius scale when he was seven or eight, and already reads at a college level, but there's some tradeoff, as I'm sure you, uh, *recall*..."

Olo spiraled up the staircase, then huffed down the hall toward his bedroom. He paused outside his mother's office, the door closed, the muted clack of laptop keys filtering beneath the door like a fairy's whispered secrets.

Tap tap tap tap tap, nearly in time with the ticking of the grandfather clock in the hall, *tock tock tock tock tock…*

He went into his bedroom, where he plucked the clown mask off his head, stripped out of his sweat-dampened shirt, and buttoned up a fresh one. He selected a necktie from the back of his closet door—a maroon one, very similar to the one Detective Lewis was currently wearing downstairs—and he stood before his mirror as he clipped it on.

Reflected in his bedroom mirror was what might appear, to the uninitiated, to be a large picture book set upon one corner of Olo Tiptree's bed. Closer inspection would show that the book appeared to be handmade, with a child's handwriting in black crayon the only thing on the otherwise blank white chipboard cover:

This book belongs to Olo.

And below that:

Do not open.

As he stood before the mirror straightening his clip-on tie, Olo's gaze shifted to the reflection of the book. Once more, that strange brain-shout intervened—

(BEWARE)

—and for the first time, he wondered if Detective Lewis had a gun in a holster beneath his suit jacket, like the detectives in Mother's novels.

(BEWARE)

"Go away," he told the brain-shout. He liked Detective Lewis and didn't appreciate the brain-shout trying to convince him otherwise.

He returned to the parlor to find Roger smoking a cigarette and pacing the floor beneath the watchful, disproving stare of Grandfather Tiptree over the fireplace. Detective Lewis hadn't moved from his chair, and was studying the pages of his notebook when Olo came into the room.

"Ah, now there's a proper young gentleman," Roger said, his cigarette trembling between two fingers.

"You didn't have to get all dressed up for me," said Detective Lewis. That smile was still on his face; Olo thought maybe the detective had been down here smiling the whole time he had been upstairs changing his clothes, and that in turn made Olo smile.

Olo crossed the room and sat on the sofa, in the exact spot where Roger had been sitting earlier. He kept both his feet on the floor and his hands in his lap.

Olo's first conversation with Detective Lewis had taken place less than a month before, soon after Iris's disappearance. He and the detective had talked in the dining room on that occasion while they drank large glasses of chocolate milk. On that visit, Detective Lewis had been intrigued by Mr. Tooms, the Keeleys, and Lulu the Dancer, so Olo had explained how he had found the mannequins discarded in the woods behind the house, and had wheeled them back in his wagon all on his own. He'd dressed them in old clothes and posed them in the yard. When Detective Lewis asked why Olo had done this, Roger, who had been leaning in the doorway, cut in with a comment about how creative Olo was, always coming up with new projects, what a hell of a kid, he and Maribel were both so proud of him.

Olo and Detective Lewis had also talked about Iris. That was okay by Olo, because he liked Iris—he liked her a lot—and he liked *talking* about her. In fact, he must have run at the mouth for nearly twenty minutes about what a wonderful tutor she was, and how since Mr. Cooper and Ms. Betty and the entire cleaning staff no longer came around to Helix House, Iris was his one and only true friend.

Detective Lewis leaned forward in his chair now, closing the distance between them. His coffee-colored eyes sparkled. Olo was instantly glad he'd chosen a similar necktie to the one the detective was wearing, and he wondered if Detective Lewis had noticed.

"I know we've done this once already," Detective Lewis began, his voice smooth as a fitted bed sheet, "but I wanted to go over everything that happened the last time you saw Iris. Can you talk to me about that day again, Olo?"

"Yes, sir," Olo said.

It had been a bright, sunny Friday in June, and he and Iris had gone over that day's lessons out on the back patio. History, science, math, literature. Iris had worn a lavender dress with a matching hair band (Olo told Detective Lewis this) and Olo had thought she'd looked very pretty (he did *not* tell Detective Lewis this). They had also played a game of tag in the yard after lunch (peanut butter and marshmallow sandwiches, sliced apples, fruit punch drink boxes), then a game of hide and seek (Olo's favorite) once they'd finished with the day's lessons. Both Maribel and Roger had been gone for the day—his mother had been out of town for a book event and his stepfather had driven out to Strawbridge to meet with a literary agent—so Olo had been left on his own once three o'clock rolled around and Iris had left.

"Did you watch as she left the house that day?" Detective Lewis asked.

"I walked her to the door and gave her a hug, just like always."

"Did you see her get in her car?"

"No. I just waved goodbye then shut the door."

"Did you happen to notice if anyone else was outside your house that day? Maybe someone in a car or someone just standing there?"

Olo knew the Keeleys, Mr. Tooms, and Lulu the Dancer had been out there—just as they were right now—but he knew that wasn't what Detective Lewis was asking. Saying something like that would be like saying one of those WEIRD THINGS his mother disapproved of. Instead, he said, "No, sir."

"No, there wasn't anyone there? Or no, you didn't notice?"

"Well, I guess I didn't notice. I didn't see anyone."

Detective Lewis smiled and nodded his head. He was tapping his ballpoint pen against his little notepad; Olo liked the *chik-chik-chik* sound the tapping pen made. He also liked Detective Lewis.

The ash at the tip of his cigarette lengthening exponentially, Roger said, "Olo is a pretty perceptive child, has been since I've known him, those eyes always whizzing about, taking things in and soaking things up, just incredibly observant, which is to say, I mean, that if someone had been out there where someone might *see* them, uh, hanging around, and certainly a *car*, I mean, I would suspect Olo here would have, uh…had there *been* anyone…"

Detective Lewis ignored Olo's stepfather. "Did she come back to the house at any point, Olo? To use the telephone or anything?"

Olo said, "No, sir."

"Did she receive any phone calls that day?"

"On her cell phone," Olo said.

"Do you remember who called her?"

"It was Tony."

"Her boyfriend," Detective Lewis said.

"Her fiancé," Olo clarified.

"Ah, yes. I didn't know if you'd know that word."

"I know most words," said Olo.

Detective Lewis smiled wide enough to show a sparkle of tooth. "So it was Tony who called?"

"Yes, sir. He called her just after lunch."

"Did she seem upset when he called her?"

Olo frowned. "Upset?"

"Like, were they fighting? Arguing?"

"Oh." Olo shook his head. "No, sir. She didn't seem upset."

Overhead, a floorboard creaked. Roger looked up, his moist eyes scanning the crossbeams in the ceiling. He was gnashing his teeth together. More to himself than anyone else, he muttered, "That's my wife…"

"Do you remember what time your stepfather came home that evening?" Detective Lewis asked.

"I've already said—" Roger began, but Detective Lewis raised a hand, silencing him.

"It was at six o'clock exactly," Olo said, feeling quite proud. "I remember because I was getting hungry—we always eat at six o'clock, even when Mother is out of town—and I looked at the big grandfather clock in the hallway just as I heard Roger's car coming up the driveway."

"That's when I noticed Iris's car was still parked outside," Roger interjected. He was chasing a fresh cigarette around with his lighter. "She's stayed for dinner a few times in the past, usually at Olo's behest, so that wasn't unusual. But I'd picked up a pizza, just enough for the two of us, and thought, shoot, I don't have enough food." He cleared his throat then added, "The meeting was a bust, by the way."

Frowning, Detective Lewis said, "What meeting?"

"My meeting with the literary agent," Roger said. "The great Jack Baer, up from New York. He used to rep my wife and we sort of *fell into* this meeting since he was coming up this way on business. We came to the mutual agreement that we wouldn't be a good fit for one another. You see, my latest manuscript, it's fairly complex, eschewing all genre expectations, which is grand, but it also makes people uncomfortable. Every agent wants something *new* and *original*, but then you give it to them, and they're instantly intimidated because it's like nothing they've ever seen before…"

"Did you become concerned once you learned Iris had left the house at three o'clock, but that her car was still outside?" Detective Lewis asked.

"I guess I didn't give it much thought," Roger said. "You see, I'd made some edits to my novel after my meeting with Mr. Baer—edits in my head, I mean—and I was anxious to get back to it. I spent the rest of the evening writing in my office. Until that Tony fellow showed up, anyway."

"Around what time did Iris's fiancé come around?"

"It was after nine," Roger said. He looked at Olo, perhaps for confirmation, but Olo's face remained expressionless.

"Walk me through what happened when he showed up."

Roger shrugged. "He asked to see Iris, but I told him Iris wasn't here. Tony asked why her car was still here if she wasn't—you see, I'd forgotten about the car by this point—and so I told him, you know, I really don't know. He said he'd been calling her cell phone all evening but she hadn't answered. We went out to look at the car and that's when we noticed it had a flat tire. And that was when Tony called the police."

"So you didn't notice the tire was flat when you first arrived home that evening?"

"I guess I didn't."

"You guess or you didn't?"

Roger cleared his throat again, and said, "I didn't."

"What happened when the police arrived?"

"They asked me the same questions you did the following day," Roger said. "Olo, too. They said it was odd for Iris to wander off instead of calling for roadside assistance—or calling her fiancé to come pick her up—and that she would have most likely waited in the house. Strange, in other words, that she would decide simply to wander off because she had a flat tire."

"Yes," Detective Lewis agreed. There was something stern in his face now. Olo wasn't sure he liked it. "Very strange."

"The police took photos of the car then had it towed away," Roger continued. "The next day, like I said, you came around, detective. And that brings us up to speed, I believe."

"At any point in time, Mr. Smalls, did you touch Ms. Garin's vehicle?"

It sounded strange to Olo to hear the detective refer to Iris as Ms. Garin.

"No, sir," Roger said.

"Not even casually? Maybe you brushed a hand along the trunk as you walked around it? Leaned on the hood? Anything like that?"

"I don't really recall, now that you mention it."

"What about the tire itself?" Detective Lewis asked. "When you examined the flattened tire, did you touch it?"

"No, I didn't. I mean, I didn't really *examine* it, as you say, is what, uh, is my point. I believe Tony did, though."

"Did you notice anything peculiar about the puncture mark on the tire itself?"

Roger's features drew together in an approximation of a frown. "Peculiar?"

"Anything at all," Detective Lewis said.

Slowly, Roger Smalls shook his head. He poked his fresh cigarette between his lips and sucked at it. The tip glowed red.

"Typically," Detective Lewis said, "a car tire is punctured along the tread. You drive over something sharp in the road, and pop. But Ms. Garin's tire was punctured along the outer wall."

"What does that mean?" Roger asked.

"It means that someone deliberately flattened Ms. Garin's tire," said Detective Lewis.

Olo stiffened in his seat.

(BEWARE)

From across the room, Roger stared at the detective. The cigarette dangled limply from his mouth. "Are you saying someone came *onto my property* to do that to Iris's car? To do...whatever it was that has happened to her..."

"I'm not ruling anything out at this point," Detective Lewis said. He closed his notepad and tucked it inside his suit jacket. "In the meantime, I'd like you to come down to the station at your earliest convenience to provide your fingerprints. Forensics has been dusting Ms. Garin's vehicle, and we'd like to eliminate yours from any others that might appear on it."

"My fingerprints?" said Roger.

"If it's not a problem," said Detective Lewis.

"Well, of course not, I'm more than happy to assist with the, uh, with this whole matter..."

Detective Lewis said, "Thank—"

"Only I should probably discuss it with my wife first," Roger added quickly.

Detective Lewis leaned forward in his chair. Olo watched as one of his slender eyebrows arched.

"Hello," Maribel Sinclair said, startling all three of them.

"Ma'am." Detective Lewis stood from his chair.

Maribel came into the parlor and shook the detective's hand. She was dressed casually in jeans and a flannel shirt, the first few buttons open to reveal a slender gold chain about her neck. She had her platinum hair piled atop her head in a bun.

"Please tell me there's been some good news, detective," Maribel said.

"Nothing to report, ma'am. Sorry to say."

"Poor Iris. I've just been sick to death over this whole thing."

"And now we've got some potential foul play to contend with," Roger spoke up. "Someone apparently came onto the property and deliberately flattened the poor girl's tire. I can't even imagine what reason someone would have for doing something like that..."

Maribel said, "*What?*"

"I didn't actually say that," said Detective Lewis. "Only that the puncture mark on her tire wasn't in line with the type of puncture you typically see when—"

"What about that Tony fellow?" Roger cut in. His head was wreathed in a cloud of cigarette smoke.

"Yes," Maribel agreed. "Poor Tony, too."

Roger shook his head. "No. I mean, what *about* him? Is he, like, a *suspect*?"

The grin that came to Detective Lewis's face now was humorless. To Olo, it looked like the man was sucking on something sour. He didn't answer Roger's question, and instead thanked them all for their time. Then he turned to Olo. His smile looked genuine once again. "It was a pleasure seeing you again, Olo, my man. I'll just leave the cowboy hat here on the floor, in case you decide Mr. Keeley might want it. Okay?"

"Okay," said Olo.

(BEWA—)

"Nice tie, by the way," Detective Lewis said, and winked at him.

Olo felt suddenly buoyant with positivity.

4

The boy in the Thrasher T-shirt, whose name was Terence, eventually skated back through the park on his way home for dinner that evening. His two chums, Elliot and Sid, brought up the rear, their oversized black T-shirts kiting in the breeze. The wheels of their boards rumbled over the blacktop.

When Terence spied the discarded construction-paper invitations still scattered about on the ground, he pointed them out to his buddies. They all shared a good laugh at that. Elliot began making fun of the chunky weirdo in the *clown mask*, if you could believe such a fucked up thing—a goddamn *clown mask*? What was *wrong* with that kid?

They knew of the boy's house, of course. Everyone in town did. It was practically a mansion, nestled up there on a hill wreathed in trees. The boy's mother was somebody famous—a book writer or something—which meant the family must be rich. As for the little turd in the clown mask, Terence had seen him only once before, standing at the foot of the gravel driveway that led up the hillside to the great big house. Terence had been in a car with his parents, zipping right by, when he happened to glance out the car's window. The boy's round, smudgy face had been there, staring right back. He had what Terence liked to think of as a punchable face.

"What a dipshit," Sid said, skidding to a stop on his deck. He snatched one of the discarded invitations off the ground, crushed it into a ball, and tossed it at Elliot.

Elliot caught it, peeled it open, then read aloud (in a babyish voice) from the invitation: "'There will be cake and ice cream and games and prizes and surprises!'"

"And gay butt sex, too!" Sid chimed in.

Elliot laughed.

"Prizes and surprises," Terence said, peeling another one of the invitations off the ground. He unfolded it and that glittery construction-paper house sprang out. "Fucking lame."

"*So* lame," Sid agreed.

"I can't even," Elliot chimed in.

Yet they each put an invitation in their pocket.

5

That evening's music selection was Nigel Kennedy's recording of Vivaldi's *The Four Seasons* performed with the English Chamber Orchestra.

"I think we should consult with Seth before you go surrender your fingerprints to the local police," Maribel said.

The three of them were seated around the large dining room table, an assortment of sushi set out on various ceramic platters in front of Maribel and Roger. Olo, seated at the head of the table with his clown mask propped on the top of his head, slurped up lo mein noodles.

"You're not concerned that might make us look suspicious or guilty or something?" Roger said.

"I'm not saying we deny the request outright. I'm simply suggesting we speak with my attorney first before involving ourselves in this mess any further."

"If I understood that detective correctly, it sounds like we won't be involved at all moving forward," Roger said. He shook the ice around in his rocks glass. "Iris's *fiancé* is apparently the involved party. The detective all but said as much."

"He didn't actually say that," Maribel corrected. "Not from what I heard."

"Of course it's the fiancé," said Roger.

"That's morbid."

"Sure it's morbid, but it happens. You know that."

"Of course I know that. I'm not an imbecile." Maribel set her chopsticks down on her linen napkin. "Just for clarity's sake, Roger, your prints *won't* be on that girl's car, correct?"

"Of course not." He sounded more confident than he had when Detective Lewis had asked him the same question earlier, Olo thought.

"Not even *inside* the car?" Maribel said, a curious uptick to her left eyebrow.

A darkness flickered behind Roger Smalls' eyes. When he spoke again, his tone was flat. "No, Mare. I've never been in the girl's car."

"I've been in Iris's car plenty," Olo offered. "She sometimes takes me to get ice cream. And once we went on a field trip to the aquarium to see sharks. It was fun!"

"Well, as insensitive as it sounds, it would be nice to have the focus shift to Iris's fiancé and off us for a while," Maribel said, after granting her son a tired smile. She'd been upstairs writing most of the day and her exhaustion was palpable. "I don't like the attention. The whole thing is untenable. I've already told Alicia that I'll be doing no more interviews for the foreseeable future, until this whole sordid affair gets squared away. I nearly bowed out of this weekend, in fact, but Alicia's assured me there will be no questions—absolutely *no questions*—about this incident from the media. Those savages can skin the bones of some other carcass."

Roger, who was on his third or fourth gin and tonic, looked up from his plate and stared blearily at her. "What's this weekend?"

Maribel's wineglass froze midway to her lips. "I'm in New York for the book expo. Did you forget?"

Olo sucked a lo mein noodle into his mouth then tugged the clown mask down over his face.

"I'm..." Roger began, his eyes searching the tabletop, the platters of sushi, the packets of soy sauce, for the right words, "I'm...uh, *this* weekend? *All* weekend? Are you sure?"

"Christ, Roger." She set her wineglass down beside her plate. To Olo, she said, "Mask off at the table. I've warned you about doing weird things."

Olo pushed the mask up over his forehead. His eyes volleyed between his mother and Roger as he sat there at the head of the table.

"This Saturday is no good for me," Roger said. "I've got that publishing event in Haymarket. That upstart indie press that's interested in my manuscript?"

"You've never mentioned any event until just now."

"Like hell, Maribel." He slammed a hand down on the table, and Olo jumped in his seat. "We *talked* about this. We *discussed* this. I watched as you typed it into your goddamn day planner. I got a shot at getting this novel *off the ground* here. This is *important*."

"It's written on Roger's desk calendar in his office," Olo interjected. He'd seen it written there himself over a week ago.

"While I'm sure your stepfather appreciates you rushing to his defense, Olo, whether it's written on his desk calendar or not doesn't mean he's ever mentioned it to *me*."

"I'm sitting right the hell here, Mare," Roger groused.

"Yes, I can see that."

"You talk to the boy like I'm not in the room. It's demeaning."

"I'm sure it is," Maribel responded.

Something dark rippled beneath the surface of Roger Smalls' face. He jolted out of his seat, the legs of his chair scraping along the hardwood floor. Olo watched him stagger over to the wet bar where he dumped ice cubes, one by one, into his glass—*clunk! clunk! clunk!* He refilled his drink, then returned to his seat with an audible huff.

"You never listen to a word I say," he grumbled, hoisting his drink to his lips. He gazed off into one dark, faraway corner of the dining room.

Maribel had her cell phone out and was scrolling through her calendar with her middle finger. Olo admired the way the light from the screen made her face look ghastly.

"This Saturday," she announced. "There is nothing here, Roger, to suggest you—*oh for shit's sake!*"

Now it was Roger's turn to freeze with his drink halfway to his mouth. He did this, however, with less grace than his wife, sloshing some booze onto the tablecloth.

Maribel turned to Olo. "Why didn't you mention your birthday was this Saturday?"

"Birthday?" Roger said. He was blinking and screwing his head around like an owl. His big, confused eyes settled on his stepson. "Is it really? *This* Saturday?"

Olo resisted the urge to tug the mask back down over his face. Instead, he grasped his glass and took a few thirsty gulps of his chocolate milk.

"Your mother's right, sucker punch. You should have said something to remind us. You know how your mother and I get when we're knee-deep in our writing."

"Well, now I just feel awful," Maribel said. "Did you want to come with me to New York, darling? Celebrate in the city?"

"No, thank you."

"Are you sure? You could have a grand time, walking around and taking in the sights while I'm at the expo."

"We can just celebrate my birthday when you get back," Olo suggested. "This way Roger can attend his publishing event and you can go to the expo and there won't be any conflicts."

Roger slapped his hands together, loud as a pistol shot. "Stellar! The boy's a goddamn genius, as we know! And of course this means we'll have to go doubly big when your mother returns. I'm talking balloons, presents, a dinosaur cake or whatever your little heart desires, Olo. The whole nine yards. And you can invite whomever you'd like. We'll throw a wild bash right here at the house, just like the old days."

The wild bash that had been thrown for Olo's birthday last year had involved Roger in a pointy hat drunkenly singing "For He's a Jolly Good Fellow" out on the patio while Mr. Cooper, their former groundskeeper, led Olo in circles on the back of a rented pony. Ms. Betty had dressed one of the outdoor picnic tables in all of Olo's favorite foods, while Olo's mother had smoked cigarettes and argued on her cell phone from beneath the shade of a large oak. After the pony rides and the presents, they had all watched Olo devour an entire carton of chocolate fudge ice cream capped in a summit of whipped cream and rainbow sprinkles.

"You mean it?" Olo said. "I can invite anyone I want?"

"Well," Maribel said, resting one cold hand atop Olo's. Her palm was ice. "I think your family is all the friendship you need for the time being. Not to mention the characters in your books, of course— Robinson Crusoe, Henry Fleming, Humbert Humbert…"

Roger made a sour face. "He's read *Lolita*?"

"The point is," said Maribel, "we don't need another incident like that time I mistakenly sent you to public school."

"That was a long time ago," said Olo. "I was only six."

"Nonetheless, it's still left a bad taste." She tilted her head back slightly, as if tempting him to continue his argument. "You're sure you don't mind both of us being out of the house for your birthday, dear?"

"I don't mind," he said, reaching again for his chocolate milk.

"Then it's settled," Roger said, his loud voice echoing throughout the room. "Crisis averted."

"I'll make a note and have a cake delivered," Maribel said, typing into her phone. "I assume chocolate will suffice?"

"Double chocolate," Olo said.

"Now the boy's thinking," Roger said, grinning. There was a comet's tail of soy sauce on the front of his oxford shirt. "Goddamn it, why shouldn't there be double chocolate?"

"Fine by me," Maribel said, still typing.

"Ten, right?" Roger said. He was grinning drunkenly and wagging a finger in Olo's direction. "The big one-zero. Double digits. My God, you're practically a man now." Then he shouted, "Hey!" and ratcheted up off his chair. He wandered into the kitchen where he began slamming cupboard doors and rattling plates over the Vivaldi music.

Olo reached up to pull his mask back down, but his mother cleared her throat, so he left it.

When Roger returned to the dining room, he was crooning a boozy rendition of "Happy Birthday" and balancing a wedge of week-old chocolate muffin on a cutting board. The candle he'd speared through the center of the muffin was clearly from the brass candlestick on the mantelpiece in the parlor. Maribel smiled sourly at the display, her eyes on her husband as he set the cutting board on the table with a loud thud. The candle, too heavy for the cake, began to tip over.

"Happy birthday, Olo!" Roger boomed while Maribel appraised her husband from across the table with slatted eyes. "Make a wish, old man!"

Olo made a really good wish. Then he leaned forward and blew out the candle a moment before it fell into his stepfather's sushi.

"Bravo!" Roger cheered, applauding. Maribel was still looking at him the way she might look at something that had just crawled out of a sewer grate. "Goddamn brilliant, son! Goddamn brilliant! *For he's a jolly good fellow…*"

6

The inimitable Lucy Betancourt, detective and ten-year veteran of the Kansas City Police Department, had once slain a man in self-defense by driving a fireplace poker through the perp's abdominal cavity to the tune of a wetly audible *glughsh!* This man was by no means an innocent victim: he had murdered an untold number of young women in and around Missouri and, just moments before meeting his own demise at the business end of that fireplace poker, was about to end Lucy Betancourt's as well.

The serial killer's name was Devon Loxley, but the Kansas City Police Department had dubbed him the Slice-and-Dicer. His weapon of choice was a seven-inch fillet knife made of high-carbon stainless steel. His modus operandi was to creep up on women in a dark alley or parking garage, snatch a handful of their lustrous hair—they all had lustrous hair—and draw the gleaming steel blade of that knife across their pearly white throats. Their blood always shot out in warm spurts, but somehow Devon Loxley never got any on him. Not even a single drop on his shoes.

Loxley didn't stop with a simple slicing of the throat: once his victim was prone on the ground, old Slice-and-Dicer would set to work filleting the woman's face from her skull. He'd poke the woman's eyes out, too, just for good measure. Anything for a juicy headline, one might suppose.

Devon Loxley was one of a long line of serial killers, mass murderers, domestic terrorists, and even a crazed politician, who had nearly gotten the drop on Detective Lucy Betancourt. But of course, Lucy, highly decorated and perpetually at the top of her game, always managed to turn the tables on them at the last moment. (That stunt with the fireplace poker was just another trick up Detective Lucy

Betancourt's smartly tailored sleeve, executed with the same air of nonchalance one might demonstrate when vacuuming a carpet.)

Moments before turning Devon Loxley into a human shish kebob, Detective Lucy Betancourt had, in a climactic final denouement, revealed to him that she knew the truth about his twin sister, Delilah: she had been Devon Loxley's first victim.

"How...how do you *know* that?" Loxley growled, his body shuddering in the firelight coming from the hearth.

"Because I've got a shock-proof, built-in bullshit detector, Loxley," Lucy Betancourt responded. "The only reason you've gotten away with it for all these years was because no one knew Delilah was dead. After all, there was only her abandoned car, an aquamarine Nissan with a COEXIST sticker on the bumper, left overnight in a deserted parking garage...*with a flat tire*."

"Stop!" Loxley shouted, clamping his hands to his ears. His face was twisted in a snarl of agony. "I don't want to hear you say it!"

"A tire that *you*, Devon Loxley, had gone back and punctured *yourself* in order to confound the *police*!" Lucy revealed. From the corner of her eye, she noticed a fireplace poker leaning against the hearth within arm's reach. "A sadist's ploy, making everyone believe she had wandered off looking for help after discovering the punctured tire, when in reality she was already lying dead in the root cellar of your ancestral home!"

"Goddamn you, Betancourt," Loxley growled through clenched teeth. Spittle flung from his thin lips.

Detective Lucy Betancourt was not to be deterred: "It was a plan you might have gotten away with, too, had it not been for the trail of *missteps* you've left in your wake, Loxley, glowing like phosphorescent plankton on the surface of a dead black sea!"

"I said goddamn you!" Devon Loxley screamed, and rushed at her. And then it was poker time: *glughsh!*

7

Later that evening, as Olo sat reading Roald Dahl in the parlor, he could hear his stepfather's furious hammering upon his typewriter, *shick-shick-shick-shick-shick*, interspersed by moments of complete silence during which Olo imagined the man trembling with anger like some obstinate, tantrum-prone child. When that silence persisted for several minutes and there was no more *shick-shick-shick*, Olo set his book on the coffee table and ambled down the darkened hallway that led to his stepfather's writing room.

The door to the room was closed, a pale light seeping out from beneath the door. Olo pressed an ear to the door and heard the sonorous rumbling of his stepfather's snores.

He went upstairs and found the door to his mother's office standing open, the lights off. The screen of her laptop glowed with a screensaver of a tropical island, and Olo thought, *That's nice*. She had an early flight to New York tomorrow, so having completed her night's work, she'd gone to bed.

Olo went into his own bedroom and switched on the light. The large handmade book with his handwriting on the cover still sat on the edge of his bed. Olo picked it up and tucked it under one arm.

He carried the book down the winding staircase and into the dining room. The dinner plates were still on the table, the leftover sushi rolls hardened to briquettes. Olo placed those hard little discs of sushi onto a clean plate, along with the rest of the chocolate muffin he hadn't eaten. In the kitchen, he got a carton of chocolate milk from the refrigerator and a handful of chocolate Kisses from the canister on the counter. He placed all these items on a TV tray, then set the tray down on the dining room table next to his very special book.

Olo opened the book.

The house that popped up from between the book's covers was a miniature version of Helix House. Olo had made it himself, painstakingly cutting out all the doorways and windows, penciling in the pattern of concentric stones on the outside, culling the corkscrew shrubs along the driveway from green construction paper. It wasn't just the facade of the house, either, but rather the whole thing— peering down into it, one might marvel at the labyrinth of paper hallways and arched doorways, the multitudinous little rooms, the twirling paper fan that served as the spiral staircase at the center of the house. That paper staircase was affixed to a slender wooden chopstick, the tip of which poked straight up in the air.

Olo reached over the top of the paper house and took the tip of the wooden chopstick between his thumb and forefinger. Gingerly, he gave it a twist.

The paper staircase rotated in its base.

Out in the foyer of the real house, the spiral staircase did the same.

As always, Olo was aware of a shift in the world around him—a subtle yet undeniable alteration that he sensed somewhere in the center of his skull more than he observed with his eyes or heard with his ears. In his stomach, too, for it felt like he was suddenly in an elevator that was descending too quickly down its shaft. Both sensations passed in less than thirty seconds, but what lingered was a vague lightheadedness that he did not find wholly unpleasant.

Olo picked up the tray of food and carried it through the kitchen, beyond the parlor, and down a hallway that hadn't been there a moment ago. To the casual observer, there was nothing to differentiate this new hallway from the rest of the house—the floors appeared to be the same dark chestnut color, the walls the same unblemished ecru—but to travel down it, one might find themselves overcome with disorientation. Panic might set in. The temptation to flee might be great. Yet much in the way a fly will only trap itself further in a spider's web the more it struggles, an attempt to flee would only result in that someone becoming more lost.

There were many doors—all closed—lining both sides of this strange corridor. Olo carried the TV tray past each door until he arrived at one with a deadbolt on the outside. A smiley face had been drawn on the center of the door in red crayon. Above the smiley face, in Olo's handwriting, it said:

Iris

Olo unlocked the door and stepped inside.

It looked like the bedroom of a young girl, spacious, with a purple shag carpet and a four-poster bed frilled in pink-and-white tartan. Christmas lights hung from the ceiling, and a small music box tinkled softly atop a white vanity table. There was a collection of Mother's novels on one shelf, a heap of stuffed animals on another.

"Hello, Iris!" Olo said, merrily.

There was only one window in the room, framed in pink taffeta. It was tiny and circular, like the porthole on a steamship. Iris stood before it now, gazing through the glass. She didn't even turn to face him as he came into the room.

"Boy, it's so good to see you again," he said, his words coming out in excited little gasps.

Iris's reflection peered out at him from the windowpane. Beyond her reflection, dense white smog pressed against the glass, swirling like a million bad dreams. Whatever was out there, it was nasty as a bruise, and it looked alive.

Olo set the TV tray on the vanity table, then closed the music box, silencing that discordant tinkle of sound.

"Are you hungry, Iris? You must be. You haven't been eating at all. I'm sorry I didn't come around yesterday. But I brought you some food! Some chocolate Kisses as a treat, too. Kisses are the best! Yum."

Iris turned around. A set of dark eyes peered out at Olo from a frizz of black hair. Iris's face looked ashen, and her lips were thin and pale. There were still bits of Sheetrock in her hair from when she'd gone through the wall last week, back when she'd been more mobile. There were streaks of dried blood running down the length of her lavender dress, too.

Still, despite her appearance, Olo felt his heart beat more prominently in his chest. *IRIS IRIS IRIS!* cried the brain-shout.

"Olo," she rasped, her voice a rusty hinge. "Olo, this has to stop. Please."

"Chocolate milk!" Olo grabbed the milk carton from the tray, opened it, then set it down on the table beside the music box. "Go on," he said, pointing at the carton. "While it's still cold and scrumptious."

"I don't want chocolate milk, Olo. I want to *go home*."

Olo chewed on his lower lip. He looked around the room, saw the checkerboard on the furry pink ottoman at the foot of the bed, and broke into a huge grin. He went over to it, dropped to his knees, and began setting up the board. "I'll let you be red this time, even though it's my favorite color in the whole wide world," he said. The checker pieces went *clack* as he placed them, one by one, on the game board.

"Olo, please. Listen to me." She took a step in his direction, her feet crackling through the static charge in the shag carpet. Her right ankle was still badly swollen and she walked with a noticeable limp. "You can't keep me here. Whatever you're doing, whatever this is, it's time to stop. It's time to let me go home."

Olo's gaze unfocused. One white, pudgy hand hovered above the game board, a giant red blood cell of a checker clutched in its grasp.

"Olo, I can't *breathe* in here. I feel trapped. I *am* trapped. I asked for a window, and *that's* what you gave me? What's going *on* out there? What *is* that? What is this *place*? Where have you taken me?"

Slowly, Olo's hand descended to the board. He placed the red checker on the appropriate tile, *clack*, then snapped his head up in Iris's direction. "Don't be a sore loser, Iris. You might win this time."

"Are you even *listening* to me?"

He pointed to her side of the checkerboard. "Smoke before fire, but I'll let you go first."

"I'm not playing fucking *checkers*, you little shit! I want to go *home!*"

If someone completely detached from this scenario—say, for example, Detective Lucy Betancourt—were to observe it, they would see a woman clearly helpless and in distress, sure, but they also might see an almost ten-year-old boy growing fuzzy around the edges. The boy's eyes turning dull and dreamy, while his perfectly round head with its godlike cap of golden curls began to sway back and forth on the short, thick stalk of his neck. Had this detached observer been the same person to see him standing beside Detective Lewis's police car earlier in the day, a similarity might have been detected in the trancelike state that had, from seemingly nowhere, overtaken the boy.

But then, just as quick, clarity filtered back into Olo's eyes. He stood up and dusted pink fuzz from the knees of his slacks.

"You *can't* go home, Iris," he told her, quite matter-of-factly. "You're part of a story now. You're in my book. Your place is here now. *This* is your home. I've tried to make it as nice for you as possible. I've given you books to read and all those nice dolls to play with. I've even given you a window, although I can't help what's on the other side. That part's beyond my control. But I really do try to do my best for you, Iris."

"Olo, please, listen to me," and now she was on *her* knees, clutching her hands before her as if in prayer, "if you let me out, I won't tell anyone about this…this *place*. Not a soul, I swear it. And I won't leave you! I won't go to California. I won't even see Tony anymore if you don't want me to. I'll cancel the wedding! But I can't stay here, Olo. It's killing me…"

Olo cocked his head to one side. Great torrents of thought were whipping through his skull. Finally, he said, "I don't believe you, Iris. I know that's not true. All of what you just said—it's not true."

"Olo, I *swear* it! Jesus *Christ*!" And she began to weep.

Olo said, "In every one of Mother's books, Detective Lucy Betancourt says the same line at some point, usually near the end when she's confronting the bad guy. 'I've got a shock-proof, built-in bullshit detector.' It's like her catchphrase. Some other writer came up with that before Mother did—I think it was the guy who wrote about the old man and the fish—but it works in Mother's books, too."

"*Olo, pleeeease…*"

"I think maybe I have one of those, too, Iris—a shock-proof, built-in bullshit detector. I wish I could believe you, but I don't."

Iris's black eyes hung on him, her mouth ajar. She looked like she wanted to scream or laugh or maybe do both at the exact same time. Or maybe rush at him again, attack him, try to escape down the hallway.

"I know what you're thinking," Olo said. "You remember what happened last time you tried to run off? It wasn't fun. It wasn't olly olly oxen free. And if you hurt me, Iris, then you'll be trapped in here forever. You'll never find your way out. Not ever. If something bad happens to me…" And then he shrugged, because Iris was smart, and he didn't have to explain things like that to her anymore than he already had.

In the end, she just whispered, "*What the fuck are you?*"

He was just a boy, of course. That was no secret. Couldn't she see that?

"I'm your best friend, Iris," he said. "And you're mine. Best friends forever."

He went to the door, opened it, was about to step through…but then paused. He turned around to find her still kneeling on the shag carpet, hands clasped, tears streaming down her face. "My birthday is on Saturday, Iris, and I've got a wonderful surprise planned. You'll see. You won't have to be alone in here for much longer. I promise."

"I don't think I'm alone now," she said. The words shuddered out of her. "There are other people in here with me, aren't there? I hear them sometimes, through the walls. At least, I used to. I think they hear me, too. Who are they?"

"Goodnight, Iris."

"*Goddamn you, Olo—*"

He stepped back out into the hallway, closed the door, and turned the deadbolt. *Click.* He could hear Iris shrieking on the other side of that door—

"*Who are they? Who the fuck are they? Let me out of here! I want to go home, you little shit! I want to go home!*"

—and then she was right *at* the door, her shadow moving beneath it, followed by a—

—*bang!*—

—against the doorframe.

Bang! Bang! Bang!

"*You little son of a bitch, let me out of here!*"

Humming "For He's a Jolly Good Fellow" under his breath, Olo turned and wandered off into the darkness.

8

One month earlier, beneath a bright June sky, Iris Garin was hiding behind a shed in the backyard of Helix House, smoking a cigarette. She never liked to smoke in front of Olo—she felt shameful smoking in front of any kid—so she'd welcomed Olo's game of hide and seek. The game afforded her the opportunity to slip away behind the shed and suck in a lungful of carbon monoxide without feeling guilty.

They'd finished the day's lessons, so she'd allowed him twenty minutes of playtime before she headed home. He was a nice kid, if a little strange—well, okay, a *lot* strange—but he was *smart*. Math wasn't his strong suit—he struggled with even the simplest concepts—but he possessed an aptitude for reading, writing, and the creative arts like no other kid his age she'd ever seen. Heck, some adults she knew couldn't hold a candle to him.

She'd only been tutoring him since last fall, but they'd formed a quick bond. Early on, she'd made an error in judgment when she assigned books that were recommended for his age. Olo had whizzed through them, understanding concepts and words that were far above his age group, and seemed overall bored with the rudimentary subject matter.

They soon read other books together—Conrad's *Heart of Darkness*, Golding's *Lord of the Flies*, and Orwell's *1984*. Olo read and understood these books without difficulty, but he described them as "too angry." He was a bright, sunny kid (despite having no friends), always quick with a smile and his own brand of infectious laughter, so maybe these books *were* too angry. When she asked him what sort of books he enjoyed reading on his own, he told her he'd read all of his mother's books.

Iris knew Maribel Sinclair was an author, but she'd never read any of the woman's work. One afternoon, Olo had lent her a hardback copy of *Death on a Meat Hook*, the first Detective Lucy Betancourt novel. Cheese-ball title, and the text itself was rife with purple prose and mixed metaphors, but Iris had secretly enjoyed it. Strange, though, that Olo enjoyed them as well, given the gratuitous violence, foul language, and explicit sex scenes. Or maybe he only liked them because his mother had written them. Was Maribel Sinclair okay with her son reading these books? Iris never asked.

Now, as she smoked behind the shed, a part of her felt guilty for having to leave him at the end of the month. She'd discussed it with him earlier in the year, explaining how she and Tony were going to get married this summer and move to California. A long way away, true, but maybe Olo could come and visit once she and Tony got settled?

Olo had been upset, and rightly so. She was all Olo Tiptree had. The kid didn't attend public school, had no friends, and his mother and stepfather were practically MIA most of the time. The few occasions she'd walked down to the park with him or took him out for ice cream, the other kids steered clear of him as though poor Olo radiated noxious gas.

"When will you leave?" he'd asked her.

"At the end of June," she'd said (and they were here now).

"I turn ten in July. Can't you at least stay and come to my birthday party?"

"I wish I could, sweets. But Tony starts a new job at the beginning of the month and I need to plan the wedding."

She'd felt like a heel, all right, but was telling the kid the truth worse than lying to him? She hoped she'd done the right thing.

Her cell phone chimed in her pocket. She dug it out and saw Tony's name on the screen.

"Hey, baby," she said, then took another drag of her smoke.

"I'm thinking tacos from the Exxon station and a bottle of cheap sangria for dinner," Tony said. "Tell me that doesn't sound glorious."

Iris laughed. "I'm not eating gas station tacos. Are you crazy?"

"You judge, but you don't *know*, girl. There's a *legit* Mexican restaurant in the back of that Exxon station. Mexxon food! I'm telling you, Iye, these tacos are to die for."

"Okay, but if I get botulism and kick the bucket, I want you killed and buried along with me."

"What are you, an Egyptian princess?"

"And a foot rub," she added. "I want a foot rub. Individual toes."

"Now you're pushing it."

"You want me to eat gas station tacos and *I'm* pushing it?"

"What time are you getting out of there, anyway?"

"I'll head out by three."

"That creepy kid put the moves on you yet?"

"Cut it out. He's not creepy," she said, taking another drag of her cigarette. "He's just a little weird. Well, maybe a lot weird. He's got no friends. I feel sorry for him."

"Kids like that grow up to become mass shooters and serial killers."

"That's awful, Tony. Don't say that."

"I heard he got kicked out of elementary school when he was just in first grade. I don't know what he did, but it's gotta be pretty fucked up to get you expelled in *first grade*."

"That's not true. He's always been homeschooled." Although even as she said this, she didn't know if it was true or not. *Had* he gotten kicked out of first grade?

"Anyway, Iye, the kid's not your problem. Don't feel bad."

"I know. It's just that his parents don't give a shit."

"Can't save the world, babe."

"Yeah, well," she said…and then she looked up to see Olo watching her from between two of those ugly, sculpted hedges. Watching and listening. "Shit, Tony, I gotta go."

"Try not to break the little weirdo's heart," Tony said, and disconnected the line.

Iris slipped the cell phone back in her pocket. A moment later she realized she still had the cigarette between her lips, so she plucked it out and pitched it around the side of the shed.

"Hey," she called after him, no different than she'd call after a timid puppy. "Did you hear any of that, Olo?"

He said nothing.

"Olo?"

"Who was that on the phone?" He was peeking tentatively at her from between the hedges.

"That was Tony."

"That's the guy you're going to marry."

"That's right." She went over to where he stood, wedged between those two weirdly sculpted hedges. Almost like he was hiding there. Or like he'd snuck up to listen to her phone conversation on purpose. "Listen, Olo, I didn't mean what I said on the phone. I was just goofing around. You know I love the heck out of you."

The boy's face was stoic. "I didn't hear anything," he said.

He's lying, she thought. *I've hurt his feelings.*

"I can stay an extra half hour, if you want," she told him, by way of apology. "How's that sound? We can play any game you want."

Olo sucked on his lower lip as his eyes narrowed in thought. A small white booger popped in and out of his left nostril as he breathed.

Such a weird kid, she thought, not without pity.

"Can we play hide and seek in the house?" he asked eventually.

"Sure."

"But can I show you something first?"

"Abso-surely," she said, and tousled Olo's curly blond hair.

The thing he showed her was up in his antiseptic little bedroom on the second floor. Iris had always thought Helix House was disturbing in its hugeness and sparseness, and Olo's bedroom was no different—there was simply a bed, a desk, a bookshelf, and a closet filled with Olo Tiptree's peculiar brand of clothing, all in a bedroom about the same size as her entire apartment. The rank of clip-on neckties hanging from the kid's open closet door was both comical and sad.

"Here," he said, opening his desk drawer and taking out what looked like a large photo album. He set it on the desk as Iris came up behind him to see what it was.

A plain white cover with Olo's handwriting on it in rigid black crayon:

> This book belongs to Olo.
> Do not open.

"I made a book, just like Mother," Olo said. "Only this one has no words."

"If it has no words, what's it—" Iris began, but then her breath caught in her throat as Olo opened the front cover.

When she was a child, Iris and her sisters had owned an elaborate princess-themed board game. When you opened the board, a majestic castle unfolded, and you could move your tiny princess figurine across the drawbridge and up and down the castle's passageways until the game was won by reaching the top of the tower. The thing that popped out of Olo's book reminded Iris of that very game, only Olo's version was even more impressive.

The house had been meticulously cut from cardstock and colored to resemble Olo's *actual* house—Helix House. There was no roof, so she could peer down into it and marvel at the intricacies within—the cardstock hallways with their paper doors, the tissue paper staircase wound around a narrow wooden stick, the checkerboard tiles drawn in red and black crayon in various rooms, brown construction paper to represent the dark wooden floors in other rooms. There was a drawing of the grandfather clock in the foyer, its hands frozen at either midnight or noon, and what she supposed was the portrait of Olo's grandfather over a meticulous sketch of a fireplace in the paper parlor. All of it—simply magnificent.

"Wow, Olo, you *made* this?"

"I did! It's my house. Do you like it?"

"It's unbelievable. Did you show this to your mother?"

He hesitated, then said, "Not really."

"I can't believe you did this on your own." She pointed to four small figures made out of wire twist ties from loaves of bread. "Who are these? Your family and me?"

"That's Mr. and Mrs. Keeley, Mr. Tooms, and Lulu the Dancer."

Ah, sure. Those creepy mannequins he'd cobbled together in the front yard. They'd never failed to give Iris the creeps, and she'd begun mumbling goodbye to them at the end of each day as she walked quickly to her car. Iris dismissed them now, and instead reached out and fingered a small tab sticking out from one of the walls of the paper house. "What about this?"

"Don't," Olo said quickly, pushing her hand away.

"Sorry, my dude. I was just curious." And even as she said this, she noticed there were several other tabs—tabs all over the place.

"They make the rooms change," said Olo. He pulled one of the tabs, and to Iris's amazement, the walls of the tiny paper parlor rotated so that the cut-out windows repositioned themselves, as did the entryway to the room. The portrait over the fireplace was replaced by a panel of black construction paper. Most impressive was that a new corridor now branched off from the room and wound deep into the center of the paper house.

"My God," Iris said, peering closer at the pop-up house. She pointed to the top of the thin wooden stick running up the center of the house, the one that the winding staircase was glued to. "What's this one do?"

"Watch," said Olo. He pinched the tip of the stick between two fingers and turned it slightly. The motion caused the tissue-paper staircase to rotate, as well as all the other rooms in the house to change at once. It was as though Olo had constructed a fully functional zoetrope in the center of this diorama. Rooms were reconfigured, corridors vanished, new hallways appeared. Iris couldn't wrap her head around it.

"Olo, this is really unbelievable. I don't know what to say."

"You really like it?"

"I do. I'm blown away, my dude." She studied the system of new rooms and hallways. One of the new rooms in particular jumped out at her. It was colored completely black, from the floors to the walls, and even the little flap of a door. She pointed it out to him. "What is this one supposed to be?"

Olo said nothing.

She looked at him and noticed his eyes had grown distant and foggy. His face was slack and his head was tilted ever so slightly to one side. It was as if he'd fallen instantly under a hypnotist's trance. This sometimes happened to him, Iris knew; she'd witnessed him zone out on occasion while doing his schoolwork or reading a book or sometimes even while drawing. Many kids tended to zone out from time to time—there was nothing unusual about that—but Olo always did so with such...*alacrity*...that even now, with her having grown accustomed to it, Iris still found it unsettling.

"Hey," she said softly, touching his shoulder.

Olo began clicking his tongue against his teeth—a steady, metronomic ticking that for some reason reminded Iris of the grandfather clock downstairs in the foyer. A spit bubble glistened in one corner of his mouth.

"Olo?"

He came out of it with a rapid blinking of his eyes. That prideful smile was back on his face. It was like nothing had ever happened.

"Look here," he said, reaching over the top of the pop-up house and pointing down into one tiny square room surrounded by a dozen others. This particular one was colored in various shades of pink and lavender. "That room right there is *your* room, Iris."

"Aww, my dude. Pink is my favorite color."

"I know!"

She reached up and tugged playfully at his mop of golden curls. "You're a sweet kid, you know that?"

"And now?" he said, his face so close to hers now that she feared for one second that he might actually try to *kiss* her.

That creepy kid put the moves on you yet? she heard Tony saying in her head, and while he wasn't completely wrong in his assessment of Olo Tiptree's weirdness, Iris Garin suddenly felt a swell of maternal compassion for the boy.

"Now what?" she said.

"Hide and seek in the house. Before you have to go home. You promised!"

She checked the time on her cell phone. "Okay. Five minutes, all right?"

"All right!" he cheered, and he ran out into the hall.

Iris followed him out. She heard him *thunk-thunk-thunk* down the winding iron staircase. More than one shadow shifted along the hallway, as if Olo had instantly fractured into many different Olos. A trick of the light, no doubt.

"Am I hiding or counting?" she shouted after him.

Olo did not respond.

"Olo? What's the deal, my dude?"

Still no answer.

She stepped onto the spiral staircase and was halfway down when she realized Olo was standing directly below her, gazing up through the slats in the stairs. Gazing straight up her dress.

Jesus, she thought, and tucked one hand and a bit of fabric between her legs to cut off his view. Whatever maternal instinct she'd felt a moment ago fled quickly from her, leaving her feeling hollow and tricked, somehow.

"Go run and hide, Olo…"

But he had already vanished down the hall on silent feet.

Her own plodding footsteps coming down the metal stairs: *thunk-thunk-thunk*.

She felt lightheaded when she reached the ground floor. Had that weird spiral staircase made her dizzy? Directly across from her and nestled in a shadowed corner of the front hall, the second hand of the ancient grandfather clock chugged with steady precision; its ticking echoed throughout the foyer.

She crossed down the hall and past the parlor, down another corridor where doors lined both sides of the hallway. Roger Smalls' office was back there somewhere, she knew; she'd gone in there on one previous occasion when Olo's parents hadn't been home, and pored through a few raunchy, poorly written pages from a bloated manuscript that sat on Mr. Smalls' desk. She'd been curious to read his work, but Roger Smalls' writing had turned her off; it was disjointed, messy, and the characters' names kept changing. There was something indescribably desperate about it, and it had left her uneasy.

"Ready or not, here I come," she said, her voice echoing down the hall ahead of her.

She went to open one of the doors, but found it was locked. A second door was locked, too. As was a third.

The hallway cut sharply to the right, and she followed it. Which room was Roger Smalls' office again? She couldn't remember. The goddamn house was so *big*.

Here, she thought, and gripped a cool brass doorknob. Turned it. It *was* Roger Smalls' office, or at least she thought it was, but it looked different now. The walls were bare. The large mahogany desk was gone, as were the bookshelves she recalled from her previous visit. Mr. Smalls' typed manuscript pages were still in here, only now they lay scattered about the floor—damn near papering the entire floor, in fact. She picked up one of the pages, her head beginning to spin a little bit faster. A part of her still felt like she was going down, down, down that spiral staircase.

Typed in the center of the page was:

```
myself asks
am i here?
i've lost myself
i fear
```

She let this page waft to the floor. Those words had made her uncomfortable, although she couldn't say why. She looked down at her feet, noticing that every single page had that same queer little poem—or whatever it was—typed onto it.

Iris stepped back out into the hallway.

"Come out, come out, wherever you are," she called.

…ever you are…ever you are…ever you are, replied her echo.

She went back down the hall, expecting to come out past the parlor again. Instead, the hallway cut to the left. *Yes, okay, I cut right, so now I cut left to get back*. She turned the corner, then went still.

The hallway stretched on ahead of her for an impossible distance. She hadn't come this way after all, yet she couldn't figure out how she had gotten so turned around in a hallway. Moreover, *this* hallway seemed longer than the whole goddamn *house*.

"Hello? Olo, my dude? Are you down there?"

She didn't like the tremor she heard in her voice.

…own there…own there…own there…

Echoes never ask questions, she found herself thinking, and it was an unexpected thing to think, something that only served to unsettle her further. *They only respond…respond…respond…*

She turned back around and hurried now in the direction she *believed* to be the way back toward the center of the house. But ahead of her was nothing but hallway, and more hallway, and more hallway. Farther ahead, she could see a *second* hallway intersecting with *this* hallway, and *that* couldn't be right. Could it?

The hallway is the echo, she thought, and this thought incited a finger of panic to rise up in her. What it meant, she had no idea, but she couldn't deny that she was perspiring like a hostage now and fresh out of patience. Where *was* that goddamn kid?

Had he shut a door on her?

To confuse her?

To lock her in this hallway?

To mess with her head—

How big is this house?

"Olo! Enough, now! Where are you? Let me out of here!"

…ere…ere…ere…

"Help! Hello!"

…elp ello…elp ello…elp ello…

She raced back down the hallway, yanking on doorknobs to see if any might open. None did. Behind one, she heard the slow lament of the grandfather clock out in the foyer. *A-ha!* She grabbed the knob, twisted it…but it wouldn't budge. This was the way out, wasn't it? She could *hear* the goddamn *clock* in the goddamn *foyer*. Impossibly slow and growing impossibly slower, that second hand nearly grinding to a halt, as though the clock was winding to a stop, but it was *still out there*. It went *tick-tock*, and not *tock-tick*, because—

—*because the order is always I, A, O, or simply I, O in this case, it's the unspoken grammatical rule of English, the ablaut reduplication, and it's never the opposite, never the flip side of a—*

(world)

—word, unless of course that clock is, in actuality, going tock-tick, tock-tick, tock-tick, *and I'm lost somewhere on the other side of it all, on the other side of the wor—*

—because he *had* locked her in here, hadn't he, the little weirdo?

The clock stopped ticking.

…eirdo…eirdo…eirdo…

Iris screamed.

9

Maribel Sinclair left for the airport Friday morning in a big white SUV that pulled up to Helix House and idled in the driveway like some large predatory cat. She gave Olo a stiff hug, and with all the tenderness of an automaton, administered a cold, emotionless kiss to his forehead. Olo was wearing his favorite necktie, the bright red one with the thin gold stripes. He had his clown mask perched atop his tangle of blond hair.

The driver of the SUV—a big fellow in a pale blue turban—got out and carried Maribel's bags to the car. He loaded them in the back, then turned around to stare with unmasked bewilderment at Mrs. Keeley with her pruning shears and Lulu the Dancer frozen in mid-pirouette, her peeling gray torso tethered in ivy.

Roger watched from the porch. He was smoking a cigarette and leaning against one of the wrought iron helixes, a medicated look on his face. It wasn't until the SUV was halfway down the driveway that Olo's stepfather raised his hand and muttered a barely audible, "Safe travels, love of my life. Bon voyage."

Olo joined Roger on the porch.

"Don't look so morose," Roger told him.

Olo didn't think he looked morose at all. In fact, he was feeling pretty upbeat.

"Seriously," Roger said, staring down at him with hard, dark eyes. "Lose the face, kid."

Olo pulled the clown mask down.

10

Olo didn't see his stepfather for the rest of the afternoon, which was just fine by him, since he had so much to do to get ready for tomorrow's party. The machinegun rattle of Roger's old typewriter filled the hallways and corridors and echoed up the spiral staircase to the second story of Helix House for much of that day, pausing only when his stepfather staggered to the wet bar to refill his drink.

Olo set to work baking himself the first of several birthday cakes. Double chocolate with fudgy brown icing and chocolate sprinkles on top. He was giddy the entire time he mixed the batter. He readjusted his clown mask so he could read the baking instructions on the back of the box clearly, then relished the smell of the cake baking in the oven. He ate spoonfuls of sugary chocolate icing straight out of the container while he watched the timer.

Once the cake was taken from the oven and sat cooling on a rack on the counter, Olo set to work preparing dinner for him and his stepfather—chocolate chip pancakes with whipped cream and extra syrup, and two tall, frosty glasses of chocolate milk (also with whipped cream on top). As the gooey pancake batter burbled and hissed in the hot skillet, Olo sprinkled handfuls of chocolate chips into them, then shoveled a handful of chocolate chips up under his mask and into his mouth.

Just as Olo was setting the table in the dining room, he noticed a peculiar smell in the house. Had he left something burning in the oven? No, the oven was clear. So where was that burning smell coming from? Olo went to find out.

Roger swayed drunkenly in the parlor, his body a dazzling orange in the glow of the fire dancing in the hearth. He was clutching a thick ream of paper, and as Olo came into the room, Roger stripped a few sheets off the top and let them sail to their fiery deaths into the fireplace.

"What are you doing?" Olo asked.

Startled, Roger whirled around. Black tendrils of smoke spooled up out of the hearth and formed a screen in front of Grandfather Tiptree's portrait. Olo guessed that Roger hadn't opened the flue all the way.

"Do you want to know a secret, Olo? A grown-up secret, since you're poised to be ten years old tomorrow?" There was a low, sandpapery quality to his stepfather's voice. He often sounded like this when he was wrestling with a particularly uncooperative piece of fiction, be it a short story or one of his many unfinished novels.

"What are you burning?" Olo asked.

"My novel. The one I was going to take with me tomorrow. It's useless. I don't know what I was thinking. I don't know why I bother trying." He stripped another sheet off the top of the stack and let it flutter down into the flames.

"You don't have another copy, do you?"

"All first drafts must be written on a typewriter, Olo," he instructed, and whipped another few pages into the hearth. "You know that. Otherwise, I'm just *processing* words instead of *writing* them."

"What's the secret you wanted to tell me?" Olo asked.

"Your mother is a vampire."

Olo laughed. He thought his stepfather was joking.

"I'm not joking," said Roger. "She's not the kind that bites your neck and sucks your blood. Would almost be better if she was, this way people would *see* the damage she's done to me. No, sir. All she needs to do is get close. Sit right next to you and invade your aura. Soak up all the gamma rays that make an artist an artist. Took me *years* to realize this, but I finally have, son. Your mother is a vampire of deep thought and dreamy abstraction. A *creativity* vampire, siphoning the artistry right out of my soul. She's the goddamn anti-muse, Olo."

"*Mother* is?" Olo said, making sure he understood what his stepfather was saying. Sometimes, when Roger was in one of his MOODS, Olo wasn't sure he understood him completely.

There was a glass of some amber liquid on the mantelpiece; Roger snatched it up and dumped its contents down his throat as Olo watched. The flames in the fireplace grew taller and brighter, hungry for more pages.

"When I met your mother, I had grand notions. I had *talent*. I was a writing *machine*, Olo, riding a wave. Do you know I once wrote an entire novel-length manuscript—I'm talking just over eighty thousand words, okay?—in exactly four days. That's the God's honest truth. Back then, my creativity was always hungry. That was me, just feeding the muse. Grist for the mill, never batting an eye. Feed, feed, feed. It came so goddamn *naturally* that it never felt like work. It never felt like…like cutting your wrists and bleeding on the goddamn page…"

Roger tossed the empty glass into the fire, where it shattered against the brickwork.

"The real fucking kicker, Olo, is that I'm still sitting here, letting it happen. I *feed* it to her. I've been letting her drain all my talent from me, some unwitting slab of meat living under the same roof, ignorant that she was dining on my soul, bit by bitter bit. And now that I've figured it out, I'm still goddamn doing it. Because what a goddamn sucker I am."

"If Mother is the vampire," Olo said, "then *she's* the sucker."

Roger studied him blearily from the opposite end of the room. His Adam's apple juddered, and then a laugh wrenched itself free of his throat. "Christ, that's funny, Olo. You're a funny kid."

Olo gave his stepfather a proud smile.

"Do you know what it's like existing as a life-support system for an anti-muse?"

"Nope," said Olo.

"I'm a shell. A husk. I'm no different than those creepy-ass dummies you got out front. Word of advice, now that you're ten and practically a man? *Don't be a writer, Olo*. It ain't worth it."

"I already made a book," Olo told him.

Roger waved a dismissive hand at him. "Christ, Olo, you don't *make* books. You *write* them. You're not a fucking printing press. You're not Johannes Gutenberg." He fed more manuscript pages into the fire.

"If you burn your novel," Olo said, "then what will you bring to your publishing thing tomorrow?"

"There *is* no publishing thing tomorrow, Olo. It was canceled weeks ago."

Olo didn't understand. "Then why did you tell Mother you had to go?"

"Because what's left for me to say? 'Have a lovely trip, dear! I'll stay home and play house with your son! Go on and *be a writer*!' My bloody soul trembles from all that she's stolen from me."

He tossed the remaining pages into the fire, then leaned with his hands braced against the mantelpiece as he watched them burn. From the parlor's entryway, Olo watched them burn, too.

"Books are magic, Olo, which makes writers the only true magicians. Dark, terrible magicians."

The wheels were turning in Olo's head. "If Mother is a vampire, does that make me a vampire, too?"

Roger peered at his stepson from over his shoulder. Half his face was lit by firelight, the other half awash in shadow. "Could be, son," he said, his voice low. There was something wolf-like in the one eye that Olo could see. "Could be."

The two of them watched the fire until there was nothing left of Roger Smalls' manuscript but a snarl of gray smoke clinging to the rafters.

"Can I show you what my book does?" Olo said eventually.

11

The venerable Lucy Betancourt was once trapped in an underground bunker, a prisoner of the cannibalistic serial killer Joseph Janx. She'd been on Janx's trail for months, but in typical Lucy Betancourt fashion, she'd gotten in over her head. Now, she was trapped in the madman's dank concrete bunker one hundred feet belowground, surrounded by the half-eaten, rotting corpses of Janx's prior victims. The smell was gag-inducing; fortunately, Lucy Betancourt had long ago mastered control over her olfactory sense while under the tutelage of a blind *shinobi* in the Shimōsa Province of Honshū.

Janx preferred to eat his victims alive. He liked to carve off bits and pieces of them while they watched in horror, shrieking with terror and writhing in pain. He found the nipples the most delectable, with the genitals (of either gender) coming in at a close second. Judging by the decomposition of some of the corpses in the bunker, old Janx had been at it for a very, very long time.

Lucy Betancourt was not repulsed by the dead. In fact, the sight of all those bodies only fueled her will to survive. She would never give up. At the very least, she'd take the son of a bitch to hell with her, if it came to that.

"It's only a matter of time before he comes for me with his knife and his cutting board and his KISS THE COOK apron," Lucy muttered to herself, searching the cinderblock walls of the bunker for a way out. There was none, of course; the only way out was the way *in*, which was through a steel door by which Janx might arrive at any moment.

Yet maybe the way out *was* through that door. That door would have to open in order for Janx to step through. Only problem was that Janx weighed a cool three hundred pounds, easy. Even with all her *ninjutsu* training, Lucy didn't think she could overpower Janx in mere hand-to-hand combat. She needed to be *smarter* than him. Defeat him with her *brain power*.

One corpse buried far in the back of the room caught Lucy's attention. Unlike the others, which lay about in various stages of decomposition, choice cuts removed from their bodies, stripped down to the bare, bite-marked flesh, this corpse was nothing but a skeleton dressed in a filthy gray sweater and slacks. Its eye sockets were spongy with spiderwebs. It was the oldest of all Janx's corpses by far. The only one still dressed, too.

That's because he didn't kill that one, Lucy realized.

Which meant the bones belonged to Janx's *mother*.

The psychological profile cobbled together by the FBI stated that Janx had most likely been reverential toward his mother as a child, even fearful of her. He wouldn't have dared harm her, and would have actually done anything within his power to please her. Once she'd died, he would have kept her corpse close by.

"I'll use his weakness against him," Lucy said aloud, her voice reverberating off the walls of that small concrete chamber.

Moments later, when Joseph Janx came squeezing through the metal door, a ravenous gleam in his eyes, the blade of his knife shining, he was shocked to find a woman standing before him wearing his mother's sweater. Was *this* his mother?

"Put down the knife, son," said the woman in the gray sweater.

Never one to disobey his mother, Janx let the boning knife clatter to the cement floor.

The woman in the gray sweater—his *mother*?—approached. She held her gaze on him, and he shied away, ashamed.

"Put down the cutting board, son," she said.

Janx opened his large hand and let the cutting board strike the floor.

When the woman in the gray sweater bent down to retrieve the boning knife, he remembered there had been *another* woman down here, a police detective that he had hoped to eat, so where had *she*—

Lucy Betancourt thrust the knife into Joseph Janx's belly.

Janx screamed.

Lucy grabbed the cutting board and used it to hammer the blade deeper into Janx's guts. Blood gushed from the rent in Janx's KISS THE COOK apron, and Lucy didn't stop until the handle of the boning knife was swallowed up inside the wound.

And while several critics would go on to complain that Lucy Betancourt's escape from the dungeon of the cannibalistic serial killer Joseph Janx plagiarized from the conclusion of *Friday the 13th Part 2*, Lucy Betancourt in fact *did* escape, and all because she'd used Joseph Janx's one weakness against him…

12

"What the hell am I looking at?"

Olo had his special book opened up for his stepfather on the dining room table. Up until now, Iris had been the only other person to see it, and her reaction had been wholly different than Roger's. His stepfather stared down at the paper-and-cardboard house poking up from the pages of Olo's book, glancing at it from various angles, running the palm of one hand across the tops of the paper spires. It was as though he were unable to see it properly no matter which angle he viewed it from.

"It's our house," explained Olo. "I made it."

"This isn't a *book*. This is…is…I don't know *what* this is…"

"Watch what it does," Olo said. He reached over and took the tip of the chopstick between two fingers. Gave it a firm twist.

The little paper staircase twirled around. At the same time, a sound like metal scraping against metal echoed into the dining room from the foyer.

Roger looked up at the sound. "The hell was that?"

"Go see," Olo told him.

Roger stared at the darkened doorway that led to the foyer for several drawn-out seconds. Then he crossed the room and stepped out into the front hall. Olo grabbed his clown mask from the table and pulled it down over his face as he followed his stepfather into the foyer.

Roger Smalls stood at the foot of the spiral staircase, staring up into a black chamber of nothingness high above his head. The entrance to the staircase faced a different direction now, but that wasn't the only difference; dark bruise-colored smoke pressed against the second-story windows and, from Roger's and Olo's vantage down here in the foyer, the upstairs landing looked somehow more spacious than it had just moments ago.

"What…what the hell's going on?" Roger uttered.

"Go on up and see," Olo said from behind his mask.

Slowly, Roger ascended the staircase. He wound around and

around, Olo following not too far behind, until they were both upstairs and gazing at a half dozen corridors that branched off from the staircase, like the spokes in a wheel.

Olo heard his stepfather's sudden intake of breath.

"*What in the world…?*"

A series of wall sconces blinked on along the length of the corridor directly in front of them. Even with this sudden illumination, it was impossible to see to the end of the corridor. What they *could* see were the rows of doors on both sides of the hall, each one as white as bone and with a shimmery brass lever for a handle.

Moving with the lassitude of someone in a dream, Roger advanced down the corridor. He grazed the wall with his fingers, touched one of the glass sconces with its dancing flames, and paused before one of the closed doors. His shadow was fractured into many, spearing out from him in all directions.

He reached out, gripped the nearest door handle, tried to crank it.

"Locked," Roger muttered. It sounded like he was talking to himself, as if he'd forgotten all about Olo.

"That door is not for you," Olo said from somewhere behind him.

Roger was panting with either fear or excitement, or maybe a cocktail of both. "What's going on? Are we still in the house?"

"Sort of," Olo said. "A house in a book."

"How…?"

"You can't be here tomorrow," Olo said from behind his clown mask. "You'll mess up my birthday plans. You need to go to your publishing party."

"What are you—"

Olo lifted a hand and pointed farther down the corridor.

Roger turned, looked to where his stepson was pointing—

13

—and saw that someone had written something in black crayon on one of the doors farther down the hallway. Wooziness pulsed inside the confines of his skull, not all of it due to alcohol. As he drew closer, the words on the door took shape, rising out of the gloom until they revealed themselves in the flickering glow of a pair of wall sconces:

Roger's Publishing Party
(have a good time!!!)

I'm drunk and I'm dreaming, he told himself. *I'm passed out with my face on the keys of my typewriter. I'll wake up hung over in a few hours with QWERTY imprinted on my forehead…*

Here, in this drunken nightmare, he reached out and gripped the door's cold brass lever. Unlike the previous door handle, this one rotated easily in his trembling hand. It felt to Roger as though the door had been *waiting* for him to open it.

He looked over at the smallish clown in the necktie standing in the dimness of the hallway behind him. Hadn't Olo been there just a moment ago? Where had the boy gone? Who was this small clown staring up at him with those blank, ovoid eyes?

"I can't go in there," Roger said. "I…I've burned my manuscript. They'll all laugh at me. I'm such a fool."

A sob trembled up his throat. A part of his mind told him that he didn't need to sob, this was all an alcohol-fueled nightmare, and that his novel was safe and sound in his office. Another part of his mind told him that the figure standing with him in this hallway *wasn't* a clown, not really. It was just a child wearing a plastic mask. Of course it was. He'd already known that, hadn't he? Also, why was he so damn *lightheaded* all of a sudden? He felt as though he were in a continuous freefall, picking up speed as he plummeted to greater and greater depths.

Picking up speed...or freezing in time?

He squinted at the child—

"Olo?"

—but the clown was gone.

No, Roger thought, amid a throb of panic. *No!*

He moved sluggishly back down the corridor in the direction he had come. But now there was nothing but a chasm of lightlessness where the second-floor landing should have been. He hesitated before crossing into that darkness, but ultimately went, groping blindingly for the handrail of the spiral staircase.

A door slammed behind him, loud as a gunshot. He jumped and cried out.

A second door slammed.

A third.

But all those doors were closed! his mind screamed, trying to mine some reasonableness out of all this sudden madness. *What doors are slamming? What nightmare is this? Where am I?*

He was disoriented, unsure if he had actually reached the landing after all. He turned and jogged back down the corridor, those flickering wall sconces impossibly far away now, *and how had that happened?*

He whirled drunkenly around—

—only to slam against another door. A door that hadn't been there a moment ago.

Something shifted in the darkness behind him. He twisted around, and a sense of relief flooded through him as he recognized his surroundings: he was downstairs in the parlor. The fire had gone out in the hearth, dousing the room in a pearlescent gloom. A dense white fog had rushed up to the bank of windows and the glass patio door, occluding the moon. But it was the parlor, all right.

How did I get downstairs?

His eyes jittered up at the oil painting above the mantelpiece. The thing on the canvas was no longer Maribel's father, Bartholomew Tiptree, but a thing that had retreated into the black depths of the painting itself. Roger could make out only its eyes, glowering mistily like a pair of distant headlamps cutting through fog.

Roger spun around again and found that he wasn't in the parlor at all, but up against the wall of a small, square room, hardly bigger than an upright coffin. There was no source to the light now, and it was fading fast. Panicked, he turned back to the door, but now there was nothing but a blank wall there—not even a door handle for him to futilely grope.

"*Hey! Hey! The hell's going on? Let me out of here! Let me out of here!*"

He slammed his fists against the wall—

14

—while in that shocking pink bedroom, Iris Garin bolted upright on her tartan bedspread and listened in horror to the muted cries reverberating from somewhere deep within that strange and terrible house, while—

15

—Maribel Sinclair, just a few blocks from the Javits Convention Center in New York City, sat drinking a glass of cabernet at a hotel bar, having deliberately chosen a seat beside one of the more notable, award-winning novelists of our time, not to talk, not even to observe, but to solely subsist in this novelist's gravitational pull, never drawing attention to herself, not even making eye contact, but merely existing within this artist's proximity, breathing him in, while—

16

—the final vestige of that meager light fled completely from the tiny coffin-sized room, dousing Roger Smalls in the blackest darkness of his life.

17

The clown mask still secured to his face and his blood-red clip-on necktie perfectly straight, Olo Tiptree descended the spiral staircase and arrived in a bleak and desolate foyer. All the lights were off, and a swirling darkness—a darkness tinged with violent streaks of purple—pressed itself against the windows. Hallways were laid out in every direction, while the massive front doors of Helix House— of *this version* of Helix House—stood as impervious as the doorway of an Egyptian tomb.

Olo wandered back into the dining room to find his book still splayed open on the table, exactly where he'd left it. He peered over the top of the paper-and-cardboard pop-up house, his eyes tracing the mazelike construct of tiny paper rooms and hand-cut hallways, where even the cleverest of mice would be forever lost. The paper house tantalized him, with its congestion of windows and hallways and dark, hidden rooms.

With great care, Olo tore around the perimeter of one room,

amputating it from the rest of the hallway. It came out as a small cube of paper held together by tabs of scotch tape. The door with Olo's tiny, meticulous writing on it was just a paper flap, nothing more.

Olo carried the tiny paper room into the parlor, where he pitched it into the fire that still burned in the hearth.

TWO:

THE BIRTHDAY PARTY

1

Saturday morning saw Peyton Joya rise earlier than normal. It was summer vacation, and when she didn't have to get up early for a baseball game, she enjoyed sleeping in. But something had roused her earlier than usual on this particular Saturday, and it was no use lying in bed, trying to go back to sleep. Particularly when the sun had found a hole in her dark curtains and drilled a beam of white light into her left eye.

It's not the sun that woke you, girlie, she told herself, rolling over so that the javelin of daylight couldn't stab at her. *You had one shit show of a nightmare. That's what woke you*. Or were they called daymares—or morningmares—when they happened in the early hours of the morning?

She climbed out of bed and stood before the full-length beveled mirror that was angled in one corner of her bedroom. She was more than halfway to twelve, and much to her displeasure, she was beginning to notice the discrepancies between her body and those belonging to the grimy, smelly boys on her team.

Mom had big boobs, she thought, and not without a touch of despair. *Will I have big boobs, too?*

It seemed like a criminal sentence.

Also, what else is there? Something on the tip of my brain. Ha ha, is that a thing? Tip of the brain? Brain-tips? Whatever it is, there's something I'm forgetting today. Or is there?

She hit the bathroom, cleaned herself up, then crept down the hall toward the kitchen. Her sisters were still asleep, and her father's bedroom door was closed, which meant he was still sawing wood, too. Peyton didn't want to wake them—more for her own peace and quiet than anything else—so she kept silent.

In the kitchen, she switched on the small TV on the counter, muted it with the remote, then dug a bowl out of the cupboard. She relished the *shwwwsh* of her favorite sugary cereal filling the bowl—it was the only vice she allowed herself, food-wise—then she drowned the whole mess in almond milk. On the TV were yesterday's box scores; she studied them while she ate.

Twenty minutes later, she was in the garage doing chin-ups on the bar. Eleven of them today. Three weeks ago, she could only do four. That was progress. She'd also added an average of thirteen yards to her hits, and that was *also* progress. If you were to rank the best hitters on the Bristol Bangers, Peyton Joya might not have been number one, but she'd be in the top three for sure.

Her father was still asleep but the twins were up by the time Peyton came back into the house, her shoulders sore and her arms turned to jelly. Ceshia and Callie were in their PJs watching *True and the Rainbow Kingdom* as they sat cross-legged on the couch in the living room. They giggled when they saw how damp and frazzled their older sister looked, then knocked their heads together to whisper conspiracies about her. Peyton made them breakfast— two more bowls of cereal, *shwwwsh* and *shwwwsh*—then warned them not to spill any on the couch unless they wanted to incite Dad's wrath.

More whispers and giggles from the twins.

Peyton took a quick shower then got dressed in her Bristol Bangers jersey and ball cap. Today's game was at two o'clock, which meant she could spend the rest of the morning down at the batting cages on Fleet Street practicing her swing. Just as long as Daddy didn't insist she take the twins someplace.

As she sat on the edge of her bed and laced up her sneakers, she saw the folded piece of red construction paper on her nightstand. The happy face smiled up at her.

That's right! That weird kid's birthday party is today. Is that what's been on my brain-tip all morning?

Was she actually going to attend?

She'd seen the kid around town before, skulking by himself along the outskirts of the playground, or standing by the road that ran in front of his big house while he watched the cars drive by. He was homeschooled, which meant he was a social misfit as far as the kids in her class were concerned, but that didn't mean he should have to spend his birthday all alone. Did it?

He must have some *friends*, she told herself.

If he did, would he have showed up at the park to hand out birthday invitations to a bunch of strangers? countered a different part of her.

If he doesn't have friends, then it's for a good reason, she rationalized.

Or maybe no one has given the poor dummy a chance, came the counterargument.

He wore a stupid clown mask to the park! she insisted, and there it was—game, set, match.

Because he's ashamed and lonely and doesn't know any better, came the counterargument.

Game? Set? Match?

"Craaaaaap," she groaned, and stuffed the invitation in the pocket of her jeans.

2

Disregarding Detective Lewis's advice that he stay away, Tony Davis pulled his car up the long gravel driveway of Helix House at around eleven o'clock that Saturday morning. He'd been up to the house on three or four occasions in the past, whenever Iris's banger of a ride was in the shop. His last trek out here had been the night Iris had gone missing. She'd failed to show up at his apartment after work and all of his calls to her cell phone had gone straight to voicemail without ringing, as though she'd had the thing turned off.

He'd been worried about her when she hadn't answered any of his calls, but when he pulled up in front of the large house and saw her car parked out front, relief had washed over him. But when Mr. Smalls answered the door and told him Iris wasn't there, a host of fresh worry accosted him. He and Mr. Smalls examined Iris's car and saw that the driver's side front tire was flat. There was an inch-wide gash along the tire's outer rim. That explained why the car was still here...but where the hell was Iris?

Mr. Smalls didn't know. Neither did that strange kid, Olo, whom Tony had spoken with before calling the police. His mild concern had quickly elevated to panic.

I'm looking into it, Tony, Detective Lewis had promised him. *You just gotta let me handle it and leave those people alone. I don't need you going up to that house seeking your own answers and making things more difficult for me.*

But it had been nearly a month now, and Detective Lewis wasn't any closer to finding out what had happened to Iris. The police were unable to trace her phone and they'd uncovered no footage of her on traffic cameras in town, be it on foot or in someone else's car. Tony Davis felt as though he were wading through a swamp while the flesh was being nibbled from his bones. He'd postponed moving to California, his new employers agreeing to delay his start date, because he knew he couldn't leave without Iris. There was no *life in California* without Iris. His apartment was still filled with all her wedding magazines.

Where are you, Iris? What the hell happened to you?

Tony had begun to wonder if Roger Smalls hadn't done something to Iris. And even though Detective Lewis wouldn't come right out and say so, he knew the detective was thinking that, too. Iris had never complained about Smalls, but she *had* said he was a drunk and on a few occasions she'd heard him ranting to himself behind the closed door of his home office. Detective Lewis had said they were "working on" getting Roger Smalls' fingerprints. If Roger Smalls hadn't done anything wrong, why the holdup? It felt suspicious to Tony.

There was a boy standing on the front porch, tying a bundle of underinflated balloons to the railing. This was Olo Tiptree, whom Tony had met on a few occasions, although most of what he knew about the boy had come from listening to Iris's stories. Iris had a soft spot for the helpless and the downtrodden—it was one of her more endearing qualities, Tony would have to admit—and friendless, overweight Olo Tiptree certainly fit that mold. Even now, as Olo heard the vehicle approaching, the boy looked up and Tony saw that he was wearing a creepy plastic mask. A clown mask. He was a strange goddamn kid, for sure, and the sight of that mask caused the palms of Tony's hands to perspire.

No creepier than these monstrosities, Tony thought, rolling slowly past the quartet of mannequins that stood frozen in the overgrown, weedy flowerbeds that flanked the driveway. If this wasn't the most *Twilight Zone* thing he'd ever seen…

Tony parked, got out of the car, and strode up the cracked flagstones that led to the porch. "Hey, there. Olo, right? Do you remember me?"

Olo plucked the mask off his head. His blond curls shined like pyrite, and his face was blotchy from the heat. He wore a preposterous clip-on tie, red as a rosebush.

"I'm Tony, Iris's boyfriend."

"Fiancé," Olo corrected.

"Yeah, that's right. Are your parents home?"

"No, sir."

Aren't kids always supposed to say their parents are home when a stranger asks? Growing up, if Tony and his brothers had been home alone and someone came knocking on the door, he always told the knocker that his mom was in the shower. That was one of Mom's rules. Did kids not do that anymore?

"Any idea when they'll be back? Your dad in particular?"

"Stepdad."

"That's right," Tony agreed.

"Um," Olo said.

Tony Davis felt something cross the space between them, snapping like sparks.

"Mother is in New York," Olo said. "Roger went to a publishing event in Haymarket."

"They left you home alone?"

"Roger will be back this evening."

Tony peered up at the house, and at the ranks of dark windows, where he anticipated seeing a face returning his gaze. Because he felt like he was being watched from some improbable distance. But there were no faces in the windows. There was no one there.

Tony got back in his car and headed down the sloping gravel driveway toward the bottom of the hill. Those faceless mannequins observed his departure, and there was something about one of them in particular—the one posed as a ballerina—that struck him as inexplicably significant. He even slowed the car as he drove by so he could get a good look at its ivy-wrapped torso, its outstretched wooden arms with those crude, fingerless hands. The way it balanced on one formless leg…

Something about it…

What is it what is it what is it?

He kept driving, even though a part of his brain urged him to stop, to get out, to go over and study that terrible thing more closely. Because he felt like he was overlooking something—something important. When he glanced up at the rearview mirror, he saw the boy still standing on the porch, watching his retreat.

He had put his mask back on.

3

The man's car had already disappeared from view, leaving a rooster tail of dust in its wake, when Olo lifted his hand and waved goodbye. He wondered if the man—Tony—was lonely now without Iris. It made Olo sad to consider this, but then he wondered whether worrying about someone else's loneliness was yet another one of those WEIRD THINGS his mother was always reprimanding him about.

Iris was lonely, too, Olo knew. She'd been tucked away by herself in there for too long. That wasn't good, but he was going to fix that today. After today, she wouldn't be alone in there, and Olo would have a whole bunch of NEW FRIENDS.

It made him think of poor Mr. Cooper—

BAD IDEA, interrupted the brain-shout. But Olo couldn't help but think about the old man now. If he tried hard enough, he could almost imagine him sitting at the bottom of the porch steps, drinking from a bottle of chilled Coca-Cola.

Once upon a time (before Iris arrived), Mr. Cooper had been Olo's best friend. He was a ruddy-faced, cheerful old man who not only cut the lawn and trimmed the trees around the property, but also sculpted the topiaries that flanked the long gravel driveway. Mr. Cooper had possessed more than just a green thumb; he'd had an artist's eye. He taught Olo the names of all the flowers on the property—those that grew wild, such as the New England asters and the fiery blanket flowers, as well as those that Mr. Cooper had planted here himself, "for a little zip." Mr. Cooper had also done a lot of repairs around the house, and he often let Olo watch as he replaced rotted wood on the porch or applied a fresh coat of paint to the railing.

Mr. Cooper had always worn faded overalls and a straw cowboy hat. The hat was in awful shape, and there were sections where the weave had come apart, allowing tufts of Mr. Cooper's cottony white hair to poke through. One afternoon, as they sat on the porch steps drinking Coca-Cola from cold bottles, Mr. Cooper told Olo that the sick in his belly was getting worse and he wouldn't be coming around anymore after this week. This terrified Olo, since Mr. Cooper was his only friend. Olo had wept and Mr. Cooper had slung an arm around the boy's shoulders to comfort him. Before he left that afternoon, he'd placed his tattered cowboy hat on Olo's head.

Lying in bed that night with his clown mask on, Olo allowed a strange little plan to formulate inside the confines of his skull. That odd pop-up book he'd been compelled to create? The one he'd worked on for the past several months, hidden away in his bedroom as if committing some dark treachery? It did strange and wonderful things to the house—things he hadn't told anyone about. More and more frequently he would slip down one of those impossible hallways and wander around in that other world for incalculable amounts of time, lulled into an inexplicable state of serenity by the dizzying, ambrosial nature of that other world.

WHAT IF, said the brain-shout...only this time it was less a shout and more like a secret whispered across the undulating contours of his gray matter. *What if you can keep Mr. Cooper in one of those rooms and see him anytime you want?*

And just like that, lying there in the dark on his bed, Olo Tiptree's eyes had grown large behind the eyeholes of his plastic mask.

He had told Mr. Cooper about the crack in the wall at the end of the hallway, and Mr. Cooper had went in search of it, a small tub of spackle in one liver-spotted hand. There had been no crack, of course. Once Mr. Cooper had turned down the hall, Olo got out his special book and proceeded to rearrange things. The echo of Mr. Cooper's sluggish footfalls vanished in an instant.

Olo visited him later that night, the old man tucked away behind a door with his name on it. Olo brought him a Kit Kat bar and a carton of chocolate milk. But Mr. Cooper hadn't been hungry. The old man was seated on the floor, his head slouched against one wall. His legs were splayed out in a V in front of him, and there was a glassy, faraway look in Mr. Cooper's eyes.

"Am I dead?" Mr. Cooper asked. His voice sounded thin and shaky. "Have I died?"

"No, sir," Olo told him. "You're in my book. Safe."

Something akin to a smile spread across Mr. Cooper's sallow face. His cotton-white hair stood up in whorls on his head. "Thank you, son," he said, and touched Olo's cheek with a burlap-rough hand.

Olo would visit Mr. Cooper in that tiny room whenever he could. Sometimes he would bring his checkerboard, and he and Mr. Cooper would play. Mr. Cooper always beat Olo at checkers, but after a while, Olo began turning the tables on him. He thought this was because he'd gotten better, but in reality, he saw that it was because Mr. Cooper had gotten worse. After only a few weeks in that room, Mr. Cooper had forgotten how to play checkers altogether.

Things only got worse from there. Olo wasn't sure why, but he surmised that he had left poor Mr. Cooper tucked away in that paper house all alone for too long, allowing for something inside Mr. Cooper's head to unravel. Loneliness was like that—a thing that plucks at a thread and begins the process of unraveling. Olo understood how that could happen sometimes. The old man began to rant and scream and gibber like an imbecile. He would try to grab and hurt Olo whenever Olo would visit, and he would also hurt himself. Once, Olo watched poor Mr. Cooper dig one of his own eyes from his skull while screeching like a madman, blood spurting down the front of Mr. Cooper's overalls.

GONE MAD, said the brain-shout. *GONE ROTTEN.*

It wasn't until Olo had tucked Iris away in a room of her own did he realize he no longer wanted to be friends with Mr. Cooper. The old man's screams unsettled Olo, and even Iris had commented on hearing him shrieking through the walls from time to time. Olo wondered if he should just let Mr. Cooper go, sending him back out into the *real* world. But Olo was a bright boy, and he'd read enough Lucy Betancourt novels to know that Mr. Cooper might tell Mother what he had done. Or maybe even the police. So instead of letting Mr. Cooper go, Olo took a black crayon and colored in Mr. Cooper's tiny paper room. The next day, when Olo slipped into that world and went up to the door that said—

Mr. Cooper

—on it in Olo's own handwriting, he pressed his ear to it and listened. He could no longer hear the mad ramblings and shrill cries, the gouging of fingernails in wood and flesh alike, from the other side. He dared to open it, and just as he'd suspected, looked upon an endless black void. Poor Mr. Cooper was gone.

Now, a curious white fog settled over Olo's mind as he stood on his porch in the bright sunshine, thinking of all this. His eyes unfocused, blurring the world around him. In that blur, and for the briefest of moments, it appeared as though his friends out in the yard had begun to move about: dear Mrs. Keeley began snipping at those weeds while Lulu the Dancer finally completed her pirouette.

(GONE MAD GONE ROT—)

But then everything snapped back to normal, and Olo was smiling again, and still waving at Tony Davis's car that was now long gone.

4

"The truth is, you may already be dead, and this is hell," said Detective Lucy Betancourt.

Iris turned away from the woman, and gazed back out the misty porthole in the wall. The fog was so great, she couldn't tell if it was nighttime or daytime out there; if there was a torrential downpour or a blistering summer sun. That swirling mist against the glass was as thick as milk, and it reminded her of the fog that had been misting through her own mind for however long she'd been trapped here.

"I mean, it's time to face facts, kiddo," Detective Betancourt said. Her tone was no nonsense, edged in disappointment. "How long you think you've been in this place?"

"I don't know," said Iris.

"Take a guess."

It seemed like an eternity. Yet, at the same time, it seemed like the blink of an eye. Time was nonexistent in this place. When she'd first been locked away, she tried to keep track of days by counting how many times Olo came through the door. If he showed up wearing a different outfit, she considered it a new day. She'd lost count at some point—the fog was sometimes very dense and muddling in her head—but it had surely been weeks. A month? More?

The thing was, she'd hardly eaten. Whenever Olo would come, he'd bring her a tray of food—if you could call candy bars and chocolate milk "food"—but she couldn't remember the last time she'd eaten or drank anything that he had brought her. People died if they went more than three days without water, didn't they? Yet here she was, locked away for an unknowable amount of time, and she'd maybe sipped what amounted to half a carton of chocolate milk. And even that carton was small—the size they give out with school lunches. How was that even possible?

"It's not just the food, and you know it," said Lucy Betancourt. Iris listened to the detective shift across the carpet, the shag as high as an unkempt lawn. Static electricity crackled. "I don't mean to be crass, but when was the last time you copped a squat, kiddo?"

It was true. Iris hadn't felt the need to cop a squat—as Lucy Betancourt had so courteously put it—since she'd been in here. Under normal circumstances, she had the bladder of a hyperactive hummingbird, and couldn't even make it the whole trip to Tony's parents' house in Haymarket without having to pull over at a gas station at least once. But in here? Nada. Zilch. Zip.

"Sleep, too," Lucy Betancourt tossed out there.

Also true. There was the ugly pink bed that had somehow found its way into this room, and while Iris sometimes lay on it to read or to stare forlornly at the ceiling, she'd never slept in here. Even now, exhausted as she was, sleep seemed a thing too far out of her reach. Didn't people die after too many days without sleep?

"Die or go crazy," Lucy Betancourt said.

"I'm not dead and I'm not crazy," Iris told her.

"Yeah? Well, if I were a betting gal," said Lucy Betancourt, "I'd say you're teetering on the precipice of purgatory as we speak. What do you think finally did you in? It must have been something sudden."

"I'm not dead," Iris insisted.

"Struck by a bolt of lightning?" Lucy Betancourt went on. "Gruesomely decapitated? Or perhaps something as pedantic as your basic car accident. Didn't Olo say something about your car getting a flat tire?"

After she'd found herself trapped in this place, Olo had come to her, passing easily through a door Iris herself had been powerless to open. She'd been such a fool back then that she'd actually rushed over to him and scooped him up in a tight embrace. She'd chastised him for tricking her like that, and where the heck was she, anyway?

You're in my book now, Iris, he'd said.

The little shit.

It took some time for her to realize that she was now Olo's prisoner—that *he* had caused this to happen to her. At first, he had kept her in an empty room, where he would visit her periodically. Iris asked him why he was keeping her here, and he'd said it was because he didn't want her to go to California. She kept asking where she *was*, but he kept saying she was in his *book*, and what the hell did that mean?

Each time he left, she tried the door, but it wouldn't open. It was as if only Olo possessed the power to come and go as he pleased. She banged against it, but the door was solid wood. Days went by. Days? She wasn't sure. Hours? Weeks? Time was all messed up in here, and something was intercepting her thoughts, twisting them into knots, and dumping them pell-mell back inside her skull. She sometimes thought she heard other people behind those walls, moaning and crying out, although she couldn't be sure if those sounds were real or manufactured inside her own increasingly unstable mind.

He brought her food, which she didn't eat, and a game of checkers, which she refused to play. She shouted at him and grew angry. That only served to upset Olo, and there were longer stretches between when he'd come to see her again. That would have been fine, but those periods of isolation tore at her mind. Strange thoughts, like calculating the hypotenuse of a triangle or the chemical makeup of magma, kept infiltrating her consciousness. It was as though these strange, unanchored thoughts existed in the air, and she was only breathing them in.

The next time he returned, she pummeled him until he fell to the floor, crying. Then she ran out of the room, straight down a hallway as dark and as bleak as a mineshaft. She slammed up against a wall, turned, and found that all the walls were closing in on her. The ceiling, too. Iris had screamed as the hallway turned into a coffin all around her. She remained there in that tiny rectangle of space, her shrieks muted, her breathy gasps moistening the air around her, claustrophobia suffocating her. He kept her there for some time, though exactly how long, she never knew. When the walls finally widened all around her and Olo was there in his clown mask to lead her back to her room, she was quaking like a puppy. It had been her punishment for hitting him and trying to escape, he'd explained.

She thought maybe she'd catch more flies with honey, as the saying goes, so on his next visit, she played checkers with him. She smiled, although it hurt her face and weakened her spirit to do so. When he asked if she was his best friend, she told him *yes*. And, in turn, *she* kept asking him that same question, over and over again—*Where am I, Olo? Where have you put me?*

His response, never changing: *I told you, Iris. You're in my book. You're a part of my story now. This way, we can be best friends forever. Isn't that nice?*

"Isn't it?" said Lucy Betancourt.

Iris closed her eyes. Sometimes Lucy Betancourt frustrated her, but that was only because the detective was logical, and she enjoyed poking at all of Iris's weak places. Not to torment her, but to clear the fog from her brain and help her think straight.

"Stop it," Iris said, her voice small. Despite Lucy's intentions, it was all a little too much at the moment. "Please."

"Telling me to stop won't help you. You need to think, girl."

Those first few hours, when she realized Olo had trapped her: *You can't keep me in here, wherever we are. People will come looking. Tony. The police. They'll see my car out front and ask questions, Olo.*

But Olo had taken care of that, hadn't he? He'd learned how from one of Maribel Sinclair's novels. Flatten the tire. Say the woman walked off into the night on her own. Who's to say what happened to her from there?

"I see where this is going," Betancourt groused. "You're going to blame me for all this, aren't you? Because he got it from one of my books."

Iris shook her head. Hot tears streamed down her face.

"I can't be responsible for what that kid does," Betancourt said. "He shouldn't even be *reading* those books. Speaking of, how many of my novels have *you* read since you've been in here? Twelve? Fourteen? It's the only thing you can do to while away the hours—*but how many hours has it been? How many days?* Can't read fourteen novels in just a couple of days, kiddo. You've been in here much longer than you realize."

Yes, she knew this to be true. She'd felt this for some time now.

When catching flies with honey proved to be unproductive, she'd tried to escape again, only this time on the sly. Early on, she'd still had her cell phone with her—although it got no signal and the screen was scrambled with strange characters—so she smashed it until it was nothing more than a jagged blade of glass and metal. She used it to dig right through a wall, cutting herself up and bleeding on her dress in the process. But in the end, she clambered through a hole in the drywall and out into a dim hallway with flickering sconces on the walls. The moment she hit that cool, tiled floor, she'd bolted.

She ran through a seemingly never-ending corridor, one that turned and twisted and doubled back on itself. It took her around and around and around. She never reached her own room again—never saw the hole she'd climbed through in the wall—but somehow she knew she was just going in circles.

At some point, she'd staggered out onto the landing. She saw the spiral staircase and the darkened chasm that was the foyer below. Somehow she was on the second floor of Helix House. She hadn't bothered to question how that could be; instead, she dived down the stairs, taking those wrought iron risers two at a time, cackling shrilly as she sank lower toward the foyer, toward freedom, toward—

But she kept going, going, going. Beneath her, the staircase kept rotating. No matter how fast she ran, she made no progress. A goddamn hamster in a wheel.

At some point, overcome by vertigo and sheer exhaustion, she collapsed and tumbled the rest of the way down the stairs. When she finally struck the floor of the foyer, pain exploded in her right ankle. She feared she'd broken it, but it only turned out to be badly sprained.

Sobbing and full of pain, splayed out on the hardwood floor like something shot down from the sky, she looked up to find a slight figure standing above her. He was wearing his clown mask. At the sight of him, she'd started shrieking.

The next thing she knew, she was in this new room. Not a punishment coffin, but something so much like her own childhood bedroom that it was uncanny. He'd somehow given her a bed, and a shelf of Maribel Sinclair's novels. Imprisoned and bored to tears, Iris had read every single one. And when she finished the last one, she had started over again with the first.

"I mean, we're practically soul sisters, you and me," Lucy Betancourt said now. "You know all my deep dark secrets, all the italicized thoughts in my head, straight from the pages of my books. And I, of course, know all your bullshit, too, Iris."

Iris shuddered. "I don't want to talk about you or your books anymore," she heard herself say.

Lucy Betancourt laughed. "Really? Because *Publishers Weekly* calls me compulsively readable. But forget all that. The only question here, Iris, is: *What the fuck are you gonna do?*"

She had planned to launch herself out a window, so she'd asked for one. But the window that appeared in her wall the next day—and was it a day or a week or a minute later?—was no bigger than a hole tunneled by a rabbit in the earth. And whatever the hell was swirling around out there…well, that wasn't freedom.

Lucy Betancourt cleared her throat, and repeated her question: "*What the fuck are you gonna do, girl?*"

Iris knew what the fuck she was going to do. She was going to kill the little shit, that's what she was going to do.

"How?" Lucy asked.

Good question. Iris had attempted it once before, wrenching a leg off her vanity, ready to bludgeon him with it the next time he stepped into the room. Yet the second she broke that vanity's leg free, it crumbled to ash in her hands. It seemed that anything Olo had provided to her could only be used for its intended purpose. Vanity legs weren't meant to bludgeon, so it had crumbled. Bedposts weren't meant to be used as a cudgel, so those, too, crumbled to ash. The only thing that had maintained its integrity had been her cell phone, which she had brought in here with her from the outside, but she had lost it during her attempt to escape this place.

Somehow, Olo had known she'd planned to harm him: he'd arrived later that afternoon, his thick, sweaty neck bulging over his ridiculous clip-on tie, his eyes the color of metal shavings. He'd told her, quite plainly, *If you kill me, Iris, you'll be trapped in here forever. Alone. You won't die, but you'll go quite mad, Iris, and you'll stay that way for an eternity.*

And she knew he was right.

"So what's changed now?" Lucy Betancourt wanted to know. "What's got your ire up enough that you're willing to put that to the test again?"

"I'm dying in here," Iris said. Her voice was barely audible, even to her own ears. "It's only a matter of time before I lose my mind completely anyhow. I gotta get out." She swallowed a lump in her throat formidable as a potato, then added, "Maybe if I kill him, this whole place will cease to exist."

"Do you really believe that?"

Iris didn't know what to believe. She said, "I'd rather kill him and hope I can find my way out than stay here another minute. I'd rather die trying."

"And how will you do it? Another leg off your vanity? Perhaps pelt him to death with my novels over there on that shelf?"

"I'll kill him with my bare hands," Iris said.

And then she began to sob.

5

Howie's was a low-rent sundries shop in downtown Bristol, tucked between the First National Bank and an apothecary that had what looked like dried eucalyptus hanging in the window. Peyton usually visited Howie's to pick up paper towels, toothpaste, cleaning supplies, and other assorted items whenever her father asked. As of five weeks ago, Peyton could add sanitary pads to that list. She'd known what to expect and hadn't freaked when she first saw the bloody asterisk in her underwear, but it would be a lie to say she'd been happy about it. It seemed to be one more reminder of who she *actually* was, instead of who she *wanted* to be, which was the next Jackie Robinson.

Her father had smiled and hugged her when she'd told him what had happened. "Perfectly normal for a girl your age," he'd said, "although I'd be lying if I said I wish your mama wasn't here. But wish in one hand, spit in the other, and see which one fills up faster. I guess you and I will just have to make the best of it, huh?"

Because that's what they'd been doing ever since Peyton's mother had died—they'd been making the best of it.

Peyton still thought of her mother often. She tried not to remember her the way she'd looked near the end, as the cancer turned her into an all-you-can-eat buffet, but instead as she'd been for much of Peyton's life—spry, quick to laugh, a sparkle in her deep brown eyes.

Peyton walked up and down the aisles of Howie's, taking in all the random junk that kids a little younger than herself might care to play with. Boring yo-yos and sidewalk chalk and airplanes made of balsawood—was this junk from the 1980s or what?

"Listen," she said, startling the middle-aged white woman behind the checkout counter. "I need to get a birthday gift for a ten-year-old boy. You got anything besides yo-yos and chalk?"

The stony expression on the woman's face suggested she didn't appreciate having her morning disturbed by the inquiries of children. Peyton didn't recognize her, so she assumed she must be new. The woman gestured with one plump hand toward a rack of Amazon gift cards. The smallest denomination was twenty-five bucks.

"I don't think that's a good gift," Peyton said. "Anyway, they're pretty expensive."

"Exactly how much are you willing to spend, young lady?"

"I was thinking more like four bucks?"

"I'm not sure you could even afford the yo-yo," said the woman. "This isn't a toy store, you know."

Peyton frowned. She glanced down at the shelves of candy in front of the counter, but even that stuff was crap: Necco wafers, Trident gum, packets of breath mints. Where were the sleeves of Reese's Cups and the bags of Skittles?

"You want to turn out your pockets," said the woman behind the counter. It wasn't a question.

Peyton thought she'd misheard her. "What?"

"First of all, it's 'excuse me,' not 'what.' Second of all, I know you took something off that shelf back there. So turn out your pockets."

"You mean, did I *steal* anything?"

"You heard me, young lady."

"I didn't steal anything. I don't steal."

"Turn out your pockets and let's have a look."

"No. I will *not*."

"If you don't," said the woman, "I'll call the police."

"Go ahead and call the stupid police," Peyton said. She turned and marched to the door.

"Got you on camera, too, sweetheart," the woman called after her.

She left Howie's feeling ashamed and defeated, but also wondering if this was a sign. Like, maybe she didn't *have* to go to that weird kid's party. She gave it a try and came up empty-handed. Was accused of stealing and nearly had the cops called on her. Goddamn it.

I guess you and I will just have to make the best of it, huh? she heard her father say, and could even see his warm, tired smile in the forefront of her mind.

She realized she was trembling. Her face burned. She hurried down the block, anxious to put distance between her and the horrible woman behind the counter in Howie's. She didn't care if she bled like a stuck pig all over every pair of underwear she owned, she'd never go back in there again. *Never.*

Three boys on skateboards bolted down the street. She recognized the one at the head of the pack as Terence Lawson from school. He didn't really give Peyton shit at school, but she thought that if he saw her here now, he might stop and rag on her. Another thing her father had told her was: "Some boys don't like a girl who's strong. And some *white* boys certainly don't like a *black* girl who's strong. But you pay that no mind. You, Peyton, be strong."

She watched the trio of skaters zip around the corner of a building. Across the street was Tito's Sporting Goods. She'd forked over plenty of her allowance buying baseballs there (not to mention the money she'd had to lay out not once but *twice* when she drove a pop-fly into Ms. Harmony's front window).

Tito was perched on a footstool assembling a rack of golf clubs when Peyton entered. He looked up, a smile stretching the lower portion of his face. He began shaking his head solemnly at the sight of her. "Don't tell me you sent another one into Ms. Harmony's living room, Peyton."

"Nope," she said, looking around, "but the day's still young."

Tito laughed. Then he noticed something was out of sorts with her. "You okay? You look upset."

"I'm fine," she said, and then quickly switched gears: "I need to get a birthday present for someone. A boy. Ten years old."

"What does this boy like?"

"Beats me. I don't know anything about him. I don't even think he has any friends."

"Do you know him from school?"

"No, he doesn't go to my school. He's the kid who lives in that big house on the hill. You know the one?"

"I sure do. Those people are rich."

"Shoot," she said, feeling this new dilemma rear its head. "You're right. I forgot about that. Like, what do you get a *rich* kid? I don't got much money."

"Maybe don't worry so much about the money," Tito said. "Maybe think more about the friends part."

Peyton frowned. "What do you mean?"

"You say he's got no friends," Tito said, "so why don't you get him something you both can do together? This way, *you* be his friend. That's a better gift than anything you can put in a box. And it don't gotta cost you a lot of money. *Comprende?*"

"*Sí, amigo, pero* what do you have in mind?"

Tito twisted his large body around on the footstool. He pointed to a wall teaming with baseball gloves. "Teach the little *chamaco* how to catch a ball."

She approached the wall of gloves, gazing up at them all. She didn't much care for the idea of playing catch with this kid—it sounded almost like babysitting—but she also knew how excited she'd been when she'd gotten her first glove. It had been a gift from her mother, just before she'd died. In fact, it had been her mother's glove, her name still visible on the leather in faded ink—*Alice*. Her mother had gotten a thick black marker and had printed Peyton's name over her own. It was a great glove, well-worn, and it smelled of her mother's history. It was how Peyton had learned to love baseball.

"They're expensive," she said, disappointed, gazing at the price tags.

"Those kiddie ones are cheaper," Tito said, motioning toward a wire carousel where smaller gloves hung from plastic hooks. They were done up in assorted neon colors and looked ugly as sin, but the price was right.

Peyton took a bright red one down off the rack. Smaller than hers and made of cheap vinyl or plastic instead of cowhide, but it was only six bucks. She had a ten-spot in her pocket, although she'd only planned on spending four. Oh, well…maybe there would be rich kid goodie bags for all the guests at the party and she'd make out in the end.

Tito followed her to the register and rang up the glove. She handed him her cash.

"What's this *chamaco*'s name, by the way?"

It occurred to her that she didn't know. She reached into her pocket and tugged out the birthday invitation. The paper had begun to fray, but that happy face's smile didn't falter. When she opened it, the little paper house popped out, and glitter rained down on Tito's carpet.

"Bartholomew 'Olo' Higgins Tiptree, and then there's three *i*'s after it."

"Eyes?"

She showed Tito the invitation.

"Ah, that means 'the third,' like his daddy and his daddy's daddy all have the same name." Tito whistled, shaking his head again. "And what a name it is." He handed Peyton back her change, and also the glove in a plastic bag.

"Thanks," she said, tucking the rest of her cash back in her pocket.

"Some woman went missing from there last month, you know."

"From where? The house?"

"*Sí*. I read something about it online." He got his phone out and thumbed through the screen. When he found what he was looking for, he said, "Yeah, okay. She was the boy's tutor. Her name was Iris Garin. Ring a bell?"

Peyton shrugged. The name wasn't familiar. Maybe she wasn't from town.

"Article says she was last seen at the house, then got a flat tire and went off somewhere. No one's seen her since. This was last month, and still no news. Her fiancé is offering a reward."

"How much?"

"Doesn't say."

"Do you ever watch those true crime documentaries on Netflix?"

"Who doesn't?"

"I wouldn't trust that fiancé, if I were the cops."

"You read my mind, *chiquita*." He tucked his phone back in his pocket. "Hey, you sure you're okay? You looked upset when you came in."

Be strong, she heard her father say.

"Just got today's baseball game on my mind." She beamed a smile at him. "See you around, Tito!"

"*Adiós, chiquita!*"

She headed toward the door, the plastic bag with the baseball glove swinging at her side. Just as she opened the door and was about to step out onto the sidewalk, she recalled a single detail from the nightmare that had woken her so early this morning: a snakelike appendage, not unlike the tentacle of a giant octopus, unspooling down a long, sinister hallway, blindly probing the darkness for her.

"Peyton?"

She snapped back to reality, turned, and waved goodbye to Tito.

Then it was back out into the bright sunshine.

6

At the playground, a slight breeze caused the swings to sway and the seesaws to question their alignment with the earth. Skateboard wheels trundled along the pavement, a sound like distant thunder, as a trio of eleven-year-old boys swerved toward the perimeter of the park. Two girls of roughly the same age as the boys came slinking out from beneath the cover of dense trees, spritzing themselves with cheap perfume to mask the odor of cigarettes. Another boy, a bit younger than the rest, came bopping up the block with his eyes glued to the frenetic screen of his phone, his ropey, untied shoelaces slapping the asphalt.

The day was cloudless and sunny and hot. Over a scrim of trees along the opposite side of the street, where a row of tidy A-frame houses stood together like mugs on a shelf, Helix House, perched venerably on its hill, was visible to them all.

The two girls claimed the swings. The skaters did kickflips and ollies along the pavement, pretending to ignore the girls, though they occasionally peeked at them from the sides of their eyes. The boy entranced by the game on his phone nearly waltzed headfirst into a tree, only to redirect as if by sonar at the last second. They were all aware of why they were here, yet there had been no discussion about it between any of them. They had merely flocked to this locale at the same date and time, much in the way birds will migrate to warmer climes, or how ants know to fall in line to carry out an order.

Those bright red birthday invitations were no longer strewn about the ground. They had either been scooped up by a night wind and trucked off to some other part of the neighborhood, or they had been collected surreptitiously by anyone who happened to see them and found themselves enticed by the happy face drawn in black crayon.

Kickflip: "Good one!"

Ollie: "Yeah, bruh!"

On the swings: "TBH, it's so *awks*, I mean, I literally *hope* my parents *do* get a divorce."

After a while, they all graduated across the road, and began migrating in the approximate direction of the mansion on the hill.

7

Olo watched them come.

A giddy sort of triumph bubbled up inside him. The balloons that he'd found in an old junk drawer sagged from the porch railing, but the HAPPY BIRTHDAY sign above the front doors shone gold. As his NEW FRIENDS made their way up the driveway, Olo stood from where he'd been perched on the porch steps. His armpits were swampy with sweat and the air inside his clown mask was muggy. He straightened his clip-on necktie, a smile poking out from the sides of his mask.

"What...the...holy...*fuck*?" said Minecraft, just as Olo's mannequins came into view.

Thrasher and his friends, each with a skateboard propped under one arm, gazed confusedly at the headless Mr. Tooms, the fellow's sun-bleached overalls splattered with dried bird shit and a dusting of pollen.

The girls covered their mouths and giggled. The one with glittery cheekbones went over to Lulu the Dancer and tugged a string of sticky red ivy from Lulu's torso—*tunk-tunk-tunk-tunk*. Lulu, in her frozen pirouette, didn't seem to mind.

Minecraft kicked the rake out of old Mr. Keeley's hand. Poor Mr. Keeley's plastic fingers snapped off as the rake fell down atop a mattress of purple foxglove. Minecraft tossed his head back and cawed—an ugly, spiteful sound—then crouched down to hunt for the amputated digits.

It would have been nice had they arrived singing a chorus of

"Happy Birthday," or even "For He's a Jolly Good Fellow," but they didn't. That was okay. The thing about NEW FRIENDS, Olo understood, was that you had to like them despite their foibles.

Olo stripped the clown mask off his face. He was smiling so broadly his cheeks ached, but he couldn't help himself. He was bouncing on the balls of his feet with excitement.

HAPPY BIRTHDAY TO ME! screamed the brain-shout. *HAPPY BIRTHDAY TO MEEEEE!*

"You *live* here?" said Minecraft, still crouched in the grass. He found one of Mr. Keeley's amputated fingers among the weeds, puzzled over it, then chucked it at one of the second-story windows of the house. The finger struck the windowpane with a dull *tink!*

"So *sketch*," said the girl with glitter on her cheeks.

"What's with your clothes, bruh?" asked one of the skaters.

"Nah," said Thrasher. "That tie is on fleek." He went halfway up the stairs and extended a fist in Olo's direction.

Olo stared at Thrasher's fist, unsure what to do.

"Nah, bruh, you pound it," Thrasher said.

"I don't understand," Olo said, still staring at his fist.

Minecraft looked agitated. He kept throwing stuff at the house. "He's a hurb, Terence! I want cake!"

"*Caaaaake*," moaned the two other skaters. They dropped their boards and began bumbling around like zombies.

"So *basic*," said Glitter.

When Olo spoke again, his voice was so low he'd hardly heard himself.

"Whazzat, bruh?" asked Thrasher. "What'd you say?"

Olo readjusted his tie, stood perfectly straight, and found his orator's voice: "Welcome to my birthday party!"

The kids laughed, then charged past Olo and into the house.

8

Minecraft made bug eyes as he stood gawping in the front hall. "Holy *shit*, how rich *are* you?"

"My parents are rich," Olo clarified.

Olo's NEW FRIENDS walked around the base of the spiral staircase. There were some balloons tied to the handrail (they were black and said HAPPY NEW YEAR! in silver lettering) and some crepe streamers woven between the wrought iron balusters. Olo's NEW FRIENDS took turns shouting obscenities toward the vaulted ceiling. Their echo-voices thundered, and Olo laughed and shouted right along with them. (He let loose some whoppers that he'd only heard from Roger when he was drunk, and his NEW FRIENDS laughed and pointed at him and the girl with glitter on her cheeks actually blushed.)

"This place is lit," said Thrasher.

Minecraft tugged a safety pin from his T-shirt and executed every single balloon in assembly-line fashion—*pop! pop! pop! pop! pop!*

The girls danced their way into the dining room, where Olo had laid out an impressive feast: six chocolate cakes with double fudge icing and chocolate sprinkles; the foil teardrops of Hershey's Kisses in countless plastic cups; Nestlé Crunch bars in their weirdly patriotic wrapping fanned out like playing cards upon the sideboard; a pyramid of chocolate-milk cartons at the head of the table.

"We can sing to me!" Olo said, hurriedly lighting the candles on one of the cakes with a lighter he'd found in his stepfather's study. The smell of the burning candles thrilled him. "We can sing 'Happy Birthday' or 'For He's a Jolly Good—'"

Something shattered and broke. A sardonic howl followed—*oooooooh!* Olo saw one of Mother's fancy plates from the china cabinet in pieces on the hardwood floor. Filthy sneakers bolted around the room, rubber soles squeaking.

"Look at this fuckin' dinosaur," Minecraft said, appraising Mother's antique Victrola. Minecraft grasped the crank and gave it a whirl. The turntable began to rotate, the draggy rumble of music slowly gathering momentum until Olo recognized Chopin's "Revolutionary" Étude. One of Mother's favorites.

Thrasher came up to the table. He swiped an index finger through the fudgy icing on one of the cakes then popped it in his mouth. "Where are your parents?"

"They're not home," Olo said.

"They're not home on your *birthday*?"

"No, sir!" Olo said, a bit too enthusiastically.

Thrasher picked up a handful of Hershey's Kisses, tossed them in the air, and gave them a thwack with his skateboard. Tiny foil-wrapped bullets shot across the room. The girls screeched, laughing.

"We can sing to me," Olo said again. He looked down at those mismatched candles burning atop the cake. His excitement was so great—

(!!!MY FRIENDS!!!)

—that his vision began to tunnel. Heart whump-bumping in his chest, he looked up and surveyed his NEW FRIENDS through pinprick pupils. His head was dizzy with elation.

And then, to Olo's even greater delight, they *did* sing. All of them, in a chorus of discordant, screechy voices—

> *Happy birthday to you!*
> *Happy birthday to you!*
> *Happy birthday, dear, uh, umm…*

They all turned and stared at him.

"Olo!" Olo shouted.

"*Olo!*" repeated the others.

"*Olé!*" shrieked Mineshaft.

More Kisses went caroming across the dining room.

Another expensive plate shattered on the floor.

(MY FRIENDS!)

Olo Tiptree was in his glory.

9

They gorged themselves on cake and chocolate, and when they were done, the silk upholstered cushions on the dining room chairs bore smeary brown stains, and the lush oriental carpet was soggy with spilled milk.

They took off in every direction from there, a cavalry of trumpeting sneakers and whooping catcalls. Someone started banging on the piano while someone else raided the refrigerator. Thrasher was in the parlor, flipping the switch to the gas fireplace on and off in an effort to impress the girls. He kept pretending it was a magic trick, bowing with a flourish each time the fire ignited, which made the girls laugh.

Minecraft was suddenly in Olo's face. He had one of the crepe streamers from the staircase tied around his forehead like a bandana. "Why do you always wear that stupid mask?" he asked. His breath was rancid.

"It's a metaphor," Olo said.

Minecraft made a puke-face. "The fuck's *that* mean?"

"It means that what's on the outside isn't always what's on the inside," Olo explained.

"You," said Minecraft, jabbing a finger into Olo's chest. Hard. "You are a fucking loser."

And then Minecraft twirled away, the streamer streaming out behind him.

The two skateboarders rolled past Olo down the hall. He watched them slow to a stop as they came upon the arched entryway to a vast corridor that, from where they stood, seemed to go on forever. As they gazed down the throat of that hallway, a series of wall sconces winked to life, filling the corridor with a shimmery, incandescent light. It looked almost inviting.

Smiling, Olo meandered into the parlor. He climbed atop the piano while his NEW FRIENDS looked up at him in heady anticipation. They began chanting *jump jump jump jump*.

Olo jumped down on the piano keys, then fell to the floor. The sound that burst from the piano was akin to an agonized roar. His NEW FRIENDS coughed up a similar sound, pointing and laughing at him.

Olo, also laughing, stood up. He went to straighten his tie but found it was no longer clipped to the collar of his shirt. He was trembling with glee.

"Time to roll," Thrasher said. He spit into the fire that still burned in the hearth, then staggered toward the hall, skateboard tucked under one arm. The girls followed him.

"Wait!" Olo shouted after them. "There's games, too! Games and prizes! Hide and seek! It's my favorite!"

They laughed at him.

"The hide and seek winner gets a great prize!"

They kept laughing, but some of the zeal was zapped from it now. Prize? What prize? Thrasher had turned around and was evaluating him, his brow furrowed. The girls were watching Olo, too. The others crept back toward the parlor until they were framed in the doorway.

"What kind of prize?" Thrasher asked.

"How about more candy?" Olo offered.

Hands cupped around his mouth, Minecraft shouted, "*Fuuuuck yoooooou...*"

"Or," said Olo, reaching into the breast pocket of his button-down shirt, "would you like a nice hundred dollars?" He withdrew the crisp hundred-dollar bill—one he'd found next to the lighter in his stepfather's study—and held it above his head with both hands.

"He *is* rich!" Minecraft said. He sounded angry, like Olo had tricked him somehow.

"There's a grandfather clock in the front hall," Olo told them. "That's home base."

"Rich bitch!" Minecraft crowed at him.

"*Riiiiich biiiiitch*," chanted the two girls.

Olo covered his eyes with both hands. The hundred-dollar bill felt damp between his fingers. He began counting aloud with all the confidence of a tent revival preacher: "One! Two! Three! Four!"

Nothing happened at first...

Then: the hurried cavalcade of footfalls thundering up and down the hallway, still close by, still close by, but then fading as all his NEW FRIENDS, all of them, raced down that seemingly endless corridor. Olo heard doors slam, *wham wham wham*, followed by muted laughter. By the time he'd finished counting and dropped his steamy hands away from his sweat-slick face, the parlor was empty, the house silent, his NEW FRIENDS all tucked away in their hiding places.

Olo went behind the couch and lifted his very special book off the floor, where he'd hidden it earlier. It was already splayed open, the paper version of Helix House straining toward the parlor's vaulted ceiling. The secret corridor tab was already pulled.

Olo set the open book down on the floor of the hallway, directly in front of the entrance to the corridor. His heart filling with joy, he began to manipulate additional tabs along the perimeter of the paper corridor at the center of the paper house. Tiny doors were pulled shut.

He tugged at a tab and a wall appeared out of nowhere. He pulled at another tab and a different wall vanished.

MY NEW FRIENDS MY NEW FRIENDS MY NEW FRIENDS, screamed the brain-shout—so loud that it hurt Olo's eardrums.

He went out into the dining room and found his clown mask under the table. There was chocolate smeared across it, so he got one of the nice linen napkins and cleaned it off. His birthday necktie was down there, too, so he wrung the spilled milk out of it and clipped it back onto his collar.

When he stood up, there was a girl standing there, watching him. Olo recognized her as the girl from the park, though only because she was wearing the same clothes she had been on that day—the ball cap with the stylized red B on the front and the unbuttoned baseball jersey. She had a backpack slung over one shoulder and was clutching a gift-wrapped package to her chest.

"The door was open so I just came in," said the girl. She looked at what remained of the food on the dining room table, the broken dishes on the floor. In one corner, the Victrola went *shhht-shhht* over the record. "I'm sorry I'm late, but I had a game. Is the party over?"

Olo twisted his head from side to side. "No, it's not over. We're playing hide and seek."

"Ah, that's right." The girl smiled. She was dark-skinned and pretty. Like Iris. "That's your favorite game. I remember. Your name is Olo, right? I'm Peyton. Thanks for inviting me to your party. Happy birthday."

She extended the brightly wrapped package toward him. Olo stared at it. His heart was galloping now and a queer, high-pitched ringing had risen to his ears. "That's for *me*?"

"Sure. Should I put it with the others?" She looked around. There were no others.

"I want to open it now!" Olo said, yanking the box from her. He set it on the table and tore apart the wrapping paper to reveal a nondescript cardboard box. Anything—*anything*—could be inside that box.

"You gonna stare at it or are you gonna open it up?" the girl—

(PEYTON MY FRIEND PEYTON)

—asked.

"I'm gonna open it up!" Olo crowed. He tore open the flaps of the cardboard box and peered down inside. "What *is* it?"

"It's a baseball glove," Peyton said. She shrugged the backpack off her shoulder and set it on the table beside Olo's gift. She unzipped the backpack and took out her own baseball glove—this one worn-looking and the color of butter, as opposed to Olo's, which was bright red (his favorite color!) and brand new. She took out a baseball, too. The ball was scuffed and grimy, and some of the red stitching was coming loose. JOYA was written on it in black marker.

"You play baseball?" Olo asked her.

"I do."

"With other kids?"

"Of course."

"I can play, too?"

"Well, sure. Have you ever played before?"

"No! But I would love to play baseball with you and other new friends!"

Peyton nodded at the box. "Go ahead and try it on."

Olo took the glove out of the box and squeezed his hand into it. "It fits!"

"Cool beans," Peyton said. "Here—catch!"

She lobbed the ball underhand in his direction. Olo jumped out of the way and the ball thumped to the milk-sodden rug.

"Toss it back to me," Peyton said. "I'll show you how it's done."

Olo picked up the ball—that word, JOYA, pretty as a poem—and tossed it back at her. Peyton caught it in her glove and Olo cheered.

She told him to "keep your eye on the ball, not on your glove," and pitched the ball to him again.

Olo's glove made a satisfying smack as the ball landed snugly inside the pocket.

"I caught it! I caught it, Peyton!"

"You're a natural," Peyton said, smiling.

In that moment, Olo Tiptree forgot all about Iris, as well as all his other NEW FRIENDS secreted away in various rooms throughout the house, holding their breath, stifling laughter, waiting for him to come find them. But then a part of his mind stretched like taffy. His vision grew fuzzy. The high-pitched ringing in his ears was replaced by the steadfast ticking of a large clock.

When he came back to reality, his NEW FRIEND Peyton was staring at him with a quizzical look on her face. Olo tugged the baseball glove off his hand and placed it back in the box. "Do you want to play hide and seek with the rest of us?"

"Sure," Peyton said.

"Come on," Olo said, picking up his clown mask.

She followed him down the hall, tossing the ball in the air and catching in her glove, until they reached the entrance to the corridor. Olo's pop-up book was still splayed out on the floor, and Peyton paused to study it. She asked him what it was and he said, simply, that it was his own special book. He'd made it.

"Wow," Peyton said, and Olo's heart fluttered.

He pointed down the corridor. "Everyone else is already hiding. I'll count to thirty then it's ready or not, here I come."

Peyton shrugged her narrow shoulders. "Okay," she said, and skipped down the corridor.

Olo strapped the clown mask over his face. His voice muffled, he began counting out loud. As he did so, he crouched down and gave the paper staircase on its chopstick axel a decisive turn. Once he'd counted to thirty, he bellowed, "Ready or not, here I come!" then hurried off down the corridor with all the authority of an assassin in search of his NEW FRIENDS.

10

Iris, who stood peering out at the surging white fog on the other side of the tiny porthole window, looked over at the door. A strange sensation flooded her body—a numbing lightheadedness that she'd come to recognize as the precursor to Olo's arrival in this place. She felt it the way you might feel if a door suddenly opened in your own home.

Something, she knew, was about to happen.

11

Terence hid behind a large wooden desk with an old-fashioned typewriter on it. He tucked himself inside the desk's footwell then held his breath as he listened for the sound of approaching footsteps out in the hall.

When he next looked up, he saw that the texture of the light in the room had changed. Had he actually fallen asleep in here? Was it dark out now?

He crawled out from under the desk and saw a pale white cloud pressing against the solitary window, dense as blackout curtains. The room was gloomy and silent. Terence went to the window, cupped his hands around his eyes, but couldn't see beyond that swirling white cloud. He dug his cell phone from his pocket to check the time, but when he powered it on, the only thing that flashed across the screen was a series of nonsensical characters:

SH%AMSA <, TWSWSV

10287346012837461097391 7

It wasn't just the texture of the daylight that had changed, he realized, but random items throughout the room had also been altered. When he had first come in here, the bookshelf had been messy with tattered paperbacks, magazines, and stacks of typewritten pages. Now, a file of glossy hardcover novels sat on the shelf, neat as you'd please. The author's name, Maribel Sinclair, was stamped on each spine in gold foil. There'd been a fan in the ceiling, too—he was certain of it—but now there was only a recessed pocket, dark as an abyss, above the desk. A dim bluish light glowed far up in that pocket. Lastly, there had been some yellow legal pads on the desk when he'd come in here, as well as a coffee mug bristling with pens and pencils beside the old typewriter. The typewriter was still here, but the legal pads and coffee mug were gone. In their place was a stack of crisp white paper. A single sheet now poked up from the typewriter itself. Terence peered down at what was typed there:

```
myself asks
am i here?
i've lost myself
i fear
```

He stepped out into the hall, then froze.

This isn't the same hallway.

Of course, it *had* to be the same hallway. There was only *one* hallway, and one door leading to this room…yet Terence couldn't deny that this one looked completely different. Earlier, he'd come straight down the hall, hooked a sharp right around a corner, then shoved open the door to this very room to hide. Now, however, he was staring down a straight passageway that went on for such a distance that it looked like an optical illusion. Was the floor different, too? A red-and-black checkerboard pattern instead of hardwood floors? And where were those weird wall-mounted lanterns?

He ran one hand along the wall as he started down the hallway... but then quickly jerked his hand back.

The wall had flipped like pages in a book.

He kicked it, and the wall was solid. The kick's echo bowled down the gloomy passageway.

"Hello? Hey! Where is everybody?"

But the corridor *wasn't* straight on till forever, was it? Because it turned and turned and turned, so many corners, and Terence was turning with it, gaining momentum, moving quickly, his breath rasping from his parched throat. He was beginning to feel lightheaded, his thoughts growing jumbled and confused. Distantly, he thought, *Where is my skateboard?* And somewhere in the background of that thought: *kickflip ollie goofyfoot nosegrind rotational inertia an object will remain at rest or in a uniform state of motion unless that state is changed by an external force and for every action in nature there is an equal and opposite re—*

Terence turned the corner to find a smallish figure standing before him, wearing a damp, wrinkled necktie and a clown mask.

"Found you," said the clown.

The corridor went dark.

Terence felt something rush at him.

12

The girls, Julie and Casey, stuck together. Giggling and whispering secrets (Julie had a crush on Terence, but shhh, don't tell), they meandered down the corridor until they came upon a dark, musty library whose shelves were teeming with books. A wooden sign above the library door read BŌCHORD, whatever that meant, and the books looked positively *ancient*.

Julie tugged one of the books free. Dust rained down from the shelf and she hopped back so it didn't get on her UGGs. The book was heavy, the cover looked made of tanned leather, and it had about a gazillion pages. She opened it and found that the pages were made of that same leathery material. The text—strange symbols as opposed to words—looked like it had been seared onto the pages with a branding iron. She ran the palm of her hand over the page and felt— or imagined she felt—tiny hairs rise up and stiffen at her touch. She turned to another page and felt a wobbly sense of dislocation occlude her thoughts:

> Once upon a time, Bartholomew "Olo" Higgins Tiptree III dreamed about a book that was really a house, and a house that was really a book. There were many rooms inside the house (and the book), and in each one, a NEW FRIEND awaited Olo. How joyous it was to visit them and play with them whenever he wanted. In return, Olo kept his NEW FRIENDS close and as safe as chocolate milk inside the book that was really a house that was really a book.

"Casey, come see this."

But Casey was no longer with her in the room.

"Casey?"

The doorway was gone, too. Was this some kind of prank? She was surrounded by ceiling-high bookshelves, no windows or doors, and no way to get back out into the hall. Did the bookshelves *slide*? Had Casey rolled one of the shelves across the doorway by accident? Or even on purpose, just to fuck with her?

Because she likes Terence, too, Julie thought, and it wouldn't be unlike Casey to be a basic bitch about it. *Because she likes Terence but Terence doesn't like her because she tries too hard and because a clockwork motor consists of a spiral torsion spring of metal ribbon wherein energy is stored by manually winding—*

Wait—where the hell was she? Why was she holding some book?

Silverfish swarmed across the page, and she dropped the book to the floor. It struck the old hardwood with a loud *thump*, and a cloud of dust rose up off the boards. She watched in horror as the silverfish abandoned the book, skittering across the floor, the baseboards. Julie shrieked as they swarmed over the toes of her shoes.

Some of the other books on the shelf started moving around. *More bugs*, she thought, the concept so horrific—*so many bugs they can move the books!*—that she became momentarily paralyzed with fear.

Small white fingers poked between two of the books, causing Julie to suck in a sharp intake of breath and take a step back. More dust trickled to the floor. As she stared, those white fingers parted the row of books down the middle to reveal a face—a *clown* face— peering out at her from between them.

"*Found you*," said the clown.

13

Sid shouted curse words down the corridor at the top of his lungs. He had skated down the hall, passing door after door after door, but the hallway had no end. Every door he tried was locked. He skateboarded back in the direction he had come, logic dictating that he'd have to come out into the main part of the house if only he backtracked, but the freaky hallway just seemed to go on forever.

Another door: locked.

Another door: locked.

"Goddamn it!"

He jumped off his board, picked it up, and shattered one of the glass lamps that hung from the wall. The lamp went out...as did every single one running up and down the hall. The darkness that swallowed him up was absolute. Fears he'd had of the dark when he was younger returned to him now, weakening his knees and causing a sob to ratchet up his throat. Sid's body broke out in a clammy sweat.

He grabbed his board—a vintage Tony Hawk deck that had previously belonged to his older brother, Mitch—and swung it wildly in the dark. It struck the wall and Sid felt a puff of plaster dust belch into his face. More strikes, more strikes, more strikes, until he had carved a chasm in the wall. He felt around for it with one hand, his fingers stripping away loose chunks of plaster.

I can climb through, his mind yammered, *I can crawl all the way out into the yard and just run and not look back because something is wrong here something is messed up something is akin to the state of human happiness which is a wall impenetrable which is the disposition of mind and not of circumstance which is the little red invitation with a black smiley face which is—*

A light shone from the chasm he'd bashed in the wall. It was dull and bluish white and distant, and there was something celestial about it. If houses had souls, Sid would have been certain he had bashed his way straight to the center of this one's.

Behind him, in the dark, it sounded like the doors were rearranging themselves.

14

Casey followed the dulcet melody of a piano. The melody grew louder as she turned a corner, but then it stopped altogether. She stood staring at a blank wall. No, not a wall—a door.

So many doors, she thought. She felt dizzy and outside of herself, like that time she'd snuck over to Linda Harrison's house and they'd drank all that old booze Linda's dad kept in an armoire in the basement. No lock on Mr. Harrison's liquor cabinet. No lock on this door, either.

Casey turned the lever and found herself in the parlor, staring at the grand piano. There was no one seated before it. No one else in the room, in fact. Just Casey and the curmudgeonly old goat in the oil painting above the fireplace.

Only the painting above the fireplace was blank. Just a velvety black rectangle in a gilded frame. As if the old curmudgeon had stepped out of the painting and crept away while no one was—

"*Found you*," said a voice.

Casey whirled around, but there was no one there. A heavy mist hung in the windows, so thick it obliterated the sun. The room was growing darker by the second.

"Terence?"

Why'd she say that? It wasn't Terence. It was no one. No one was in here with her.

But then she caught movement in the corner of her eye. She whipped back around in time to see something shifting about in that panel of dark space that was the empty painting over the fireplace. Something *in* there, moving about.

Casey dragged the piano bench over to the hearth and climbed atop it. The painting at eyelevel now, she gazed into its bottomless

...d deep within, swirling in cyclonic rotations.

...er, and her breath caught in her throat.

..., paused, then sent her fingers through the

...nt air greeted her fingertips on the other side

...ame.

...oice again, calling to her from the depths of that swirling

...k miasma: "*Founnnnnnd yooooouuu...*"

"Yes," she said, and crawled into the painting.

15

Elliot stumbled out onto a second-floor landing, which disoriented him. He'd been on the first floor of the house, so how had he gotten up here?

A twisting helix of cold black iron spiraled down into the throat of an inky, sightless pit. Those stairs led to the first floor—he remembered seeing the spiral staircase when he'd first entered the house—which meant the *front doors* were right down there, too. Which meant *escape...*

He grabbed the railing and thundered down the iron risers, around and around, his head giddy, his thoughts tangled up in knots. Sweat peeled down his forehead and stung his eyes, but he hardly noticed. He was driven by a single-minded purpose—to *get out, get out, get out.*

Something was wrong. He stopped running down the stairs and looked around. He was still on the first step, level with the landing, as though he hadn't yet descended a single riser. How was that possible?

(get out get out get out)

He ran down a few more steps, stopped, and looked around again. Still on the first step.

Still level with the landing.

Slowly now, just one foot down onto the step below, the go, right there, easy as pie, one at a time, while—

—the spiral staircase rotated him back up to the top.

The ugly sound that burst from Elliot's throat was arguably a laugh, though it possessed all the qualities of a lunatic's scream.

He began running as fast as he could, fast as he could, fast as he could, while the staircase kept rotating him back toward the top. The faster he ran, the faster the staircase spun. When he lost his footing and rolled headfirst down that iron helix, he felt the metal stairs jabbing at his ribs and taking gashes from his forehead. The pain was instantaneous and tremendous, and he thankfully lost consciousness before he struck the floor.

16

Her ear against the wall of her ugly pink room, Iris heard the grind of twisting metal. It was the staircase, she knew, though she imagined it was the sound of many voices screaming at once.

17

Whistling "Take Me Out to the Ball Game," Peyton Joya walked down a seemingly endless hallway, occasionally tossing her baseball into the air and letting it crash back down into the snug pocket of her well-worn glove. She came across none of the other kids from the party during her solo trek down the hall, so she concluded that they all must be really good at hiding. But after several more minutes had passed, she started to wonder if there were any other guests here at all. Would any of those kids at the park actually show up? Had they all really been playing hide and seek when she'd arrived, or had Olo been lying to her because he'd been embarrassed? She hadn't seen any other gifts lying around.

"Olly olly oxen free," she said, her voice bouncing down the hall ahead of her.

And then, out of nowhere, she found herself standing before a closed door with her name written on it in crayon:

Payton

Misspelled, sure, but her name nonetheless.

She was dimly aware that she should have found this unusual. Maybe even a little frightening. Yet there was some transmission interfering with her logic—she could feel it like a sort of mental tug-of-war—and she ultimately surrendered herself to it. Curiosity propelled her to open the door and step inside.

It was a square, empty room, with startling red walls and red-and-black chessboard tiles on the floor. There was a single window set against the far wall, the size and shape of a stop sign. A white sheet of fog stood behind the glass.

The door slammed shut behind her. Spooked, she spun around and jostled the lever, but it wouldn't budge. There was writing on this side of the door as well, in that same childlike scrawl:

Once upon a time, I am so happy to have a very best
NEW FRIEND!

Panic closed cold, bony fingers around Peyton Joya's throat.

Yet at the same time, a fog misted through her skull, confusing her emotions. Her hand fell away from the lever on the door. For some reason, she was thinking about stopwatches, and the *snick snick snick* of the second hand. How Coach Faber would bark at her to *push it, Joya,* her arms and legs pumping, *snick snick snick, cross that finish line, get that speed up, round those bases, smack a homer over the event horizon of the observable universe which subsists as the theoretical boundary of a black hole beyond which no light can escape because it is trapped within a point of no return trapped like a rat in a maze of hallways trapped like a trapdoor trapped—*

Trapped, she thought, her gaze trickling down to the baseball glove she wore on her left hand. That faded cowhide with its frayed brown laces. Her name, PEYTON, printed there in black Magic Marker overtop her mother's faded name, ALICE, printed *by* her mother in the weeks before her death. Cozy in that glove sat the baseball, her own handwriting on this item, JOYA. Both items, magic totems, coming together to spell out her name.

Her name.

Her identity.

Her brain shouting: *PEYTON JOYA!*

She spun around, assuming her pitcher's stance, and fired that baseball at the octagonal window at the opposite side of the room. The ball smashed through the glass, and triangular shards rained to the checkerboard floor.

She rushed up to the busted window and screamed for help. At the same time, she realized she was far from anyone within earshot, and that her cries were futile. This house stood on its own distant hill removed from the rest of the town, and there was no one out there who would hear her no matter how loud she screamed.

At the same time she realized this, she also felt those alien thoughts attempting to invade her mind and confuse her again. She fought them off, bulldozing against them, pushing back with a set of facts of her own: *Jackie Robinson hit a total of 137 home runs throughout the entirety of his career with the Dodgers, which began in 1947 and ended in 1956, with an overall 734 runs batted in and a .311 batting average...*

Tendrils of white mist snaked into the room through the broken window. They moved with undeniable sentience, and the sight of them brought to the surface of Peyton's mind the dream she'd awoken to that very morning, of a pale tentacle of smoke chasing her down an infinite corridor...

Peyton turned and gripped the door handle again, tried to force it to turn, but it resisted. Behind her, those filaments of white smog caused the hairs on the nape of her neck to stiffen into quills. That terrible phrase written on the back of the door in black crayon struck her like a death sentence now, blurring her vision with tears.

Not gonna see Daddy again, not the twins, never sleep in my room again, never play baseball again, never—

"Baseball," she said, the word wheezing out of her.

She lifted her gloved hand and swiped at the door handle.

The handle responded, and the door swung open.

18

She ran down the corridor, blank white doors whipping by on either side of the hallway, tears streaming from the corners of her eyes. She didn't slow down to see if the white smoke was chasing after her nor did she pause when the baseball cap was stripped from her head.

Yet when she glimpsed a name printed on one of those doors, she stumbled to a stop. Her breath ragged in her throat and her lungs aching, she swiped the tears from her eyes with the back of her glove, and allowed a moment for her vision to focus:

Iris

It was the name of the missing woman from the news article Tito had told her about earlier that morning. *Iris.*

She swatted at the door handle with her baseball glove, and the door sprung open.

Something feral rushed out at her, screeching and flailing. Peyton cried out and fell backward against the wall as the thing clawed at the air between them.

It was a woman in a lavender dress. They both stared at each other, their heartbeats in perfect synch, the atmosphere pulsing all around them.

"*Who...are...?*" the woman managed. There was dried blood on her dress and her hair looked like an explosion. Her eyes blazed with a combination of madness, terror, and rage.

"Found you," said a small voice.

Peyton turned her head and saw Olo watching them from the far end of the hall. He was wearing his clown mask so she couldn't see his face, though his clip-on necktie and his head of bushy golden curls left no room for speculation.

"Found you. Found you *both*."

Peyton climbed to her feet. "Olo, where are we? What's going—"

"*Run!*" Iris screamed, clawing at Peyton's arm. "*He's a monster! We have to run!*"

Iris's fingernails drew blood down Peyton's arms. A second later, the woman was racing down the corridor while the lights in their little glass casings on the walls guttered and threatened to blink out.

"Hey!" Olo called after them. He was moving quickly down the hall in Peyton's direction now.

Forget this, Peyton thought.

She turned and sprinted after Iris, that *snick snick snick* in the back of her head now keeping time, and there was Iris right up ahead, shouting and tugging on a locked door. Peyton rushed up beside her and opened the door with her baseball glove. Iris grabbed Peyton around the wrist and dragged her through the open doorway.

They were in another hallway, no different than the previous. Peyton was instantly terrified that they were running in circles, and that there'd be no escape from this impossible place. Iris's fingernails bit into her wrist and she cried out in pain.

Others were screaming and pounding on doors. Peyton could hear them but she couldn't discern which doors they were trapped behind. Instead of guessing, she slashed at every door handle with her glove as she bolted by, each door swinging open in a shower of green sparks, until the walls trembled and the checkerboard floor tiles began to buckle.

Longhaired skater boys leapt out into the hallway from a pair of swinging doors. A girl with glitter on her cheeks ran screaming from a narrow passageway while another girl, silent as a mime, sprinted alongside Peyton for all that she was worth.

An aperture of light shimmered up ahead. Only then did Peyton risk a look back, and what she saw would haunt her subconscious for many nights to come.

There was Olo chasing after them as best he could, his arms flailing, his short, stout legs unable to keep up. He was crying out for them to *stop please no don't please my friends my friends please no please* and Peyton could hear the agony in his cries. Behind him whipped a mass of smoky white octopus tentacles as the opposite end of the corridor filled up with smog.

"*Run, goddamn it, run!*" Iris screamed.

They burst from the corridor as a mob of pinwheeling arms and twisted ankles. Shrill, desperate cries keened through the air. Iris tripped over the open book that lay spread out on the floor, her bare feet slicing through the paper house, dashing it apart—

19

—and Olo watched the others topple down all around Iris, sneakers scrambling atop the chipboard book cover, rubber soles and groping hands shredding the paper house with its multitude of passageways and antechambers and hidden rooms to bits in their collective haste to flee, the sharp bone-like snap of the chopstick keeping it all together, while Peyton, bringing up the rear, turned as she crossed the threshold of the corridor, glancing at him from over one shoulder, one final glance, terror and confusion in her eyes, and Olo's brain-shout hissed one last time, *MY FRIENDSSSS*, just before his special pop-up book was demolished, and the world around him slammed to black.

20

It was Iris's lavender headband that came to Tony Davis later that evening, as he prepared to microwave a bowl of chicken noodle soup in his small downtown apartment. That was what he'd glimpsed on the head of that faceless ballerina mannequin—Iris's headband. It struck him now less like an epiphany and more like a smack across the jowls.

He hopped in his car and sped across town. The sun was setting in the car's rearview mirror while up ahead the sky had fallen to a depthless naval blue punctuated with stars. By the time he spun the wheel and skidded up the gravel driveway toward Helix House, it was fully dark.

He had no game plan, no idea of what he'd do once he arrived at the front doors, but he knew he couldn't let it go. That headband had been *Iris's* headband. She'd been wearing it with her lavender dress the day she'd gone missing. Tony was sure of it.

The car's headlights washed over the overgrown corkscrew topiaries as he sped toward the house. When the mannequins came into view, he slowed a bit. Then he stomped down on the brake and cried out in terror. The mannequins had come to life and they were rushing toward his car.

But no—not the mannequins. These were *children*, and they were screaming and waving their arms above their heads as they ran toward him. He shoved the gearshift into Park then bolted out of the car. The kids were streaming toward him while the night trembled with heat lightning.

Iris was among them. They saw each other from across the yard, and like two lovers in a romantic period film, began running toward each other with their arms wide. Only Tony didn't get more than five steps before he struck that wall of shouting, sobbing children. They clutched at him, clawed at him, begged him for help. He told them it was okay, he wasn't going to let anything happen to them, they were safe, they were safe.

Her hair a frizzy black mop and her dress streaked with what could only be pennants of dried blood, Iris made her way toward him across the yard. She walked with a limp, and he could see one of her ankles was swollen.

"Excuse me," he said, and squeezed through the mob of clutching hands, sour breath, and damp, squinty faces. He looked at Iris while a tumult of emotion rumbled through him. Then he grabbed her, held her tight. "Where," he whispered into her wild black hair, "in the hell have you been?"

What she said made no sense, but it didn't matter to him, because Iris was safe. Iris was *safe*.

"In a book," she whispered back.

From over Iris's shoulder, Tony could see a young girl staring up at the house. She wore a baseball jersey with the number 11 on the back and a worn glove on her left hand.

21

Tony dialed 911, followed by Detective Lewis's cell phone number, then told Iris and the children to wait by his car.

"Tony—"

"It's fine, Iye. Just wait with the kids. I'll be right back."

The front doors of Helix House stood wide open. Above the doors was a sign that read HAPPY BIRTHDAY in gold foil. Tony stepped through the doorway, and was shocked to feel how *cold* the interior of the house was. No lights were on inside, but the floor was spangled in moonlight from the high windows. He crossed into the front hall, his footfalls wincingly loud in the deafening silence of that grand mausoleum. Buried in one dark corner of the foyer, a large clock ticked.

They had been prattling nonsense out there, Iris included—something about a hallway that didn't end and rooms that kept shifting and changing where they'd been held prisoner. Iris said something about a book with a house in it and told him that Olo was dangerous. Was a *monster*, was how she put it. She had spoken calmly and quite direct, yet Tony couldn't reconcile any of what she had told him. She was clearly in shock.

He called out for the boy now, his voice playing off the walls and reverberating off the high, vaulted ceiling.

A sound high above his head snared his attention. He turned and looked straight up the spiral staircase to a figure that stood on the second-floor landing, peering down at him. As he watched, the figure began descending the stairs. It wasn't the boy, but someone else. Someone who moved with a stupefying, lobotomized lethargy. The person all but collapsed into Tony's arms at the bottom of the stairs.

It was a woman, late sixties, though her face looked haunted and ancient with fear. Her fingers bit into the muscles of his upper arms while her terrified eyes searched every inch of his face. When she spoke, her voice was a grating rasp, her breath caustic.

"*Help...me...*"

She wore a faded pink blouse and a threadbare knee-length dress. Harsh black shoes on her feet. There was a name embroidered in red on the front of her apron—BETTY.

"It's okay," he told her. "You're safe."

"*Where...is...the...boy?*"

He didn't know.

"Come with me," he said, and put an arm around the woman's waist.

As he led her from the house, he could hear sirens in the distance.

THREE:

AFTERMATH

1

The following Saturday, Peyton Joya hit her first home run of the season. Her teammates went wild, her daddy pumped the air with a fist, and her twin sisters, who had been catcalling her from the bleachers throughout the whole game, spilled their popcorn as they jumped from their seats and shrieked with glee. Coach Faber slapped her a high five as she burned across home plate.

Iris Garin and Tony Davis were in the stands, too. Tony was wearing a Bristol Bangers baseball hat and was clutching a large soda between his knees. Iris looked resplendent in a floral summer dress. She'd gone crazy with a pair of hair clippers since Peyton last saw her, buzzing her hair nearly down to the scalp. Peyton didn't know what to make of it at first, but after a while, the new look sort of grew on her.

After the game, with her family waiting for her in the car (they were going to head out to the Purple Panda for some celebratory ice cream), Iris and Tony came over to her. Tony tapped the brim of her baseball hat and said, "Looked great out there, Pey. You'll make the all-star team, no question."

"Well, we don't have an all-star team, but I appreciate the confidence," she said, smiling up at him.

Tony kissed the side of Iris's face, then strolled toward the parking lot. He waved to Peyton's father, who waved back.

"I decided I like your hair," she told Iris.

Iris laughed. When the laugh faded, there was a sadness behind her eyes. Peyton wondered how much Iris remembered from her time spent in that house. She'd been in there a whole month. Peyton had been inside that place for an hour, two at the most (it was hard to judge), and that had been enough to rattle her cage.

"How you holding up?" Iris asked her.

"Me? I'm peachy. How about you?"

"I'm hanging in there." Iris's tone was confident but that sadness was still hiding behind her eyes, peering out. Peyton didn't need to study her face for long to see it. "I think maybe I want to share something with you, Peyton, although I don't know if I should. I discussed it with Tony and he said I shouldn't bother you with it— that we're all just trying to get over this thing and have been through enough, and I shouldn't add any fuel to the fire—but I don't know if he's right. I think maybe I should tell you. I'm not even sure why, but it's something I feel."

"Okay," Peyton said. "So then tell me."

"I was two months pregnant when he locked me away in that place, Peyton. That was five weeks ago now. Yesterday I had a follow-up visit with my OB/GYN, and it turns out I'm *still* two months pregnant. Everything's fine—my numbers are all good and the baby is strong and healthy—but it's inexplicable." She paused, then added, "Well, almost."

She's going to talk about a clock, Peyton thought. It came to her out of nowhere. She remembered nothing about a clock from her time spent in that house, yet for the past week, an incessant ticking had been chasing her from nightmare to nightmare, along with images of a small figure in a clown mask pursuing her down a long hallway on a carriage made of smoke. She couldn't shake it.

"I think time stood still in that place," Iris said. "I don't know how that's possible—Christ, I don't know how *any* of that was possible—but I believe that to be the case. No question."

"It felt weird, for sure," Peyton agreed. "It was like something kept trying to get inside my head, too, and mess with my thoughts."

"I know exactly what you're talking about. Whenever I tried to think logically—to think of a way out of that place—I felt my mind go all...well, messy." That sadness still danced behind Iris's eyes. "How are your friends doing?"

Peyton shrugged. In the dugout, her teammates were collecting the equipment, dumping batting helmets and aluminum bats into mesh bags. "I guess they're mostly okay. They weren't really my friends. Just some kids from school."

"Well, I'm glad they're okay."

Peyton gave her a smile. Truth was, she didn't know how the others were doing. She'd heard through the grapevine that one of the girls—Casey somebody—had been admitted to a hospital for a psychological evaluation. She kept claiming she'd crawled through a painting and into another dimension. Certainly sounded ridiculous when you said it out loud, but Peyton had no reason to disbelieve her.

"What do you think happened to him?" Peyton asked. "The boy?" She didn't want to say his name.

Iris's eyes grew distant. "I don't know, Peyton. Maybe he just... disappeared...along with that hallway. He was still in there when it all went away, wasn't he?"

"Yes, he was," Peyton said. She'd been staring at him when the corridor vanished, taking the boy along with it. "You don't think he's, like, still trapped in the walls of the house somewhere, do you?"

"I don't know for sure, but I don't think it worked that way. Wherever we were, Peyton, it wasn't behind a wall. Not really."

Peyton glanced down at her cleats before meeting her eyes again. "Yeah, I guess I knew that."

Iris gave her a tired smile. "Listen, you call me if you need anything, okay? No matter what. Even if it's just to talk."

"I will."

"You saved my life in there, you know. Those kids' lives, too. I don't know how you did it, but you did."

Peyton shrugged and looked down at her sneakers again.

"Great game, too. I'm impressed."

"Glad I could send one over the fence for you."

This time, Iris's laughter held no hidden secrets. It was pure.

"What're you reading?" Peyton asked, pointing to the book poking out of Iris's purse, although what she'd meant was *Why are you reading that?* She recognized the author's name on the spine, and it gave her a chill. Maribel Sinclair.

"A Lucy Betancourt detective novel. Kinda trashy, but I guess you could say I got hooked. And it might sound strange, but it's like visiting an old friend."

"Don't sound strange at all," Peyton told her. "Mom used to say a similar thing. Reading good books is like visiting good friends."

And what about bad books? Peyton wondered. *What do you visit when you open a bad book?*

The notion sent another chill rippling down her spine.

"Take care, kiddo," Iris said. She touched the side of Peyton's face—her hand was warm—and then walked across the field toward the parking lot, where Tony Davis watched her with a desperation that said he would never again let her out of his sight.

"Hey! Peyton!" It was Coach Faber, waving her over to the dugout.

Peyton jogged over, feeling a bit ashamed that she'd allowed her teammates to clean up while she stood around chatting with Iris.

"Excellent game, as usual," Coach Faber said.

"Thanks, coach."

"Here. Don't forget this." He handed over her baseball glove, which she'd left on the dugout bench. "See you Monday for practice."

"Abso-surely," she said, which was an Iris-ism she'd unconsciously adopted.

Across the parking lot, her father honked the horn.

"Gotta go," Peyton said.

"Go on," Coach Faber said. He pulled a stopwatch from his pocket. "Run and I'll time you."

Peyton Joya ran.

2

The question at the forefront of Detective Eugene Lewis's mind was: *How the hell am I going to write this goddamn report?*

Okay, so it wasn't exactly *the* question at the forefront of his mind, but it was certainly lurking around back there, causing him some mild agitation. He'd already gone through an entire bottle of Maalox over the past week, and he was worried he was courting an ulcer.

What had happened in that house?

For starters, there was Betty Barnes, Maribel Sinclair's housekeeper who'd supposedly retired and went down to Florida roughly one year ago, shell-shocked and on the verge of madness. He'd visited her in the hospital and tried to piece together the woman's story, but it was so erratic and nonsensical that he quit taking notes midway through her rambling recitation. The only thing Eugene was able to cobble together was that the boy, Olo Tiptree, had somehow trapped this woman in a room of the house where he'd kept her prisoner for an entire year.

He interviewed the children one at a time, each one with a parent present, and received a series of similar stories. Olo Tiptree had invited these kids to his house to celebrate his birthday, only to trap them in a series of strange rooms deep inside his house. When Eugene asked them to elaborate, he was chagrined to receive stories of shifting walls, never-ending hallways, and an oil painting that led to another dimension.

And then there was Iris Garin. The woman who'd been missing for a month, having seemingly vanished without a trace.

"That's exactly what happened, detective," she'd told him. "I vanished without a trace."

"How does a ten-year-old boy keep all those people prisoner in his house all on his own?" he had asked her.

"I don't think he did it on his own," Iris said. "Did you find a book at the house?"

Eugene had gone back and bagged the book as evidence, although he didn't believe Iris's story. He didn't think she was lying—he didn't think *any* of them were lying—only that she, like the others, was in shock. *Something* had happened to them in that house, of course, and clearly Iris and Betty Barnes had been kept in isolation someplace… but a magic pop-up book?

Where was the boy now? Where was his stepfather, Roger Smalls? Those were the big questions. Eugene wanted to find them.

He contacted Maribel Sinclair, who returned from New York with questions of her own. Where was her son? Where was her husband? When she'd learned that both Iris Garin and Betty Barnes had allegedly been kept prisoner in her home, Maribel Sinclair stared at Eugene with cold, gray eyes, and told him that was preposterous.

According to Mrs. Sinclair, Roger Smalls had gone to a publishing event in Haymarket the day of the birthday party, which might account for his whereabouts. But Eugene soon learned that the event had been canceled weeks ago. So where exactly was Roger Smalls? Had he and Olo left town together?

"Perhaps your son has been having problems with his stepfather?" Eugene suggested. "Maybe he's staying in secret at a friend's house?"

"Olo has no friends," Maribel assured him.

At his request, she provided him with a photo of Olo and one of Roger, too. Eugene dispatched them as a BOLO, and their grainy images appeared on the nightly news for the next week or so, along with a telephone number people could call with any information regarding their whereabouts.

An elaborate conspiracy started coming together in Eugene's head: Olo luring people to the house, while the stepfather drugged them and kept them locked away someplace. Yet both Iris and Betty claimed they'd never seen Roger Smalls while held prisoner. Only the boy.

Maribel Sinclair allowed for a search of her house and surrounding property. (Just to be sure, Eugene filed for a search warrant, too.) Cops crawled in and out of Helix House, searching the place from top to bottom, but found no evidence of any hidden rooms. Nor could they find a room resembling the one Iris Garin had described—pink shag carpeting and a small porthole window in the wall. There was absolutely nothing in that house that corroborated any of their stories.

"Because those rooms are not *in* the house, detective," Iris had told him the last time they spoke. "They're in that *book*."

Sure they were.

His coworkers and fellow detectives printed stories from the internet and left them on his desk—stories about mass hysteria, and how groups of people can all suffer the same hallucinations if the circumstances were right. Half of the stories were about UFO sightings. Eugene fed each one into the shredder.

Just when things couldn't get more perplexing, a woman arrived at the police station to speak with Eugene. Her name was Karen Michaels, and she was nervous. "Maybe it's nothing," she said, "and my husband has warned me not to come here and talk about it, says it'll just bring me trouble talking about it, makes me sound loony, I don't know, I mean, maybe it's nothing or maybe it's *something*, but I *did* read an article about what that Iris woman said, and those children, and I just couldn't shake it, just kept thinking, just kept—"

Eugene told her to calm down.

She'd been Olo Tiptree's teacher in first grade, back when the boy had attended public school. A bizarre and inexplicable incident had occurred one afternoon that resulted in Maribel Sinclair removing her son from the school. Karen Michaels described Olo as a very smart young child who had difficulty making friends. None of the other students in his first-grade class played with him, and he'd often sit alone at recess and during lunch. One afternoon, Olo drew a picture of their classroom. He showed it to her, then asked if she would pin it to the bulletin board for the whole class to see. She agreed, but then she looked more closely at the drawing. She asked him why there were no doors or windows on the drawing of the classroom. Olo responded, "So no one can get out."

It was here that Karen Michaels paused and examined the ball of Kleenex she was picking apart in her lap. Eugene filled a paper cup with water from the water cooler and set it on the edge of his desk in front of her.

"The next thing I know," she said, her voice shaking, "the windows in the *actual* classroom were gone. So was the door. I...I can't explain it. I started freaking out, feeling the walls for where the door had gone, the windows. I was sure I'd lost my mind. But it wasn't just me. The other kids saw it, too, and they all got up and starting looking for the door and the windows, too. They were crying and I was crying and my head started feeling really weird, like I wasn't getting enough oxygen or something. The clock over the chalkboard got really loud, and I could hear it slowing down, slowing down, until it stopped completely. And the kids and I, we were just *so upset*…"

"What was Olo doing during that time?"

A terrified little laugh came out of Karen Michaels's mouth. "He was setting up a checkerboard. Right there at his desk near the back of the room. And I remember when he was done, he looked up at us—we were all huddled against the chalkboard at this point, as far away from him as we could get—and said, 'Who's first?' I remember that. 'Who's first?' He wanted to play *checkers*."

"How'd you get out of the room?"

"I tore up the drawing and everything went back to normal. The kids ran out into the hall and I went straight to the front office. But by the time I got there, I realized I didn't know exactly what had happened. I felt like I was cracking up. I wound up telling the principal that he'd locked us in and wouldn't let us leave, and that it had upset the children. Upset me, too. It was the closest thing to the truth I could muster."

Eugene thanked her for coming in, and walked her to the door. He couldn't believe such a story, of course, but it did convince him to go into the evidence locker and page through that strange pop-up book Iris had insisted the boy had used to trap her in that house.

No, he thought, closing the book. *What is going to happen is someone will recognize Roger Smalls' photo and will phone it in. We'll find him and the boy holed up in some motel somewhere. Roger Smalls will be arrested and will likely admit to administering hallucinogenic drugs to Iris Garin, Betty Barnes, and the children at the birthday party. Maybe he even put the drugs in the birthday cakes. And that will explain everything.*

It made good sense.

3

It was a cool day for the end of summer, and the sky was silver with rain. Maribel Sinclair stood smoking a cigarette on the covered porch of Helix House as Detective Lewis's unmarked sedan crawled up the driveway. He parked beside Olo's dreary, faceless mannequins, and climbed out of the car. He looked defeated, walking with his head down and his shoulders slumped, although it could have been just to keep the rain out of his face. He carried something under one arm.

It had been weeks since the incident yet there had been nothing further from the police. No clues as to the whereabouts of her husband and her son, no clarity as to what had actually happened in this house, if anything at all. She had begun to think Detective Lewis wasn't the best man for the job. A case like this required someone with a little more panache, a little more open-mindedness. Someone like Detective Lucy Betancourt.

The thing Detective Lewis carried under his arm was Olo's book. He returned it to her with an apology for holding on to it so long. She probably would like to have it. When she asked if there had been any further developments—a habit that fostered no real hope—Detective Lewis just shook his head and found it difficult to meet her eyes.

Once he left, Maribel carried the book into the dining room. She opened it up on the table, and stared down at a jumble of crumpled paper and torn paperboard. Some random slips of paper fluttered out onto the table. A broken chopstick poked crookedly from the center of the two pages, like the busted mast of a shipwreck. Torn in half was a cardboard likeness of Helix House, stamped with footprints.

The ticking of the grandfather clock out in the front hall was suddenly very noticeable. As she listened, she swore the second hand was slowing down, grinding time to a halt. She swore, too, that a drunken fog was slowly creeping into her brain. Disorientation pulsed briefly inside her, and for a fleeting second, she forgot where she was. But, no—she was right here in the dining room, listening to the clock *tick, tick, tick*, slower and slower. She waited for the ticking to stop altogether...but it never did. The clock regained its normal tempo, and that sense of disorientation dissipated.

She closed the book, tracing her fingers along the front cover:

> This book belongs to Olo.
> Do <u>not</u> open.

She went out into the hallway and stared up at the spiral staircase. The grandfather clock ticked with doggedness at her back now— *tick-tock* and not *tock-tick*...

"Where are you, my love?" she called up through the winding iron stairs to the second floor of Helix House. "Where did you go?"

The only answer was the ticking of the clock.

4

Through the forever darkness: a pinpoint of light.

Faint, but there. Undeniable. Olo went to it, saw it was a keyhole, and peered out.

White smoke swirled against a midnight sky.

Olo backed away from the keyhole and watched as a meager beam of bluish light fell upon the face of the grandfather clock. The clock's hands were frozen at midnight. The front hall was silent.

Olo opened the front doors and stepped out into a wall of white mist. He sensed it was nighttime and the air was cold, but Olo hardly registered it. He reached up and felt his clown mask atop his head. He pulled it down over his face. There, that was better.

He felt around for the porch railing in all that fog, finally found it, then went carefully down the steps, the soles of his cordovan shoes thudding dully on the wooden risers. He could see nothing as he stepped down into the yard. The fog was so great that when he looked down, he couldn't even see his shoes.

Something moved off to his right; he sensed it more than saw it. A slight alternation in the mist—a thing in motion. Olo took a step in that direction, his hands groping blindly ahead of him in the fog, until he felt something gently strike his open palm. He felt it and realized it was a foot, only made of plastic. Olo released it, and the foot rotated past his face as Lulu the Dancer completed her pirouette.

Movement all around him now. A ruined, fingerless hand rested on his shoulder. A pair of gardening shears sailed like a dorsal fin through the fog directly ahead of him. He heard the jangle of the buckles on headless Mr. Tooms's overalls, and the stiff rustling of Mr. Keeley's straw cowboy hat. A plastic hand found one of Olo's own, the fingers closing around his with a series of brittle snaps. And somewhere in all that mist, Lulu the Dancer kept dancing, dancing, dancing.

Surrounded by his friends, Olo Tiptree's heart swelled with joy.

THE STORY

1

I'm in the thick of it, bobbing and weaving like a prizefighter, when my cell phone vibrates in the pocket of my sports coat. It's a quarter to midnight and I'm at one of those lavish Upper East Side parties that don't start to gutter out until well after three. I know practically no one, am a guest of Karen Boyd, my editor, and I'm God knows how many drinks in the tank. Much of my evening has been spent avoiding conversation, and in devising the most effective circuit to and from the bar. There's a chandelier above my head that looks like something NASA has launched into orbit, and as I dig the phone from my coat, I slosh some whiskey out of my rocks glass and onto the floor. A vampiric old crone in a blood-red gown sees this and somehow manages to scowl without altering the expression on her mummified face.

It's Sammy Deane calling. That alone is cause for alarm. In the five years I've known him, he's never once called me on the phone. Countless text messages, sure, but never phone calls. He's a tech-head, a computer geek of the highest order, and he'd sooner tap out a salutation in Morse code than pick up a telephone. Moreover, we haven't spoken since I left *The Spectral* seven months ago.

There's a small balcony overlooking East 74th Street, so I weave through the crowd to take the call out there. There are flower boxes on the railing and a short, chunky fellow in a rumpled suit is having a cigarette while watching the traffic lights below.

"Grady? Grady?"

"Sammy, what's up? Is something—"

"Look, I'm just gonna say it, okay? I'm sorry, Grady. I'm sorry."

I screw a finger into one ear so I can hear him better. "Sammy, what—"

"Taryn's dead," Sammy says. "She's killed herself."

The world seems to tilt at a precarious angle. I find myself staring at the chunky fellow in the rumpled suit. He's staring back, his face a dark web of shadow. Only his eyes sparkle, reflecting the never-ending traffic below. Smoke envelopes his bald head. He looks like something belched up from the depths of hell.

I must have asked Sammy to repeat himself, because he does.

She's dead. Suicide.

Taryn.

2

There's no next-of-kin, and Sammy's got the constitution of a humming bird, so I'm suddenly in a cab on my way to the morgue somewhere in the fetid, steamy intestines of the Bowery. Still in shock, I sit in the back of the cab clutching my cell phone, as if expecting another call, from Sammy or anyone, telling me, no, so sorry, but there's been a mistake, Taryn is still alive and well and as headstrong as ever, and we're so sorry for the confusion, Grady, have a good night. I pray for that call. Pray for it. But no. I've got my drink from the party in my other hand; the ice has melted and the octagonal glass replicates the lights of the city like a prism. It's like a tiny galaxy resting on my knee.

The morgue is housed in a stone building that looks like it could be a bank. Inside, I'm greeted by walls of bulletproof glass, which surprises me, and it's like I've been tricked into imprisoning myself. I feel like if I turn back around, the door I've just come through will no longer be there. I stand there in a stupor, expecting Rod Serling to appear at any moment and begin a narration of my sins.

It's not Rod Serling who approaches, but a tall black man with a tired face. Like the guy on the balcony having a cigarette, he's got on a rumpled suit, only this one looks much cheaper. When he extends his hand to shake mine, I catch a glimpse of a gold shield clipped to his belt.

"Grady Russo? I'm Detective Mathis."

I realize I can't shake his hand because I'm still occupied with my whiskey and my cell phone. I drop my phone into the side pocket of my sports coat and, for some reason, feel the sudden and uncontrollable urge to apologize. So I do.

"You got any ID on you?" the detective asks.

I fumble my wallet out of my pants, show him my driver's license. It causes me to wonder how many people falsely identify bodies in morgues in New York City.

He leads me down a claustrophobic little hallway comprised of dingy aquamarine tiles. The air reeks of ammonia. He tells me how Taryn's landlord called the police after finding her hanging from a beam in her apartment. I'm confused and ask how long ago this happened. Because it seems like it's in some other lifetime, that if it actually happened—did it actually happen?—then surely I'm a week or a month or even several months late to the party. Surely this wasn't as recent as—

"Earlier this evening," says Detective Mathis.

"Earlier this…excuse me?"

"A few hours ago."

I let this sink in. It sounds wrong. That Taryn should have killed herself while I was drinking whiskey at some ritzy party on East 74th Street is wrong.

"You an ex-boyfriend?" Detective Mathis asks me.

I fumble through a response in the negative. My hesitation makes me sound guilty of some crime. I realize I'm still drunk.

"We used to work together," I say. "Coworkers. But friends, too, I mean…yeah, we were friends." As if I'm trying to convince myself instead of this cheap-suited police detective.

"When was the last time you saw her?"

I do the quick mental math. "Around March, I think."

The detective just nods his head.

We stop before a metal door. I expect big bolts and locks and all that jazz, but no, there is only a slender handle with a little lever that Detective Mathis depresses with his thumb. Taryn's in my head now, looking just as she did the last time I saw her, which was at some hipster bar in Greenwich. That was…what? Five months ago? She tried to get me to come back. I tried to be kind to her. Neither of us were successful.

Detective Mathis opens the door to reveal a sterile room with alabaster walls. The rear wall is comprised of steel drawers. There is a white curtain and a sink and jittery fluorescent lights in the ceiling. Centered in the room is just what countless television shows and movies would have you expect: a gurney covered in a white sheet. There is a figure beneath the sheet, and my eyes run from what I assume to be head to toe, immortalizing in my brain the crenellations, the peaks and valleys, the full-length contour that makes up the body underneath. Taryn.

Suddenly, I'm sober.

I expect a guy in a white lab coat to show up, but no. Detective Mathis takes me over to the shape beneath the sheet. He asks if I'm ready.

I want to ask, *Is she bad?* I want to ask, *Will this haunt me?* I want to ask, *Will I ever forget what I'm about to see?* But I don't ask any of those things. I simply nod my head, feeling like I'm being manipulated by a puppeteer tugging on a string. I say, "Yeah." I say, "I'm okay." I say, "I'm ready."

Detective Mathis folds down the white sheet.

A thing very much like Taryn Donaldson is under there. It's funny, but I don't look at her face. Not right away. Instead, I stare at her clavicles, those delicate sloping collarbones just below her neck. I can't look at her face because that will force home the fact that she is gone, and maybe I'm not ready for that just yet. So I stare at those oblique little bones, and in my increasing panic, I think, *Wow, they look like the arms of a rocking chair just under the skin, those bones. How have I never noticed that before on any human being? Does it take death for the beauty of collarbones to reveal itself? Jesus Christ.*

It's inevitable: my eyes tick up toward her face. I pass her neck to get there and see the stark black rind of flesh there, where whatever she used to hang herself with abraded and squeezed her throat. Was it a rope? A bed sheet?

"How'd she do it?" I hear myself ask the police detective. It's my voice, but it's also not my voice, issuing from the end of some long pipe.

"Electrical cord," says Detective Mathis.

For some reason, this jabs me like a white-hot poker in the center of my chest.

Her face, then. Someone, I assume, has gone to great lengths to make her look presentable. Because surely someone who hangs herself from a ceiling rafter by an electrical cord around the neck does not look so peaceful. Her eyes are closed, of course, and there is actually still some color on her skin. Her dark, spriggy mop of hair frames her face, and for some reason it is that hair more than the sight of her face that causes a sob to lurch from my throat.

Our relationship, I realize now, was many things. Complex. No, we were never boyfriend and girlfriend, although we shared those intimacies on occasion. It's that hair—recalling the smell of it, the texture of it, the way she'd come into the bunker every afternoon in the wintertime with that hair bristling like springs from beneath a knit cap—and just like that the floor pulls away from my feet and I'm suspended in some vacuum, unable to look away, to think away, and there's Taryn talking in my ear, calling me an asshole, saying I only think of myself, and what was the matter with me, because this thing we've created is *real* and it's *great* and what the hell was I doing?

I notice something strange—not about her face, but about her hand, which pokes from beneath the white sheet on the opposite side of the table. The palm of her hand is black. I ask Detective Mathis what it is.

"Paint," he says. "Black paint."

I accept this as if it's procedure, as if it's the most normal thing in the world. I am not thinking rationally or coherently now.

"Well?" Detective Mathis says. His deep bassoon voice sucks me back down through the layers of atmosphere until I'm back on solid ground. I actually feel the earth thud against the soles of my feet as I come in contact. "I need a verbal."

"Yeah," I say. "It's her."

The detective nods then covers Taryn's face back up.

But it's still there. I can see it beneath the sheet. Her visage is burned onto my retinas. *Will this haunt me?*

I guess I have my answer.

3

Detective Mathis follows me out to the street. It's like we're on a date and he's trying to be chivalrous. I feel like there's something more.

I like to think it's the reporter in me, the newsman who senses a story beneath the story. But in truth, it's as human and feral as eating and screwing and shitting.

As I hail a cab, Detective Mathis clears his throat.

"If you've got some time tomorrow," he says, "I'd like you to come by her apartment and have a look at something."

"What is it?"

"Hard to explain. Let's say around noon?"

My head is a cascade of piñata candy and sharp javelins of disco-ball light.

The taxicab pulls up to the curb, some rousting Middle Eastern music spilling from the open windows.

"Mr. Russo?" says the detective.

"Yeah, okay. Noon. See you there."

I get in the back of the cab and before I can blink my eyes, we're away from the curb and merging with traffic. Unsettled, I twist around in my seat. Through the rear windshield I stare at Detective Mathis in his cheap, crumpled suit, standing on the curb with his hands in his pockets, looking like the most downtrodden son of a bitch who ever lived.

I look down and find that I'm still clutching the rocks glass. It's empty now, so maybe I guzzled the remnants at some point back at the morgue. But it's still here. It's still with me. And for whatever reason, this causes a laugh to ratchet up the stovepipe of my throat.

"Hey," I shout to the driver. "Hey!"

"Hey!" he shouts back over one shoulder. He never really takes his eyes off the road but also somehow glances at me, too.

"Turn the music up," I tell him. "Turn it up. Up! Up!" I thump my hand against the ceiling of the cab.

"Up, up," says the driver, motioning with his hand. "Louder, yes? The music?"

"Yes!"

"You like?"

"Louder. Louder."

"Up," says the driver, and he cranks the Middle Eastern music louder, louder.

Satisfied, I sob like a child in the backseat of the cab.

4

I meet Sammy for coffee the next morning. He looks like someone who's been shoved off a subway platform for being a shithead. Truth is, he's always looked like that. This is Sammy Deane: about six-foot-three with a white-boy Afro, thick and pasty jowls, black-framed Buddy Holly glasses, and if you were in a band that had a hit single in the seventies, Sammy's wearing your T-shirt. He's got this way of taking up more room than necessary, as if there is a small force field that surrounds him, and I watch now as a mother attempts to maneuver a stroller out of his way. She carves a wide berth, as if Sammy's made of uranium. He's got the straw of his Frappuccino in his mouth as he approaches my table.

I get up and give him a hug. He clubs me once on the back. We sit, and it's almost impossible that we are here together. I feel like I'm sliding backward in time. None of this is right.

"How you holding up?" I ask him.

He hoists one big shoulder then sets his drink down on the table. "You go to the morgue last night?"

"Yeah."

"Sorry. I just couldn't do it."

"It's okay."

"It was…her, right?"

I nod.

"Well," he says, but then says no more. He gazes out the window of the café and watches the people out there on the sidewalk and in the street.

We're only four blocks from the bunker. I used to stop in this café every morning and sometimes I'd ditch out for a fresh cup of coffee midday, if the work brought on too much of a headache, which it often did.

"I just don't understand it," I say. I'm watching the people out there now, too. "Did you notice anything different about her in the past couple of days?"

When he doesn't answer, I turn and find that Sammy is staring right at me. I can't tell if he's angry or upset or just nonplussed.

"What?" I say.

"Yeah, man. She'd been losing her shit for weeks. Didn't she call you?"

"Call me? No. Why would she call me? I haven't talked to her in like five months."

"No shit?" One of his caterpillar eyebrows arches toward his Afro. "She said she called you, talked to you."

"When was this?"

"I guess about a week or so ago. When she really started getting messed up. I made her do it. She said she would, and that after, she said she spoke to you and everything was cool." He glances at the fluffy white cloud of whipped cream atop his Frappuccino. "I guess she was just bullshitting me."

"She never called. I never spoke with her. I wish I had."

"Yeah," Sammy says. His lips move around like he's trying to work a sesame seed out from his teeth. I can't tell if he's fighting off a swell of emotion or if he's turning some particular thought over in his head.

"What did you mean, she'd been losing her shit? What was going on?"

"I don't know, man. It's hard to explain. That's why I wanted her to talk to you. In the beginning, she just got, like, really obsessed."

"With what?"

"With work."

This is nothing new. But there is a flicker of apprehension behind Sammy's eyes now, even as he thinks of it.

"She'd stay late at the studio and even had me transfer files so she could take stuff home," Sammy says. "A few mornings, I'd come into the studio and she'd be there at the console, sleeping. Like, drooling all over the system."

It's a little much, I agree, but it's not out of the realm of normalcy for Taryn. When she got hot on something, there was no slowing her down, until she collapsed from exhaustion. She once fell asleep standing up in the middle of a party and didn't even drop her drink.

"But then," Sammy continues, and I watch as that flicker in his eyes darkens, "there was this shift. A complete one-eighty, man. She started not coming into the studio at all. I'd have to send her like a billion texts just to get her to come to work. I thought maybe she had the flu, and she sure looked like it when she eventually showed up, but you know...I just figured maybe she was dating some dude and things were going bad, or maybe she had burned through her savings quicker than she had anticipated. Stuff like that. I never asked her about it. I guess I should've."

"*Was* she seeing someone?"

"Not that I know of. I never saw her with anyone. And the way she looked the past couple weeks, man..." His gaze flits up at me, which is when I realize he's been mostly talking to his Frappuccino. "She looked like wrung-out shit, man. Even smelled bad, like she quit taking showers."

"That's not like her."

"That's what I'm *saying*, man. She was all over the place. Like… like…nervous about something, you know? I thought maybe, you know, drugs or something. The medical examiner gonna run a toxicology?"

The question catches me off guard. "I don't know. I forgot to ask. But I'm seeing the police detective later today. He wants me to see something at her apartment."

Sammy leans toward me, his big hands on the table. "What's at her apartment?"

I shake my head.

"How'd she do it, Grady? Pills?"

I tell him about the electrical cord.

"Oh." He sits back in his chair. His big hands drop into his lap.

I wonder if it might have been money problems, but that doesn't seem probable. Taryn's parents died years ago. They were wealthy when they were alive, plus they left her with quite an insurance windfall following their deaths. She singlehandedly bankrolled *The Spectral* for the entire first year it was on the air, before we got sponsorship. Including my meager salary.

"What are you going to do?" I ask Sammy. He's just an engineer. When I left the show back in January, Taryn became the sole producer, program director, and on-air talent. There is no one left to run the show now. No one left to host it, either, of course.

"I'm halfway through post on our last episode. I guess I could finish it, upload it. Cobble together some eulogy or something on the end of it. You wanna come back and record a few words or something?"

I'm nodding my head. It seems fitting. Yet the thought of setting foot back in that studio—the "bunker," as Taryn and I always called it—causes my armpits to leak sweat down my ribs.

"She made me co-producer after you left," Sammy goes on. "Guess that might look sexy on a résumé."

"You going back there today?"

"You know, I think I'll give myself the day off." He's gazing out the window, watching men and women move up and down the sidewalk as if on a conveyor belt. "I don't want to go back there just yet. Not alone. Not for no reason other than it just feels weird, you know? Maybe I'll catch a movie or something."

"That's a good idea," I tell him.

"How's the life of a real journalist, by the way?" It's not meant as a dig, but the tone of his voice and the timing of the question couldn't have been more misplaced.

"I've been busy," I say.

"It's cool, though? I mean, you dig it?"

"Yeah. It's cool."

"You're with *NewsBlitz*, right? You do a lot of traveling?"

"A few places. It's a big organization. I'm not really involved with the radio folks, but I can put in a good word for you, if you'd like."

"I don't know. It's worth it?"

I try to read between the lines, wondering if what Sammy is really asking is whether or not my decision to leave *The Spectral* was worth it, given this sudden and irrevocable outcome. As if my departure from the podcast had doomed Taryn.

Or maybe Sammy hasn't meant that at all.

Maybe it's just me inferring things that are not there.

Things I now feel guilty about.

"It's what I needed to do," I say. "I loved the podcast, Sam, but that was Taryn's baby. It always was. I was never in it for the long haul, and I never kept that a secret from her. I know she was pissed when I left, but you guys kept doing good stuff, and I was hopeful that she'd moved past all that."

He's staring at me like he wants to say something but he's not quite sure what.

"I didn't want to spend my life chasing ghosts," I tell him.

Yet now look where you are, his eyes say back. *Look at this ghost we have to share between us now.*

"Was good seeing you again, Grady."

"You, too."

"I'll shoot you a text about doing that recording."

"All right."

He gets up and carries his Frappuccino to the door. He doesn't even look at me one last time before he leaves.

I lean back in my chair and watch him step out onto the sidewalk. He's got the invisible force field up to full power now, I see, and as he lumbers down the block, I watch men and women unconsciously swerve to avoid him, like guided missiles that don't want to strike the wrong target.

5

I'm crouched on the floor with my back against Taryn's apartment door when Detective Mathis arrives with the landlady. The detective's suit is a bit less wrinkled than the previous one, but his face looks just as tired as it did the night before. Taryn's landlady is a relic from communist Russia, a sturdy woman with a beehive hairdo so black it's almost Superman blue. She wears a purple velour jogging suit and carries a jumble of keys on a brass ring the size of a basketball hoop. As she approaches, she eyes me with distrust. Her red-painted lips twist into a knot.

I climb to my feet and shake the detective's hand.

"Thanks for coming out," Detective Mathis says.

"Of course."

The landlady unlocks the door and lets us into the apartment.

"Keep in mind," Detective Mathis says. "This is exactly how we found it last night."

It's a spacious corner loft, which means windows make up two of the four walls. The ceiling is high, all exposed ductwork and iron crossbeams. There's the old futon, the Crypt Keeper pinball machine, the Tarantino movie posters. All the things I recognize that are in their proper place, that anchor my suddenly weightless body to something real, something familiar, something solid. It's everything else that hits me like a hammer.

The first thing I notice is one of the walls has been painted black. It's a hasty job, done with a brush and not a roller. The painter had given up before the entire wall was covered, and instead has completed the job by painting, in three-foot-tall letters, DO NOT READ, along the wall.

I realize I'm about to have my world shaken apart.

Taryn was never a meticulous housekeeper, but the next thing I notice is just how ruinous the place looks. There are clothes everywhere, and books and papers and other junk scattered around. I wonder if the place has been ransacked. There is a smell in the air, too—one that suggests cleaning wasn't a priority in her final few weeks, mingled with the throat-thick stink of drying paint. Probably a fridge full of rotting food, too. It makes me sad to take all this in, because it strikes me as clear evidence of a declining humanity, a weakening of spirit, a person on the brink. This apartment is like a blazing neon sign warning someone—anyone—that its occupant is headed for disaster.

"Jesus," I say, looking around.

At first, I think it's the state of this place that Detective Mathis wanted me to see. *It's not just me, right? Your friend was living in a shithole, right?* Some kind of corroboration. But that's not it. I realize what it is when I walk halfway across the room and see Taryn's desk, the one with the two computer monitors on it, the recording equipment beside the desk on a metal shelving unit. Her stereo and bookcases, which also look ransacked. The desk is shoved against a cinderblock wall, and the light from the opposing wall of windows casts it in an angelic light. Ironically so, because—

"What the hell?" I mutter, pausing in midstride. I stare at the desk. I suddenly don't want to go near it.

It is as if the desk itself was ground zero for some explosion of mad, erratic thought—a detonation of mostly indecipherable words and phrases and collections of random numbers that had erupted from the desktop and sprayed like shrapnel onto the walls, the baseboards, the exposed ductwork and I-beam rafters.

It's writing, furious writing, scrawled in a panicked version of Taryn Donaldson's blocky print. It's all over the desktop, not just filling the pages of the stacks of yellow legal pads there, but on the desktop *itself*, printed in black permanent marker, although a few phrases in bright green and red also appear at random. There are Post-its all over the computer monitors and on the stereo atop the metal shelf, the print on these square colored panels too small and cramped for me to read from where I'm standing. The writing explodes from there, boils out, *roils* out, buckshot all over the walls, along the painted I-beams in the ceiling, scrawled like a mad genius's mathematical equations on the hardwood floor, *A Beautiful Mind* gone haywire. A monsoon of words. An obliterating sandstorm of words.

Detective Mathis looks over at me.

I tell him I need a minute to process all this.

I focus on the individual phrases scribbled on the walls, most of it illegible, but catch some snippets of information, of words and phrases that I can decipher, but even those do not provide much clarity. This is not a puzzle meant for piecing together. For a second, I think I might be having a stroke—that would account for my inability to reconcile what I'm reading. But no, that isn't it. Aside from phrases like *i'm already in how am i already in?* and *i can hear it behind the wall of noise* and *i am both chasing and being chased*, most of what is written on the walls of Taryn's apartment is in some foreign language. Or, more accurately, in *several* foreign languages. It's all over the place, shouting at me in visual dialects I have no way of comprehending.

I feel deaf.

"What is all this?" I say, still marveling over the mess of it all. Until now, the sight of all those words scribbled everywhere has prevented me from seeing the slender orange cord dangling from one of the exposed I-beams. I see it now. It has been cut, but it's still tied to the beam. They must have cut it to get her down. The quickest way. There is a chair nearby, on its side. It makes sense that the police have left these things as they are, I suppose, though there is something crude and hasty about it all. It makes my throat tighten.

"I was hoping you might be able to tell me," says Detective Mathis.

"This...this isn't like her. This isn't Taryn. She wouldn't have done this. This place looks like...looks like madness." I stare at the detective. "It's like she went crazy in here."

On another wall, Taryn has created what appears to be a series of seismic graphs, of sharp peaks and valleys, the charted false responses of a lie detector test. There are several of these, and depending on how I look at them, they either resemble a musical staff, brain waves, or a child's rough rendition of spiky blades of grass. Taryn was never much of an artist.

"Is it possible someone else...?"

"There were no signs of forced entry or foul play, Mr. Russo. Her door was locked when Ms. Vasiliev here came into the apartment." Detective Mathis points to the desk chair that lies knocked over on its side on the floor, just a couple of feet from where the remnants of the electrical cord dangles from the beam. "She stood on that, then—"

"Yes, okay," I say. "So why bring me here to see this?"

"Because it's bugging me," Detective Mathis says. He points to a column of numbers that have been scrawled onto the cinderblocks. They're all over the place, in tidy little matrices. The tidiness of that specific madness somehow makes it worse. "Any idea what those numbers mean?"

I tell him *no* before I actually study them. I go to the wall, look from one set of numbers to another. Each series of numbers is separated by a colon, then another set of numbers separated by a colon, then another—

"They're time codes," I say.

"Time codes."

I take a step back and take the apartment in again, this time from a different mental positioning.

"These are her work notes," I say, understanding it just as I speak the words. "This is her, breaking down audio for a segment."

"I don't follow," says the detective.

"The show," I tell him. "She hosted a podcast called *The Spectral*. Researched things like UFOs, Bigfoot, Mothman, shit like that. The audio files are time coded, and she would break down snippets of sound and help our engineer put the show together."

Just like a police detective, Detective Mathis has keyed in on one word in particular from what I just said: "Our?"

"I used to host the show with her." In my head, I'm hearing Sammy from earlier that morning, telling me how obsessed with work Taryn became in the past few weeks. *An understatement*, I think now. My knees feel weak.

Detective Mathis looks around at the insanity on the walls. "So this is normal?"

"No, not like this. Of course not." I grab one of the yellow legal pads from the desk. "She'd write it here, not on her goddamn walls."

Detective Mathis strolls over to a section of wall where the words MAN and WOMAN are printed on the brick, with hash marks and time codes next to each word. He must feel like he's trying to decipher hieroglyphics. I do.

"This is just…" I say, trying to find the words. "It's like her mind blew up in here. None of this other stuff makes any sense to me."

"What was she working on?"

"I don't know."

On the desk I find more of the strange foreign phrases littering the notebooks there, the desktop, the Post-it notes stuck to the screens of the computer monitors. One sheet of lined notebook paper says, simply, *dogs barking*, over and over again, like a mantra or a prayer, each with a strange string of numbers after the phrase. All different numbers. I cannot discern a pattern here. There probably isn't one.

There are CDs on the desk, too, and a stack of vinyl records on the floor in front of the metal shelving unit. Taryn had a decent record collection, but on close inspection, I don't recognize any of these albums. It's mostly classical music. Taryn would have never listened to any of this stuff. The record album on the top of the stack is Igor Stravinsky's *The Rite of Spring*. Beneath that is a Bach composition performed by the Munich Bach Orchestra and conducted by someone named Karl Richter. *First Movement!* is printed in Taryn's handwriting across the cover of the album, underlined multiple times.

A far cry from the Clash records Taryn always spun.

"The CPU is missing," I say.

"What's that?" says Detective Mathis.

"The computer. The monitors are here but the computer is gone. She had a big old-school tower. Did the police take it?"

"No."

I glance around, but can't find it. The only other piece of electronic equipment I can see on the shelving unit is Taryn's stereo.

I go to the stereo, power it on. There is a disc in the CD player. I press play and brace myself for the crunch of distorted guitars, or hell, maybe even the orchestral strains of classical music to come lilting through the large speakers on either end of the large apartment.

It is not classical music. It is not punk rock.

What comes is a sudden hiss of static, sharp as a slap. Sound upon sound upon sound. Layers of it. I wince. It builds in intensity until I cannot take anymore.

"Please," the landlady yells at me, covering her ears. "Please, okay?"

I turn off the stereo. The silence that follows is cottony and full.

"What does 'thaumatrope' mean?" Detective Mathis asks.

I glance at the police detective, still shaking the cottony silence from my ears. "What?"

Detective Mathis goes to another section of the wall and points to a grouping of tiny printed words. I join him and find that the words are actually just *one* word, printed over and over and over again. Obsessively. Sometimes with a question mark after it.

Thaumatrope.

Thaumatrope?

Thaumatrope.

"An optical illusion," I say. "Like, a disc with a different picture on each side. When it rotates, the pictures blend. It's…wait, hold on…"

I go to a cluttered corner of the loft, near the windows, stepping over mounds of unwashed clothes, a suitcase, and a trail of paperback books splayed out like a hand of playing cards. Taryn's bed is here, nothing more than a mattress and box spring on the floor, the sheets twisted into balls. I try not to look at the bed too long because it bothers me. Summons too many emotions, I guess. There is a thaumatrope hanging by a string near the windows—a bird on one side, an empty bell-shaped birdcage on the other. Detective Mathis steps around the clothing and books and watches as I pull the string and the disc spins. The bird is now in the cage. Trapped.

Seeing this, the look on Detective Mathis's face is clear. There is no mystery to be solved in this apartment. Here lived a woman who went mad and left behind her last fleeting thoughts all over the walls, whatever mental jetsam she had clogging up the byways of her gray matter sprayed like buckshot on a road sign. But hell, Detective Mathis has probably seen worse.

"Who pays?" the landlady says, her voice like the report of a pistol breaking the quiet. "Eh? This mess. Who pays for clean?"

The detective and I exchange a look.

"Ma'am, uh," I begin.

"Vasiliev." She says it like she's casting a spell over me.

"Ms. Vasiliev," I say, then proceed to ask her if she noticed anything unusual about Taryn's behavior in the past few weeks, or maybe any strange people coming up to her apartment.

"Everybody in building is strange."

"I mean someone who looked like they didn't belong here. Like they were up to no good."

"No good what?" She doesn't understand me.

Detective Mathis has lost interest in my line of questioning. He's lost interest in it all. Perhaps he's already asked these questions himself. Whatever the case, the mystery has vanished for him. He wants to pop smoke, and I don't blame him.

"No no no no no," Ms. Vasiliev says, rat-a-tat, like firing a machine gun. "Only music. Plays the music. Loud. Loud."

I hold up one of the record albums. Stravinsky. "This music?"

"Da." But she also points to the CD player. "And that other," she says.

"What other? The CD I just played?"

"Da."

"She's blasting white noise?"

"What?" Ms. Vasiliev barks, confused. She pronounces the word with a *v*.

I don't bother to pursue this line of questioning. My mind hurts. My heart hurts. Now I'm back to looking at the segment of extension cord hanging from the beam. It gives me vertigo.

What the hell was going through your head, Taryn?

"Is Russian," Ms. Vasiliev says.

Both Detective Mathis and I look at her.

"What's Russian?" Detective Mathis asks.

"Here. Here. This one. Only this." She walks to the wall, that blue-black beehive hairdo leading the way like a mystical orb, and slaps a pale white hand against one particular foreign phrase printed in five-inch-tall letters on the cinderblocks.

Zdrávstvuyte privétstvuyu vas.

"Is greeting," Ms. Vasiliev says. "Is hello." The *h* is hard, and comes out on a spray of spittle from the back of her throat.

"Hello," both Detective Mathis and I say at the same time.

"Da." She points to each individual word as she speaks it. "Says, 'Greetings. I welcome you.'" *Velcome.*

"Welcome who?" Detective Mathis asks. "Us?"

Ms. Vasiliev says no more.

I feel like someone is slowly driving a needle behind my left eye.

I see something else now, too—a set of black handprints stamped on a closed door. The bathroom door. Something clicks in the back of my throat as I recall Taryn's blackened palm from the morgue. *Black paint.*

I go to the door, grab the knob. Deep breath. Twist it and shove the door open.

It's dark. I flip on the light.

Taryn's computer is in the bathtub, soaking beneath a foot and a half of water. In smudgy black paint on the shower tiles, inscribed there most certainly by a finger, like someone finger painting, is that phrase again, repeated as if for emphasis.

DO NOT READ.

Detective Mathis joins me in the bathroom doorway. Stares from over my shoulder.

DO NOT READ.

"I think I wanna get out of here now," I say.

6

You freelance on a circuit. Many cars on many tracks, all whizzing by each other, never colliding, only glancing at each other as you swift by the ramparts. Except sometimes you *do* collide. Because there are always exceptions.

I met Taryn Donaldson eight years ago, back when we were still in our twenties. I was juggling freelance assignments for about a half dozen different city papers while hoping to work my way on as a staff reporter with any of them. Maybe sometimes you see faces or you get to shake someone's hand at a party, but really, you get to know your competition from their bylines. You get to know whose forte is politics, who is an avowed art critic, who takes out their personal vendettas by penning scathing reviews of new restaurants, nightclubs, books, independent films.

I'd seen her name as a byline many times, but she was not competition. She was too eclectic—stories about the underbelly of the New York Racing Association, political corruption conspiracies, rumors of secret locations throughout Manhattan where bizarre religious cults supposedly gathered to perform black masses. She penned an exposé on a filmmaker whose movies were supposed to cause seizures. She wrote another story about a saxophone player who could play multiple notes simultaneously, and the story, in no subtle terms, suggested this fellow was the devil incarnate.

She was nuts.

She was also standing like a mannequin before a duo of classical guitarists at a publishing bazaar hosted by the Museum of Natural History one evening. Two stories above her head was a life-sized model of a blue whale. She was not interested in the blue whale, but in the guitarists, who kept eyeing her like she was the heavy here to collect a vig.

One of the editors who had purchased a few of her articles had pointed her out to me through the crowd, and so I went over to her to introduce myself. I extended a hand, but she ignored me.

"They're summoning Magog," she said, not looking at me. This afforded me an opportunity to study her profile—the small, upturned nose, the frizz of black hair whose style was completely outdated, and her narrow little chin. She was pretty in an aloof, unconventional sense. Her body wasn't bad, but it looked like she'd borrowed the blouse and slacks from a roommate, because they were a bit too big for her slight frame. The blouse was open, revealing a faded black Misfits T-shirt underneath.

"These guys?" I said, glancing at the guitarists. They were maybe in their forties, with matching gray ponytails and beaded bracelets. They both gave me hard stares. "They seem pretty harmless."

"Subterfuge," Taryn said.

"Can you get her out of here?" one of the guitarists mouthed to me.

I looked at her. "Can I buy you a drink?"

"Generous. It's an open bar."

"I read your piece about the devil-worshipping saxophonist."

"You read it wrong. He wasn't a devil worshipper. He was the devil."

"Come on," I said. "Let me pretend to buy you a drink."

We slept together that night. She was one of those girls you knew you could sleep with right away. Not because she was easy, but because she wanted to sleep with you just as much as you wanted to sleep with her, and she made no attempt to hide it. We went back to my apartment, and she was this wily, pale, frizzy-haired thing in flaking black nail polish. When we were done, she dressed, pressed the tip of her nose to mine, and said, "Don't fall in love." Then she fled.

I had no phone number or address for her, and she maintained no online presence on social media, as far as I could tell. Email addresses that I obtained from editors bounced back undeliverable. I could only assume she was deliberately cloaking herself, having dissolved into some version of the Bat Cave deep beneath the trembling sprawl of the city. Of course, this was counterintuitive to our line of work—we all survived off people who contacted us with potential leads, so we needed to make ourselves accessible—so it only served to heighten my curiosity about her.

I resorted to tracking her through her published news stories like a bloodhound tracks a scent through the woods. East Side, West Side, she popped up like a bad penny throughout the city, almost tauntingly so, and I had no recourse but to document her appearances through her bylines like an epidemiologist charting pockets of a disease outbreak. Here and here and here. I found myself asking the few editors we had in common about her, but they had no information to offer, or weren't keen on providing it if they did. I felt like I was trailing a ghost. Begging for a haunting. Because that was it—Taryn Donaldson was haunting me.

"Do you know her?"

It became a question I asked other freelancers on the circuit, trying to make the question sound casual, off the cuff, like hey, just trying to share some common knowledge about one of our peers, right? This batso chick I hooked up with after some publishing event. Anyone? Anyone? Spreading the stories beneath the stories, the under-city that makes up the city, the frills of a blossoming disease throughout the stinking, rat-infested alleyways of Manhattan. Trying to convince myself that she was, in fact, a ghost. Because that would make things easier.

They're summoning Magog.

Most people didn't know her. A few did. One guy said he'd fucked her in the restroom of Jem's Pub on 15th Street, and I thought maybe this was a possibility. He described her the best he could, given how drunk he'd been. Shorn black fingernails and a Ramones T-shirt. Sounded about right. He didn't know her whereabouts either. Didn't care. Inconceivable to think these story-hungry vultures showed so little interest in the inexplicable disappearance of one of their own. Yet I guess some people resonate more powerfully with some than others. Depends who you are, and who they are with you. Or who they let you be. Depends on a lot of things.

About a year went by, maybe more. Of course, I eventually gave up my obsession, though, in truth, I never truly forgot about her. Even on the rare occasions when I would glimpse her byline in one of the local papers, I read it with a sense of bittersweet nostalgia, the way you look at pictures of ex-girlfriends in old high school yearbooks. I convinced myself she was a praying mantis, and I was lucky she hadn't eaten my face.

"Do you know her?"

I quit asking that question, too.

At some point, her bylines vanished altogether. She'd gone off the track. Her name was no longer below the printed mastheads, her decidedly dour photo no longer comprised of digital pixels among the online journals. Fleetingly, I wondered if the polytonal saxophonist had dragged her to hell, or if she'd become the unwitting sacrifice of that clandestine group of cultists she'd been surreptitiously tracking throughout the city. Anything, anything.

And then, like some lightning strike, she came up beside me at a bar, just pocketed right into place, *snick*, and she wasn't glammed up or turning any heads, and in truth I didn't even know it was her until she started talking.

"I've been thinking," she said. "What the fuck are we doing, man?"

I looked at her. Swear to God, it took me a second to place her. Even though she still looked the same.

"Taryn," I said.

"Answer me. What are we doing?"

"We? What we? Where'd you go?"

"Not 'we' as in 'us,' but 'we' as in our *individual* we. You and me *separatum*. You dig?"

"You're nuts," I told her.

"True fact, Jack. Buy me a drink? A real one this time?"

I bought her a beer and we vanished to a booth at the rear of the bar. I'd come with friends, but they'd disappeared. I didn't care.

"You had a neat name. What was it? It's on the tip of my tongue."

"Grady."

"Yes! Right. Grady."

"You're something else," I told her.

"Oh yes," she said.

"Still tormenting lonesome guitar duos?"

She frowned. "I don't know what you're talking about, but I bet it's clever." She took a pull on her beer.

"I tried to find you, you know," I said, then realized, as soon as the words were out of my mouth, that it sounded a bit desperate. Or maybe even a little stalker-ish. "I mean, after that night, I wanted to call you."

"How come?"

"I guess…well, to see you again."

"I told you not to fall in love, didn't I?"

"I'm not in love."

"I warned you."

"I'm not in love."

"Yeah?"

"You stopped writing," I said, by way of changing the subject. My face was already beginning to grow hot.

"Have I?"

"I mean, I haven't seen any of your stories in months."

"You know what my biggest regret is?" she said.

"Uh, what?"

"Not bringing a video camera."

"What? Tonight?"

"On assignment." She winked at me and said, "We're gonna do something, you and me. It's our destiny. I can feel it."

"Is that right?"

"It's in the stars, Grady."

I made a show of glancing at my watch. "I'm free if you are."

"I'm serious. We're gonna dig through the crust and arrive at the meaty truth."

"You're a nightmare."

"Oh, I am," she said, "but I'm yours. Not right at this second, but soon. My head feels like a beehive. Swimmy. So many thoughts."

"What's going on?" I asked her.

She ignored the question. "You still freelancing?" she asked instead.

I told her I was. Sort of disappointed she hadn't been keeping tabs on my bylines like I'd been keeping tabs on hers. Ghosts haunt people; people generally don't haunt ghosts.

"When was the last time you wrote something you really gave a shit about?" she asked me.

"I don't know," I said. "Maybe never."

"Exactly." Her eyes lit up. For an instant, she looked like something designed by Jim Henson—big eyes, bright face, that frizz of wild hair that was now down past her shoulders. "Do you know what I'm doing tomorrow?"

"What are you doing tomorrow?"

"I'm getting on a train to Indiana."

"What's in Indiana? Family?"

"A woman who murdered her two children," she said.

I guess I laughed. Maybe I thought she was joking. Or maybe I was growing uncomfortable.

"Boom, boom, boom," she said, making stabbing motions toward my solar plexus with one hand. "Twenty times each, right in the chest. One right after the other. I guess you do the older kid first, right? Less of a fight to contend with."

"Jesus Christ, Taryn…"

"Come with me," she said.

"What? I'm not going to Indiana. Come back to my apartment instead."

She narrowed her eyes. She wasn't beautiful, but in certain moments, she could stop your heart. Now was one of those moments.

"I'm serious," I said.

"So am I," she said.

"What paper is paying you to cover a murder story in Indiana?"

"None. And I'm not covering a murder story. I'm covering a possible demonic possession."

"What're you talking about?"

"Woman claims her children were possessed. That's why she killed them."

"Like, *Exorcist* possessed?"

"Is there another kind?"

I thought about my nearly year-long obsession with the girl staring at me right now but said nothing of it. "I don't get the point," I said instead.

"Come with me and find out," she said.

"Can't happen."

"Can't?"

"Won't."

She arched a slender black eyebrow. "Scared?"

I laughed.

We had some more beers and then we got in a cab. Before I could say a word to the driver, Taryn gave him an address on Chrystie Street. It was a loft apartment that she shared with no one. I whistled as I came through the door and looked around. What was her rent, five grand a month? I barely made enough cash to scrape together my portion of the rent for an icebox apartment I shared with another guy, and I could forget about those student loan payments.

"You live here alone?"

"Just me and the dust bunnies."

"How the hell do you afford this place?"

Her parents had been very wealthy. They'd died a few years earlier in an automobile accident and left Taryn not only their fortune but the payout on a sizable life insurance policy. It was suddenly apparent that Taryn Donaldson didn't have to work at all, which made her inclusion in the freelance rat race all the more curious.

I watched as she went around the loft, switching on little lamps in various corners. There was a desk in the middle of the room on which sat two chunky computer monitors, a stack of notebooks, a nice pair of headphones, and some audio equipment I couldn't name. A CPU tower stood on the floor beside the desk, as old as Moses.

"Wine or beer?" she asked as she went to the kitchen nook.

"Beer's fine." I went over to the desk. On the wall behind it were sheets of yellow legal paper with columns of numbers printed down them in meticulous handwriting.

Taryn returned with two Michelobs, handed one to me.

"What's all this?" I asked.

"Christ, I don't even know anymore." She stared at the computer monitors, the stack of notebooks, the pages taped to the wall with something akin to disappointment. Then she went around to the other side of the desk, set her beer atop the stack of notebooks, and tapped a few of the keys on the computer's keyboard.

I was startled when the voice of God came through the walls. An ancient voice, old and whiskeyed, rough as a foot callus and wise as a turtle. I saw there were speakers on a shelf behind the desk and some more across the loft, near Taryn's bed, which was just a mattress on the floor below a wall of windows that overlooked the Bowery.

"Ever notice how pretty much all accounts of ghost sightings, supposed alien encounters, all that shit, it's always the *same*?" she said. She was staring at one of her computer monitors, her face lit with a pale bluish glow from the screen. "Like, if all these people are crazy, then they're all crazy in almost the same exact way."

I came around the other side of the desk and saw that she had opened a file on the computer, which contained countless audio tracks. When the old man paused in his speech, Taryn's voice replaced it with a question, coming through the speakers that were now right behind me.

"Is this an interview?" I asked. "Who is this guy?"

"An old man who saw a ghost in Washington Square. He's one of four."

"Four what?"

"Four people who've seen ghosts in Washington Square."

"Okay. But what's the point of all this?"

"Could've been a documentary, if I'd had a video camera."

Suddenly, the video camera comment from earlier in the evening made sense. Talking with Taryn was sometimes like traveling through time, where she gave you the answer to a question hours before it was asked. Or before you even knew there was a question at all.

"Anyway, it's all over the place," she said, hitting the spacebar, which paused the audio. "There's nothing cohesive about it. And some of it's just crap, really. I've got an hour's worth of a woman who claims she saw a sea monster in the Hudson."

"Is this why you're going to Indiana tomorrow?"

She picked up her beer, took a swallow, then offered me a wan smile. "I can't help it. I love the stories. I just don't know what to do with them."

"That old guy's voice was magic," I told her. "I think maybe a video camera might take something away from the mystique."

"You think?" She set her beer back down on the desk.

"Sure. Then again, what the hell do I know?"

She kissed me—a quick peck on the lips. When she drew back, she said, "I'm not looking for a boyfriend."

"I'm not looking for a girlfriend."

"Good," she said, and proceeded to unbutton my jeans.

Sometime later, I was awoken by a cold breeze coming from the open window above my head. I rolled over and blinked up into the darkness. There was a little wooden disc with a bird on one side, a birdcage on the other, that hung from the ceiling and twirled lazily in the breeze. The faster it rotated, the more it looked like the bird was trapped in the cage.

I propped myself up on my elbows and saw Taryn across the room in the dark, surrounded in a nimbus of bluish light. She was stark naked and curled over her keyboard, staring at the computer screen. She had the big headphones on.

A bit more self-conscious than she, I wrapped the bed sheet around my waist and crept over to Taryn in the darkness. She looked up from the computer as I approached, her face pale and plain in the digital light. She was as young as a child in that moment.

"Group them together," I said.

She removed the headphones. "What?"

"Group them together. All the ghost stories in one segment, all the UFO stories in another. All the Hudson River sea monsters in another."

"Segments?" she said.

"Yeah. Like…episodes."

"Of what?"

"Of whatever you want it to be. Podcasts are getting pretty popular."

The idea struck her in some profound way; I could see the wheels turning behind her eyes. Slowly, she began nodding her head. She wrote the word *podcast* down on the yellow legal pad she was balancing on one pale, naked thigh.

I walked back toward the bed, ready for at least another hour or so of sleep. I was physically exhausted; we had torn into each other and I'd been woefully out of practice.

"What time does that train leave for Indiana?" I asked as I dropped back down on the bed. "I guess I could tag along."

Taryn Donaldson smiled at me through the darkness.

7

STAND UP AND TAKE NOTICE! is written in stark black letters on the door of the bunker. Below that is a picture of Homer Simpson being hauled toward a burbling caldron by two gelatinous green aliens in spacesuits. And below the picture is a bumper-sticker proclaiming that mankind is the unwitting main course in a grand galactic banquet—so fatten up.

The bunker. It's just how I left it, as if it's been cryogenically frozen and awaiting my return. It's a windowless Bleecker Street foxhole with sound-dampening foam on the walls, pegboard partitions, *X-Files* posters and Todd McFarlane figurines, all of it garlanded together by a cat's cradle of Mardi Gras beads, Christmas lights, and dangling pine-tree air fresheners. The air fresheners, profuse as they are, cannot mask the staleness of the air down here, the heated sizzle of electrical equipment commingled with body odor and a less identifiable pungent funk. There is the table at the center of the room, the laptops and recording equipment still right there, the dual microphones arching on their long metal elbows toward empty chairs. Two sets of headphones are on the table, their cords curled on the laminate tabletop like delicate black snakes. It's as if she has left my seat open and ready for me, in the event I might return. I never planned to return. Taryn isn't going to return now, either. *The Spectral* has died with her. The whole place looks like a museum diorama immortalizing the show that had once been recorded here.

Sammy's engineering booth is set up on a small platform against the far wall, behind a partition of Plexiglas. He's there now, slouched in his chair with the cans on, and in an old Lynyrd Skynyrd T-shirt speckled with some kind of dried rust-colored sauce.

In a way, this is worse than being in Taryn's apartment, even with all that madness scribbled out along the walls, even with the section of orange extension cord dangling from the I-beam and her computer in the bathtub. There is a history here—the history of *us*—that is so profound it feels like the air is different, that the colors are brighter, that the smells in this place have the power to transport you to a wholly different dimension.

I try not to think about it.

Sammy gives me a perfunctory nod from behind his wall of Plexiglas. It's as if I've never left. I've got a six-pack of Miller, and I hand him one as he comes down from the platform. He thinks I'm here to record a eulogy for Taryn, which he can tag on to the end of the final episode that is still yet to air, but that's not exactly true. I thought I might summon the courage to do it on the cab ride over, say a few quick words before my emotions got the better of me, but being here, now, I find that I have chickened out. Besides, there are other pressing matters on my mind.

As we sit at the table in the center of the room drinking our beers, I say, "What was she working on just before she died?"

"Well, we were finishing up postproduction on the current episode and batting around ideas for what to do next," Sammy says. "She hadn't really made a decision one way or the other."

"The other day you mentioned she had become obsessed over something she was working on. Do you know what it was?"

"Well, she really didn't go into it with me, but…" He trails off, his gaze shifting toward the engineering booth.

"But what?"

"About two months ago she asked me to make copies of a bunch of files. Put them on an external drive. You remember me telling you?"

"What files?"

"Audio files."

"Audio of what?"

"White noise," Sammy says, and I pause with my beer halfway to my mouth. "Like when you run to the end of a reel of tape but you still got the speakers cranked? You know what I mean? That hissing sound?"

I'm nodding my head, thinking of the CD in the stereo back at Taryn's apartment.

"Here, hold on," Sammy says. He gets up from the table and saunters back behind his partition of Plexiglas. There's a filing cabinet back there, and a bulletin board bristling with flyers, takeout menus, business cards, and reams of handwritten show notes. There is a dry-erase board back there, too, and I can see the details of the episode that was currently in postproduction—the mapping of random and seemingly unrelated concepts and ideas into a pie chart of semi-coherency. Chaos into comprehension. That's how stories are made.

Sammy taps a few keys on his console. There are a half dozen Bose speakers mounted around the room, strategically placed for optimum sound, and they instantly come alive. The sound is at once familiar yet wholly alien to me—a drone-like hum combined with a sharp hiss. It is the same sound that issued from Taryn's CD player back at her apartment the other day, yet it is also different, too. I recall how the audio track back at the apartment grew louder, a crescendo of static that, in hindsight, reminds me of the conclusion of the Beatles' song "A Day in the Life," the way the orchestra builds into controlled madness before it all slams to an end. This sound is different. It doesn't build, but remains a steady drone.

It hurts my head.

I wave a hand at Sammy to turn it off. He does.

He returns with a stack of yellow legal pads. I can make out the handwriting on the pages from where I'm sitting, and I can tell that they belonged to Taryn. He tosses them on the table in front of me. I see that the first page is crowded with groupings of numbers, of time codes. Each grouping consists of five or six time codes corralled in a circle. I flip through the pad and find that the same stuff is written on subsequent pages. It's similar to what was written on the notebooks and even on the walls back in Taryn's apartment, but with one major difference—these notes seem controlled, thoughtful, precise. The notes back in Taryn's apartment were madness, scribbled as if in a panic, like someone cranking out an SOS before their ship goes down. Not to mention half of her notes had been printed in marker on the walls of her apartment...

"She was taking notes on this stuff," Sammy says, dropping back down in his chair. He's killed his beer and goes for another.

"This white noise? What exactly is there to take notes on?"

"I don't know, but I asked her about it. She said there was more to it. If you listen. Other sounds. Like, sounds behind sounds, masked by other sounds. A collage of sound, Taryn called it. She was trying to find some pattern in it all."

"*Is* there a pattern?"

"Beats me. If I listen to that shit for more than thirty seconds, I get a pounding headache."

"Where'd they come from?"

"The audio files? A listener sent them in. As email attachments. Nearly a hundred of them."

I feel myself do a double take. "A *hundred*? A hundred different audio clips of white noise?"

Sammy pulls one of the laptops on the table in front of him. The blunt pegs of his fingers rattle the keyboard. I glance back down at the stack of yellow legal pads. Something occurs to me. "When did the first email from this listener come in?"

"A couple months ago," Sammy says, "but I can get you an exact date in just a sec."

A couple months ago. There are three legal pads sitting here in front of me. Every page of each pad is filled. Toward the back, the notes start to get sloppy, and more reminiscent of what was on the walls of Taryn's apartment. As if she started losing her shit toward the end.

"She filled up three notebooks in just two months' time?" I say. I do not mention to him the state of her apartment.

"Like I said, she was obsessed."

"I don't get it."

Sammy turns the laptop around so that we can both view the screen.

Unless things have changed in the seven months since my departure from the show, this is what I know: On any given month, *The Spectral* receives approximately two hundred emails from listeners. A large portion of these are your basic fan mail—praise of a particular episode or a show of appreciation for the work done—while others are suggestions for episode ideas, for topics that are of interest to the show's listeners. A smaller portion of the emails are from people proposing that *The Spectral* should investigate their *own* story—that something inexplicable or seemingly paranormal has materialized in this particular person's life, and they are calling on the hosts—or host, since my departure—of *The Spectral* to come investigate and hopefully bring some closure to whatever might be haunting them. This might sound crazy, but it is from this last category that Taryn and I would get most of our episode ideas.

We would also receive our fair share of rambling, nonsensical, gonna-shoot-the-president emails, which we kept in an ironically named digital folder we called the Forget-Me-Nots. As a rule, we never deleted any emails, but the Forget-Me-Nots folder was as good a cyber wastebasket as you'll ever find. It's a black hole. All *was* forgotten. And I cannot recall a single time I've ever gone fishing in that macabre little pond for something after it had been unceremoniously dispatched into those murky depths.

But that is exactly what I'm looking at now. Sammy has opened the Forget-Me-Nots folder, and has scrolled to a series of emails from someone called the Night Listener. When Sammy scrolls to the bottom, I see that there are exactly 119 emails from this particular individual. Every single one was sent on the same date—June 9, a little over two months ago.

"That's a hundred and nineteen emails of white noise," I marvel aloud.

"No, man. It's crazier than that. It's a hundred and nineteen emails of white noise *that Taryn wanted me to make copies of*. She was listening to this shit for months."

"That's enough to drive anyone crazy." And even as I say this, I hear how it sounds. I want to backtrack, to change it, but I can't. Sammy just looks miserable. I clear a lump from my throat. "And then what? A hundred and nineteen emails in one day, and then nothing else? They just stopped coming?"

"Just stopped coming," Sammy says, nodding his shaggy head.

"Night Listener," I mutter, reading the name on the screen. For some reason it rings a bell for me, although I cannot figure out why. "Who *is* this guy?"

"Just that," Sammy says. "A listener. A fan."

I see that every email has a file attached. I point to the little paperclip icon. "Those are the audio files, I assume? There's a file attached to every single one?"

"Yes. Sometimes more than one."

"What does he say in the emails?"

"Well, he says nothing in the later ones, just sends the file. But he makes a half-assed introduction in the first email."

Sammy clicks on the email dated June 9. It loads on the screen:

> Greetings, Ms. Donaldson,
>   As discussed, attached are the first few audio files I have recorded. I will send the others in separate emails.
> Things have changed. Warning: DO NOT LISTEN TO

RECORDINGS ALL AT ONCE! It is best to do so in
three-minute intervals with at least a twenty-minute
break in between.

Have you been approved yet? If so, I hope you are
being careful.

Awaiting your reply,

The Night Listener

"Approved for what?" I ask.

"Beats me."

"You said this is the first email from this guy?"

"Yeah."

"Because he opens with 'As discussed,' which suggests they've
talked previously."

"If they did, it wasn't through this server or this email account.
And Taryn never said anything about it."

"And she never said why she was listening to this stuff?"

"She just asked me to download all the files this guy emailed to
the show. So that's what I did. She's the boss. Or *was*."

"And they're all like the one you played for me? Static?"

"Well, I didn't listen to every single one, but I'm guessing yeah."

I'm confused why this is something Taryn keyed in on. What
about this scenario had piqued her interest? What am I missing that
Taryn could see?

"'Awaiting your reply.' Did she ever write back to the guy?"

"Not that I know of," Sammy says. "There aren't any responses
to him through the show's email account."

"We must be missing something obvious here," I say. "Something
in the recordings themselves that Taryn heard."

"Well, Grady, you're welcome to listen to them if you want,"
Sammy says. "As long as they don't make you crazy."

We look at each other just as he says this. No doubt the same thought has sparked to life inside both our heads. *Taryn.*

But it's too preposterous for either of us to speak it aloud.

8

For the second time, Sammy Deane copies all of the Night Listener's files onto an external hard drive. He gives this one to me, but not before wrapping it in a brown paper sandwich bag, presumably because he feels this is akin to some illegal transaction. As for myself, as I step out of the bunker and onto the sidewalk, I try not to feel like I'm hauling around a bag of plutonium. I've got Taryn's legal pads with me, too, although I'm not quite sure what my intentions are. Maybe I *have* no intentions. Maybe I just want to take a piece of her madness with me, out of that bunker and into the real world. Set it free like some caged bird.

I'm still not sure what I'm doing when I hail a cab then tell the driver to take me to Chrystie Street. To Taryn's apartment.

I've still got the key to her apartment on my key ring, though I suppose it's possible she's had the locks changed since last I used it. But she hasn't: the tumblers roll and the door squeals open. I take a deep breath before stepping inside; the state of the apartment is still too fresh in my memory, and I'm not quite sure I'm ready to look at it all again. Not this recently, anyway. But I'm not sure how long it will be before the apartment is repainted and cleaned up, and before all of Taryn's stuff is shipped off somewhere. Before some stranger is living here. Taryn had no living relatives, at least as far as I know, so I can't begin to wonder what happens to all the personal items she's left behind. Is there some great donation bin where it will all go? Will I inadvertently stumble across homeless people and hookers in Times Square donning her wardrobe? Or is it just all off to the city dump?

Because I assume it's the latter, what I am about to do does not feel even remotely like stealing. Stealing from whom? Who cares about this stuff, anyway? I take the CD from the stereo (even though I have a copy of the file on the hard drive Sammy gave me, or at least I should), as well as the stack of notebooks from her desk. I root through a closet and find a small suitcase, which I fill with the classical music records and CDs that teeter in tiny towers around her workstation. I feel only slightly like I'm overreacting when I snap several photos with my cell phone of the craziness sketched on all the walls. I do my damnedest not to stare at the I-beam and the partial length of electrical cord still hanging there—

When will someone take that down?

—and then pluck the Post-it notes from the computer monitors and stuff them in the suitcase, too.

Taryn's cell phone is on the floor near her mattress. It looks almost hidden there, a secret from a dream poking out from beneath a pillow. *Goddamn it, Taryn*, and just like that, I'm furious at her.

After some minimal deliberation, I shove the phone in my pocket. Then my gaze rises until I'm staring at the thaumatrope hanging by a string in front of the wall of windows. Bird on one side, birdcage on the other. It reminds me of our first night together all those years ago. I tug gently at its string. Bird, cage, bird, cage.

It is the floorboards settling, of course, but when I hear that loud creak in the otherwise silent apartment, I freeze. Then I turn around to see if Taryn will be standing there. I almost expect it. That shock of black hair, those eyes that suck thoughts from your head. In a ratty Black Flag T-shirt and baggy jeans, maybe, or perhaps nude except for the bed sheet twisted about her pale, narrow frame.

And for a moment, I almost see her. Tears burn in my eyes.

But of course, I am alone. The only ghosts here are the ones I've brought with me.

Before I leave, wheeling the suitcase behind me, I pause and stare at the condition of the place one last time. Not just the jumble of words and numbers and madness sketched on the walls, but of the swatches of black paint that Taryn had lathered closest to the door, and those words in stark black lettering, more prominent than the rest of the writing she'd printed on the walls: DO NOT READ. Now, in the light of a new day, I feel I am very close to seeing things from a different light. A different perspective.

Do not read, I think. *Do not read what?*

It occurs to me that, perhaps very near the end, Taryn came upon some realization and tried to cover it up. She purchased black paint to cover up what she had printed all over the walls. But the grip of her madness was too strong, and she never finished. Instead, she left that ominous warning—DO NOT READ—before killing herself.

What did she hide beneath that black paint?

What did she not want someone to read?

What secrets was she keeping?

Who was she warning?

Anyone who might listen, I tell myself. But I don't believe that to be true. Not really.

Because: me.

She was warning *me*.

9

As I wait for a cab outside Taryn's apartment, I am struck—irrefutably—with the sensation that someone is watching me. Sure, it's a busy Manhattan street, populated with scores of people with countless peering eyes…yet I'm suddenly certain that at least one person is gazing at me from some remote distance. It's a feeling that accosts the animal part of my brain and sends a shiver down to the base of my spine.

I look around, see no one of any consequence—just New Yorkers perambulating along the sidewalk, doing their New York thing. Yet I still sense those eyes, radiating from some hidden pocket of the city, watching me…

A cab pulls to the curb and the driver lays on his horn, startling me.

Nothing, I tell myself as I climb into the cab. *It's nothing.*

10

I give Taryn's cell phone to Sammy Deane, in hopes that he'll be able to bypass the password-protection. None of the combinations I've typed have worked, and I'm reluctant to keep going and risk crashing the phone. He's skeptical, eyeballing me like I'm a grave robber, or some pervert on tiptoes gazing through a lighted window. I tell him I want to see whom she was in contact with during the last few days of her life. The expression on his face is telling—*What's the point?* it says. And maybe that's a fair question. What *is* the point? I can't bring her back.

In an effort to lessen his suspicion, or to perhaps arouse his own curiosity, I show him the photos I snapped of Taryn's apartment—the crazed scribbling on the walls, the filthy state of the place, the goddamn CPU in the bathtub, which for some weird reason the police have just left there. This seems to sell it to him; he shakes his woolly head, looks interminably sad for a moment, then agrees to crack open her phone and get back to me.

I've got some deadlines for stories I'm writing for *NewsBlitz*, but I've got a long lead time and I'm not under the gun. So I take a few days and hunker down in my apartment where I comb, page by page, through Taryn's notebooks and legal pads. Because it's kitschy, I've also got an old turntable near my bed, and I find myself playing the LPs I took from Taryn's apartment, one after another, like it's some factory assembly line. I have always been lukewarm on classical music, but I find these records gradually lulling me into…well, if not a trance, then certainly a peacefulness that seems juxtaposed only by the increasing calamity of Taryn's handwritten notes.

There is little sense to be made from her notes. What is clear is that she was attempting to dissect the audio clips sent to her by the Night Listener. What is *unclear* is *why*. I plug in the external hard drive Sammy gave me and pull up all the files. I listen to snippets of the audio recordings, each one a frizz of static, and one thing becomes instantly apparent—I can only listen to this madness for brief periods at a time, because the sonic hiss-drone-crackle of that white noise causes my head to throb. I think of the Night Listener's warning in his email about listening to the files for periods of three minutes at a time with a twenty-minute break in between and decide that maybe there is some good advice in there. Because the alternative is what? Hanging from a rafter with an extension cord tied around my neck?

That's terrible.

I feel…unhinged.

I spend some time composing an email to the Night Listener, tweaking it and second-guessing myself. Finally, I send it. Almost immediately, it returns undelivered. I wonder if this is a sign from the cosmos. *Back off, Russo. Did you not read the literal writing on the wall?* I resend the email and it bounces back again without hesitation. It seems the Night Listener is not accepting unsolicited emails. Either that or maybe he's shut down the account.

On a particularly warm evening, I stand out on my fire escape with a glass of Woodford Reserve and watch the menagerie of traffic lights swipe back and forth beyond the mouth of the alley. I've got Taryn's CD—the one I took from her stereo—playing in my apartment; I find I can listen for longer periods of time with a buffer between me and the sounds on the disc. In this case, the buffer is my closed window. That pane of glass is like a radiation shield. And even then, as the white noise rises in strident peaks, I can feel it *through* the windowpane. It's less a sound and more a tremor in my back teeth. A tiny oral earthquake.

I happen to look down and see a figure standing in the alley, staring up at me. It's dusky enough so that I can't make out details from such a height (except that I sense the figure is male), and he's directly below me, so that he's partially blocked by the grate of the fire escape. Immediately, I think back to the sensation I'd felt upon leaving Taryn's apartment, that I was being watched by unseen eyes. I feel it now all over again, tenfold.

I lean over the rail for a better look, which is when the figure shifts closer to my building. He moves with a stiff gait, like someone in physical pain or distress, but he's still quick about it. It's like whoever it is, he doesn't want me to see him. Like my having spotted him was an accident, was a mistake. Like he's being cagey now.

I call down to him, a generic salutation, my voice reverberating off the brick facade of the building across the alleyway. But that only causes him to press closer to the building. I go around to the other side of the fire escape and peer down, just in time to catch him vanishing behind a dumpster. I wait for him to reemerge, but he doesn't. He must have headed in the opposite direction, toward the street.

There are sometimes homeless people who wander down the alley to sift through the dumpster. This person, with their furtive movements and their reluctance to be seen, did not strike me as one of the homeless, which only serves to heighten my suspicion. But then I think, *Suspicion of what?*

Am I making myself paranoid?

I finish my drink, pour myself another, and stand out there while Taryn's CD continues to spit static from my stereo.

It's when I'm lying in bed one night while *not* looking at Taryn's notes that I suddenly realize how the puzzle is constructed. I flip the sheet off me and stagger in my boxer shorts into the miniscule living room, which doubles as my home office. The desk is shoved against one wall, overflowing with Taryn's notebooks. Her records—*my* records— are spread out everywhere. Because it has become confusing keeping track of all these notebooks and legal pads, I have started maintaining my own notes on the dry-erase board above the desk. I have transposed a series of time codes from one of the legal pads to the dry-erase board. These are all labeled "dogs barking" in Taryn's chicken-scratch handwriting on the legal pad, and in my more cautious printing on the dry-erase board. Yet when I pull up the audio files and scroll to the time codes mentioned in her notes, I hear nothing but static. In other words, without knowing which audio file corresponds with each time code, I am at a loss.

It is only now, in the desperate and widening hours of night, that I understand her system—that each *notebook* corresponds with a particular file. The notebooks themselves contain a number on the first page that corresponds with the specific email sent by the Night Listener. Notebook #5 corresponds to email #5, which in turn connects to the attached file of said email, and so on. On the occasions more than one file was sent in a single email, she has denoted this with a series of sub-numbers at the top of each notebook. It is suddenly right there in my face.

I pull up an audio file, scroll to the corresponding time code, and play it through my laptop's speakers. Fuzz and hiss, boom shaking.

I plug in some heavy-duty headphones and strap them on. Here we go.

It takes a couple of listens until I hear it, but it's there, buried beneath all those layers of hiss and static and industrial washing machine sounds: the faint din of a dog barking.

I repeat this process all through the night. It's not just the dogs. I find that there are languages being spoken behind the wall of white noise; there are snippets of classical music, some of which I recognize from Taryn's records, which I've been playing on and off; the rumbling of a distant thunderstorm; even what sounds like the metallic, fuzzed-out screech of an electric guitar.

I suddenly feel feverish with excitement. I'm sweaty and achy and my head hurts, but something inside me now feels connected, albeit tenuously, with Taryn's spirit. I'm not a religious person, and despite having been a co-host and co-producer of *The Spectral* for years, I do not believe in the supernatural. However, I am suddenly compelled to dash about my tiny apartment, switching on all the lamps, flipping all the light switches, just to confirm that Taryn isn't *right here with me*, spying on me from the shadows. A ghost. Or a demon.

They're summoning Magog.

"Of course," I mutter into the darkness. "Of course they are. Aren't we all?"

My head feels like it's been squeezed in a vise.

11

I'm dreaming about someone banging on my door. But in reality, it's someone banging on my door. I jump out of bed, pull on a pair of jeans, and hurry down the hall.

It's Sammy Deane. He's got a bag of McDonald's in one hand and Taryn's cell phone in the other. "Here," he says, thrusting the cell phone at me. "It's done." He seems disgusted by the whole transaction and just wants to be rid of it.

"You're a hero," I tell him, taking the phone.

He follows me inside, looking around. For the first time in days I am aware that my apartment is wrecked. It stinks, too—I haven't done dishes or laundry since I returned from Taryn's apartment with her notes. I try to recall exactly when that was, but I cannot be sure. Three days ago? A week?

"The hell happened here?" Sammy says. He clutches his McDonald's bag to his chest, as if fearful some of my filthiness might infect his food.

"Been working. You want some coffee?"

"No way."

I pour myself some from the pot and drink it cold.

Sammy goes to the dry-erase board, where I have continued my decoding of Taryn's notes. I ran out of room on the board, so much of my writing has leaked out along the drywall in crooked sentences. Sammy stares at the writing on the wall, so close that his nose nearly touches the ink, and then he straightens up. He looks at me from over the half-wall that separates the living area from the kitchenette.

"What?" I say. I manage a grin for his benefit.

"Now I'm worried," Sammy says.

"About what?"

"About you, Grady. This place looks like the pictures you showed me of Taryn's apartment. Is that…is that what you're trying to do?"

"I'm not trying to do anything. Here—let me show you what I figured out."

I spill some coffee on my rush toward my desk. The audio files are already on the laptop screen, so I consult my notes and play a series of files that I have edited together in a nearly seamless loop. There is the white noise, of course, but there is also the orchestral strains of Bach's Brandenburg Concerto no. 2 beneath it. I have manipulated the audio to bring the music to the forefront.

"First movement," I tell him, and hold up the Munich Bach Orchestra record album that sits atop the stack of records beside my desk. "That's what she was doing with all these classical records. She was trying to identify the music hidden on the audio files."

"Sounds like shit," Sammy says. "Shut it off."

"Not a classical fan, huh?"

"That's no music, Grady. That's just…that's *noise*. I can't listen to it."

"Yeah, it hurts my head, too. But it's in there. You just gotta *listen*."

"Don't wanna."

"Yeah, well, that Night Listener guy was right; you can only listen to it in short bursts. Gave me a few nosebleeds, too, when I first started."

"Shut it *off*, bro."

I turn off the speakers. It feels like my skull expands in the aftermath.

"You need to get out of this apartment," Sammy tells me. "Open a window, at least." He glances down at his bag of food, and I can tell his appetite has fled.

I pry open a window. There is no breeze; the city outside feels like a kiln.

"What are you trying to do here, man?" Sammy says. "Like, look…I get it that you feel a little guilty. I do, too. But you're not gonna find any answers here, Grady. You're not gonna come to understand what she did to herself. It'll never make sense. Stuff like this never does."

I guess I'm just staring at him, not saying anything.

"I know you loved her, man," Sammy goes on. "So did I. But you can't go losing your own mind looking for answers."

A part of me knows he's right. Another part of me wonders if that is, exactly, what I've been doing. Looking for answers? Searching for absolution by inserting logic into an illogical situation? Because what Taryn did to herself was not logical. Suicide? I could search forever and never arrive at a conclusion.

"I didn't have to walk away completely," I hear myself say. My body suddenly feels loose, like it's being held together by pipe cleaners and stretched-out rubber bands. "I didn't have to walk out of her life when I walked away from the show. I get it now. I get it."

"You can't do this to yourself, man. Let's go out, have some lunch."

I set my cold coffee on the desk and stare out the open window.

"C'mon, Grady. Let's put it to rest. Go grab a shower and we'll get out of here for a while."

So that's what we do.

12

When I return home later that afternoon, I see my apartment for how it really is. *Jesus Christ*. I clean it up a bit, tucking Taryn's notebooks in my desk, her record albums in my hall closet. I do the dishes and stuff my dirty clothes in the laundry hamper. I remove the Bach record from the turntable and replace it with a Thin Lizzy album. I open all the windows and smell the city as it crawls inside, hot and steamy and summer-damp. With a sponge, I scrub the writing off my wall.

Truth is, I do not give Taryn's obsession a second thought until later that evening, when I notice her cell phone on the coffee table. I pick it up, power it on. Sammy successfully bypassed the login screen, so it opens to all her social media applications, her email, her music and audio books and downloaded podcasts and whatever else she kept on her phone, with ease.

Okay, so I *do* feel a bit like a Peeping Tom as I scroll through her phone. I make it a point not to access her photos. I *do* access her text messages, though. Not to sound overly dramatic, but it's true that text messages are repositories of our personal and professional exchanges, a snapshot of someone's life, a digital fingerprint that we leave out there in cyberspace. Communiqués that sum up the existence of our lives.

Taryn Donaldson was a loner with no living relatives (as far as I know) and very few friends. The cache of text messages in her phone are testament to this, and I feel miserable as I note that the majority are spam—boilerplate missives about fluctuating mortgage rates and medications that will prolong erections. There is a string of messages between Taryn and Sammy, entirely work-related.

I keep scrolling until I see my name. It shouldn't bother me, but it does—pummels me like guilt, in fact. I notice the date of the texts go back to March, when I agreed to meet her at that bar in Greenwich Village. She had tried to convince me to come back to the show, but I had refused. I had dismissed her. When she got up to use the restroom, I paid the tab and left. That was the last time we spoke.

I close out the messaging app and set the phone back on the coffee table. I lean back against the couch, unable to shake the image of that cut piece of extension cord hanging from the beam in Taryn's apartment. I'm thinking, too, of the Night Listener's email, the one Sammy showed me at the bunker. I'm thinking about the words *as discussed*.

I sit forward and snatch up the phone again. Open Taryn's

phonebook, scroll through all the names of contacts, thinking that this is surely a futile effort, but then I see it—NIGHT LISTENER, followed by a phone number.

No fucking way.

The Night Listener is right here, in her phone.

Who are you? I wonder. *What poison had you sent to Taryn in those audio files?*

Using Taryn's cell phone, I dial the number.

I wait.

It doesn't ring. It doesn't disconnect. It doesn't seem to do anything but remain in suspended animation.

Maybe the Night Listener's got Taryn's number blocked, so I switch to my own cell phone and dial the same number.

And am greeted by the same result: nothing.

I try to locate the owner of the number online—I even feed my credit card number into one of those search engines—but there are no results. The Night Listener has gone to great lengths to make sure his or her privacy remains private.

Who are you? The thought keeps rolling around and around in my head. *Who are you and what have you done?*

13

A strange chirping sound fills my apartment later that evening, as I'm getting out of the shower. It takes me a moment to realize it's the ringtone on Taryn's cell. The caller has concealed their number, but I answer it anyway.

"Is this Grady Russo?" says the person on the other end of the phone. The voice is soft and paper-thin. Male. Deliberately quiet, I think.

On my end of the line, I whisper back: "How do you know my name?"

Instead of answering my question, the caller says, "If you're calling, then she's dead." It's not a question, but there is a slight inflection in the caller's voice that suggests he's not one hundred percent sure, either.

"How do you know that?" I ask. Then: "Who *are* you?"

I can hear him breathing on the other end of the line. If I could take on any comic-book superpower in that moment, it would be the ability to siphon people's thoughts straight out of their heads and pull them through their cell phones.

"Answer me," I demand.

Just when I think he will hang up, he gives me the name of a bar on the Lower East Side, and tells me to meet him there in one hour.

Then the line goes dead.

14

The bar is called Ill Will's, and it's not the type of establishment I would ordinarily patronize. To be frank, it looks like a murder might happen here at any moment. It might even be me.

I squeeze through the narrow doorway and survey the dimly lit atmosphere, the stink of body odor in the air. The buzz-haired bartender looks like she can crack walnuts under her chin, and she's probably the most delicate flower in the place.

I'm twenty minutes early for my rendezvous with the Night Listener. Part of me wanted to scope out the place ahead of time, but really, my mounting anxiety wouldn't allow me to hang around my apartment once I got off the phone. I had to get dressed and get here, to see what this was all about. To find out how this guy knows my name and knows that Taryn is dead.

I go straight to the bar and order a scotch and soda. I might have ordered a fetus in a football helmet judging by the look the bartender gives me, but she obliges. When the drink arrives, I toss back a healthy swallow, then peer down at a phrase carved into the lacquered wooden top of the bar: STAND UP AND TAKE NOTICE! It's the same phrase that's on the sign that hangs on the door of the bunker. Its appearance here in this place—perhaps carved with a knife that has seen some action—strikes me as a bad omen. It's almost as if it's telling me to wake the fuck up and get out of Dodge.

There is a man seated on a stool at the far end of the bar, watching me. He's maybe in his fifties, but he looks like they've been harsh years, so it's difficult to tell for sure. A tuft of sagebrush beard sprouts from his chin, and he's got his hair pulled back in a ponytail. He's got large, blue-collar hands, too, only the fingernails on his wide, blunt fingers are painted black.

I watch as he empties his beer glass, only to receive a refill from the bartender without having to ask. She brings him a shot of something dark and menacing, too, and I watch him knock it back like someone taking liquid Tylenol from one of those tiny plastic measuring cups—a quick jerk of his fingers and then the booze is history. He even swabs the inside of the shot glass with his tongue.

It's him, of course. The Night Listener. He must know it's me, too—I stand out like a freak show attraction in this place, or whatever the opposite of that analogy is—but he doesn't come over to me until twenty minutes go by. So, in that regard, he's right on time.

He's got on large black forester boots, a chain wallet, and a belt buckle that might actually be a pewter serving tray. The pièce de résistance is his grimy black T-shirt that says RUBY COX, a pinkish red cartoon chicken that looks unambiguously phallic below the text.

"What're you lookin' at, Charlotte?" the guy asks, coming up beside me. He reeks like a pigsty and his arms are dressed in intricate tattoos. A diamond stud winks at me from one earlobe. "You gaming to get your eyes poked out?"

"Are you…the guy who called me?" I ask. I'm aware the bartender is watching this exchange, as are the other patrons. I'm aware, too, that my voice is a bit unsteady.

The guy laughs, and I catch a glimpse of teeth that look like pinto beans. Then he settles one of his sturdy mitts on my shoulder. Gives me a squeeze. "You are in deep, my sister," he tells me. He raises his other hand in a fist, but casually. I watch as his pinkie finger pops up and down, up and down, in the suggestion that either he or I have a small dick. I can guess who.

"Leave him alone, Quinn," the bartender says, though I can tell it's with some reservation. She's enjoying this nearly as much as the foul-breathed beast with his hand on my shoulder.

I shrug the guy's hand off my shoulder then get up off my stool. The guy's eyes are locked on me as I dig my wallet from the rear pocket of my jeans, then dump more than enough cash on the bar to cover my drink as well as a generous tip. It occurs to me that I might not leave this place with that wallet, but in the moment, I don't care. I feel like I've been set up, like I've been led here the way you'd lead a cow to slaughter. Oblivious.

"Where're you going, Charlotte?" the man—Quinn—calls after me as I weave around the tables toward the door. Hands swat me on the ass as I go, and their harsh laughter follows me out onto the sidewalk.

The night is humid, and there is an oily quality to the air; it tastes like a buttery version of soot at the back of my throat. I stand there, perspiring, my sense of self-preservation changing places with anger now at having been duped. And for what purpose? Why the hell would the Night Listener tell me to show up here just to stand me up and maybe even get me beat to a pulp? I don't understand any of it, and I certainly—

There is a man waving at me from across the street.

He's got the hood of his sweatshirt up over his head, so I can't make out many details, but he looks to be about my age. Also, he's leaning on a cane. As I stand there staring at him, he keeps waving me over with mounting urgency. Before I know what I'm doing, I'm hurrying across the street and nearly trip over a mound of plastic trash bags on the curb.

"You're Grady Russo," the guy says. Again, it's not a question, although he doesn't sound completely confident. He's a little breathless and looking me up and down.

"What the fuck is this all about? You told me to meet you in that place, and I almost got myself killed."

This close, I can see that he's maybe even younger than me. Maybe middle to late twenties. Someone's done a tune on his face— he sports a prominent black eye and the right side of his jaw looks swollen. He's wearing a navy blue hoodie and gray track pants, the tear away kind with the snaps down the legs. Pristine Air Jordans on his feet, startlingly white; they appear to radiate with their own internal light in the dark.

"Those dudes wouldn't kill you," he says, though he looks uncertain as he says it. "Maybe do some other stuff, but not kill you."

"What's this all about? Who the hell are you? How do you know who I—"

The guy lifts one hand, motions for me to slow down. "Look, I'll explain whatever I can, but you gotta understand I'm not making the rules here. I'm just going along with it, same as your friend was doing, given choices that I gotta pick from. Sometimes I pick the right one, other times, well…"

"What choices? What are you talking about?"

He turns and looks up the block, to where the front windows

of a Chinese restaurant lay a rectangle of soft blue light onto the sidewalk.

"You hungry?" he says.

15

Once we're seated in a booth and a waitress has taken our drink orders, I ask him his name.

He's already shaking his head. It's as though he's anticipated this question. Prepared for it. "No," he says. "No way, man. No names. I've made that mistake in the past and it's cost me." He leans over and pats the head of his cane, which leans against the outside of the booth. He's got his hood down now that we're inside, and I can see someone has pummeled his right ear, which is red and swollen, to go along with the damage they've done to the rest of his face.

"You're the Night Listener," I say.

"Yeah, okay, we'll stick with that. Might as well. Hey, look, I'm sorry about your friend. If you don't mind me asking, how'd she do it?"

I tell him about the extension cord tied to the I-beam in her loft.

"Extension cord, right," he says, and it's like he's ruminating over something. I get the sense there's some detail here I'm not privy to, or maybe something I've missed, and it's making me anxious. "You used to co-host the podcast with her," he says. "*The Spectral*. I'm a huge fan, you know. Or was. I've listened to every episode. How come you quit?"

"What is this, a job interview? How did you know Taryn was dead?"

The Night Listener leans forward across the table. When he speaks again, his voice is just a notch above a whisper. "You ever hear of the Story?"

"What story?"

"An electronic, interactive book, that exists solely online. I don't know who created it, who maintains it, or how long it's been circulating out there. It's not for sale at any bookstore and you can't check it out of the New York Public Library. It's not something you can just Google and find on the internet."

"You're talking about the dark web," I say.

"I'm talking about whatever exists *behind* the dark web."

"What does this have to do with Taryn's death?"

"I'll get to that," he says, "but first, you gotta keep an open mind, man. Don't be like you were on that show."

He's referring to my persona on *The Spectral*. Whereas Taryn was the wide-eyed believer, I was the pragmatic skeptic. It wasn't an act; it's who we are. Or were.

Our waitress arrives with our drinks—scotch and soda for me, a beer and a porcelain flask of hot sake for my companion. She bows demurely, but before she can leave, the Night Listener orders the Fun Yum Dinner Platter #7, extra spicy. He asks me if I want anything, but I shake my head. The young woman bows again then glides soundlessly across the dimly lit restaurant. On a small stage at the rear of the place, a man with a round, sweaty face is adjusting an elbowed microphone stand in preparation for karaoke.

The Night Listener takes a sturdy gulp of his beer, then pours some sake into a small ceramic cup. I watch the steam billow out. "You remember those old Choose Your Own Adventure books that were popular, like, a million years ago? All those easily digestible little adventures where every chapter ended with a decision to be made by the reader? If you want to slay the dragon, turn to page seventy-one. If you want to run like a little coward bitch, turn to page eighty-two. Well, the Story, it's like that. You read the Story, follow the prompts, make a decision. If you make the correct decision, you're allowed to continue, and you're rewarded with a clue, which, in theory, will help you make the correct *subsequent* decision."

"What happens if you make the wrong decision?"

Something stiffens behind the bulwark of the Night Listener's face. "You don't want to do that," he says.

"How do I know which is the right decision?" I ask.

"You won't. Not until after you've made it. Go with your gut, I say. Intuition. Or flip a coin, whatever. Thing is, when you make the right decision, the clues are provided to the reader in a series of audio clips."

"Those are the audio files you emailed to Taryn," I say. "But they were nothing but white noise."

"No." He shakes his head. "Not at first. They only turned to static once I copied the files. They *changed*, is what I'm saying. It's like they're not meant to exist outside the Story. You take a fish out of water, it *dies*, man."

"What were they before they changed?" I'm thinking of the distant sounds of dogs barking, of classical music, all of it. Now, in this Chinese restaurant, so removed from the craziness I have invited into my apartment, I can't be sure I heard any of that, or if I only convinced myself that I had.

"Forget it."

"Because I think I hear sounds behind the static. Classical music. Dogs barking. Foreign languages."

He looks distressed. "You should be careful listening to that stuff."

"What am I hearing?"

"You're hearing *nothing*, man. You're wasting your time. That's some cosmic gibberish they use to block the *real* sound."

"Who?" I ask. "Who's blocking the sound?"

"That's a question that's beyond me. I don't know."

"Tell me what was on your audio files before they got corrupted."

He considers this—I can see the thought muscles flexing behind his bloodshot eyes—but then ultimately shakes his head. "Forget it. I already know I'm not supposed to tell you."

"Says who?"

"Never mind. Point is, those clues were mine and mine alone. Just like Ms. Donaldson's clues were hers alone. It was a mistake sending my clues to Ms. Donaldson, although I didn't realize it at the time. It was the wrong choice and I wasn't thinking clearly. And now I feel bad that she wasn't more cautious. I tried to warn her."

"You met her in person?" I ask him.

"Only once. I was hanging around Bleecker—I knew you guys recorded there 'cause you said it on the show sometimes—and when I saw her come out, I approached her. Said I had a crazy story for her to pursue. *The* Story. She didn't think I was some nut, and she listened to me, man. Like, really *listened*."

Yes, I think. *Taryn would have listened. That's who she was. That's what she did. She listened.*

"I told her everything I'm saying to you," he says. "She asked me to send her those audio clips, and that's what I did. A little bit at a time, so I wouldn't fry her circuits, you know? But like I said, I told her to be careful."

"You're telling me those audio files caused her to kill herself?"

"No," he says. "Not the audio files. It was the Story."

"How does a story make someone commit suicide?"

"You're not *hearing* me, man." He actually pounds the table with a fist. A few heads swivel in our direction. "It's not just a book. It's something more. It burrows in your brain. It feeds you things and you find yourself trying to digest it all. Next thing you know, you can't tell what's real and what's part of the Story."

"If this book is so hard to find, how did Taryn get a hold of it?"

A muscle spasms in one of his lower eyelids. "It found her," he says.

This guy's crazy, I think.

But I'm also thinking about the state of Taryn's apartment. I'm picturing that phrase painted as a stark black warning throughout Taryn's loft—*DO NOT READ*. I'm seeing her computer soaking in a foot of water in her bathtub, and those indecipherable notes scribbled madly on the walls. Taryn hanging from an I-beam, a length of extension cord tied around her neck. The way she looked lying on that stainless steel slab in the morgue. Nothing sane about any of that, either.

The Night Listener's food arrives, a steaming bowl of flat egg noodles and vegetables floating in a thin brown sauce. The smell of it makes my stomach clench and my eyes water. He shovels a forkful into his mouth then reclines his head and closes his eyes in ecstasy. At the back of the restaurant, karaoke commences with two drunk middle-aged women singing "I Will Survive."

"So what's this Story about? Plot-wise, I mean."

"It's different for everybody. What you'd read is different from what I'm reading is different from what Ms. Donaldson read."

"So there's more than one book?"

"No, man. It's all the same book. It's all one Story."

"Then how's it different for different people?"

"It's a chameleon," he says. "Ever-changing."

"Why did you send Taryn those audio files in the first place?"

"Because that's what she *does*, man," the Night Listener says. And then he catches himself: "I mean, that's what she *did*. She dug deep into the occult. All the mysteries of the unknown universe. She was the one who *believed* in this stuff. Who else was I gonna go to with all this?"

"Why go to anyone?"

"Because I was losing myself in the Story and I needed someone to ground me. My problem was I didn't take any notes. Not at first, anyway. I told Ms. Donaldson about that—'make sure you take notes,'

I said. It's important to keep notes. Do it in your own handwriting, so you can trust what you read. Do it whenever you feel the need, even if you don't have any paper handy. Write it on your fucking arm, if you have to."

"Notes about what?"

"About what's real, as opposed to what's fiction. The Story will mess with your mind. The more time you spend inside it, the more you'll become disoriented and confused. The more likely you're liable to wander out into traffic, or tie an electrical cord around your neck. Some folks, they don't last long. Your friend Ms. Donaldson lasted about two months. I've been in it for about six. I've heard stories of people losing themselves in a matter of hours. It's all subjective."

"Based on what?"

"Based on who you are, I guess. Based on what you bring to the Story."

"I don't get it," I say. "I don't get any of it."

He tugs up one sleeve of his hoodie to reveal an arm covered in ink, though not tattoos. He has written on his arm in pen, the countless words smudgy and erratic. He rolls his hand over to expose the pale white flesh of one wrist. On it, he's written:

GR scotch & soda

"The hell's that?" I ask him.

"Your drink order."

"Mine?" I don't understand.

"You're GR," he says. "Grady Russo."

"When did you write that?"

"Earlier tonight," he says. "When I knew you'd be the one to answer Ms. Donaldson's phone."

I glance at the scotch and soda sitting in front of me now. I suddenly don't want to touch it. Then I look up and spy his cane leaning against the outside of the booth. It's a simple wooden affair with a curled handgrip. Yet something occurs to me.

"You were outside my apartment," I say. I'm recalling the stiff gait of the figure in the alley between my building and the next. The way I called to the figure, and the way they shuffled awkwardly behind a dumpster to escape. "That was you…"

"My God, this is *soooo goooood,*" he says, and crams another forkful of noodles into his mouth. "You don't know what you're missing, man."

"Have you been watching me?"

"This is all part of the Story," he says.

"Then tell me how to get a hold of this Story. I want to find it."

"I already told you," he says around a mouthful of food. "It finds you."

"Then tell me how it finds me."

That muscle spasms in his lower eyelid again. He stops chewing and just stares at me from across the table. "It already has," he says.

He sets his fork down in his bowl, dabs the corners of his mouth with a linen napkin, then produces a handgun from inside his hoodie.

"Jesus Christ," I croak, my whole body stiffening in the booth. I want to run but I can't move.

"You're already inside the Story, Grady," he tells me, and then he puts the barrel of the gun in his mouth and pulls the trigger.

16

I'm sitting on a fire hydrant with blood spatter on my shirt when an unmarked police car pulls up in front of the Chinese restaurant, a bubble light on the dash. There are already about a half dozen police cruisers blocking the street, two ambulances, a fire engine, and a cluster of shell-shocked people milling about. One of the drunk women who had been singing Gloria Gaynor only moments ago is standing near me, hugging herself beneath the spotlight of a streetlamp, her face stone sober now.

There's no one in the restaurant now except for a few uniformed police officers, and whatever is left of the Night Listener's body, slumped in a ruinous, bloody heap in the booth where we had been sitting. Each time I close my eyes I see him poke the barrel of the gun in his mouth, his eyes wide as if he's surprised to be doing this, and then a sudden flash as he pulls the trigger. A moment after that, and everybody's shrieking and running out of the place, the abandoned karaoke mics looping feedback into the air.

Detective Mathis climbs out of the passenger side of the unmarked sedan. A female detective gets out of the driver's side, and they both confer briefly with a uniformed officer in the street before marshaling toward the restaurant. Before they go inside, Detective Mathis happens to look over at me. An expression of surprise washes over his face, as if he's just been kicked in the nuts and the pain hasn't hit him yet, only the absurdity of it. He says something to his partner then comes over to me.

"Grady, right?" He's pointing at me, and then he's pointing at the restaurant. "Were you in there?"

I don't know what to say. I guess maybe I'm in shock, too.

"You need a medic? Are you hurt?" He's looking at the blood on my shirt.

I manage to shake my head.

"Listen," he says, and rests a hand on my shoulder. I don't realize I'm trembling until his hand steadies me. "You sit tight. I'll be with you shortly, all right?"

Numb, I feel my head bob up and down. I'm a marionette and someone up there's tugging at my strings.

Detective Mathis follows his partner into the restaurant. I'm not so far away that I can't still see the shape of the Night Listener's body slouched in the booth. The female detective is there, latex gloves on her hands, and someone else is taking photos. I watch as Detective Mathis joins her, pulling on his own pair of latex gloves.

I decide I can't sit here a moment longer. I get up off the fire hydrant and wander across the street, where a mob has formed to watch what's happening. The door to Ill Will's stands open, and there's my friend in the RUBY COX T-shirt and the black nail polish standing on the curb; he's got his big sledgehammer hands on his hips and a look of dim consternation on his face. As I wander by, his eyes meet mine, and then his gaze skirts down to the constellation of blood on my shirt.

There is a diner on the corner, the place mostly empty. I sit at the counter and order a cup of coffee. My hands shake and I slosh it everywhere when I bring it to my mouth.

The skinny guy behind the counter stares at my shirt.

"You should see the other guy," I say, and then a strange sort of sob creaks out of me.

I'm not sure how long I sit there spilling coffee on the countertop, but when I amble back out onto the sidewalk, I can still see police cars at the intersection. As I get closer to the scene, I see what can only be the Night Listener's body being loaded into the back of an ambulance. There is still a crowd across the street, but my friend in the RUBY COX T-shirt is gone. So is the woman who had been singing karaoke.

Detective Mathis is standing with his partner beneath the awning of the Chinese restaurant. His latex gloves are off and he's furiously scribbling in a small notepad. Backlit by the lights of the restaurant, his shadow looks long and sinewy on the pavement.

He looks up, sees me, waves me over.

"Grady Russo, this is my partner, Detective Betancourt," Detective Mathis says.

"Hello," says Detective Betancourt. She is African American, short of stature, with wide hips.

I say the first thing that comes to mind: "There's a series of bestselling novels about a detective named Betancourt."

"Honey, I've heard all about it," she says, not unpleasantly. "Someday, I'm gonna sit me down and read one."

"Witnesses said you were with the guy," Detective Mathis says. "He's got no ID on him."

I shake my head. "I don't know his name. I just met him tonight."

"What exactly happened, Grady?"

I tell the detectives exactly what happened—that the guy took out a gun and shot himself in the face. No, I didn't know he had a gun. No, he didn't give any indication that he was going to do something like that.

"How do you know him?" Detective Mathis asks.

For a second, I can't remember how I know him. How do I know him? Even when it comes back to me, it sounds preposterous and like something out of a fever dream. I tell them about the email the Night Listener sent to Taryn, and how I'd found his number in her cell phone. How I called the number and how he called me back.

"And you came out here to meet with this guy…why?" Detective Betancourt says.

Again, it's all confused in my head.

"Do you need to sit down?" Detective Mathis asks.

"No, I'm fine. I wanted to meet with him to find out what he and Taryn had been doing before she died. He sent her a bunch of weird emails. I guess I was just trying to make sense out of what happened."

Detective Mathis leaned over to his partner. "That's Taryn Donaldson, the suicide downtown."

Detective Betancourt is nodding her head. She's looking at me, though, and not at her partner. When her cell phone starts ringing, she excuses herself and steps away to answer it. I find I am grateful for her departure.

"Do you still have Ms. Donaldson's phone?" Detective Mathis asks me.

Do I? I can't even remember.

I search my pants and find it's wedged in the right-hand pocket of my jeans. I hand it over to Detective Mathis, and he tucks it away inside his suit jacket.

"I'd really like to go home and change my shirt," I tell him.

"All right," he says. "I'll call you if I have any further questions."

I just stand there, staring at him.

"You sure you're okay, Grady?"

"Yeah," I tell him. "I'm fine."

Yet I'm thinking of the Night Listener's last words to me, just before he put that gun in his mouth and pulled the trigger.

You're already inside the Story, Grady.

17

I arrive home to an apartment that is a black void, except for the dreamscape of city lights that glows beyond the windows. I'm thinking of Taryn as I go to the kitchen and take down a handle of Dewar's from the cabinet. I empty a few fingers into a drinking glass then gulp it all down. *Slug, slug, slug.* Then I go straight to the bathroom, where I dry-swallow a few aspirin, then strip out of my blood-splattered shirt and climb beneath a hot stream of water. I let the bathroom fill with steam, and I don't adjust the temperature even when it becomes uncomfortable on my flesh. It feels like penance.

I can't reconcile the Vegas odds of witnessing someone commit suicide in front of my face while I'm still mourning Taryn, who had also just taken her own life. Until recently, I had never known anyone who had killed themselves. Now I know two. It seems unfathomable. A cruel cosmic joke.

When I return to my bedroom, a towel around my waist, there is a square of light shining through the darkness. It is the glowing screen of my laptop on my desk. A single phrase floats in stark white letters against a black background on the screen. It says:

You have been approved to read the Story.

Below that is a button that says, simply, BEGIN.

I stare at it from across the room for a very long time. My mind attempts to cobble together the pieces of this puzzle, arriving at some notion that the Night Listener had somehow hacked into my computer and allowed for this website to appear to me this evening, as the *coup de grâce* to his bizarre story. I am by no means a computer guru—that sort of thing has always been best left to Sammy Deane—but I assume such a feat isn't impossible. Yet if I am right in my assumption, it begs a bigger question: *Why?* Why would the Night Listener go through the hassle? What sort of payoff is there for a morbid prank like this, particularly since the prankster himself is at this very moment growing cold and stiff in the city morgue?

I'm trembling as I cross the room and sit in front of the computer. I consider closing my laptop and crawling into bed, praying that the nightmares that are already clawing at the door decide to grant me reprieve. But before I can think straight, I'm dragging the mouse to the BEGIN button, and clicking it.

18

Welcome to the Story! Your journey begins NOW!

You are an investigative journalist looking into the mysterious disappearance of a man named LONNIE BELKNAP. You have not been hired by any parties associated with the deceased, but are instead investigating this disappearance for PERSONAL REASONS. While you have some contacts in the local police department, your gut instinct steers you away from seeking their help on this particular matter. Moreover, due to your PERSONAL REASONS, your own mental stability may become COMPROMISED throughout the course of your investigation, so BE CAREFUL and REMAIN VIGILANT!

A piece of advice, intrepid journalist, as you begin your quest: you must use COMMON SENSE to weed out FACT from FICTION. You must be careful NOT TO TRUST ANYONE. You must follow the clues no matter how difficult it may be to do so at times. Simply stated, intrepid journalist, you must STAND UP AND TAKE NOTICE!

As we begin, you are already in the midst of your investigation, having collected information from sources and having conducted several interviews of people with potential knowledge about the missing man, LONNIE BELKNAP. You arrive home one evening, ravaged by exhaustion, and go to have a drink on the fire escape of your apartment building. As you do so, you are alerted to a MYSTERIOUS FIGURE standing down below in the alleyway, watching you. As you call out, the figure hides behind a dumpster. This arouses your suspicion.

If you wish to pursue the MYSTERIOUS FIGURE, CLICK HERE.

If you wish to ignore the MYSTERIOUS FIGURE and finish your drink, CLICK HERE.

19

A part of me is still convinced this is some awful joke, although I can't for the life of me figure out how it's done, or what the payoff is. Another part of me isn't so sure.

I slide the mouse across the screen and make my selection.

20

You have chosen to pursue the MYSTERIOUS FIGURE.

You hurry down the fire escape and jump down into an alleyway swollen with trash. The figure is no longer hiding behind the dumpster, and for a moment you think he's given you the slip. But then you see him running deeper into the alley. You know he won't get far, unless he can scale the eight-foot chain-link fence back there.

You run after him and grab him just as he's halfway up the fence. He falls backward onto a pile of trash bags, crying out in pain. His hands are up, covering his face, as though he expects you to attack him. You don't attack him, but merely swat his hands away so you can get a good look at his face.

You do not recognize this man, but it occurs to you that this isn't the first time someone has been loitering around in the alley outside your apartment like someone casing the joint. This isn't the first time someone has been keeping tabs on you.

You ask him why he's been lurking around your apartment, and he tells you he was just out for a stroll and got lost. You don't buy this story and decide to go hands-on with the guy. Not accustomed to having his face broken, the man begs you not to strike him. You ask him again what he is doing here, and this time he confesses.

He tells you his name is JACKSON WEEKLEY, and that he was hired by an ANONYMOUS SOURCE to break into your apartment and rob you. You press him on the identity of his ANONYMOUS SOURCE, but JACKSON WEEKLEY does not know who his employer is, nor does he know why his ANONYMOUS SOURCE wants to stage this robbery. JACKSON WEEKLEY only knows that his ANONYMOUS SOURCE is willing to pay him BIG BUCKS for the break-in. Something stinks, and it's not the trash in the alleyway.

If you want to call the cops on JACKSON WEEKLEY, CLICK HERE.

If you want to let JACKSON WEEKLEY go, CLICK HERE.

21

I am about to select "call the cops," but then I change my mind at the last second.

22

You have chosen to let JACKSON WEEKLEY go and to NOT call the cops. This is a wise choice, because as JACKSON WEEKLEY gets up and dusts the trash from his clothes, he tells you that he believes his ANONYMOUS SOURCE may actually be a POLICE OFFICER.

CONGRATULATIONS! For selecting an action that has advanced your quest, you have received a CLUE.

CLICK HERE to receive your CLUE.

23

I click the "clue" button and an audio box populates the lower half of the screen. Sound is filtering through the laptop's speakers, faint at first but growing louder.

It's music.

A pair of classical guitars. The melody is only vaguely familiar. It sounds like a live recording, perhaps in a nightclub or dinner theater, because I can hear the clinking of glasses and the murmur of unintelligible conversation in the background. I listen for a while, trying to place where I know the piece they're playing, but I can't. It's familiar, but I'm no connoisseur.

A woman's voice comes through the speakers. Unlike the murmured conversations buried beneath the din of the music and the other ambient noise, I hear every word she says with perfect clarity:

"*They're summoning Magog.*"

And just like that, the recording ends.

24

My hand shaking, I click on the button again to replay the audio clip, but it does not play again. I keep clicking the button, keep clicking the button, keep clicking the button, wondering if it's a glitch, but it still won't replay.

And then the screen goes dark. My laptop shuts itself off, and I'm left sitting in my pitch-black bedroom wearing nothing but a towel, my heart smashing in my chest.

Did I hear what I thought I heard?

Taryn?

When I turn my computer back on, I hope to see the Story's website load on the screen, but it doesn't. I check my browser history, but there's no record of it. How the Night Listener managed to hack this system yet leave no trace of doing so behind is beyond me. As I sit here in the dark, I wonder if I am still in shock from having witnessed the Night Listener shoot himself, and if I simply hallucinated reading the Story and hearing what I thought I heard on that audio clip.

There is a small spiral-bound notebook on the desk beside my laptop. I dig a ballpoint pen out of the desk, then write down the names Jackson Weekley and Lonnie Belknap. As I do so, it's the Night Listener's voice I hear: *It's important to keep notes.*

25

I'm on my way to the bunker the following morning when I receive a call from Detective Mathis. He asks if I'll meet with him at some point later that afternoon to provide a more cogent statement than the one I gave him and his partner the night before. I agree, after I take care of some business. Detective Mathis thanks me for my cooperation.

Sammy Deane is in the studio, a pair of chunky headphones on. He's twisting the knobs on the console when he looks up from behind the wall of Plexiglas and sees me standing down in the bunker. He holds up one finger, *give me a sec*, and I try not to look at the two microphones that still sit on the table in the center of the room. Those two empty chairs. Mine and hers. Neither to be filled again.

Did I really hear what I heard last night? Because that's impossible.

Taryn Donaldson dead is impossible, too, yet here we are.

Sammy comes down from the booth with an audible huff. He

looks exhausted, like he's been up all night running around the city. He's got some dried chocolate sauce or something on his Lynyrd Skynyrd T-shirt. "You look like shit, Grady."

"I didn't get much sleep last night."

"*NewsBlitz?*"

"Not exactly," I say, and then I tell him how I located the Night Listener's phone number in Taryn's phone, how I went to meet him, and how he swallowed the business end of a handgun while in the middle of his Fun Yum Dinner Platter #7, extra spicy.

Sammy Deane drops down into Taryn's old chair. His jaw has come unhinged and his eyes are clouded with a blind, disbelieving fogginess. "Jesus *fuuuuuck*," he intones, rubbing one side of his face with a club-like hand. I can hear his palm scrape along his beard stubble.

"There's more," I say, and then tell him all I can remember from the Night Listener's spiel about the Story. I ask Sammy if he's ever heard of such a thing, but he just shakes his head. He's listening to me in a stupor, trying to wrap his head around it all. I conclude by telling him how the Story appeared on my laptop, how I followed the prompts, and how I was rewarded—*rewarded?*—with an audio clip that I swore contained Taryn's voice. "Only not just her voice, Sammy. It sounded like a recording from the night Taryn and I met."

Sammy's big eyes roll up in my direction, magnified behind his Buddy Holly glasses. "I...don't know...what that means," he says haltingly.

"'I don't know what that means, either," I confess. I've got a backpack over one shoulder, which I dump onto the table now. It's got my laptop in it as well as a stack of Taryn's notebooks. I take everything out and set them down in front of Sammy. "If there's any evidence of where that website came from or how someone could bring it up on my laptop, can you figure it out?"

"Uh…" Sammy says.

"And if there's some way to retrieve that audio clip from my computer's memory," I say.

Sammy shakes his head, blinks his big eyes. "I mean, I can dupe the hard drive, see what's on it. Are you sure you…you heard what you think you heard?"

I'm sure, I think, but I can't say that. Not for Sammy's benefit, but for my own. I can't bring myself to admit the impossibility of it all. Even if it's someone messing with me…*how?*

"I don't know," I tell him. "I need to hear it again. See what you can do."

He nods at the stack of Taryn's notes. "What about this stuff?"

"I need them out of my apartment. I don't want to confuse her notes—" *with my own*, is what I planned to say, but I catch myself there, too. "Just hang on to them, will you?"

"Yeah. Sure." He drops a meaty hand atop the notebooks and slides them closer to him.

"Thanks, Sammy. Owe you one." I head to the door, push it open, am knifed in one eye by a blade of sunlight.

"Hey," Sammy says. "You wanna cut that eulogy for Taryn before you go? I'm splicing together the episode now."

I'm standing there on a pair of unsteady legs, a tornado whirring through my skull. I feel like someone has taken an ice cream scooper and hollowed me out. "I can't right now. Soon, though. I promise."

My departure from that place feels like a coward's retreat.

26

I show up at a coffee shop on Mott Street, only a few blocks from the precinct. I expect to find Detective Mathis already waiting for me, but instead I see his partner, Detective Betancourt, seated at a small table against a smudgy window. She sees me and smiles. I join her at the table, the sun so potent it sets the right side of my face on fire.

"Detective Mathis got a last-minute call," she says, by way of explanation. "I hope you don't mind."

"Fine by me."

"How are you today? Get any sleep last night?"

I shrug. "Some."

"I know about what happened to your friend," she says. "Taryn Donaldson. I'm sorry for your loss, Grady."

"Thank you."

Detective Betancourt takes a small notepad from her sports coat. "Let's just get it done, shall we? Start from the beginning, Grady. Tell me how you wound up getting in contact with the guy, and what happened at that restaurant."

I tell her about how I had been digging through some of Taryn's things in the aftermath of her death, to include some of her work stuff. I explain about the series of emails Taryn received from someone calling himself the Night Listener, and how I found a phone number for the guy in Taryn's cell. It's a rehash of what I told her and Detective Mathis the night before outside the Chinese restaurant, only now I'm more collected and feel like I'm making sense. As much sense as any of this can make, anyway.

Detective Betancourt asks what the connection was between the Night Listener and Taryn Donaldson.

"He was a fan of the podcast," I say. "He didn't really know her, only that he met her just once, in person. Said he waited around outside the studio one day because he had a story for her."

"A story?"

"Yeah, it's not unusual for listeners to submit story ideas to the show."

"By showing up at the studio in person?"

"No. Mostly by email."

"So it would be odd for this fellow to show up at the studio to meet with Ms. Donaldson in person?"

I think about what I want to relay to Detective Betancourt. Tales of a magic ebook? Audio clips that change to static when they're downloaded from some mysterious server? Taryn's own disembodied voice coming through the tinny speaker on my laptop?

I say, "The show has always attracted some weird elements. Our listeners were generally levelheaded, normal people, but there were some who were…well…"

Detective Betancourt nods her head. I don't need to continue; she gets it. "Did this fellow intimate that there was something more between him and Ms. Donaldson? A relationship, maybe?"

"No. Why?"

"Just looking under every stone." She smiles at me again, but there's little humor in it.

What she's getting at hits me like a slap across the face. "Wait, do you think this guy did something to Taryn? That it wasn't suicide?"

Detective Betancourt's humorless smile widens. There's pity in it now, which I don't like, but I understand. Instead of answering my question—or maybe that pitiable smile was supposed to answer it—she says, "Any chance you still have Ms. Donaldson's cell phone? I'd like to have forensics take a look at it."

"I gave it to Detective Mathis last night."

"Did you?" She seems surprised. "Well, I guess I'll check with him, then."

"Tell me—do you think this guy actually killed Taryn and made it look like a suicide?"

"No," she says. "I don't, Grady. I'm sorry. I'm just asking questions."

I don't know what I expected her to say, but that leaves me

unsettled. And I don't one hundred percent believe her.

I ask her if we're done. I'm roasting in this window seat.

She closes her notepad. "We're done. Thank you, Grady."

I shake her hand, rise up from the table. Before I head to the door, however, I turn and ask if they were able to identify the Night Listener's real name.

"Jackson Weekley," she tells me, and I feel the whole world tip to one side.

27

When I get back to my apartment, I dig an old PC out of my closet, connect it to the internet, then conduct a search for Jackson Weekley. After some digging, I come across his Facebook page. It's a private account, though some of the photos are public, and I recognize him right away. Mostly, he's giving the camera the peace sign. He's with some friends in a movie theater. He's wearing a Viking helmet and fake beard at a Halloween party. He almost looks like a different person in these photos, even though I know it's him.

The most recent photos show him in a hospital bed. He's still giving the peace sign, but his face is puffy and bruised, and one of his eyes is swelled shut. His left leg is in a cast and suspended by a network of wires off the bed. I think about his response when I asked him his real name: *No way, man. No names. I've made that mistake in the past and it's cost me.* And then he patted the head of his cane.

Did someone do that to you? Did someone smash you to bits because you said the wrong thing? Because you gave them your name?

It doesn't make sense.

I also locate his alias on a Reddit post from last year:

TheNightListener1127
Subject: interactive online book The STory
Anyone familiar with this? Supposed to be an online
version of a choose your own adventure or secret path
book. Only it's real.

LuisKhanIn6969
Subject: Re: interactive online book The STory
What do you mean its real?

Hemmingson_M_anon
Subject: Re: interactive online book The STory
old vintage choose yur own adventure books worth
alot of $$$ today

TheNightListener1127
Subject: Re: interactive online book The STory
Real like it makes things really happen. The story
becomes part of reality. Or the other way around.

Hemmingson_M_anon
Subject: Re: interactive online book The STory
check ebat

Hemmingson_M_anon
Subject: Re: interactive online book The STory
*ebay

G_L_Poach_writer
Subject: Re: interactive online book The STory
????

TheNightListener1127

Subject: Re: interactive online book The STory

Won't be on ebay. This is dark web sh!t. I want to find it.

MyselfAsksAmIHere

Subject: Re: interactive online book The STory

it finds you

I click on the name MyselfAsksAmIHere, which should show me all the posts this person has made, but according to this, the author has only made this one post. This one reply. Nothing else. It's like some phantom swooped in to comment only to vanish just as quickly.

I don't know what to make of any of this, except that it leaves me feeling vulnerable and exposed. Helpless. Also, like I'm missing something, something important. I glance down at the notepad where I had written down Jackson Weekley's name the night before. There is the other name there, as well—Lonnie Belknap. The "missing person" from the Story.

Do I want to do this? I wonder. *Do I want to travel down this road?*

I search for Belknap's name and am immediately provided with several news stories—one even from *NewsBlitz*—about a missing man. At this point, I am beyond surprise; seeing this only causes a numbness to infiltrate my body.

Lonnie Belknap, a forty-six-year-old business owner from Queens, went missing a little over a month ago. According to the news articles, police suspect Belknap disappeared to avoid paying back a series of business loans. Lonnie's ex-wife (who isn't identified by name in any of the articles) goes further, asserting that her former husband's business dealings weren't all completely aboveboard, and that she believed he'd met a terrible fate. *Murdered*, is what the former Mrs. Belknap is suggesting. Belknap's neighbor in Queens makes a similar assertion, and also says the man's dogs were barking nonstop the night he went missing.

Dogs barking, I think, and write that down on the notepad.

I scroll down the page and find a photo of Lonnie Belknap. He's mostly bald, with a wreath of grayish hair around the sides and back of his head. He looks older than middle-age, with an alcoholic's meshwork nose and dark black pockets beneath his eyes. I read a subtle smirk on his lips, which suggests to me that he's more of an asshole than he immediately lets on.

What does this mean? That the Night Listener—Jackson Weekley—inserted himself into the Story, and tossed Lonnie Belknap into it, too? Even if I could force myself to believe that, the Reddit post seems counterintuitive. It's proof that, one year earlier, Weekley was searching for the Story himself. It lends credence to what he told me last night before blowing his brains out.

Out of nowhere, I become convinced someone else is in the apartment with me. It's a small place, so it only takes a handful of minutes for me to poke my head around, peer under the bed, look behind the shower curtain, pull apart a closet full of clothes, to convince me that I am alone. Because of course I am. Who else would be here with me?

I pour a glass of scotch, then drink it on the fire escape. It's late afternoon, which means the alley has grown dark as the sun rolls its way west of the city. I watch the steam rise from grates, listen to the traffic on the street, watch a street gang of pigeons balancing on a clothesline. I think I see someone hiding from me down there in the alley, but I can't really be sure. I'm trying hard not to spook myself further, not to buy into this paranoia. So I finish my drink, climb back inside, and nail the window shut. Better to be safe than sorry.

When I go back to my bedroom, I find the next part of the Story up on my computer screen.

28

The following evening, you take JACKSON WEEKLEY out to dinner in order to pump him for additional information. You see he's got a black eye and walks with a limp now. Someone has really given him the business. You ask him what happened, and he says he was jumped by a guy in a ski mask last night. He says it happened soon after he called his ANONYMOUS SOURCE and explained that he had been unable to break into your apartment. JACKSON WEEKLEY says that the man who beat him up was also a cop—possibly the very same ANONYMOUS SOURCE who had initially hired him for the break-in—because he happened to glimpse a gun in a holster and a gold shield beneath the man's sweater during the fight.

You ask JACKSON WEEKLEY what this ANONYMOUS SOURCE wanted him to steal from your apartment. JACKSON WEEKLEY says it was a cell phone that once belonged to YOUR FRIEND that is now in your possession. You ask why, but JACKSON WEEKLEY doesn't know. You ask him for the phone number of his ANONYMOUS SOURCE, and JACKSON WEEKLEY nods his head. When he reaches beneath his sweatshirt, you think it is to retrieve his own cell phone so he can give you the number, but instead he produces a PISTOL. Before you can stop him, he puts the barrel of the gun in his mouth and pulls the trigger.

When the cops arrive at the scene, a POLICE DETECTIVE asks for YOUR FRIEND's cell phone.

If you want to comply and give the POLICE DETECTIVE YOUR FRIEND's cell phone, CLICK HERE.

If you want to lie and say you don't have YOUR FRIEND's cell phone, CLICK HERE.

29

The next thing I know, I'm across the room staring at the lighted square of the computer screen while my heart bangs a rhythmic tattoo against my ribcage. Time has passed without me knowing, although I'm not sure how that's possible. It's much darker now beyond the windows.

I'm clutching something so tightly in my right hand that pain pulses up my arm. I look down and find I'm holding a ballpoint pen. Beside me, on the bedroom wall, I've hastily copied some of the text that's still on the computer screen. I don't remember doing this, but it's also not my most pressing concern.

I go back over to the computer and stare at those two choices radiating from the monitor:

If you want to comply and give the POLICE DETECTIVE YOUR FRIEND's cell phone, CLICK HERE.

If you want to lie and say you don't have YOUR FRIEND's cell phone, CLICK HERE.

It's true that a laugh erupts from my throat. There's nothing remotely funny about any of this, of course, yet I feel that laughter is the only reasonable response. After all, it's the best medicine, isn't it? Maybe I'm sick. Either that, or I'm going mad.

I've already given the police detective my friend's cell phone, I think.

TRUST NO ONE

is written in my own handwriting on the wall above the computer.

STAND UP AND TAKE NOTICE!

is written in ink on my left arm, but also on the wall.
I reach out to the keyboard and make my selection:

You have chosen to lie to the POLICE DETECTIVE. You do not give him YOUR FRIEND's phone.

This is good, because there is something IMPORTANT on YOUR FRIEND's cell phone.

Prepare to receive your CLUE.

I wait for the little audio box to pop up, but nothing happens.

There's nothing left on the screen for me to click, either. Just as I'm about to tap the space bar, the screen goes dark. The computer shuts down.

"No!"

I press the power button but the computer doesn't respond. It's dead. It's silent.

"Goddamn it, no!"

I'm angry, I'm confused, I'm flooding with a cocktail of terrible, poisonous emotions. I pace back and forth like a lion in a cage. Every time I pass by the computer I jab at the power button, but still nothing happens.

God only knows how long a strange chirping sound is echoing throughout my apartment, but when I finally realize I'm hearing it, I also realize that I have been hearing it for some time now. I shamble around the apartment in search of the sound.

It's coming from Taryn's cell phone, which sits on my coffee table.

An impossibility, because I gave this phone to Detective Mathis.

Or did I?

You have chosen to lie to the police detective, I think. *You do not give him your friend's phone.*

I pick up the phone and answer the call.

Whoever's on the other end is in a restaurant or a bar or someplace where people are laughing and clanging silverware in the background. No classical guitar music this time, but a conversation between two people:

—I tried to find you, you know. I mean, after that night, I wanted to call you.

—How come?

—I guess…well, to see you again.

—I told you not to fall in love, didn't I?

—I'm not in love.

—I warned you.

—I'm not in love.

—Yeah?

—You stopped writing.

—Have I?

—I mean, I haven't seen any of your stories in months.

—You know what my biggest regret is?

—Uh, what?

—Not bringing a video camera.

—What? Tonight?

—On assignment. We're gonna do something, you and me. It's our destiny. I can feel it.

30

Because there must be a logical explanation for this, I return to Taryn's apartment. My key still works, so I let myself in. I'm holding my breath. The place is still as it was when I came here with Detective Mathis. This seems impossible—how long will it remain in this condition, unrented, with a segment of electrical cord dangling from a rafter?—but it also strikes me as terribly *fitting*. It's as if this place is a stage outfitted in all the proper dressing and appurtenances, and I'm the actor here to go through the motions. I can almost imagine an audience watching me from inside that swath of black paint slathered across Taryn's wall.

That patch of black paint triggers something inside me. I suddenly know what Taryn has covered up: the transcribed handwriting of her *own* story. Just as I have been writing mine on my own walls, she had been doing so on hers. Only, in the end, she covered it up. *DO NOT*

READ. I wonder if I've been careless, left myself open to problems, leaving those words out there for anyone to see. My landlord. A burglar. Anyone.

I literally shake my head to clear it. Maybe coming back here was a bad idea. It's messing with my head.

Someone is fucking with me. That is the only plausible explanation. It seems less likely now that it is Jackson Weekley, a.k.a. the Night Listener, who has set this whole thing in motion prior to his death for some unknown reason. It's too elaborate, too complex. But what I really mean is it's too *personal.*

When I try to break it all down, the only thing that makes sense to me is that Taryn recorded our conversations from back then without me realizing it. She even hints at it in that last recorded snippet that came through her cell phone when she says, *You know what my biggest regret is? Not bringing a video camera.* Because maybe all she had on her that night was a hidden audio recorder. Had she been surreptitiously memorializing all our conversations? The *why* of this doesn't trouble me as much as the *how*—namely, *how* someone would have known those recordings existed, and *how* they would begin the process of taunting me with them. The *why* boggles me, but the *how* seems impossible.

I pull open her drawers, her file cabinet, ransack her shelves of recording equipment. I'm not sure exactly what I'm looking for—a USB drive, a collection of unlabeled audiocassettes, the audio recorder itself—but I think I'll know it when I find it.

Above Taryn's mattress, the thaumatrope spins. Bird in the cage. Bird in the cage. Bird in the cage.

Suddenly, I'm thinking about the computer in the bathtub. I took for granted that, given the state of this apartment, Taryn had submerged the computer herself. But what if she hadn't? What if she kept all those hidden files on her computer, and *someone else* had come in here and taken them, then drowned the hard drive so no one else could attempt to retrieve them?

It all seems unnecessarily convoluted, yet I'm one hundred percent convinced of this when I step into the bathroom and find the computer missing. Everything else in this apartment has been left unchanged since Taryn's suicide, yet the computer is now gone. This seems to validate my theory, although it doesn't make me feel any better. Who would be doing this to me? What reason would someone have to fuck with my head in this way? If Taryn had audio recordings of us saved on her computer's hard drive, who would know to come in here and steal it?

I step out of the bathroom, register a quick blur in the periphery of my right eye, then everything goes black.

31

I come to with a pounding headache. I'm splayed on the floor, staring up at the section of extension cord that hangs from an I-beam in the ceiling. I remember arriving at Taryn's apartment, but everything else is a blank.

My attempt to sit up sends a lightning bolt of pain through my head. I touch a tender bump above my right eye and fireworks explode. My vision is a little wonky, too, because for a moment I think I'm seeing a troll hunkered down in one corner of the apartment clutching a golf club.

The troll is Ms. Vasiliev, the landlady with the jet-black beehive hairdo, and she *is* clutching a golf club. When she sees I'm awake, she scurries toward me brandishing the club while unspooling a string of angry Russian epithets. I think she is going to strike me again, so I raise my hands to block the blow.

Two figures come into the apartment. One is a policewoman in uniform, the other is Detective Mathis. Upon seeing him, I think I am suffering a hallucination. The policewoman tells Ms. Vasiliev to drop the golf club, which she does. The policewoman asks her what happened, and Ms. Vasiliev begins yammering like a sewing machine.

Detective Mathis kneels down beside me. He's studying the contusion on my head. Then he meets my eyes, checking them for signs of concussion, I suspect. "How do you feel?"

"I'll live," I say, and prop myself up against the wall.

"What're you doing here, Grady?"

I'm not too messed up from the blow to my head to know that if I tell him the truth, he's going to think I'm crazy. Instead, I tell him I came here to make sure I hadn't left any of my stuff in Taryn's apartment, assuming the place will be cleaned out soon.

"It's called breaking and entering, Grady," he tells me.

"No, it's not. I have a key." I dig it out of my pocket and hold it up so that it catches the waning sunlight coming through the wall of windows. Detective Mathis plucks it from my fingers, and I guess that's that.

"You need an ambulance?" He's back to studying the bump on my head.

"No, I'm good."

He nods, satisfied. Then he joins the policewoman in interviewing Ms. Vasiliev. The old Russian is talking fast and angrily, and her heavily mascara'd eyes keep flitting in my direction. I get up and wander back into the bathroom, where I examine the lump above my right eye. The skin isn't broken but it's one hell of a knot, and it'll probably bruise like a bastard.

Over my shoulder, reflected backward in the mirror:

DO NOT READ.

What happened to the computer?

DO NOT READ.

Why would someone be messing with me like this?

DO NOT READ.

Detective Mathis appears in the bathroom doorway. "Ms. Vasiliev won't be pressing charges. But you can't come back here, Grady. Not anymore."

"Understood."

"You told Detective Betancourt you gave me Taryn's cell phone?"

"I misspoke."

"Misspoke?" He folds his arms and leans against the doorframe. I glimpse his badge and his gun on his hip.

That's what Jackson Weekley saw when the guy in the ski mask was beating him up, I think. *That's how he knew he was a cop.* But then I realize that didn't actually happen. Not in real life. That was part of the Story. I make a mental note to jot that down on my notepad for clarity's sake when I get back to my apartment.

Detective Mathis says, "You sure you're okay? I can drive you to have your head looked at."

I tell him I'm fine.

"I *would* like to take a look at that cell phone," he tells me. "Think you can get it to me?"

"I guess so," I tell him, although I have no intention of giving him that cell phone. Not again. "I gotta find it."

"You don't know where it is?"

I open my mouth, but the only thing that comes out is a hiss of hot air.

Detective Mathis is smiling almost imperceptibly at me. "You're not lying to me for some reason, are you, Grady?" he asks.

"Why would I lie?" I tell him.

"All right." Yet I don't like how his eyes linger on me. He turns to leave but I call him back.

"What is it?"

I point to the empty bathtub. "Did someone come and take the computer?"

He peers into the tub.

"There was a computer in there," I remind him. "Soaking in about a foot of water. Don't you remember?"

His expression remains unchanged. "No," he says finally.

Who's lying now? I think. But then I also think: *Was that part of the Story, too? Am I getting things confused?*

"Don't come back here," he tells me, and then he leaves.

32

Back at my apartment, I've got an icepack on my head and a glass of Dewar's in my hand when Taryn's cell phone chimes. I look at the screen, which says:

> If you'd like to call KAREN BOYD about LONNIE BELKNAP, CLICK HERE.

> If you'd like to ignore this message, CLICK HERE.

I click the first button and Taryn's cell phone immediately dials the desk of my editor at *NewsBlitz.*

"Grady Russo! I nearly took out an APB on you! Everything okay?"

I tell her everything is fine, I've been busy with work, and I apologize for not coming by the office. I'm still ahead of my deadlines, so she's not concerned. Though when I ask if she knows anything about a missing man named Lonnie Belknap, there is a pause on her end of the line.

"Are you joking?" she says.

"Why would I be joking?"

"You must have heard something. Are you saying you want the story? I've already assigned it to Linda—"

"Are we talking about the same thing?" I ask her. "Lonnie Belknap. Businessman from Queens who's been missing?"

"Yeah, right," she says, "only he's *not* missing. Not anymore. His body was pulled from the East River earlier this morning. Single gunshot wound to the head. Execution-style."

I try to reconcile what this means in the grand scheme of things, but find myself powerless to do so. What does *any* of this mean?

"Can't say I'm surprised," Karen is saying on the other end of the line. "Information has come to light that Mr. Belknap wasn't the most upstanding of citizens. Had some crooked dealings with some bad people. Back when he first went missing, we received an anonymous tip that there might even be some crooked cop involved."

"Crooked cop?" I feel like a parrot, spitting Karen's words back at her without substance.

"It's nothing we've been able to verify, and the anonymous source has quit communicating, but we'll keep digging and see what we can find." A pause. "You sound funny, Grady. Is everything okay?"

I catch my breath as the world spins. Tell her I'm fine, everything's fine, I'll talk to her soon. Before she can say anything more, I disconnect the call.

33

There is a steady pounding at the center of your skull, and someone is calling your name over and over again from some nearby distance. A veil is shucked away from your eyes, or maybe it's like a fog lifting. You realize you are lying on the floor of your apartment, staring at the ceiling.

When you sit up, you see there is more writing on the walls. Some drawings, too—most notably a crude rendition of a bird beside a bell-shaped cage. You glance down at your left arm and see more writing there, too—phrases that are simultaneously important yet mean nothing: "Ruby Cox" and "Indiana = possessed children." The hamster going around on the wheel inside your head has died.

Taryn's cell phone is on the floor at your side. Its screen is cracked. You pick it up as you rise wobbly to your knees, and stuff it in the back pocket of your jeans. You realize you're still listening to someone banging on your door and shouting your name.

You have a choice to make here. A decision. Open the door, or ignore the person on the other side and hope they go away? You decide to—

34

—open the door.

It's Sammy Deane, red-faced and sweat-shiny. There is a Superman shield of perspiration darkening the center of his faded Rush T-shirt. He's got his man-bag over one shoulder and a look of irritation on his face.

"I been knocking for like five minutes."

"I didn't hear you."

"You said to come over."

"I did?"

"When I called." He frowns. "What's the matter with you? What happened to your head?"

This baffles me—I recollect no phone call from Sammy—yet I let it go. Regarding the bump on my head, I mutter something about a clumsy accident, and leave it at that.

Sammy shoulders through the doorway but stops only a few feet into the apartment. "Christ, Grady, what's going on here?"

He's looking around at the state of the place—the walls inked in their litany of handwritten notes, the filthy dishes stacked on the counter, even the scribbled phrases on the flesh of my left arm. It occurs to me that my clothes smell—my *skin* smells—and I can't remember the last time I took a shower. Or even what day this is.

It's not day, it's night. The city presses its black face against my windows, a million spider-eyes of light peering in.

Sammy goes to the drawing of the bird and the cage on the wall. He looks so closely at it that his nose nearly touches it. I go to the kitchen and grab two beers from the fridge. I have a vague recollection of decorating these walls, though it's fuzzy, like something remembered after a night of heavy drinking. What *is* perfectly clear to me is the recording that played out of Taryn's phone. A conversation between the two of us. I keep trying to convince myself I hallucinated it, but I know that's not the truth.

I go over to Sammy, hand him a beer. He takes it without looking at me; he's backed up a few steps from the wall in order to survey all the words and phrases there. They're mostly snippets from the last recording, the words I want to remember because, for some reason, I feel they are important. I have also attempted to transcribe the text of the Story, but each time I do that, my mind gets murky and my writing becomes nonsensical. For example, next to the drawing of the bird and the birdcage, I have written, over and over again, the word *thaumatrope*.

"Are these all from Taryn's notebooks?" Sammy wants to know. He's scrutinizing one handwritten phrase on the wall in particular that, I admit, out of context might seem a little bit odd. It says:

JW (NL) beat up by cop IN STORY & LB shot in
head 4 REAL
    don't be fooled!

"Forget that stuff," I tell him. There's no way for me to give a suitable explanation without sounding like a lunatic.

"Because it looks like all that crazy rambling from her notebooks," Sammy says. "And those pictures of her apartment that you showed me." He's not letting it go. "*Who* was shot in the head? What *is* this?"

In an effort to change the subject, I say, "Hey, listen, I'm gonna speak with my editor at *NewsBlitz* sometime this week, see if I can get you an interview. I've already put in a good word, started talking you up, so—"

"I don't wanna work at *NewsBlitz*, Grady."

"How come?"

He hoists both his shoulders, which makes him look like an overgrown child. He's stopped reading the missives written on the wall and is now examining the window, all those bent-angle nail-heads poking out from the frame. He flicks one of the nail-heads and I expect it to make a *thwang* sound, like in a cartoon, but it doesn't. "It's just not where I wanna be," he says absently.

"Then what are you doing here?"

He turns and stares at me with a mixture of concern and frustration. He sets his beer down on the coffee table, then slides the man-bag off his shoulder, opens it, and places my laptop on the half-wall that separates the kitchenette from the rest of the apartment.

"What'd you find out?" I ask him. I forgot I gave it to him.

"No one's hacked your rig. Everything's normal."

"What about that audio file?"

"Grady, there's nothing there."

"That's not true," I tell him. "Someone's fucking with me."

"Well, then it's someone who's really good, because they covered their tracks and left no evidence behind."

And that's when it hits me. How could I have overlooked something so basic? It could be because Sammy Deane is now standing directly below a handwritten phrase on the wall instructing me to TRUST NO ONE, or simply because my mind has finally made the only logical leap here.

"It's *you*," I say. I even point at him.

He's pretending to be confused. "Me, what?"

"*You're* the one messing with me. You've got the computer skills. And you found those recordings of Taryn and me with all her stuff, and so you figured you'd spook me. This whole thing's about revenge, is that it?"

"The fuck are you *talking* about?"

"Because you blame me for her death," I say, and now my whole body is shaking. A molten-hot fury is rising through the core of my body. The pieces fit. "Because she kept coming to me for help, and I kept ignoring her. Because she cried on my shoulder back in March, and I snuck out on her when she went to the bathroom to clean herself up. Because you think I'm a horrible fucking person who needs to be punished for all—"

I can't continue. I drop to my knees, my body wracked with sobs.

I feel my heart beating inside the bump on my head. Across the room, Sammy stares at me. He looks terrified, too. A mirror reflection of my own feelings. I wait for him to tell me I'm wrong, to tell me I'm not to blame, to say all is forgiven.

But he doesn't.

He tugs the strap of his man-bag over his shoulder then saunters quietly to the door. Once he's gone, it's like he's never been here.

After a while, I get up off the floor and go to the bathroom. I wash my face and hands. I press some fingers against the tender bump on my head. I imagine myself as a bird in a cage, only it's really just an optical illusion. I'm really free, I just don't know it.

The computer screen in my bedroom glows in the darkness. My body shaking, my mind a wreck, I approach it and read the text that's on the screen:

> If you would like to play the video clip that is on TARYN's phone, CLICK HERE.

My hand is vibrating as I reach out and press the button.

Nothing happens.

Not on the computer screen, anyway.

But I hear a noise coming from the next room. I go there, see Taryn's cell phone on the coffee table beside Sammy Deane's unfinished beer, a fuzzy video playing on the cracked screen.

I pick it up and stare at the video.

It's dark and grainy. Whoever's filming—it must be Taryn, it's her phone—is partially hidden behind a tower of shipping crates. It's nighttime and she's at a deserted wharf. I see the moonlight reflecting off black water and, in the distance, the lights of the city.

The video focuses in on a swarthy figure standing at the edge of a dock. No, not just one figure—there are two. The second figure is kneeling before the first, hands on his mostly bald head. The man on his knees is Lonnie Belknap; I know this not because I can see him so clearly on the video, but because of some inkling of intuition that sparks to life inside me.

The man standing above Belknap takes out a gun, presses its barrel to the back of Belknap's head, and fires one shot. There is a quick muzzle flash and then Belknap's body goes limp. He falls forward into the river.

There is the sound of someone gasping very close to the camera. It's Taryn. The phone shakes in her hands, the video momentarily blurring. She's doing her best to stay hidden behind those shipping containers while continuing to film.

The figure on the dock tucks his gun away then strolls across a gravel lot. He's masked in darkness for much of this, except for when he passes beneath the harsh sodium glow of a lamppost.

It's Detective Mathis.

Just as I'm staring at his face on the screen, the phone goes dead.

I try to power it back on, but it won't go. Are there more cracks in the screen now than there were before, or is it just my imagination?

A message dings on my bedroom computer. I go into the bedroom and see the next page of the Story on the screen:

> At this moment, DETECTIVE MATHIS is walking toward your apartment. He knows you have the video and he is planning to shoot and kill you.
>
> If you wish to retrieve a weapon and kill DETECTIVE MATHIS before he can kill you, CLICK HERE.
>
> If you wish to flee down the fire escape, CLICK HERE.

I click the button for "flee," which prompts the screen to change:

> You cannot flee down the fire escape; you have nailed
> the window shut.

I stare at the text with mounting horror. As I stare, it changes:

> You are a bird trapped in a cage.

Someone is knocking on my apartment door. My whole body stiffens. I creep out of the bedroom and walk slowly toward the door. I can see the movement of feet beneath the door, can hear a man's impatient breathing accompanied by the creaking of floorboards. Another knock, and I feel it reverberate through my bones. I pray that it is Sammy Deane, coming back out of pity.

"Grady? It's Detective Mathis. Are you home?"

I can pretend I'm not here.

"Grady?"

A pause. Silence. Will he leave?

Something goes sliding into the doorknob on the other side of the door. A key? Or is Detective Mathis picking the lock? The knob jostles furtively.

I go to the kitchenette and grab the first thing I see, which is a large carving knife poking up from a butcher's block on the counter. I keep the lights off, wedging myself up against the refrigerator in the dark, both my hands wrapped around the handle of the knife.

The door squeals open, inviting a shaft of light from the hallway into the apartment. There is a shadow framed in that shaft of light. I see the shadow is holding a gun.

"Grady?"

I hold my breath.

Detective Mathis steps inside. He closes the door behind him. Takes a step into the place. Another step. From the corner of my eye, I see his dark form pass by the kitchenette. That gun is raised and scanning the darkness ahead of him. The lights are on in the next room, and he's heading now in that direction.

I launch myself off the refrigerator and plant the six-inch blade of the carving knife into the soft meat of Detective Mathis's neck.

The gun goes off, the sound deafening in the tiny apartment. I release my grip on the knife and watch as Detective Mathis staggers forward. One hand paws at the knife handle jutting from his neck. He's still got the gun in his other hand, though not for long; another couple of steps and the gun drops to the carpet. Detective Mathis drops, too—straight down onto his knees, and then wham, onto his chest. His legs swim across the carpet and he's making wet, gurgling sounds way back in his throat. He's got his head turned sideways so that the handle of the knife points straight at the ceiling, his profile like a fish's, his mouth gawping soundlessly as blood spurts from the wound and sprays across the carpet.

A moment later, and Detective Mathis is dead.

I stand there, trembling, unable to take my eyes off him. Blood continues to seep from the wound, only much weaker now. There is nothing working in Detective Mathis's chest to keep pumping it out, so it only trickles until it stops trickling altogether.

No, I think. *This isn't real. This is part of the Story.*

I look down at my left arm for something written there that might confirm this. But there is nothing.

Nothing.

From the bedroom: another ding on my computer.

I step over the detective's body and go into the bedroom. The text on the computer screen says:

If you would like to play TARYN's CD, CLICK HERE.

There are no other options, so I click here.

Out in the living room, the stereo comes alive. The CD I took from Taryn's apartment—the one loaded with static—is still in the CD player. It begins to play now, that same static at first…but then the static fades until I hear what sounds like the dull murmur of distant conversation. There *is* something there, behind that wall of white noise. People chatting, laughing, watching some sporting event. Glasses clinking on tabletops and a bar. Footsteps approach, then stop suddenly. Taryn's voice comes through the stereo speakers:

> *"What happened to the man who was sitting here?"*
> The bartender of the pub in Greenwich Village
> responds:
> *"He paid the tab and left."*
> Taryn says:
> *"He…left…me?"*

There is a beat of silence, with only the soft commotion of the bar patrons in the background. So much silence, it could be full of anything. Then the bartender says:

> *"Are you okay, ma'am? You look upset. Do you want
> me to call someone? Ma'am? Ma'am? Ma'am…?"*

Then the static is back, though just briefly. It acts as a transition, taking me from one scene to the next. When it fades again, there is my own voice, telling whoever is calling to leave a message and I'll return their call as soon as humanly possible. It's Taryn's voice again, though thinner somehow. Weakened. I remember Sammy

Deane telling me that Taryn called me in the week before her death. I remember seeing a voicemail from her, but I hadn't listened to it, had just deleted it, because I didn't want to get back into all the bullshit with her. I didn't realize what state she was in. I didn't realize all that was going on.

She's crying softly as she says:

> *"Grady? It's me. Please call me. Please. I'm lost. Help me."*

She's breathing on the line. She sounds like she wants to say more. But she doesn't. And then the voicemail ends.

The static is back, so loud I clamp a pair of bloody hands to my ears. Pray for it to end, pray for it to end, pray for it to—

It ends.

Silence fills the apartment.

I lower my hands. I'm breathing like I've just run a marathon. I look over at Detective Mathis's body, still bleeding on my rug, and feel a hard knot tighten in my belly. I glance around for the gun he'd dropped, but I can't find it. I get down on my hands and knees and peer under the couch, but it isn't there. My throat is tight with panic.

In the bedroom, the computer dings one last time.

I appear in the doorway. I can see the screen just fine from here:

> Thank you for reading the Story. You may now kill yourself.

I won't, of course. I won't do that. I've got a dead police officer in my apartment, but it was self-defense. I've got the video on Taryn's phone to prove—

The phone, I remember, is dead.

I rush to it now, try to turn it on, but nothing happens. The glass screen is coming apart, slivers of it slicing open my fingers and cutting my palms. I drop it to the floor.

Taryn stands in the open doorway to my apartment. She's wearing what she wore the night we met at the museum gala, that ill-fitting open blouse with the Misfits T-shirt underneath. I take in her face, her hair, the delicate rocking-chair arms of her collarbones, and that knot in my stomach goes even tighter.

She turns and walks down the hall.

I rush after her.

When I reach the hallway, she's already at the opposite end, passing through the door to the stairwell. I pursue, my breath ragged in my throat, my hands tacky with Detective Mathis's blood mixing with my own.

I go through the door and don't see her. I call out her name, which echoes up and down the cement stairwell, her name, *Taryn*, where did she go, where did she go?

She's moving up the stairwell. I can hear her. I can *sense* her.

"Taryn!"

I take the stairs two at a time, hurrying to catch up, yet somehow she manages to stay just out of view as we both spiral up that concrete staircase.

When I reach the roof, I see the nightscape of the city spread out before me, a thousand galaxies, the cool nighttime breeze of summer like absolution on my reeking, tired flesh.

Taryn stands on the edge of the roof. She is looking at me with a combination of pity, sadness, and something like regret...only I wonder if it is only *my* regret, echoed in her eyes, closing the distance between us, giving me back what I knew I carried in me all along.

"Taryn," I say, staggering toward her across the roof. "Taryn, I'm

so sorry. I should have been there for you. I'm so sorry. I'm so…
I'm so…"

My throat closes up, my vision blurs. For a moment, there are
three Taryns standing at the edge of the roof.

She opens her arms wide. "Try not to fall in love," she says.

I run to her, my arms out, tears streaming from my eyes. I go to
her, go to her, *go to her*—

Try not to fall in love.

But it's too late.

I'm already falling.

ACKNOWLEDGEMENTS

The last two novels I wrote dealt with heavy themes—grief and loss in *Come with Me*, addiction and childhood trauma in *Black Mouth*. I've learned from experience that when I spend several months in those dark places writing such books, my own mood tends to shift. I become furtive, restless, a thing none too pleasant to live with (just ask my wife). This is how it is whenever I write anything, but it's doubly so when the books tend to wallow in such darkness and despair.

I wrote the first novella in this collection, *The Skin of Her Teeth*, as a sort of palate cleanser after I'd finished *Come with Me* and before I began what I knew would be the arduous journey of writing *Black Mouth*. It was fun to write and I had no real expectations for it—I was just an author luxuriating in what, to me, felt like a fun and bizarre story. When I sent it to my editor at Titan, I thought maybe they'd publish it as a promotional ebook or something—an appetizer prior to the publication of *Black Mouth*. But the response from my editor surprised me: could I write three more thematically linked novellas and make this a collection?

As my British friends say, I was chuffed by the notion. It gave me an opportunity to indulge in a series of stories that dealt with all manner of haunted books, haunted writers, and the power of the written word. Is *Ghostwritten* a collection of four standalone novellas? Yes. But it can also be read as one complete novel, wherein those four novellas are loosely linked to tell a greater story—a story that stretches even beyond the pages of this book. (Astute readers might recognize references to many of my other stories embedded in these novellas, from *Little Girls* to *Snow* and many others, creating a tapestry that expands beyond the boundaries of *Ghostwritten* itself.)

I want to thank my editor, Sophie Robinson, for challenging me with this wonderful project, as well as everyone else who supported it over at Titan Books—Louise Pearce, Katharine Carroll, Sarah Mather, and all who toil behind the curtain.

Thanks to my tireless agents, Cameron McClure, Katie Shea Boutillier, and Matt Snow.

A hat-tip to my fellow Candlelight authors, who read early snippets of some of these novellas and provided priceless insight and commentary—Rhodi Hawk, David Liss, Robert Jackson Bennett, and Hank Schwaeble.

And of course, thanks to my wife and kids. I get to do this because my wife holds things together behind the scenes, and my kids keep my imagination alive.

—Ronald Malfi
Annapolis, Maryland
June 21, 2022

Ronald Malfi is the award-winning author of several horror novels, including the bestseller *Come with Me*, published by Titan Books in 2021. He is the recipient of two Independent Publisher Book Awards, the Beverly Hills Book Award, the Vincent Preis Horror Award, the Benjamin Franklin Award, and his novel *Floating Staircase* was a finalist for the Bram Stoker Award. He lives with his wife and two daughters in Maryland.

ronmalfi.com
@RonaldMalfi

For more fantastic fiction, author events,
exclusive excerpts, competitions, limited editions and more

VISIT OUR WEBSITE
titanbooks.com

LIKE US ON FACEBOOK
facebook.com/titanbooks

FOLLOW US ON TWITTER AND INSTAGRAM
@TitanBooks

EMAIL US
readerfeedback@titanemail.com